LADY ⟨ W9-CXJ-590
IS A TRIUMPH

"I have found Sasha Miller's *Ladylord* to be one of those books which enchants the reader fully and is not easily laid aside. Her evocation of a highly formal and yet utterly cruel and ruthless civilization is superb. Only the Empire series by Feist and *Takido Road* by Robeson are in the same class of making characters engaged in torturous intrigue fully believable and at the same time drawing the sympathy of the reader. This is, to my mind, something unique and reaches the top of this type of fantasy."
—Andre Norton

"A well-handled, solidly engrossing fantasy effort. Noteworthy."
—*Kirkus Reviews*

"In her skillful hardcover debut, Miller creates a socially complex world that's as vital as it is mannered, and fills it with captivating characters who are familiar with depravity as well as with grandeur."
—*Publishers Weekly*

"Nicely done adventure with a protagonist who is sharp-witted as well as a skilled warrior."
—*Science Fiction Chronicle*

"Filled with wizards, dragons, and political intrigue, this novel from Sasha Miller is a hard fantasy adventure with a decidedly feminist attitude. . . . An entertaining book."
—*The Magazine of Fantasy and Science Fiction*

"Sasha Miller's *Ladylord* has the tone and culture of the mysterious East in its bones. . . . [A] tale of high adventure mixed with a host of sensual and political intrigues.

"What Sasha Miller delivers throughout the novel is highly skilled and meticulous craftsmanship. Just as Oriental art is often exemplified by fine detail work, Miller's story consists of many small elements carefully arranged into an elegant whole."
—*DragonMagazine*

LADY LORD

Sasha Miller

TOR®

A TOM DOHERTY ASSOCIATES BOOK
NEW YORK

LADYLORD

Copyright © 1996 by Sasha Miller

Edited by James R. Frenkel

Cover art by Tristan Elwell

A Tor Book
Published by Tom Doherty Associates, Inc.
175 Fifth Avenue
New York, NY 10010

Tor Books on the World Wide Web:
http://www.tor.com

Tor® is a registered trademark of Tom Doherty Associates, Inc.

ISBN: 0-812-54949-X
Library of Congress Card Catalog Number: 95-30034

First edition: April 1996
First mass market edition: January 1997
Printed in the United States of America

0 9 8 7 6 5 4 3 2 1

To M.

ACKNOWLEDGMENTS

This work owes a lot to the Gang, who alternately pummeled me into abandoning the entire project (Kevin O'Donnell, Jr., in particular, for his infernal Standard Lecture 47) and encouraged me (Donald Robertson, crying "More dragon! More dragon!" and Marina Fitch telling me how, in spite of her being so hard on the manuscript, she couldn't get the story out of her mind). Then there was Lisa Swallow with her steadying influence, and John Staley, who translated the name of one of the characters as something really bizarre in Japanese, and Jim Aikin, who liked it from the start while being just as tough and uncompromising as anybody else in the critique group. Thanks to Tony Bryant for helping me with details of the duel and an important point of honor. Thanks also to the other dozen or so people who laid hands, one way and another, on the project and whose reaction was, for the most part, favorable. And special thanks to Susan Graham, who finally got the thing off high center, and to Jim Frenkel, who carried it through.

Because of you, and sometimes in spite of you, I got it finished—because it wouldn't let go of me, either.

1

i

*L*ady Javere qa Hyasti, known to her intimates as Javerri, hurried up the long stairs toward the Audience Hall. Her father had sent for her at last. The circumspectly worded message and the fact that he had been moved to the formal Hall from his apartments in the Residence told her clearly enough that Lord Qai qa Hyasti felt life slipping from his grasp and wanted to settle his earthly affairs before going Beyond and joining those spirits inhabiting the Ancestor Stone.

She had been busy at her studies in her room down on the second level of Yonarin Castle where the women's quarters were located, willing herself not to think about anything but the history book in front of her, when the messenger rapped on her door. Now she ran up the three red-lacquered stairs leading to the veranda of the Audience Hall and paused at the doors only long enough to take off her sandals and leave them with the dozens of others that lined the walls. The twin Guardians painted on the doors glared down at her, reminding her to smooth her hair and garments before bursting into the death chamber of Lord Qai qa Hyasti, ruler of the Third of the Five Provinces. With their green skin, red hair, and glaring eyes, they brooked no disrespect from those who would have audience with the ruling lord. She bowed respectfully and opened one of the doors, slipping inside as unobtrusively as possible, her feet noiseless in the white footlets everyone wore indoors.

"Lady Javere," one of the physicians said. He bowed so low that, tiny as she was, she could see the top of his tonsured skull. The man must have been stationed there expressly to await her arrival.

"Physician," Javerri said, inclining her head to the precise degree that good manners dictated. "Lord Hyasti is well?" It was the polite way of asking if he was still alive.

"He is well, Lady," the man said. "Though today he wishes to speak with you most urgently."

This was no news to her; his asking for her presence was surely a sign that she stood as high in his favor as anyone could ever hope to be, more significant perhaps than his action last year of marrying the concubine who had borne her. She refused to let herself speculate on anything beyond this. Not yet, not while things could yet change and she might find herself what she had always been—a daughter, treated much as a son and given the kind of education a son would have, but a mere daughter nonetheless.

"Please take me to Lord Hyasti," she said, and the physician turned away with another bow, motioning her to follow him.

The entire chamber reeked of incense, of assorted herbal infusions, of medicines pounded and blended in fatty bone marrow and applied externally, of the blood that had been let from Lord Hyasti's veins in a last attempt to revitalize him. Most of all it smelled of death. Death lay curling along the low rafters of the ceiling, hiding in the incense, lurking behind the eyes of many of the people in the room. Javerri's spine chilled; she knew she was in the presence of implacable enemies this day, enemies not entirely of her own making. She mustered all her training to keep her face expressionless. She felt as if she were traversing a field strewn with wizards' work, where pebbles could explode under her feet with the slightest misstep. The men and women waiting silently in the death chamber moved aside to let her through. Some watched out of curiosity; others stared with resentment. All observed with intense interest as she knelt beside the low bed and decorously arranged her skirts.

She scarcely recognized her father. He lay propped on a mountain of silk-covered pillows, his face haggard, his skin almost gray. She swayed slightly, willing herself not to faint.

"Shall I bring tea?" The man beside her had a concerned look on his face and she realized that her composure was not as perfect as she wished it to be.

Not trusting herself to speak, she nodded. He left her side, returning almost immediately with the scalding-hot tea. She sipped deliberately from the green-glazed cup, burning her tongue, willing herself not to show any discomfort, welcoming the pain. It acted to steady her. "Thank you," she said, making a note to remember this physician.

The man on the bed stirred at the sound of her voice.

"Javerri," he said. His voice was no louder than a whisper.

"It is a beautiful day, Father," she said. She gave him her best smile. "Much too beautiful to waste lying in your bed. I miss our rides together, when we would fly our hawks and make bets as to which bird would make its kill first."

Lord Qai qa Hyasti smiled a little in return. "You won those bets too often," he said.

"I cheated shamelessly. My eyes are better than yours, and sometimes I told you it was my hawk that struck when it was yours all along." A sudden rush of tears blurred her vision and she turned her face aside. "I beg forgiveness, Father."

The man on the bed made a wheezing sound, meant for laughter. "For the cheating, never. Thy tears, yes. Glad I married thy mother. Never could believe Crimson Lady missed so many strikes. One more question answered before I die."

His open use of the internal, personal form of address with her was not unusual; his referring to his death, however. . . . Javerri jerked her head upright and stared at her father.

"Don't look at me. Got no time for pretty manners. Never had, really. Even less now." Lord Qai coughed. Several physicians jostled one another to offer him medicines. He waved them away impatiently. "No more, no more. You fuddle my head. I want my last moments on this earth to be clear. Where's that secretary?"

An elderly man, white of beard and stooped of shoulder, made his way through the crowded room to Lord Qai's bedside. "I am here, my lord."

"You, Wande-hari? I want a scribe, not a magician."

"It is my honor to serve you, my lord," the ancient mage said. "In fact, I insist on it."

"Well then, write this as I tell it to you. On this day, at such-and-such an hour—fill in the particulars later—died Qai qa Hyasti, Lord of the Third Province of Monserria. In the knowledge of having no living son of his body, at his death he declared Lady Javere qa Hyasti to be known henceforth as his son and sole heir, that this son and heir may continue to defend the Third Province and the land of Monserria against its many enemies even as Qai qa Hyasti has done his entire life long. With his last breath he prayed the Sublime Lord of the First Province to recognize the necessity for this unusual move, and in remembrance of Qai qa Hyasti's service to the realm, to confirm his son in his inheritance. Nao-Pei stands next in line, after Javere." Lord Qai took a deep shuddering breath. The speech, obviously long in preparation and formal in tone, had nearly exhausted him. He looked at Javerri. "Are you pleased, my son? Ancestor knows it won't be easy for you. Sorry I won't be here to help you. Can't be helped, ei? Now go, all of you. I'm tired. Still have my dying to do."

"I thank you humbly, Father, for overlooking my great unworthiness. I will strive not to dishonor your trust." Behind her, Javerri heard the hiss of indrawn breaths as the news traveled through the room. She concentrated on keeping her face still, no emotion visible. It was unseemly to rejoice, yet her heart had leapt upward when she realized that everything she had worked so hard for was coming to pass. Also mixed with the joy, she discovered, was fear—fear of the unknown, fear of the responsibility that was now becoming all too real, approaching far too swiftly. Toward the rear of the stuffy chamber she heard a woman's familiar voice expressing protest, and a man's voice cautioning her to be still.

That would be Nao-Pei qa Hyasti and Baron Sakano qa Chava, her constant companion. Javerri's eyes narrowed. I must find out who in the castle is going to rally to my half sister and who is going to be loyal to me, she thought. I need every vassal I can muster for I must live long enough to receive my inheritance.

Aloud, she repeated her thanks and apologized for taking so much of Lord Qai's precious time.

"For my son, I grudge nothing," Qai said. "Want to sleep a little before I sleep forever. Wise for thee to swear thy heir's oath to me now, not wait until I waken."

"I do swear, Father," Javerri said fervently. She took his thin, wasted hands in her own and held them to her forehead. "I will protect and maintain Third Province to the last of my life's blood, always remembering the examples thou hast set, and consulting with the Ancestor Spirit."

"I could ask no more." Then the dying man's wrinkled eyelids closed and his breathing grew thick.

Javerri placed her father's hands gently on the coverlet and rose, nearly upsetting the forgotten cup of tea. She bowed low, despite the fact that her father could not see her. Unexpectedly, fresh tears dimmed her eyes and she waited until she could display a calm and unemotional face to the onlookers before turning to leave.

As she made her way back through the room, she saw Nao-Pei waiting for her—stationed, actually, where Javerri could scarcely avoid their meeting. Her face looked like a thundercloud as she inclined her head politely in Javerri's direction. The Baron Sakano stood at a discreet distance from her; he was the richest land owner in the province after the Third Lord and it was said that he crept into Nao-Pei's bed every night after his wife went to sleep. It was also said that Nao-Pei accepted his malformed Jade Stalk into every orifice of her body except the one designed for it, so that she could preserve her entirely technical virginity. That was mere servants' talk, of course, and not to be given much weight. Still, it was interesting.

Javerri paused in front of them, allowing herself the small luxury of enjoying the way they struggled and failed to control their features, and held out her hand.

"Lady," Nao-Pei said reluctantly. She put her fingertips to Javerri's. "Or should I address you now as Lord of the Third Province?"

"I am but his son and of no importance. The Lord of the Third Province is still well," Javerri said. "He sleeps."

Lady Moon and Ancestor, but how poorly thou hast learned thy lessons, she thought. She smiled sweetly at Nao-Pei. Though thy schooling was presumably better even than mine, how slight is thy control over thyself. I burn and quake, but nobody knows to look at me. I see it in thy eyes how thou dost hate standing second to me.

Not for the first time Javerri was grateful for Wande-hari's private training that allowed her to sense another's inner feelings at need. Unreliable and erratic though the ability was in her, still it amounted to the ability to read minds, if sometimes dimly; Javerri knew she would need all this and more during the days ahead. She could sense that Nao-Pei felt her lapse of control instantly; perhaps she even felt Javerri's reproof, mild though her voice had been. If so, this would bear watching. Perhaps Nao-Pei was not such a negligible enemy after all. The other woman bit her lip, furious at her breach of manners.

Baron Sakano came forward, bowing and touching his forehead to Javerri's fingers. "Surely the Lord Qai will be well forever," he said politely.

"Surely." Bowing in turn, Javerri left the death chamber, pausing a moment on the veranda to take a few breaths of clean, cool air before slipping on her sandals again and going down the stairs to the pavilion so she could light a stick of incense at the shrine in the center. Out on the path, a gardener was smoothing the pebbles that she had disturbed in the haste of her passage earlier. He retreated so she would be the only living person in the garden. Everyone knew she must pay her respects to the Ancestor at this juncture, and that she be seen doing so.

She composed herself with an effort. It was always wise to come before the Ancestor with an untroubled mind.

ii

Wande-hari gathered his hastily scribbled notes, preparing to take them to his quarters. There he could transcribe the precious document neatly, making the three copies needed to take to First City plus the most important copy, the one to go to the archives in Fifth Province, home of scholars, scribes, mages, and students of the law. That copy, if he were quick enough, would be signed by Lord Qai's own hand. The rest could be sealed with the official signet, Qai's personal chop. He paused, looking at the dying man. He could scarcely recognize Lord Qai qa Hyasti in this shrunken wreck that now lay on heaps of pillows, struggling for every breath. His hands, still lying where Javerri had placed them, looked so thin Wande-hari fancied he could see the pattern of the coverlet through them. The only mercy Lord Qai's illness had shown was that it had come upon him swiftly and looked to carry him off with equal dispatch.

Qai was of the most aristocratic of families in all Monserria, and could trace his heritage directly to Lord Yon, the almost legendary warrior who had taken Third Province for his own back when the world was newly formed. Like Lord Yon, Qai had been a vigorous man. He ruled his province with such a firm hand and sharp tongue that his troops had given him the nickname of "Old Vinegar-Piss." Officially, he ignored it even after he had learned of it. The face he showed the rest of the world was even more bellicose and unyielding than before and only a few intimates knew of Lord Qai's delight that the men he commanded liked him this well to show him such affection. Other lords bore nicknames much less flattering. Qai probably never knew that elsewhere he was also referred to as "Old Vinegar-Piss" as well, but not with any great fondness; Third Province was too rich and its ruler subject to too many jealousies from too many people who would replace him if only they had the strength to do it. Qai had survived more than one attempt. Ironic that this wasting illness accomplished what mere mortal enemies could not.

Unexpectedly, Lord Qai opened his eyes. "Stay a moment longer, old friend," he said. The breath rattled in his throat and his voice could scarcely be heard. "Isn't this the day you've worked toward so long? Your favorite has won. Your candidate. Celebrate with me."

Wande-hari bowed. "It was your choice, Lord," he said.

"Was it? Or was it entirely your doing?"

"I have trained both of your daughters to the best of my ability. Javere has more of you in her, Sire. Therefore, my efforts had better effect."

"Some think the old prophecy outdated, no meaning for us these days."

"I know some no longer believe Third Province will fall if its ruler is not wed to it first and foremost. And does not come to it not knowing the touch of love. But the secret which Lord Yon passed on to his son on his death bed is what has kept Third Province strong. Every descendant of his has honored it in his turn, even you. And now, because you leave a daughter as heir—"

"Enough, old friend." Qai's eyelids drooped with fatigue. His words came slowly. "I know. You cherish the old customs. You have done your best. Javerri is now my son. I have decreed it. We picked the most likely ones, together. Set them to their training. I die content with my choice. Tell me. Are you certain, both of them are still virgin?"

"I am as certain as I am of anything in this life, Lord." Wande-hari lowered his gaze in turn. *And that is only one of several reasons I threw my influence behind Javerri,* he thought. *She has drawn the prophecy into her very soul. Nao-Pei observes only the forms. A demon must have taken thy form in her bed and inserted Nao-Pei's soul into Lady Nao-Cha's womb for the sheer mischief of it. If it hadn't been for Nao-Cha's rank, I wouldn't even have considered her daughter when it became clear that there were to be no sons, and it fell to me to train the young woman who would be Lord Qai's successor. How we both worried, Qai, thee and me, because there were only daughters who might grow old and past their time for childbearing, waiting for thee to die. That's* one worry past both of us now, ei? Lucky for Third Province, unlucky for thee.

It is true, Wande-hari thought, I knew from the first about Nao-Pei's character. I find no comfort in this fact. Eeeei, but her conduct with Sakano is deplorable! Hard as I've worked on Javerri's training, I've worked harder keeping the truth about Nao-Pei from her father. Even Nao-Cha says Nao-Pei should have been born in a Fourth Province whorehouse, not to her. She will give my beloved Javerri a lot of trouble before she is through.

Lord Qai stirred again. "Look after her," he whispered, and Wande-hari knew which of his daughters he referred to. "Bring a new mage to Third Province. Devote your full attention to her."

"I will, Lord. It is my promise."

Then Qai fell asleep in earnest. His breath grew shallow and less frequent. Wande-hari lingered at the bedside. He called for his writing instruments. The transcribing he could do here and copying all but the document meant for the Fifth Province could wait for a little while, after all.

iii

Javerri walked down the stairs toward the pavilion where the Ancestor Stone waited. The gravel crunched underfoot, and she knew she made the very picture of humble supplication as she approached the great stone. But there was no dissemblance in her as she knelt and lighted a stick of incense from the small flame that always burned at the base of the stone.

Hundreds of years ago Lord Yon himself had stumbled upon the Ancestor—more than man-high, a column with a mushroom-shaped cap and two round protuberances at the base on either side forming a base—standing upright in the low woods a few miles to the north, where few stones disturbed the thick pine-needle carpet. At his direction, the stone was brought to Yonarin Castle at the expense of great effort by the people, as no draft animals were employed and men hauled the stone on vast sledges. It was said that Lord Yon labored alongside the humblest peasant, pulling a rope and helping bring the stone down from the ridge where it had been discovered. Further, the miraculous stone had been scarcely touched by the craftsman's chisel—just a bit, here and there, to enhance the effect. Now it reared heavenward in the place the lord had had built for it, the generative principle made manifest, Fruit and all. Men came and touched it, hoping for a semblance of its hard vigor. Pregnant women prayed and gave offerings to it in gratitude; barren ones gave in supplication.

As Javerri began murmuring the prayers she had memorized in childhood, the old welcome peacefulness came over her. She felt miles away, scarcely hearing, scarcely seeing. She had done her weeping long ago, so she would have no tears left to risk a public display that would show weakness. The incense stick burned down and she lit another and yet another. She was still kneeling there when the people—courtiers, officials, barons, hangers-on—came from her father's chambers. They put her father's famous sword, Steel Fury along with his daughter Lady Impatience, the companion dagger, into her hands, telling her that Lord Qai qa Hyasti had awakened once and then—most unexpectedly—died in his sleep, and that she was now Lord of the Third Province.

iv

The people pushed and pulled at her until the clamor made Javerri's temples throb. She was almost ready to scream from sheer frustration before she could escape from the crowd of courtiers and barons and to the privacy of her own apartment. Trying not to be as rude as she felt like being, she closed the door almost in their faces. Her head pounded unmercifully and her cheeks and eyes felt hot and dry. Not daring to call a physician lest word begin to spread that the new ruler of Third Province was a weakling, she confided only in Chimoko, her personal maid. Chimoko gave her a remedy used to calm children who became feverish from excitement, and to her relief it seemed to be working. Gratefully, Javerri lay down so Chimoko could rub her feet with perfumed oil.

"It's a good day that has finally come," Chimoko said, "not to wish bad luck on the old lord, but he was ill and is dead and now you have triumphed, Ancestor and the Six Winds be praised!"

Indulgently, Javerri did not reprove the maid and Chimoko chattered on about her mistress's good fortune until Javerri's obvious inattention caused her to subside. Javerri closed her eyes, drowsing a little from the medicine and giving in to the thrill that coursed through her and threatened to disrupt the propriety of her grief. Time enough later to think about the worries and problems her elevation brought with it. Even now that the thing had happened she still found it difficult to believe the rumors that had been on nearly every lip had proved true after all! It was said that the betting on who would eventually be declared Qai's heir spread throughout the castle and into the very kitchens and stables. First Wife Lady Halge, though well beloved by everyone, had been barren, and Qai's other wives and concubines produced no sons that lived more than a month or two. By law, each province needed sons to succeed their lord.

The Five Provinces of Monserria were founded on five great pillars; rice, oil-nut trees, sauce beans, worm silk, and vinegar. All the provinces produced these items in some degree, but each specialized in one. Oil-nut trees grew in the greatest abundance in the ruling province. Second Province, home of traders and merchants, was also home to rows of sauce beans that marked every property boundary. The best vinegar in Monserria came from Fourth Province, and only in scholarly Fifth Province did the inhabitants have enough leisure for extensive cultivation of the worms that produced the silk. Third Province was largely agricultural and owed its wealth to its vast rice fields.

It was just chance that had kept Javerri herself from being sent to the rice workers' House of Children when she was born, disappointingly, one more girl in a household that seemed destined to produce only living girl children. Qai qa Hyasti's wives and concubines regularly and habitually rid themselves of their girl children in just this manner.

Javerri's mother Shantar had also decided to dispose of her infant. Because she was high in Lord Hyasti's favor at the moment, she still hoped to bear a living son before his interest turned elsewhere. But Lord Hyasti ordered that the infant be brought to him so that he could see her.

"She has your eyes," he said, pleased. "Green as the finest jade. Third Province's color. It is an omen. Keep her and nurture her well. She reminds me of you, Shantar."

And so Shantar had bowed low and obeyed her lord's command. After all, it had been the beauty and unusual color of her eyes that had brought her to Qai qa Hyasti's attention in the first place.

When it became clear that there were to be no male heirs, a dozen daughters had been selected to be brought up with special attention, and Javerri was one of them. Wande-hari had taught them all impartially, weeding out the candidates until only two were left, Javerri and her half sister Nao-Pei, whose rank was much higher. As a courtesy, Qai had married Shantar—who then became Lady Shantar—and had given her her own apartment in honor of her elevated status. Shantar had been born, rumor had it, with dung between her toes. She had originally come to Qai as a tribute-offering concubine from the far north land of Hinstannod. Lady Nao-Cha had come to Third Province as a minor wife and Qai would not have one lording it over the other.

With only two pupils to occupy his time, the special bond that had always existed between Javerri and Wande-hari grew more firm. He began instructing her privately, in arcane matters that appeared to have no bearing on whether or not she would emerge as the unprecedented female heir.

"But how can I become Third Lord?" she had asked repeatedly. "Or Nao-Pei? Third Province has always gone to a son."

"A way will be found," he always answered.

Now Javerri wondered how much of Lord Qai's solution had been his own idea and how much had been Wande-hari's.

"My lady— My lord?"

Javerri roused herself from her reverie. To her relief, her fever had vanished. Chimoko now stood by her bedside, head bowed deferentially. "Yes, Chimoko?"

"A deputation waits outside, my, my lord."

Javerri smiled at the way Chimoko gamely struggled to use the unfamiliar and unnatural form of address. If she had been Javerri's social equal, she might have called her by name, though only close friends breached good manners this way. Even between equals, propriety indicated titles be used instead. It was a subtle suggestion that the person to whom one was speaking was, in reality, one's superior. "Who is it?" she asked.

"The magician Wande-hari, Generals Sigon and Michu, Lord Ivo, and Baron Sakano. And Chakei."

Javerri raised her eyebrows. Unexpected as Sakano's visit was, Chakei's was even more so. But it was well. She needed to speak with him to make sure he wouldn't create a disturbance at Lord Qai's funeral. She had a distressing premonition that he might try to save Qai's body from the flames.

"Did Chakei say what— Of course he wouldn't," she said. Chakei, the Dragon-warrior, was incapable of human speech.

She put on the clean white footlets Chimoko handed her, preferring to do this service for herself. Then she got up and slipped into the fresh robe Chimoko held ready for her. Even before she had finished winding the sash around her waist, Chimoko was busy with a comb.

"Shall I dress your hair for you, Lord?" she said.

"No, just make me tidy." She checked her reflection hastily in the mirror Chimoko held for her, wiped away a smudge of eye pencil on her cheek and touched up her lip paint.

Yes, her appearance was flawless. Because she was so tiny she and Chimoko relied on unwinking perfection in every detail to create the impression of greater stature than existed. Her long hair, so black it shone with blue highlights, was tied at the nape of her neck with a green ribbon in the simplest possible manner; her underdress of rose-colored silk matched her lip paint while the white overdress showed just the merest hint of green embroidery along the sleeves and hem. Javerri debated for a moment. As the new Lord of the Third Province she was entitled to wear Steel Fury and Lady Impatience in her sash; each weapon bore an identical pierced gold hilt, their beauty hidden only in time of war. And as part of her upbringing, she had been schooled in a sword's use. But something told her that a martial display was not what was called for in this case. Still, some display of her new status was called for. What would Lord Qai have done? As a compromise, she tucked Lady Impatience into her sash and nodded to the maid. Chimoko opened the panels that served as doors in a house's interior, and the Lord of the Third Province entered her private audience room modestly, ready for her first conference with her sworn leigemen.

v

" . . . and of course, we must also consider the question of your marriage," Wande-hari said. He held up his cup for more rice wine. He could use only his right hand. The left lay idle beside him, the nails grown so long they made the hand quite useless. Each nail was encased in a gem-studded guard made of the purest gold.

The table maid failed to pour the heated wine from the flask marked with the traditional nine-petaled flowers as quickly as Chimoko thought proper, and she frowned at the slip, sucking at her teeth. Amused, Javerri anticipated the scolding the girl would receive later.

They sat around a low lacquered table, all but Chakei, who crouched on his hindquarters in a far corner, to all appearances oblivious to the humans. As Javerri watched, Sakano shifted in his place and she took due note. Now we come to it, she thought. With this mention of marriage, Wande-hari has opened the heart of the matter. Sakano had no eyes for me when Nao-Pei still had a chance at the lordship, but now he offers himself as if I were a painted doll, unaware of what goes on around me. She allowed herself to smile at Sakano, so faintly her expression might not have appeared to change unless the onlooker were paying close attention. *I wonder what disposition he proposes to make of his wife,* she thought.

"My marriage, Wande-hari?" she said, turning to gaze at the elderly mage. "But surely I am not required to marry at once."

"Of course not, Lord," he said deferentially, "but times are not as peaceful as we might wish them to be. You are a woman, regardless of the title you bear, and as such—and unmarried as well—you could be spirited away and married forcibly."

Javerri nodded. She knew as well as the mage that Lord Yassai qa Chula, First Lord and Sublime Ruler of Monserria, would probably move against her as soon as news reached First City. It was no secret that he had always coveted Third Province, and had gotten on very poorly with Third Lord Qai. But politeness discouraged open discussion of this fact. Also, it was no secret that in the absence of any child of his body, he favored the sons of his sister above all others. She looked away for a moment, and the channel between the mage and her abruptly opened.

I counsel marriage, yes, but on thy own terms. It can be no real marriage. Thou must have a husband who is no husband. Until thou hast been confirmed and this confirmation ratified by a Council of Lords, Third Lordship is not yet truly thine. The ratification is just a formality, you understand.

It was the first time anyone had ever spoken to her directly, mind to mind, and it caused an intense pain that lanced straight through her head, starting between her eyebrows.

That will grow less, with practice. Open thy mind.

B-but I cannot—

Thou dost it, even now.

She felt dizzy and raised her cup to her lips to hide it. **I do not understand, Wande-hari.**

We talk between, Lord. I counselled thus with thy father often, though his replies were more often aloud than like this. I taught thee well.

But won't the others notice?

Nay, I told thee. We speak between. In two heartbeats we can say what would take two turns of the glass to accomplish aloud.

Truly, Wande-hari? Yes, I can see that it is so. The others have scarcely moved. Then I can ask how can I have a husband who is not truly a husband?

Thou wilt find a way from thy difficulty, even as thy father did, child. There is more to tell thee: Nao-Pei works at this moment to raise a rebellion against thee. She is willing to prostitute herself to First Lord Yassai and his nephews, even to sacrifice Sakano to achieve the position thou holds now.

The connection ended with a fresh flare of pain behind her eyes. Javerri took a sip of wine, grateful for the warmth in her throat. "And who could possibly want to occupy such a dangerous position as husband to the Lord of the Third Province?" she said, trying to keep her tone light. Her mind raced as she tried to think of a way out of this. The four men at the table laughed politely.

"As it happens, these gentlemen have brought formal proposals," Wande-hari said. At his signal the men took letters from the pockets in their long, flowing sleeves, placed them very properly on their fans, and gave them to the magician. Each letter was carefully folded and sealed. In turn, Wande-hari transferred the letters to his own fan and presented them to her. "Each of these four candidates for your hand has sworn with the most solemn of oaths to abide by your choice with no retribution to be visited upon the victor, so you can freely choose from among them here and now."

She nodded, unsurprised. She picked up the top letter, broke the seal, and opened it. It was from Michu, the general whose squadrons of pikemen knew no equal. Even without his chop on the letter, she would have known it was from him. From the corner of her eye she could see him, staring politely at a jar of dried flowers in the corner of the room. He wore a dark brown robe, scarcely ornamented save for the Third Province sigil embroidered in green silk over his heart. His legs were short in proportion to his body, and he had always been a man who looked finer seated than standing, the more so since he had reached the stage in life where he was beginning to put on weight. Still, there was scarcely a trace of white in the jet-dark hair he wore in the old-fashioned manner, tied back tightly against his skull. She looked at the unadorned sheet of rice paper.

"I am a plain blunt man," he had written. "So I plainly propose marriage between us. I am clearly the best candidate, a strong arm for you to lean on. . . . " She nodded at him, laid it aside and opened the next letter.

General Sigon's letter was written in graceful characters; the paper itself bore a delicate design so subtle it could have been overlooked. Its message was much along the same lines, only more tactfully phrased. "Though I have not felt moved to remarry since my beloved wife's death, I am deeply honored to present myself to you in the interests of strengthening your position and also because your person is very pleasing to all who have the honor to behold you. . . . " It was as typical of him as Michu's had been. Sigon the Excellent Strategist he was called, and for good reason. His origins may have been more humble originally than Michu's, for he was baseborn whereas Michu came of a good family, but he more than made up for his low birth these days. His robe of dark blue showed flashes of gold-embroidered lining when he moved to take more wine. Though he and Michu looked of a height when sitting, when they stood, Sigon's whip-thin figure towered over Michu's stocky one. She smiled at both of them. They had occasionally acted as tutors when she was learning her warrior skills and she thought of them almost as uncles. She recognized their offers as the declarations of loyalty they really were, and loved them for the gesture; she was certain either would be appalled if his suit met with success.

A wave of perfume assailed her nostrils even before she broke the wax seal on the third letter. As she did, a small but perfect emerald dropped to the tabletop; it had been embedded in the wax. Lady Moon and Ancestor, she thought. Sakano must really be serious about all this! Or Nao-Pei is, she amended silently. It amounted to the same thing. Curious, she scanned the letter. "The emerald pales beside thy eyes. . . . " Her lips nearly twitched as she read and she kept a smile from showing only by the greatest effort. Sakano promised to set aside his present wife and any entanglements in which he was currently involved. Also, he would return all lands and revenues he now possessed at the late Lord Qai's pleasure, in hopes that his beloved wife the present Lord Javere— And so on, she thought. The only thing he didn't specify in all this was what he expected to receive in return. In addition, that is, to my entirely virginal body which he might prefer to Nao-Pei's well-used one, she thought wryly. She set the letter aside with a courteous nod of her head in Sakano's direction and picked up the last letter, the one she had deliberately saved until this moment.

Ivo qa Gilad was heir to a line almost as ancient and distinguished as her own. Through bad luck, however, the family had become virtually impoverished and he had taken service with his liege lord as captain of Yonarin Castle's archers. It was freely said that Lord Ivo had no peer in all the Five Provinces when it came to his use of the bow. Much younger than either Michu and Sigon the Strategist, like them he had been her tutor though she had shown no great talent for the bow. During the past year at the rising of each new moon— and this was before she began to emerge clearly as the favorite to follow her father to Third Lordship—Ivo had petitioned Lord Qai for Javerri's hand in marriage. Concubine's child though she was, it was common knowledge that Javerri stood high in Lord Qai's favor. Even if Nao-Pei won as heir, Javerri could be expected to command a rich portion which would attract any suitor, rich or poor. Ivo, however, firmly renounced any claim on her dowry. He loved Javerri for herself, he declared, and not for the advantages marrying her might bring. And Lord Qai believed him while refusing him his suit.

"Not yet, my Admirable Archer," he said each time Ivo petitioned. "But you grow daily in my regard. Do not despair."

Despite the prophecy and Wande-hari's plans for her, more than once Javerri had hoped her father would relent and allow the marriage, for she found Ivo both handsome and kind. He pleased her in many ways and she had always looked forward to her lessons with him; regardless of how abominably she performed he was ever patient with her clumsiness. She looked closer at the letter on which he had written this latest proposal; he had used a strange ink that flaked at a touch of her fingernail— She set the letter aside, unwilling to commit her self, her body, just yet.

"And after I marry?" she said to Wande-hari. "What then? I can see there is something more you are not telling me."

"We shall journey to the capital city," Wande-hari said. "Not only must we make our allegiance to First Lord Yassai, but we must also seek a new magician for Yonarin Castle."

Now she looked at him fully, her surprise plain. "But why, old friend?" she said. "Of everyone living in the Third Province I thought your loyalty was the firmest!"

"It is your father's command," the magician said serenely. "He ordered me to retire, to become your counselor only. I grow old, Lord. The passing of Lord Qai informed me most clearly that all of us are but a sigh against the raging winds of time. I would not leave you without magical protection merely because I had the arrogance to think myself exempt from the fate that awaits us all, lowest to most high."

There's a clear message for Sakano in that, if he is astute enough to recognize it, Javerri thought. "Your wisdom is boundless, Wande-hari," she said. "But what of our fierce Dragon-warrior? Why has he come to this meeting? Surely he doesn't want to marry me as well."

The Dragon-warrior had been at Yonarin Castle as long as Javerri could remember. Lord Qai's father, it was said, had purchased him in the egg, the only way anyone could ever come to possess one of this incredibly rare breed, and the price had threatened to bankrupt him. But of the other rulers of the Provinces, only the First Lord himself could presently boast of a Dragon-warrior in his court. Chakei's pebbled skin, freshly oiled, shone scarlet on the head crest and ridge down his back, lightening to cream on the front of his body, while his eyes were so deep a black they gave back no gleam of light at all. He loved fire, and was unaccountably immune to its effects; more than one maidservant, new to Castle Yonarin, had screamed and fainted to discover him comfortably asleep on the bed of coals in the kitchen fireplace. The very rumor of his presence on a battlefield was enough to demoralize an enemy; he liked to rip opponents to shreds with his enormous five-clawed hands and though he never ate flesh, Lord Qai didn't discourage the rumors that criminals destined for execution were given to Chakei instead of the headsman.

Now Chakei stood up and approached the table where Javerri sat. Vaguely man-shaped though much larger than all but the biggest man, his movements suggested that his species might have gone on all fours at some recent time in its history. He swayed from side to side. He put his hand to his belly where, Javerri understood, his heart was located. Unexpectedly, her mind opened to him as it had to the ancient magician's.

ladylord honor here you i

She caught her breath, glancing involuntarily at Wande-hari. He nodded almost imperceptibly; somehow she knew that he was part of this connection, helping and guiding her. In some remote part of her mind a nagging question dissolved; though Chakei could hear and responded to commands when it suited him to do so, she had always wondered if the Dragon-warrior truly comprehended what was said to him.

always protect ladylord swear always i

She summoned her small ability, grateful for Wande-hari's help. **I thank thee, Chakei. Thou hast my loyalty in return.**

know this i, old lord say
You know about the funeral, and how we must burn him?
no but good is
I was afraid you'd—she started to say *interfere* but changed it—***object.***
is good to return to fire

The connection dissolved. She felt dizzy again and retired behind her fan to recover. At least she knew now that Chakei wouldn't make the funeral into a shambles. Speaking *between* with the Dragon-warrior was even more tiring than with the magician; still she sought Wande-hari's mind.

Which proposal should I accept? Not Sakano's, of course. But which? Would Sigon or Michu abide by the prophecy?

I cannot advise thee, Javerri. Thou knowest that. She felt an undercurrent of amusement in the old mage's thoughts. She knew he had noticed her omission of Ivo's name. He severed the connection so gently Javerri felt no stab of pain from it. She took a deep breath.

"My sincere thanks to all of you for offering to marry me. But while three of you are moved by the loyalty you must feel to Third Lord, I find that another adds to this a deeper emotion. I shall accept Lord Ivo," she said decisively, "and marry him without delay. His letter of proposal, which I shall treasure always, is not, like Michu's, the strongest or, like Sigon's, the most gracefully worded. Nor was it written in perfumed ink, nor did it bear a jewel in the wax seal like Sakano's. But it is nonetheless more precious to me than any of these, for it is written in his life's blood."

The other men turned and looked at the Admirable Archer; Ivo himself sat very still with downcast eyes. Sigon and Michu exchanged smiles, then bowed their heads in acceptance. Sakano, less disciplined, allowed a veritable panoply of expressions—relief, jealousy, thwarted greed—to race across his face before he regained control of himself. Ivo raised his head and stared at her, uncaring that his love and longing showed plainly. She had to look away, unable to meet his eyes.

Alas, my Ivo, she thought. Wande-hari hast told me what I must do. I could order the others. But thou lovest me and I will choose thee. Wilt thou look at me thus when I tell thee that I cannot allow thee to come into my bed?

2

i

*T*hough she had the power to do so, Javerri couldn't allow the marriage to proceed without telling Ivo first how matters must stand between them. Her honor demanded it. The day after she accepted his proposal she called him in for a private meeting. Without wasting words, she told him plainly, forcing a coldness she did not feel into her tone, that although custom gave him, as husband, access to her body whenever he wanted her, she as Third Lord denied him this right.

He went a little pale. She expected him to petition to leave her at once, to take back his offer of marriage. She held her breath. The only other suitor of rank was Sakano. . . .

Then Ivo bowed his head but not before she saw the pain that suffused his features. "As you command, Lord Javere," he said with stiff formality. "I will take my lead from you in this as in all other matters. This I swear."

Relief flooded through her and she struggled not to let it show. "Wande-hari has begun to call me Ladylord," she said, not seeing any reason to mention that the mage had first heard it from Chakei. "I like it well and am pleased when those close to me use it as my title." She smiled. "Come, Ivo, sit with me. We will have tea or perhaps you would prefer wine?"

"Tea, please."

She gestured to Chimoko. In seconds the maid brought the tray Javerri had told her to have prepared and waiting. On the same tray she also brought food—a small plate laden with pickled vegetables and noodles with bean sauce, artfully arranged. At a lifted eyebrow from Javerri, Chimoko disappeared, leaving Ivo and Javerri alone.

She picked up a bowl, so delicately glazed and tinted that the pale green hue showed only in the sunlight. "Allow me to serve you," she said to Ivo.

"No, it is not proper—"

"Please allow me. Let us pretend that I am still the Third Lord's minor daughter you used to instruct in the use of the bow."

"As you command," he said again.

Obediently, he sat on the cushion at her side. Good. Perhaps they could be friends after this interview after all. While they pretended to busy themselves with the vegetables, she turned the conversation to trivial matters.

"You must know that I honor you greatly," she said.

"For you to agree to marry me does me an immeasurable honor," he said.

She laughed a little. "Don't forget that before I arrived at this lofty state I was only a concubine's child. I haven't forgotten, nor will I ever. No, the honor I was referring to is the esteem in which I hold you. You wanted me when I was less than nothing. That is why I chose to accept you now."

"But—" He bit his lip on the protest.

"There are vexing questions to be answered on every side. For example, had you considered that I must decide what to do with my father's concubines?"

Glad of the change in subject, he quirked an eyebrow and began to laugh softly as the implications sank in on him. By custom, the new ruler inherited all his father's wives and concubines—excluding his own mother, of course—and disposed of them as he saw fit. Many young lords chose to clear out the women's quarters by sacrificing the luckless women on the old lord's funeral pyre, later filling the empty rooms with younger and presumably more desirable females. "Surely you won't send them all to the headsman!" he said with some humor.

"Of course not," Javerri said. "No woman has gone Beyond to join Lord Qai except by her own hand. Nor do I propose to replace them with—with male concubines, or to wallow nightly in orgies of woman love the way some wagging tongues are already having it. But it is a question that has to be addressed. And did you know that Baron Sakano has now left the court?"

"Yes. I was glad to see him go. He and Lady Nao-Pei—"

"—are better kept where I can watch them," Javerri said. She hoped he had composed himself enough so that she could broach the more serious subject they would have to discuss. "Although I do admit there is something to be said for separating those two by as many *ri* as possible. I had been thinking of taking her with me to First City, just to keep an eye on her. But that has nothing to do with the greatest problem that troubles you and me." She set aside her dish and the eating sticks of oil-nut tree wood and opened her fan.

As if he could read her thoughts, he set aside his dish as well and faced her directly, giving her his full attention. "Please. Tell me."

She took a deep breath. "Third Province is in a terribly precarious position. Despite Lord Qai's declaration, I am still a woman and there are those who will accept me only reluctantly as lord. We are faced with possible insurrection at home and threatened with absorption by First Lord's greedy nephews who want our lands only for the riches they'll bring, and who care nothing for us or our people. The Sublime Ruler is noted for his deviousness even in the nest of political intrigue that is his court; he is fully capable of finding a way around Lord Qai's express wishes. He has the authority to have me killed if he wished it and no one would lift his voice in my defense. Probably he won't do this. Such an act would cause the other three lords to unite against him out of fear for their own lives. No one, not even the Sublime Ruler, would risk a civil war for such a trivial thing as the momentary pleasure of ordering my death. But he certainly will want me out of the way. At the very least he will put me to some kind of trial, a test. And if I fail, the nephews will win. It is for this very reason that I must bar you from access to my bed," she said. "You know that I face many dangers, more in fact, than you realize. I must wed my province before I can wed you; it must be my wife, even as you are my husband. This is the law every ruler since Lord Yon has observed. Until First Lord confirms me, I must remain untouched. Ours will be a marriage of form only. And—" She bit her lip on the incautious words she was about to utter. Not yet. "And I had to know you would accept these conditions before I could tell you the reason I imposed them," she said instead.

She had another reason for maintaining her purity, more personal, much less noble. And this she dared not tell him. She barely admitted it, even to herself. She must continue to deny him, even when she had legally become Third Lord. . . .

She breathed deeply again, fighting to regain control, and fluttered her fan. "It's true that I need a husband, for all the reasons Wande-hari mentioned and more besides, but beyond this I need a friend I can count on. Will you be my friend, Ivo?"

He moved from sitting to kneeling beside her. "With every drop of blood that's in me." Without reaching into his mind Javerri knew they both thought of his marriage proposal, carefully written in that same blood. "But—but Javerri, if some day—I mean, when conditions allow, that is—"

She willed herself to stare at him coldly. "You presume too much," she said, but her voice wavered just a little.

As if he could not help himself, he reached out and took her hands in his. She dropped the fan. She could smell the clean, spicy aroma of his skin. She longed to touch him, to stroke the lean smoothness of his face, to massage the vertical line that hours of concentration with the bow had etched between his brows; but he grasped both her hands tightly, and without meaning to she leaned toward him. He kissed her eyelids and touched her mouth with the tip of his tongue. Then he held her close. She turned her head away; he brushed the back of her neck with his lips. She shivered as an unexpected flame awoke between her thighs.

So that's the Springing Up of the Jewel Terrace I've read about, she thought dazedly. It was the first time she had experienced it. Abruptly she understood why men and women never kissed except in the privacy of the bedroom. She and Ivo drew apart, staring at each other. She might have been turned to stone, her body was so stiff, except that no stone could feel as she felt. Wildly, she found herself wishing that he would disobey her orders, ignore the conditions she laid upon him—

"Forgive me, Ladylord Javere qa Hyasti, but I wanted to touch you just once," he said formally. "I know that you neither love nor desire me. You ask only for my friendship. But I do love you and will for all my life. I will honor the prophecy. I agree to your terms and will not embrace you again." He bowed his head, in control of himself once more. He released her hands, stood up, bowed again before leaving her where she sat.

Lady Moon and Ancestor! she thought in dismay. How well she'd convinced him! He had no idea how much she did love him and desire him, but then neither did she until today. Now, she didn't know whether to laugh, cry, or throw things.

She sat very still, summoning every ounce of self-discipline at her command, until she could regain control over the rebellious body that threatened to wreck her careful planning with its urgent uprush of desire. She had no time for that. Eventually her racing pulse beat slowed. She patted away a few drops of perspiration that had, unaccountably, appeared at her hairline. Then she picked up her fan and touched the small bell that signalled her readiness for the next person who had business with the Ladylord of the Third Province.

ii

According to ancient custom, a Third Lord's body was burned in the special funeral courtyard outside the main pavilion that had been constructed just for this purpose when the castle had first been built by Lord Yon. Lord Qai's reign had been a long one; the bronze doors were half hidden behind flowering vines which had to be torn down before they could be opened, and the lock yielded only reluctantly to the rusted key. Inside, however, all was in readiness, having been left so after the funeral of Jinku, Lord Qai's father. The stone-lined fire pit had only needed a new lining of dried wood, a soaking in oil, and the application of a torch.

Palace servants built a canopy over the pit, draped with white cotton and adorned with every flower that could be found, and the highest priests laid the bodies carefully in the pit. With Lord Qai were burned also the bodies of those ladies who had chosen to follow him in death—surprisingly many, Javerri noted, indicative of how beloved Lord Qai truly had been. Among them were First Wife Lady Halge and, surprisingly, Lady Nao-Cha. Nao-Pei reacted hardly at all to her mother's unexpected action, and Javerri put this fact away for consideration at another time.

Her place was in the spectator box, along with other high officials of the court. She endured the ordeal without tears, as befitting the new Lord of the Third Province, and she wore both Steel Fury and Lady Impatience in her sash.

When all had been prepared, with many prayers, the chief among the priests threw the first torch onto the pyre, and his companions threw theirs likewise. As the fire blazed, lesser priests opened wide the great doors so the Ancestor Stone could witness. This insured that the souls being released by the flames went directly into the Ancestor Spirit before they could be captured by the numberless demons that always gathered when someone died. The souls could be reborn from the Ancestor Spirit if they chose, but if the demons got them, they would be lost forever.

The pit had been cunningly constructed to concentrate the heat of the fire so funerals could go quickly. When the blaze had consumed everything, the pit was cleaned and, under Javerri's direction, prepared for her own funeral against the day when she would join the Ancestor Spirit in her turn.

Then the doors were closed again and locked, and fresh climbing vines planted to hide the spot.

iii

The following day, Ladylord Javere issued her first proclamation. The surviving wives and concubines of the late Lord Qai qa Hyasti were now free to become wives of citizens of the Third Province, according to rank and each lady's preference. Most—Javerri's mother Lady Shantar among them—immediately presented themselves for marriage, and the large Audience Hall in the castle had to be set aside for interviews as honest farmers and merchants came hurrying in hopes of winning an elegant new wife. Javerri had never gotten on well with Shantar; even before she had been named heir, Shantar had won many enemies in the women's quarter with her airs. Despite this, Javerri personally settled her mother on a wealthy landowner. He lived far away from Third City so everyone involved was happy about the arrangement. Though Ivo didn't know it, he was fortunate also not to face the prospect of living in the same house as his mother-in-law.

Talk had always been open in the women's quarters, and Javerri listened well. With this in mind, she devised a third alternative open to the widows, not widely publicized, and in this she did not—could not—rely on what her father would have done in similar circumstances. Discreetly, she invited the notorious Madam Farhat for a private meeting with her. This woman was absolute ruler of the Precinct of Women in Third City, where even the ruling lord dared not meddle. Rumor had it that Farhat's influence extended throughout the entire province as well for all that she, too, had been born with dung between her toes. Over heated wine, Javerri offered Madam Farhat a dozen or so of those women who, for one reason or another, wanted neither remarriage nor release from this world. Farhat was suspicious at first, then unbelieving, then incredulous when she discovered that Javerri wanted no more than token payment for each woman who chose to enter the Hyacinth Shadow World.

"It's a bargain, Lady," Farhat said. She carried a fan far more elaborate than her rank entitled her to, and she used it to cool herself now. "I mean, Lord. If I got even one courtesan of the second rank I would be happy. But I know of two potential first ranks among Lord Qai's younger women and many third ranks as well."

"If they want to join you," Javerri said. She fluttered her own fan gracefully. "Please remember that each woman must make her own choice."

"Of course, of course," Farhat said airily. "And why wouldn't any woman choose the Hyacinth Shadow World if it were that or marriage with some dung-smeared peasant? As for the other alternative—" Farhat shuddered.

Ah, but thou hast not come so far from being one of the peasants thou despiseth, Javerri thought. Not that I find thee an unfit tool for me to use at my need. She smiled and offered the woman more wine.

"You are very understanding," Javerri murmured.

"More so than you might think, Lord," Farhat said. She shot Javerri a keen glance; both ladies were on the third flask of heated wine and Javerri could tell it was having its effect. "There is much talk about your marriage."

"Oh?" Javerri said smiling, instantly on her guard.

"There's been *much* talk—oh, not that I ever gossip, or any of my ladies," Farhat added hastily. "But in the business I am in, one does hear many things. Please. Can't we talk frankly, one woman to another?"

"But surely that is what we are doing." Javerri poured Farhat more wine from the special flask, the one marked with the eleven-petaled flower design. She hoped the woman was too tipsy to realize the significance of the fact that the flowers on Javerri's flask had only five petals and she was drinking a beverage not much stronger than hot water.

"Of course, of course, I understand. You are a high-ranked lady—I mean—"

"In my inner circle I am called Ladylord. I would be pleased if you would address me so." Gratified, Javerri watched the other woman melt under the flattery, twisting on her cushion and preening herself openly. This might loosen Farhat's tongue even more effectively than the strong wine itself, Javerri thought.

"Ladylord," Farhat said. She smiled, the thick makeup on her cheeks threatening to crack with the movement, and waved her fan so vigorously the breeze ruffled her hair. "Thank you. As I was saying, you far outrank me, Ladylord, and did even before Lord Qai died and made you his son and heir in accordance with the prophecy. I have no illusions about that. But also I have no illusions about the peculiar position you are in and the risks you cannot afford to take."

Javerri stiffened, instantly alert. How could the woman know the other reason she must deny Ivo even after she was confirmed in her position, when she desired him so much? But then, she thought, Farhat must deal with this sort of thing almost on a daily basis.

At last she allowed the words to form in her mind, to become real. Even the best methods of preventing conception could fail. All Third Province could be jeopardized if she had to cope with a pregnancy at the same time she wrestled with the terrible concerns that must plague her until the Third Province was truly secure. A pang of pure longing surged through her as she realized how very much she wanted Ivo's child. No, she thought, shuddering inwardly. I would not take the medicines that release an unripe child from a woman's body. Not Ivo's child.

Madam Farhat seemed not to have noticed Javerri's moment of panic. "You've been more than fair with me," the woman continued. "And I am now, in honor, your debtor. Oh, yes." She laughed deprecatingly. "You may well think that there is no room in the Hyacinth Shadow World for honor. But I say to you that there would be no Hyacinth Shadow World at all if we did not deal with scrupulous fairness regarding all those involved."

"I had never a doubt." Javerri poured more wine. The

woman was tipsy enough by now that she didn't notice Javerri had stopped drinking. Even the weak brew in her flask might be too much, when she had to keep a clear head. *And what is it thou dost want from me, I wonder,* she thought sourly. *Wilt thou offer to provide the medicine? Debtor indeed.*

"I am in a position to hear much valuable information, Ladylord," Farhat said. "You understand that what goes on between a man and one of my ladies is held in the strictest privacy. You would be astonished at what some men will do with a lady to whom he owes nothing beyond payment—" She drew herself up primly and sipped at her wine. "That, of course, is not the issue. But sometimes a man will want to talk later. He *needs* to, you see, and if he speaks too freely about matters you might wish to know about, then it is nobody's fault but his, is it?"

Javerri smiled at the woman through the wave of dizziness that swept over her. *So it's nothing more than this!* she thought, relieved. *Just money. Thou art not only a procuress but a greedy sow as well. May I be reborn a back-passage whore in the dingiest waterfront brothel in the Fourth Province, birthplace of all beggars, highwaymen, and diseased preparers of food, before I fall into thy trap. Valuable information to thee. Worth far more to thee than what I'd have to pay for it. Not for anything would I put myself into thy power for any information thou couldst bring me.*

"Surely a man's words under these circumstances aren't to be taken seriously," Javerri said aloud. "And to pay money for such maunderings—" She gave a delicate shudder and hid her face modestly behind her fan. "Impossible."

"Did I say anything about money?" Farhat said hastily. "No, Ladylord, though one might hope— Well, be that as it may. I wanted only to demonstrate my loyalty, in the best way I can."

"I meant no offense." *But I did mean to pry thy grasping fingers from my purse strings,* she thought. *Thou wilt not dare ask for as much as a rice cake now, but thou must pass along an occasional bit of information I'll find useful, or prove thyself the liar thou knowest I think thou art.*

"And no offense taken, Ladylord." Farhat drained the wine cup. "See here, to show my goodwill and to thank you for your generosity with your late father's women, I will put at your disposal one of my first-rank courtesans any time you, ah, desire to reward some gentleman you esteem, and charge you only half the usual fee. Everything handled with the utmost discretion, of course."

Javerri nodded. Even if by some chance Madam Farhat actually knew how matters stood with her and her husband, here the woman was on solid ground and could not be faulted. More than one highborn woman had found herself stirred by a man and unable to gratify his passions, particularly if she were married to another. But she could send him a graceful substitute for her favors in this manner. That was only one reason tongues had wagged about Nao-Pei's scandalous conduct with Baron Sakano, when there was a perfectly acceptable substitute available. And if honor in the Hyacinth Shadow World was a doubtful commodity, discretion was not.

"You are too kind," she murmured. "If ever I have need of your services, I will call upon you with complete confidence."

"Ladylord."

At least the woman did know when an interview was ended. Farhat rose to her feet, a little unsteadily, and bowed. As she left the room, Javerri stared after her, deep in thought. Farhat represented great potential danger. Could she prove useful after all? It was possible. Much depended on the women she had put into Farhat's keeping, and whether they chose to be loyal to her or to the Ladylord. But here again, she, Javerri, would have to go carefully, as through a wizard's field of explosives. She wished there were someone to whom she could confide the events of this interview. But all her closest advisors were men. Only another woman could truly comprehend what had just gone on between the Lord of the Third Province and Madam Farhat of the Precinct of Women.

iv

On the earliest suitable day, Javerri and Ivo were married privately, in front of the Ancestor Stone. The yellow-robed priest stumbled over the words, mixing "lord" and "lady" in referring to the two of them until Javerri finally instructed him to use their names without any titles.

She had chosen the hour just before sunset when the shadows grew soft and evening birdsong floated gently on the air. A small group of specially invited courtiers stood as witnesses, among them Sigon and Michu with their personal bodyguards. According to custom, the bride and bridegroom went unattended.

Javerri's conscience lay heavily against her heart while she repeated the vows that bound her, body and soul, to Ivo, and gave him full sovereignty over her person from that moment onward. She looked at the great stone, gleaming with the perfumed oil that had been rubbed into it. Forgive me, Ancestor, she thought. But thou knowest why my vows are shallow and why my husband will not find me in his bed this night nor any other for unknown time to come. Be thou with me and hasten the time when all my vows can be fulfilled.

She glanced up at Ivo. He towered over her, as tall as Sigon, and to her eyes at least, even more elegant. His skin glowed golden from the sun's touch, and his eyes were such a dark brown that they appeared almost black. She longed to touch his hair, clubbed into a knot at the back of his head, and to feel his hands on her again. But she made the effort that kept her face still and her mind calm all during the rest of the ceremony when she became, formally, Javere qa Hyasti qa Gilad, even through the feast that followed. She excused herself at last when the serious drinking began.

She had already moved into the house her father had occupied. Within the Residence, the lord's first wife could maintain her own quarters at sufficient distance from the lord's rooms so the comings and goings of various other wives and concubines could be ignored. Javerri had given orders that Ivo be established in this area. Though other buildings within the citadel were either ornate or starkly military according to their uses, the Residence was designed to be a place of exquisite simplicity, a tranquil world of its own in the midst of the huge castle.

In the deepness of the night, lit by a single lamp, Javerri sat at a small dressing table while Chimoko took her hair out of its elaborate coif. The maid knew about the unusual arrangements that had had to be made. In fact, she had been entrusted with the extremely personal task of contacting Madam Farhat. "Is the woman here yet?" Javerri asked with elaborate carelessness.

"Yes, Ladylord. She arrived an hour ago. I took her to Lord Ivo's bedroom and saw to it that she had something to eat and drink."

"And—and what does she look like?" Javerri asked delicately. She could tell that Chimoko wasn't at all deceived by her demeanor.

"Very beautiful. But she doesn't look at all like you," the maid added. "She's tall, and full-fleshed."

"Perhaps Lord Ivo won't like her."

"The—the lady of the place from which she came said she was very skilled, very experienced. And Lord Ivo will have had plenty of wine."

Javerri frowned, irritated and uncertain as to exactly why. The whole arrangement was entirely rational, the only sensible thing to do under the circumstances. And surely she herself had drunk enough wine that her nerves should not be troubling her by now. And yet she was displeased. Chimoko hastily changed the subject.

"This same lady sent a present for you. The—the other brought it with her."

"Oh?" Javerri said, her displeasure deepening. What on earth could Farhat have sent her? Curiosity gradually got the upper hand. "Well, where is it? Surely if someone sends me a present I should have the courtesy to open it."

Chimoko hastened to fetch the bundle, covered in silk and then in paper. Javerri pulled the paper aside and stared, puzzled, at the plain wooden box. Strange. She had never before in her life received a gift in such a nondescript container. The wrapping was worth far more than the box.

"Perhaps you should look inside," Chimoko suggested.

Javerri unfastened the latch and opened the lid. She caught her breath. "Lady Moon!" she exclaimed involuntarily.

With Chimoko practically hanging over her shoulder she stared, fascinated and faintly horrified, at the contents of the box. Naturally she had heard about such things—who hadn't?—but she had never seen any. Everything fitted into its own special niche, layered in silk-lined trays. She touched the strands of beads. They were of different sizes, one strung on rough hempen cord, the other on silk. And here, this ring must go over the Night-Growing Mushroom—yes, and equipped with a knob to press against the Jewel Terrace, too. And this! She stifled a laugh. It was the Ancestor Stone complete with Fruit only smaller. It looked to be made of ivory, so heavily carved it was almost unrecognizable—almost, but not quite. She examined the carvings, feeling her cheeks grow warm in spite of herself. The carvings were extremely amusing, and completely obscene. But the size of it! How could one possibly get it inside? She found another, more modestly proportioned and just as carefully carved, and concluded that the first was intended as a curiosity only. Perhaps it was even quite valuable. There were other items, however, for which she could not imagine a use at all. She touched a third item like a Jade Stalk, but smooth and minus the spheres, and attached to the same kind of cord as the beads. Whatever did one do with this? She looked again at the beads and abruptly her face flamed as she understood. One by one, she took all the things out of the trays and carefully placed them on the dressing table. A smile started in one corner of her mouth and spread over her face. A so-called "decent" woman probably never saw more than one or two of these items in all her life, let alone had the opportunity of using them. They were definitely secrets until now confined to the Hyacinth Shadow World, seldom finding their way beyond its boundaries. Whatever Farhat's motives in giving her the box, she had succeeded in the one thing she had probably never even dreamed of. With the Ladylord's examination of the contents of the box, her dark mood had definitely lightened.

"Have a purse sent to Madam Farhat in the morning," she said, lips twitching with amusement. "And make certain it is filled with gold, not copper or silver. And send with it my thanks for her extreme thoughtfulness."

"Yes, Ladylord," Chimoko said, practically swallowing her fist to stifle a fit of giggles. Her cheeks were red, and a drop or two of sweat showed high on her forehead. "May I look some more?"

"As much as you please. Then put everything away and place the box in that clothes chest. No, I mean it," she said to the flabbergasted maid.

"Yes, Ladylord, as you command." Chimoko's demeanor clearly showed that she would have had no hesitation in exploring the pleasant possibilities Madam Farhat's unexpected gift offered and furthermore, she had assumed that her mistress would do likewise immediately. Javerri turned away, signalling that the subject was closed to discussion.

Much later, long after she had dismissed Chimoko for the night, she stole quietly from her bed and retrieved the box. She opened it and stared at the contents thoughtfully. Virgin though she was, she had been thoroughly instructed in private matters as a matter of course. Ivo's nearness and the thought of what he must surely be doing by now made sleep elude her, as she might have anticipated but had not. Farhat, she realized, understood the nature of men and women more profoundly than she had thought. In this area at least, Javerri recognized that the woman had no peer. Hesitantly she picked up the smaller of the Jade Mushrooms provided for her use, touching the ridges and bumps carefully carved on its surface, imagining how it might feel. . . .

Then she closed the box and put it away again. She would not endanger her maidenhead with any of these things; surely they were intended only for experienced women. Nor would she stoop to such expedients with Ivo as Nao-Pei practiced with Sakano, even to preserve her virginity. She crept back to her bed. Her body tormented her; she touched herself, seeking to ease the discomfort. Without conscious volition, her fingers found the Jewel Terrace and lingered there. Unexpectedly, and for the first time ever, her body arched and she erupted in shuddering pleasure. She had little time to think about it; the spasms subsided and she fell asleep at once.

v

Many *ri* separated Javerri from First City. Wande-hari urged that they depart with all due speed, before any local opposition could grow firm enough to be a real threat.

"We will have runners who can keep us in touch with the castle," he said, "and we can turn back instantly if need be."

"I don't like leaving here at all," Javerri said.

"Nor do I. But it is of the utmost importance that we attend to our business with First Lord. Without his confirmation your enemies are on stronger ground than they will be once you have it."

She nodded, knowing that this confirmation was going to be the most difficult part of their entire journey. She knew also that despite his still considerable powers, Wande-hari would be helpless to influence Sublime Lord Yassai. As in the other provinces, Javerri's lands were sorely lacking in competent magicians. Of those mages who lived elsewhere other than in the Fifth Province, Lord Yassai kept most in First City with him. He surrounded himself with them to counteract any spellcasting one of his vassals might be moved to try. Even the attempt, it was said, resulted in immediate imprisonment and slow death by torture of the unfortunate mage involved. Magicians, even his own, even the chief among them who was known only as the Scorpion, approached Lord Yassai with great care.

She had left Sigon the Strategist in charge, taking Michu and a hundred pikemen as well as Chakei for her guard. Though she was an excellent rider, she chose to go by foot instead, not only because horses' hooves were the ruination of the roads but also because the use of horses could have been interpreted as a signal of war and the necessity of moving swiftly. She made a point of inquiring about the physician who had been so courteous and thoughtful when her father was dying; his name was Lek and she added him to her entourage as her personal doctor. This pleased her; another person who traveled with them did not.

In addition to the physician, the group of travelers included the illustrious Lady Safia, that one of Madam Farhat's best ladies who had come to the Residence on Javerri's wedding night. She would ride in a palanquin carried by servants. Javerri and Ivo would go in palanquins because of their rank and Wande-hari as well because of his age, but she fretted at the necessity of having yet another palanquin in the company. Well, she could do something about that. She would get out frequently and go on foot, and nobody else dared ride while she walked. She allowed herself briefly to enjoy the picture of a delicate creature like Lady Safia being forced to walk in the dust with Chimoko, like an ordinary mortal. Ivo, standing beside her, remained mercifully unaware of her thoughts.

"I wish I could take the entire burden of this journey on myself and relieve you of it. This will be very tiring for you," Ivo said.

"I'm very strong, much stronger than I look."

"You look as frail as a flower."

She smiled at his morning gift to her, a perfect branch of late-blooming mimosa. "Well, I'm not. You'll see."

She climbed into her palanquin and, when all was ready, gave the signal to move out. She waited until she was well away from Third City before closing the curtains.

All Monserrians were enthusiastic travelers, and Javerri's entourage was only one of many journeying to or from First City. They made excellent progress, staying in one of the province's numerous roadside inns each night. Despite Javerri's remonstrances, the ever-practical Chimoko had insisted on bringing the box with them and she placed it near Javerri's bed each night. Of course, when Chimoko looked into the chest the next morning she had noticed that the box was not precisely in the spot where she had put it the night before. The maid, earthy and practical, simply couldn't encompass the notion that Javerri hadn't put its contents to use in privacy that first night nor that she wasn't doing so now.

"There will be," Chimoko said, "the time in First City before you are confirmed, when Lord Ivo will continue to be occupied with the other lady, and you deserve your pleasures as well."

Sighing inwardly, Javerri gave up trying to convince the maid otherwise. Let it be, she thought. I have other matters, more urgent, on my mind and this is trivial indeed.

Javerri, with Chimoko for company, slept in a separate room from her husband and Safia while the men disposed themselves as General Michu directed during these nights on the road. Chakei always crouched half-dozing just outside the Ladylord's door.

"There's a guard," Michu said truculently. "Why does that creature find it necessary to do this? He never guarded your father's door."

"Perhaps that's because I am a woman. It's his way of showing devotion."

"I'm no less loyal and I don't have to sleep at your feet."

"You're not a Dragon-warrior."

Michu's wide face creased in a sudden smile. "Thank all the gods and Ancestors for that!" he said. "They say there aren't any females among 'em. Still, I'd rather have him standing guard where I post him. Someone may get killed, stumbling over him in the night, and he thinks you're being attacked."

"Leave him alone. His presence pleases me, and it does no harm."

And so Michu reluctantly subsided, though he made it plain he didn't approve of the arrangement.

The general had brought up a valid point, however. She tried asking Chakei about it herself without Wande-hari to help the mind contact. In doing so, she discovered that, although she could do it alone for very brief periods, her head ached abominably with the effort.

forgive ladylord not want hurt

I'm sure it will get easier with practice, Chakei. Didn't my father talk with thee like this?

sometimes

Michu is afraid that thou wilt kill his men if they get too close in the night.

She could swear that a look of contempt crossed Chakei's rigid features. He ruffled his scarlet crest and shook off a flake of scaling skin. ***know difference i***

And that was the end of it as far as he was concerned.

On their last night on the road, Javerri invited Wande-hari to share the evening meal with her. The closer they came to First City, the more she found herself concerned that Nao-Pei would take the opportunity of her absence to move against her and she wanted to discuss the matter with him.

"I think she will do nothing," the magician said tranquilly. "At least for the time being. Since she made no move before you left, nor in the day or so thereafter, it is plain that she now wants to see what will happen between you and Lord Yassai. She must hope he won't confirm you. If he does, there's time enough for her and Sakano to raise a rebellion afterward. Also there is the chance that she'll be able to arrange to have an Illustrious Nephew on which to practice her seductions."

"In which case Sakano will have cause to mount his own rebellion."

"And lose everything? No, Ladylord. Sakano is quick to grasp any opportunity that comes his way, but even he wouldn't dare go against Yassai's full might. I think you needn't worry about either Nao-Pei or Sakano at the present time. We will arrive at First City tomorrow, barring unforeseen difficulties. You must clear your mind of everything but the matter at hand, my child. You will need all your wits in order to survive your confrontation with the Sublime Lord."

"I know," she said, bowing her head. Then she looked up at him. He sat examining the nail guards on his left hand as if the possibility of a loose jewel in one of the golden sheaths were the greatest care he had in the world. "You aren't to accompany me to First Lord's Audience Hall."

He didn't even lift an eyebrow. "Of course not," he said.

"First Lord's suspicions will be at their highest level and the mere presence of a mage who is not entirely his creature would be enough to send both you and me to the dungeons instantly. That is why I counsel you to put away your worries and approach Lord Yassai with a mind like a clear brook in a peaceful forest. Let him perceive you to be without cares, to be secure that your petition will be successful, to be confident that he will confirm your father's dying wishes. This will shake his own confidence a little, I think. He is accustomed to people, even lords of the other four provinces, coming to him full of fear. He enjoys seeing people cringe."

"But wouldn't he resent it if I showed strength? After all, I am a woman—"

"You are Third Lord!" The ancient magician sat bolt upright in his place, fixing Javerri with an implacable eye. "Never forget it!"

"Yes, Wande-hari," Javerri said, properly chastened. "I only thought that my coming before him with a show of strength, plus my happening to be female in spite of my father's having declared me his son and heir, might serve to offend instead of impress."

"There is always that possibility," Wande-hari said. He subsided a little, mollified. "Still, I think the results you seek are worth the risk. I have often heard your father declare that when all odds seem to be against you, that is when you raise your banners to their highest and blow the loudest war horns."

"Then of course I will do as you advise."

She motioned the elderly magician to keep his place while she arose to go for a walk in the lengthening evening. She watched some farmers working late in a small rice field. This was First Province; they had no House of Children here and consequently adults were forced to do this work. The cultivation of rice was a backbreaking endeavor. People of the Third Province knew this fact intimately; it was their chief crop, and the province was known as the grain basket of Monserria. Many years ago, in an attempt to find as many hands to tend the rice as possible, Lord Yon had decreed that

unwanted children should not be abandoned or destroyed as
had always been the custom. Instead, they were to be given
to the rice workers to be set to work in their watery fields.
These children, so the reasoning went, being so small, were
admirably suited to this kind of labor. And so the House of
Children was established and continued to flourish to this day.
There were always unwanted children, peasants' offspring
for the most part, though the occasional inconvenient child
of better-class parents would wind up in the House of Children. By far the largest number of them were girls. Those boys
who inhabited the House of Children were illegitimate, or
malformed, or those whose birth had been marked with un-
favorable omens.

First Province was the smallest of the Five that made up
Monserria. As far as what it could produce itself it was the
poorest as well. Yet it lay at the protected center of the entire
country; here was the Sublime Ruler's citadel and the repos-
itory of all its wealth. Because the First Lord always stood
in jeopardy, however slight, of rebellion among his vassals,
every *ri* of land capable of cultivation here groaned under the
weight of rice fields, sauce-beans or oil-nut trees. As she
watched, a man stood up, put fists to back, and called to the
rest that the day's work had ended.

Gladly, the workers climbed into an oxcart to be taken
back to where they lived. Javerri thought briefly about oxcarts
and long journeys as the heavily loaded vehicle wobbled its
way along the rutted tracks worn parallel to the road her
company camped beside. Then she dismissed the idea. No
traveler, however urgent his errand, would ever dream of ruin-
ing the roads in such a barbaric manner. She looked beyond
the oxcart and its occupants, to the line of mountains lying
purple-blue and hazy in the distance. She found them so
soothing she wished she could linger at this spot for a month,
absorbing their beauty and serenity into her inmost being.

Wande-hari was right, she thought. I must clear my mind
of every care. Oh, Lady Moon and Ancestor, please help me
find the tranquility I must have in order to live past these next
few days.

i

Stewards showed Javerri and her company to spacious apartments that occupied a full wing on the fourth floor of the immense Residence of Stendas Castle. It put to shame anything Yonarin Castle could provide. Chimoko settled the Ladylord and her consort at opposite ends of the wing and sent the somewhat road-worn courtesan Safia to her own small cubicle near Lord Ivo's room.

Then Javerri waited. One day lengthened into two; two became a week. More stewards came daily to report, oh most courteously: Various matters of state occupy the Sublime Ruler, in the meantime please consider yourself his honored guest, all the resources of Stendas Castle and First City are at your disposal. And just as courteously, she answered: But of course there is no great hurry, Third Lord's insignificant matter is beneath the Sublime Ruler's notice, Third Lord completely understands.

She maintained an even temper and, after each of these polite rebuffs, spoke with Michu and soothed him into keeping his. Lord Yassai might believe he dealt a subtle insult by keeping the new Third Lord cooling her heels, but he obviously had never dealt with a woman on these terms before. She welcomed the opportunity to rest, for Chimoko to massage her face and body so she could make herself as sternly beautiful as it was in her power to be for the interview that would, sooner or later, take place. Also, Chimoko brought her much information and servants' gossip was always amusing if not always to be taken seriously. Another week went by before a steward finally told her that Yassai would see her.

"It's humiliating, being bidden into his presence like a dog, after he's kept us cooling our heels so long," Michu said, scowling. The looks on the faces of her companions told her that he spoke for all. "Some would consider this a declaration of war."

"I am ready to fight for you," Ivo said, putting his hand on the fine new sword she had given him.

"Ready?" Michu said, and snorted with disgust. "I'd welcome it, and all those with us as well!"

She glanced at the "honor guard" of twenty, proud of the brave show they made in their green uniforms, Third Province's color. Though they had set aside their pikes on Michu's orders, each man went fully armed with sword and dagger inside the castle, as was allowed even the lowest of the warrior caste. She noted that even Lek the physician had put a dagger in his sash. Chakei, more lethal in his own way than any of the rest, hovered at her side.

"You will all have to surrender your weapons at the door," Javerri said, "except for Lord Ivo and General Michu. Please do not make any trouble about it. Surrender your high tempers also. I believe it will not become necessary for us to fight."

Hands resting on the hilts of her own weapons, she looked them over one last time, satisfied at the appearance they all made. Then she took a deep breath, and began to descend the stairs. She walked unhurriedly through the corridors until she came to the doors of the Audience Hall, recognizable because they bore painted likenesses of the Guardians, much the same as the audience chamber doors in the Residence of Third Castle. Reluctantly, her companions gave up their weapons to red-clad guards.

Under other circumstances she would have been clad in green as well, but she was still in mourning; her overdress of pure white cotton fairly gleamed among the showier brocades worn by the courtiers who crowded the audience room. Chimoko had spent over an hour getting her hair just right and applying her makeup. As a finishing touch, Javerri slipped Steel Fury into her scarlet sash beside his daughter Lady Impatience; the pierced gold hilts glittered in the light, drawing all eyes. As a member of the highest rank of the warrior caste, every lord of the province could go thus armed even within arm's length of the Sublime Ruler, though courtesy suggested they set their weapons aside into the keeping of a trusted subordinate, if allowed to approach that close. Javerri had no such intentions. She wanted it to be instantly known that, mourning her father's loss or not, she had come to claim her inheritance.

The doors opened outward, and she nearly lost her composure. On the inner surfaces, they bore the Guardians as well, only these were carved in such high relief they looked ready to step forward and physically stop any who would come into the chamber with less than honorable intentions. They were painted no less realistically than the ones on the outside, and their eyes glittered with gems. Gems also crusted the rings on their fingers and the necklaces they wore, and glinted on the hilts of the wooden weapons they carried. Javerri composed herself to walk forward at the proper time, without any visible signs of fear.

The Hall was crowded, with rows of courtiers kneeling respectfully on one side and others whose functions were less clear on the other, leaving a center passage and a narrow aisle along each wall where her guard could stand. She motioned for her companions to go ahead of her and join the courtiers. All obeyed at once save Chakei; without seeking his mind she knew he would stay with her regardless of orders. But that was the nature of Dragon-warriors. Once given, their loyalty was complete. Even Lord Yassai would understand that.

Before she could step over the threshold, the man in the middle of the dais spoke. "Come in, come in, Javere qa Hyasti!"

Yassai qa Chula, First Lord and Sublime Ruler of the lesser Lords of the Provinces of the land of Monserria, waved a few glittering fingers negligently in her direction. Obediently, Javerri entered the room and got her first look at her sovereign lord.

To her startled gaze, the First Lord looked like nothing so much as an ancient monkey someone had dressed up and put in the center of the dais. Bright, suspicious eyes peered out at her from the nest of wrinkles that was his face. Under the ornately embroidered robe, his shoulders sagged with the burden of his years. Jewels sparkled from his nail guards; unlike Wande-hari, who kept one hand free to use, Lord Yassai's nails grew so long on both hands that he was virtually helpless.

Javerri wished Wande-hari was with her. But she knew at once and instinctively that he had been correct in his estimation that neither of them would have lived past this initial interview if she had dared include him in her retinue. One look at the number and type of retainers Lord Yassai kept around him at all times told her more, perhaps, than Lord Yassai intended her to know. The mages around him, recognizable by their robes of office, looked cowed, beaten down. She thought she saw one who held his head high and a fleeting thought crossed her mind that this must be the Scorpion, but she had no time to pursue the notion.

"Forgive me if I omit your honorific," the Sublime Ruler said with exquisite courtesy. "I hardly know whether to address you as lord or lady until your exact status has been determined. Will you allow me simply to call you Javere?"

She bowed to the exact degree prescribed. "My friends have begun to call me Ladylord, Sire."

Yassai smiled, but the lady beside him covered her mouth with her fan and tittered openly. Javerri glanced at her, surprised by her rudeness. This had to be Lady Seniz-Nan. Palace gossip had already reached Javerri's ears through Chimoko about who she was and why she occupied her exalted position. Just fifteen, she was obviously pregnant; by custom, any lapses of manners a pregnant woman committed were overlooked. By a miracle, she was the first and only of countless wives, concubines, and courtesans before her to conceive. It was also said that Lord Yassai had had enormous help, quite unknown to him, in performing the miracle of the child's begetting.

"An elegant solution to an unprecedented situation," Lady Seniz-Nan said. Her voice was light and sweet, and she held up a wine cup which was instantly refilled. By the flush of her cheeks it was plain that she had already drunk a great deal.

"Correct, my dear. Nevertheless, I insist on informality." Yassai raised another finger, and a physician seated on the other side of him lifted a bit of spiced vegetable with eating sticks, examined it, and then placed it in Yassai's mouth. Behind the physician stood an enormous guard, naked to the waist. He held a sword, poised, ready to strike. At the slightest indication of discomfort on Yassai's part, the guard would decapitate the luckless physician.

"Come and join me," Yassai said to Javerri graciously. "Have you eaten?"

"I would be honored to share food with the Sublime Ruler." She approached the dais where Yassai sat on a formal cushion. There was no cushion of lower rank for her, either on the dais or in the space in front of it. Ignoring the omission, she mounted the platform and knelt deferentially on the hard surface, allowing a flash of scarlet underdress to show as she arranged her skirts around her legs. A faint hiss of breath from the watchers in the room told her this did not go unnoticed. Scarlet was the color of challenge and it had been daring enough of her to wear it as a sash; for her to have chosen it as her underdress as well made it clear that she intended to insist upon confirmation of her inheritance here and now unless Yassai could find a way to avoid it.

"Didn't I see a physician in your company of attendants?" Lord Yassai continued imperturbably. "Would you like him to examine your food?"

"When I eat from the same dish as you, Sire? I am perfectly content."

Again the intake of breath, delicate as a snow blossom, as the physician put a bit of food into her mouth as well. She chewed and swallowed with every indication of pleasure. For her to have put herself so completely into Yassai's power spoke highly of Ladylord Javere's courage in a time and place where the art of poisoning had been refined to the point that a single morsel in a dish could be made deadly without contaminating the rest. It was a swordsman's technique she used, and the warriors in the room recognized it with a certain amount of glee; by getting inside his guard, Javerri had made it necessary for Yassai to retreat before he could move against her openly—for the moment at least.

"I was desolate when I received word that Qai qa Hyasti had died," First Lord said. "I mourned that the House of Hyasti died with him for he left no living son. I thought I would have to send one of my nephews to Third Province. You can imagine my surprise when I discovered that you have miraculously become that son."

"No more surprised than I, Sire." Eeeei, Javerri thought, nor half as surprised as the Illustrious Nephew who thought he had a chance of ruling even if it were only Third Province, now that Seniz-Nan is on the verge of presenting you with an heir.

"Hmmm." Yassai shifted on his cushion and waved away the physician with the plate of food.

Seniz-Nan leaned forward and tapped him on the arm with her folded fan. "It is like a tale out of a book. You got word from Fifth Province that the will is genuine, that it bears Qai's signature even if it did look as if a spider had fallen into the inkwell. Confirm her at once, Lord," she said, smiling at Javerri a little unsteadily. "And then call the Council to ratify it. I like her."

Yassai turned and scowled at her. She merely sipped more wine, pretending not to notice. Then he turned back to Javerri and, unexpectedly, changed the subject. "Is that truly the famous Steel Fury?" he said, indicating the sword in her sash.

Javerri put one hand on the gold hilt. "Yes, Sire, and his daughter, Lady Impatience. My father bequeathed both to me as his son and heir."

"May I see him?"

For answer, Javerri slipped the sword a finger's length from the sheath, holding him so the light caught the mottling on the blade. The entire room full of people held their breaths. It was said that Steel Fury and his daughter had taken ten years for a master craftsman to make. When the craftsman had finished, he immediately drowned himself because he knew that he would never equal either of these wonderful weapons, let alone surpass them.

Lord Yassai glanced at the blade and nodded. "It is as beautiful as I remembered. And the pierced gold work is particularly lovely."

"Thank you, Sire. When my father went to war intending to join the battle personally, he wrapped the hilts with rawhide strips. It spoiled the beauty of the sword and his daughter but it made his grip more sure." She pushed the short length of exposed sword blade back into the sheath. An unmistakable ripple of amusement coursed through the audience, a sound as of held breaths being expelled. Lady Seniz-Nan laughed openly, prompting Lord Yassai to frown in her direction. A servant flicked open First Lord's gold-edged red fan and held it at his shoulder but he waved it away without touching it.

Javerri hid her own laughter. Very properly, she had displayed only that much of Steel Fury's blade and no more. To have drawn it completely would have meant that she must use it before re-sheathing, and, quite correctly, the waiting swordsman would have taken her head then and there. She silently thanked Sigon the Strategist for having taught her the courtesy of the blade. If she had been uneducated she would have fallen into this deceptively simple trap without a second thought. The approval she felt coming from those gathered to watch heartened her; surely not everyone in Lord Yassai's court was completely his creature.

"Yes, lovely," Yassai repeated. "I always envied Qai that sword. But why carry the weapons, Javere? I notice you have brought Third Province's Dragon-warrior with you on this journey. Surely he is protection enough for you."

She glanced at Chakei where he crouched at the edge of the dais. The Dragon-warrior raised his head, ruffled his crest, and hissed a little. "He would not be left behind. I wear my father's sword and dagger because he named me his son and heir to the Third Province."

The moment the open declaration left her mouth she regretted it. This was too easy; Yassai was far too wily to leave her an opportunity like this unless he had some kind of trap prepared. The stir among the watchers deepened; they too knew that she had made a misstep and leaned forward to see what use the First Lord would make of her blunder. Javerri reached out with her mind, seeking to open a channel into Yassai's thoughts, and almost cried out. It was as if she had hurled herself against a stone wall, and within herself she reeled from the impact.

Eeeei, that hurt! Wande-hari had never instructed her in this form of mental discipline and she knew she had been foolish to try it. She caught a telltale gleam in Lord Yassai's eye and knew he had felt her probing and knew how futile it had been.

"Ah, yes," the Sublime Ruler said. He smiled benignly and glanced sideways at Seniz-Nan. "We have yet to decide the question of inheritance, haven't we?"

Javerri bowed her head, struggling to maintain her composure. "You have already found his will to be authentic. And it was my father's dying wish."

"And should be given due consideration, of course. But there is also the question of fitness for such a position, Lady-lord." Not a person in the room missed the significance of Lord Yassai's sudden use of her title, nor the delicate edge of derision with which he said it. "As far as I can see, you are just a woman—a very lovely woman, but no more than that. Why don't you marry one of my nephews? Lutfu qa Masfa, for example." An extraordinarily ugly man seated on the dais nearby inclined his head in her direction. Another even uglier simply stared at her. "Or my other nephew Quang qa Masfa? That way you can return to the Third Province secure in your inheritance and bearing strong personal connections with me as well."

She looked up. "You do me too much honor, Sire. I regret that I cannot do as you suggest and either marry Lord Lutfu or Lord Quang at once for I am already married, to Lord Ivo qa Gilad."

Ivo got to his feet, bowed very low, then resumed his place. Yassai sucked his teeth. Then he allowed himself a sigh.

"Ah. I see. To give you your full formal name I should refer to you as Javere qa Hyasti qa Gilad. What a pity. If you had married Lutfu I would have confirmed you at once, of course. But now— The only reasonable thing for me to do is set you a task to perform in order to prove that you yourself are worthy to follow your father as Lord of Third Province." He stared at Chakei. The Dragon-warrior stared back without expression. The Sublime Ruler smiled, as if an idea had just struck him. "I have it! My own Dragon-warrior is, alas, not well. He is listless, his skin scaling so heavily it cracks and bleeds. I fear he may actually be dying. But then he is very old. Unfortunately, no one appears to be sufficiently daring these days to deal in eggs; perhaps the hunters are all dead. Mortality rates among these people are said to be shocking. At any rate, I have not been able to find a trader, though I have sent word in every direction that I wanted to buy another." He paused for a moment before closing the trap with exquisite gentleness. "But you could go and find one for me."

Beside him, Seniz-Nan's face contorted briefly in fury.

Javerri felt the blood drain from her own face. Lady Moon and Ancestor! Why not order my death here and now and have done with it? She quickly curbed her thoughts; though she might have bruised her mind against the wall that surrounded his, she had no guarantee that he couldn't penetrate her mind at will.

"Surely," she said, and her voice broke a little. She cleared her throat. "Surely the successful completion of such a task would prove anyone fit to rule Third Province."

"It is settled then, and our interview concluded." Supreme Ruler Yassai smiled and waved his glittering fingers at her. "You will leave at dawn tomorrow. Go and prepare for your journey."

She rose, keeping herself steady with sheer force of will, and bowed before turning to leave the Audience Hall. Her followers rose, bowed also, and left with her. As she made her way through the sea of carefully expressionless faces on either side of her, she realized that she had been incorrect in her first impression of the Sublime Lord. He didn't resemble a monkey at all; now she recognized his expression, attitude, and character in the pictures she had seen of the most terrifying creature on the face of the earth, a monster that was enough to daunt even a Dragon-warrior. Lord Yassai qa Chula, as he had sat smiling at her and ordering her into a death mission, had looked exactly like a desert shark.

ii

Elsewhere in First City, Wande-hari sat deep in an interview with the magician Halit in an audience hall he had rented in the House of Mages. A pot of tea sat nearby and both mages sipped politely from rose-glazed cups as they talked. Wande-hari's had cooled too much; with a minor spell, he warmed it again.

Halit, though new to Monserria, came highly recommended by more than one master mage of Wande-hari's acquaintance. Dark of hair, his face relatively unlined, Halit kept the nails on both hands trimmed quite short. From his appearance, Wande-hari judged he was still young enough to be subject to the temptations of the flesh, a luxury Wande-hari had discarded many years ago. Also, Halit was vain; the heavy silk brocade of his robe and the jewels on his slippers proclaimed him so. Though Wande-hari didn't particularly like Halit at their first meeting, considering him entirely too young and untried, the old man had to admit that if Halit could do the things he was supposed to be able to do, he was extremely talented as well, and therefore he could not dismiss him in favor of another, less talented, whom he liked better.

"Show me how you make exploding pebbles," the elderly mage said.

Halit smiled. "I thought you'd ask me that, so I have the materials already at hand," he said. He pulled a silk-wrapped parcel from his sleeve, opened it, and began setting out jars of various powders. "I can also do a few other small things that you might wish to examine. They are poor indeed, when put beside the wonders you can so easily accomplish, sir, but one does the best one can. . . . " The younger man let the words trail off, shrugging self-deprecatingly. He began stirring and blending, adding so much of this powder, a pinch of that, mixing it all in a stained marble bowl. He muttered a few phrases under his breath. The powders abruptly became a paste. With another word, Halit formed the paste into pebbles that looked indistinguishable from those that covered any garden path. "It is done," Halit said.

Wande-hari smiled in turn. "We shall see," he said. He selected a sample at random, noting with approval that Halit had made these pebbles both small and of low explosive force. Others he had interviewed had not had the wit to realize he would want to set one off and still not destroy the House of Mages where he now sat.

He removed the teapot from the brass tray on which it sat and replaced it with the pebble. Moving back out of the way, he murmured the words that set off a pebble without the necessity of hurling it to the ground.

A ball of blinding light briefly appeared, and a puff of scarlet smoke hovered over the spot where the pebble had been. Impressed in spite of himself, Wande-hari had to speak another word in order to dissipate the smoke.

"Alas, the tray is ruined," Halit said. "But no matter." He made a gesture with fingers, muttered something under his breath, and the warped piece of brass became a tray again. "It will have to be re-polished, though."

Wande-hari chuckled outright. With a negligent gesture of his own he rendered the tray as shiny as it had been when it was new.

Halit picked up the tray and examined it, pleased and astonished. "Will you show me how to do that?"

"Of course, of course. Later. Right now, I'm interested in what else you can do. I'm particularly interested in how and why you made the explosion without noise."

"Oh, that's a little refinement I worked out myself. It occurred to me that it is not always desirable that an explosion announce its occurrence. I'm still trying to eliminate the flash. Some of my pebbles make the smoke you saw, in various colors. Others don't. There are times when the smoke is convenient."

"Yes, I know. This is very clever." As thou art clever as well, Wande-hari thought. But art thou clever enough? He took a bundle from his own sleeve pocket. "You must make another pebble, using my ingredients. However, first I want you to show me something else, something, ah, gentler," he said. "After all, Third Lord Javere appreciates beauty as well as martial skills."

Halit nodded. "Will this suffice?" he said. He held out his hand. The air just above the surface of his palm wavered, twinkled, then solidified into a butterfly that appeared to be made of spun gold. Its wings looked like thin slices of precious gems, so delicate the sound of a footstep could shatter them.

"Lovely," Wande-hari said.

"Wait, there's more." Smiling, Halit leaned forward and slipped his exquisite creation onto the brass tray. He raised a finger and murmured a word Wande-hari didn't recognize.

The butterfly began to sing.

Entranced, Wande-hari nonetheless scrutinized the younger mage closely to see if he were performing a mere entertainer's trick, throwing his voice so that it appeared to be coming from the butterfly.

"As you may know, I live in the House of Mages," Halit said. "Please excuse me. I will return in a moment." He rose and left the room. The butterfly continued to sing.

Halit re-entered the small audience hall so quickly that Wande-hari assumed his room must have been just down the corridor. He had a number of books under one arm and a heavily carved wooden box under the other. Setting all this down, he gestured and spoke again; the butterfly abruptly stopped singing. The air around it glittered, and then the golden creature twinkled back into the nothingness from which it had appeared.

"Truly amazing," Wande-hari murmured.

"Thank you," Halit said. "Now, with your permission, I want to show you some of the sources of my study, and also to make amends for my poor manners. You must be weary, and have had nothing but tea to refresh yourself." He opened the silk package Wande-hari gave him. "While you divert yourself I will make an ordinary exploding pebble for you."

"You are very thoughtful." Wande-hari examined the books, impressed in spite of himself. "Where did you get this one? I have had a chance to look at it only once in my life, and that briefly."

"You doubtless know that I spent some time in the land beyond our borders to the south."

Wande-hari nodded. "Fogestria, yes."

"While there, I had the occasion to study with one of their foremost mages, a man called Anselme." Halit shook his head sadly. "A most wicked man. But one learns most from one's enemies, don't you agree?"

"It is useful to know what goes on in an adversary's mind. But why aren't you still in Anselme's service?"

"Oh, I never apprenticed myself to him. Indeed, I tremble at the thought. Actually, I had learned almost everything I wanted to know from Anselme by the time he discovered that I was, to all intents and purposes, a spy. I fled for my very life." Halit smiled. "And somehow these books found their way into my baggage. I must have packed in greater haste than I knew."

"I understand completely," Wande-hari said, nodding. "And the box?"

Again, Halit shrugged self-deprecatingly. "Oh, just a few other things I discovered in my sojourn. They can make life more pleasant."

Wande-hari gestured and opened the box without touching it. Naturally, he had already examined its contents before lifting the lid but saw no reason to tell Halit this. Some of the things he recognized, others he knew only from rumor; and a few he didn't know at all. "I find little use for aphrodisiacs at this stage of my life," he said mildly.

"Nor do I for myself," Halit said. "But sometimes the masters we serve have the need for a little, ah, stimulation. Not to mention— But that's beside the point."

Wande-hari nodded. The other man's attention had slipped ever so slightly with the opening of the box and with this had come the opportunity for a fleeting glimpse into Halit's unguarded thoughts. Brief as it was, it gave Wande-hari a very informative look at various matters Halit thought securely hidden behind the wall in his mind. The man had a number of startling sexual habits. In addition, Wande-hari now knew exactly how important the box and its contents really were to Halit. He had to retreat before he could see everything, however, and he had to do it without Halit's knowing that he had penetrated that wall; otherwise, his own will could have been trapped in the other's.

"Surely it is in a mage's best interests to keep his lord content," Wande-hari said. "But Lord Javere is still young and has no need of such things."

"I bow to your wisdom. Will you take *abaythim* with me?"

"Thank you, no. But pray do so if you wish."

"It is not a habit with me. Smoking *abaythim* is a soothing practice, however, and I sometimes do so when I have a particularly difficult piece of magic to work out. It clears my mind and makes it function better somehow. I thought we might share it so you could probe my thoughts with greater ease—if, of course, you find yourself sufficiently pleased with me that you wish to take this step in the negotiations." He set off the pebble he had just made and it popped and emitted a bright pink smoke.

Thou very scoundrel, Wande-hari thought, amused. Thou knowest well thou art head and shoulders above the rest who would replace me in Third Province. "Your solicitude for my advancing years is greatly appreciated, young Halit," he said aloud. "But I am far too old a dog to learn such a new trick at this late date. Never mind, for I still have enough strength that I can probe your mind in the old-fashioned manner."

"Then I am prepared."

Wande-hari sent his thoughts toward the other man, and into his mind. With Halit's full cooperation, he entered easily. The upper level was as he already knew, that of a greatly talented mage. He probed a little deeper and to his mild surprise found a portion of what he had seen previously lying open for his inspection—the usual impulses of greed, vanity, avarice, envy, and lust staining the purity of what lay above. Below this level, he knew, he would find the wellsprings of these and every other base emotion. Every person alive possessed this bestial component, and here he did not need to go. What interested him more was the well-hidden wall he had briefly peered behind earlier. Somehow Halit had managed to render it virtually undetectable now. If Wande-hari had not had the benefit of that earlier, unguarded glimpse, he might have overlooked it.

I should have taught the Ladylord that trick, he thought. It might have helped her in her interview with First Lord. When she is advanced a little further, I will. Well, no sense in lingering. He withdrew from Halit's mind, making sure Halit felt him leave.

"Are you satisfied with what you found?"

"I am satisfied."

"Then I am suitable to become a Third Province mage?"

"How courteously you put the matter," Wande-hari said with a smile. Eeeei, my young friend, he thought contentedly, thou art verily a defiler of young boys and waterfowl, and unless thou doth learn better, some day thy use of *abaythim* will fill thy days to the exclusion of even these pleasant pursuits. But I say that thou art also the most radiantly talented mage I have known with the exception of my own master, and when I have finished with thy training my Ladylord Javere can have even First Lordship if she wills, with thee at her side. "Yes, Halit, I believe that you are very suitable to become, as you put it, a Third Province mage."

"I could ask for no greater honor," Halit said, bowing low. "Master."

iii

"To find and bring back a Dragon-warrior egg!" Wande-hari repeated incredulously. "Why, that is tantamount to—to—"

"To a death sentence," Javerri said. "With no stain of opprobrium attached to Lord Yassai. Oh, he dealt with me most skillfully. For a while he allowed me to believe that I held my own in conversation with him. But then he disposed of me so quickly I knew he had been playing with me all along."

"It was ever his way," Wande-hari said. "I regret the necessity of your facing him alone. Still, I would say that you did not do too badly."

They sat in Javerri's apartment, the Ladylord and the two mages. Chakei crouched near the door, alert for any noise or unfamiliar scent outside.

Halit cleared his throat. "This has been a day filled with surprises," he said. "I thought I had reached the peak when my master selected me to assist him. But I was even more greatly astonished to discover that the new Lord of the Third Province is a young and most lovely woman." His gaze rested on her, so warmly she was nearly embarrassed at such open admiration.

"Didn't Wande-hari tell you I was female?"

"No, he didn't."

"I thought it unnecessary," Wande-hari said.

"And so it was, Master. Still, it makes some of the things you told me a little more understandable."

"I see," Javerri said, not seeing at all. "Be that as it may, we still have this question of obtaining a Dragon-warrior egg for Lord Yassai before us, and how to live through the ordeal. We must be gone at first light tomorrow and I haven't any idea of which way to start."

Halit cleared his throat again. "If I may be permitted to speak." Both Wande-hari and Javerri nodded. "As it happens, my sojourn in Fogestria proves helpful in more respects than the one my master and I discussed this afternoon. The Burning Mountains are located south of Fogestria, and it is somewhere in these that the Dragon-warrior eggs are rumored to be found."

"Do you know where the laying grounds are?" Wande-hari said.

"Alas, no, not exactly."

"Still, you have confirmed Wande-hari's good judgment in selecting you by this information alone." Javerri thought intently for a moment. "Lord Yassai was more careful not to give me the least hint of where I should start my search. Now I wonder whether to start in any direction but south so he will dismiss me from his mind as a mere annoyance, or to head directly south and arouse even more suspicions than he now has."

"The first course you mention might cause him to send Lord Lutfu to the Third Province without waiting for your return—or word of your failure and inevitable death. Lutfu," Wande-hari added in explanation to Halit, "is the Illustrious Nephew mentioned most often in connection with Third Province."

"But wouldn't my going south immediately be likely to bring about the same result?" Javerri said.

"If I may be permitted to speak again."

"Yes, Halit. Please."

"It seems to me that either action is likely to have ill results as regards Third Province. I trust that you left it in safe hands?"

"The safest, and the most reliable. General Sigon the Strategist currently commands Yonarin Castle."

Halit bowed. "Even Lord Yassai wouldn't attack lightly a stronghold commanded by the Magnificent Strategist. I think you can consider Third Province secure, for the moment. Also, I think Lord Yassai would wait for word of your success or failure. I think he feels that time is on his side, even considering his, ah, advanced years. Dragon-warrior egg seekers have notoriously short lives."

"Halit's advice is sensible," Wande-hari said. "No one—" he put a slight emphasis on the words "—no one would go against Sigon openly just now."

Javerri nodded slowly, knowing he referred to Nao-Pei and the rebellion she must be secretly working toward. She sighed. "Very well then. Tomorrow we go south, openly, for every spy in First City to see and report to Lord Yassai. But how we will fare after that, I do not know."

Chakei raised his head and hissed. **show ladylord i**

It was the first time he had spoken *beneath* to her without her having initiated the contact. She fought for composure.

But how? Thou hast never been there.

in egg i

She blinked inwardly. **Thou could see then?**

other minds also

Thou canst contact other Dragon-warriors?

some maybe

Lord Yassai's Dragon-warrior?

She felt his shrug inside her mind. **no fire in**

He's dying.

Again the shrug.

I'll be glad for thy help.

Chakei looked away and she knew he had broken the connection. She glanced at Wande-hari; not even he seemed to have noticed her silent conversation with the Dragon-warrior.

"We must seek guidance from the Ancestor Spirit," the old mage said. "Though having ourselves better equipped for a long and dangerous journey through mountains and hostile territory would be a useful thing as well."

Now Javerri smiled openly. "That is what General Michu and his men are doing at this very moment," she said. "He is finding us riding horses and pack animals, along with food and other things we'll need. Once we are inside Fogestria we can ride, as they don't care what kind of shocking condition their roads are in. Now, let us find our beds and what sleep we can. We must make as brave a show as we are able, tomorrow morning."

"And does Lord Ivo sleep as well?" Wande-hari said.

She looked at him, puzzled. "No. He is with General Michu, arranging for our supplies and equipment."

"Ah. Of course. Lord Ivo would have it so." He turned to Halit with a smile. "The Ladylord's husband is Ivo the Admirable Archer. Has word of him reached your ears as well?"

"Of his phenomenal skill with a bow, yes. But of his marriage, no." Halit inclined his head toward Javerri. "Lord Ivo is the most fortunate man in the world, surely. Is it permitted to say that I envy him?"

"Once," Javerri said.

"That will suffice."

They all rose and the two mages bowed to her. "Sleep well, Ladylord," Wande-hari said. "Let those of us to whom you have given the tasks of preparing us for our journey work while you sleep. You will need your strength in the coming days."

"Thank you, and good night."

But after they had left and Chimoko prepared her for bed, with Chakei at his new post just inside her chamber's door, Javerri lay awake for a long while.

Why had Wande-hari made such a point of telling the new mage about her marriage? What difference could it make? And for that matter, what was Ivo doing now? The courtesan Safia had been given orders to pack her few belongings, as had the rest of Javerri's entourage. But that didn't mean she couldn't drop her bundle and raise her skirts if Lord Ivo wished it— Stop it! she commanded herself. You'll wind up as common as Madam Farhat herself if you don't watch out.

A gentle scratching at the door panel made her sit up, instantly alert. Chakei poised ready to attack, crest erect, hissing.

A light, sweet voice came softly through the panel. "It is I, Seniz-Nan."

"Lady!" Javerri exclaimed. She got out of her bed at once, donning a loose robe over her sleeping garment. "No harm, Chakei. All is well."

She slid the panel and let the girl enter. Lady Seniz-Nan, red-faced and panting, allowed herself to lean on Javerri's proffered arm. "May I have some tea?" she asked. "No, make it wine. Those stairs—"

"Of course, Lady, at once. Chimoko!"

The maid hurried in with an oil-nut berry already lighted, then rushed to heat the wine. By the time Javerri had Seniz-Nan comfortably situated on a cushion, Chimoko had returned with the heartening beverage. Seniz-Nan drank one cup at a single swallow.

"The physicians say I drink too much," she said, holding out her cup for a refill. Her condition was more apparent in her loose robes than it had been in formal attire.

"Your time must be very near," Javerri said politely. She wondered why Lord Yassai's favorite wife had risked coming to her apartment so late at night. Surely it was not just to share a little wine with the Ladylord of the Third Province.

"You're so beautiful," Seniz-Nan said, sighing. "Even if you are old. You must be past twenty at least. But you're so slim, and I'm not."

"That's only temporary, Lady," Javerri said. "Once your baby is born—"

"Oh, who cares about the miserable brat! It'll just be given to a wet nurse. I won't have anything to do with it. But that's not why I came here. I came to warn you."

"Warn me, Lady?"

"My husband has given orders that nobody in Stendas Castle or all of First City was to sell or loan your party anything that would help you on your journey."

"We must leave at dawn," Javerri said quietly. "We came unprepared to hunt for Dragon-warrior eggs. Lord Yassai dooms me to failure before I begin. Is this the act of a sovereign lord who cares for his loyal vassals?"

"I'm the one he's displeased with, not you. He was furious because I liked you and showed it." Seniz-Nan wriggled a little on her cushion. "But his orders didn't mention anything about some unknown person giving you what you need for your journey. And that's what I'm prepared to do."

"L-lady!—"

"Oh, it's not as dangerous as it sounds. I've sent one of my most trusted men after your people to buy all the things you are refused. If your husband and your general are at all bright, they'll know at once what is happening. It's no trouble for me to do it. Naturally, you'll have to pick up the things on the road once you're well away from here. What direction are you taking, anyway? That's why I came, to find out."

"The south," Javerri said. Her lips were a little numb. What kind of dangerous game was Seniz-Nan playing? Javerri shuddered a little, thinking of what was at stake.

Seniz-Nan's face lighted up in a smile. "That will really infuriate Old Limp Penis!" she said with malicious glee. "He thinks you haven't any idea which way to go."

"Please, Lady, don't you think you should be careful of how you speak?" Javerri said, alarmed. "I mean, you can trust me, but someone might overhear—"

"Bah. Nobody's going to betray me. Not when I am carrying the Sublime Heir. Virtually the whole castle knows what I think of First Lord anyway. There aren't any secrets here. At least," she added, "among the women. The men still think secrets can exist. By the way, are you taking that courtesan with you when you go?"

"You know about—about Safia?"

Seniz-Nan held out her cup for more wine. "I told you, everybody knows everything that goes on here. Well, are you taking her or not?"

"I don't know," Javerri said, suddenly unwilling to commit herself to any course of action that would be merely one more move in the game the First Lord and his Lady played with each other.

"You'd be a fool to drag her with you," Seniz-Nan said. "Not with the husband you have. If I had someone like him beside me in bed I wouldn't be supplying him with a woman from the Hyacinth Shadow World just to keep from getting pregnant, or to satisfy some outdated custom. Third Province must be very backward."

Javerri struggled to maintain her composure, shaken though she was by her careful and discreet arrangements being tossed out so casually by this child sitting before her. Remember, she is the Sublime Lord's favorite, she told herself grimly, young though she is. "My reasons for keeping Safia with my company are surely not worthy of discussion in Stendas Castle."

"Oh, you're like old Lord Qai used to be—all stiff and proper! I told you, there are no secrets—except those we really wish to keep," Seniz-Nan added, smiling to herself.

With a chill along her spine, Javerri knew instinctively that Seniz-Nan meant the way she had gotten Lord Yassai's "heir," and knew also that her life depended at this moment on her not indicating in the least manner that she knew.

"As you say, Lady." Javerri lowered her gaze, and poured more wine.

"Anyway, Old Limp Penis has gotten word of Lady Safia's presence here and shows some interest. I believe he wishes to make me believe I can be supplanted, that I am not as secure in my position as I think. It would be an exceedingly gracious gesture on your part if you made a present of this lady to him."

Javerri stared at the girl. "Aren't you afraid?"

"No. His rage will pass as it always does. This takes away all fear," she said, putting her hand to her swollen belly. "You see, he is incapable of being a man most of the time. It is his age and too many aphrodisiacs. This makes him very cruel. Maybe this lady can coax a little life out of him and make him feel young again. Even if she does nothing more than harden his Night-Growing Mushroom for a few nights," the girl continued, "wouldn't you like him more favorably inclined toward you? I fear you bear the burden of some of his anger with me at the moment."

Javerri thought rapidly. The courtesan would only slow them down on the road. It would cost her little to leave the woman in First City—possibly nothing more than the full price of her contract with Madam Farhat, and that could be negotiated. If by leaving Safia she could distract Yassai for a time and even gain a possible ally in Seniz-Nan—"I'll do it," she said. "With Lord Ivo's approval, of course."

"Good. Old Limp Penis's pawings were beginning to grow tiresome."

"Do you mean that he still—I mean, in your advanced condition—"

"He tries." Lady Seniz-Nan sighed, then looked at Javerri

keenly. "A woman's life is not an easy thing, even in Stendas Castle," she said. "Your arrival, Ladylord, and the delicious problems you present have enlivened the entire women's quarters, I can assure you. And if Lady Safia does her work as well as her reputation says she should, every woman there who has had to suffer through Old Limp Penis's attentions will be your friend."

"I am very grateful."

"I must go now. Even with the precautions I took, someone may miss me and come looking for me."

"Please be careful."

Seniz-Nan let Javerri help her to her feet. "If I'm caught I'll just say I couldn't sleep and needed to walk. Good night."

"Good night." On impulse, Javerri leaned forward and brushed her cheek against Seniz-Nan's. "And thank you."

"I'll pray to the Ancestor Spirit for good luck to follow you." The girl paused at the doorway. "Even as far away as we are from Third Province, we've all heard how you dealt with your father's women. That was very clever."

Then she was gone, leaving Javerri to ponder the meaning of Seniz-Nan's last remark.

4

i

*J*averri stood looking at the door through which Seniz-Nan had disappeared. She had to act, and now. "Chimoko!"

"Yes, Ladylord?" the maid said. As always, she waited just beyond the door to the inner chamber. Presumably she had heard everything that went on between her and the Lady Seniz-Nan. If Chimoko betrays me, Javerri thought, and then set aside the thought as unworthy. Chimoko's loyalty was beyond question. She might have cause to worry about others in her company, however. Enough flattery, enough promises of wealth and power, and a weak person would be tempted. It was just as well that they would all be leaving Stendas Castle and its intrigues with first light. That lessened the time Javerri must fear an attack against her, and worry about from which quarter the attack would come. And the form it would take.

"Go and see if Lord Ivo has returned," she instructed the maid. "I must speak with him and do not wish to risk disturbing him in any way, and I wish to go to his quarters."

Chimoko bowed and hurried out in the direction Seniz-Nan had gone, giving Javerri a few moments in which to compose herself. The Lady Seniz-Nan had been very clever, really, in suggesting that Javerri leave Safia behind. Safia's world was one of pleasure, and as a Hyacinth Shadow Lady, she was accustomed to a life of ease. She had not been trained for the relentless discipline and devotion to duty Javerri's station required of her. And if presenting Safia to Lord Yassai might mellow his attitude toward the would-be Third Lord, then Javerri would do it and settle her account with Madam Farhat later. Yassai's unexpectedly mean action in closing the merchants' doors to her was an annoyance at best, but one she could ill afford. As for Safia's wishes or preferences, Javerri dismissed the matter with scarcely a thought; without her knowing it, the courtesan had now become a useful tool in the service of Third Lord. Hers would be a pleasant enough service. Life inside the luxurious Residence was bound to be even more comfortable than that in Yonarin Castle. Safia would be called upon to do nothing more strenuous than delight all who saw her with her beauty and charm. And if, from time to time, she had to coax a quaver from Lord Yassai's faltering manhood, well that was only her duty and what she had been trained to do, ei? And the prospect of having one of her own people—even if it were only one of Madam Farhat's ladies—inside Stendas Castle might even prove very useful.

The sole remaining problem lay in whether Ivo would be willing to give her up. The thought of Ivo's possible attachment to the lady, and the thought of them together in privacy, touched an unexpectedly sore place in Javerri's heart. Surely this was the only rational arrangement for them under the circumstances. And yet, and yet—

"Ladylord?" Chimoko scratched at the door. "Lord Ivo awaits."

"Thank you." Javerri smoothed the robe, touched her hair to make certain that her appearance was in order, then followed the maid through the corridor toward Ivo's apartments. Green-clad guards, her own men and utterly loyal, stood impassively at intervals, eyes fixed on nothing. They would be torn asunder before they would reveal anything that went on while they were on watch.

Her husband met her in the middle room between the corridor and the room he slept in, the counterpart to her own arrangement except for the private room that had been hastily blocked off next to his own. He had been sleeping, or at least in bed; like Javerri, he had put a loose robe over his sleeping garment. Safia was nowhere in sight, though a trace of her perfume lingered in the air; she would have been sent back to the private room and would be waiting there until called for again. "What is wrong?" Ivo said. He touched her cheek, and his evident concern gratified her.

Leaving out the name of the lady who had visited her earlier, Javerri told him about Lord Yassai's edict against anyone in First Province selling or loaning her any of the things she would need for her journey to the south.

"I know about that already," he said. "And also I noticed the man who followed after us through the city. He wore a certain livery; the, ah, person who sent him could have been more careful."

"I think that person occupies a very special position and feels safe from retribution, at least for the moment. However, that's not why I've disturbed you tonight. I have a specific request to make."

"Anything."

"Don't be so quick to agree. You might not like what I ask. I want to leave Safia here, as a gift to Lord Yassai."

She watched his face closely, but he merely raised his eyebrows a fraction. "The journey would be difficult for the lady," he conceded, "but her own wishes should be considered as well. An unwilling woman in Lord Yassai's bed would be worse than breaking your promise to the person you spoke with."

"Of course, you are correct," Javerri said, knowing that Safia would offer no objection. "We will ask her."

Ivo went to the door panel and tapped lightly. Safia slid the door aside and entered the room immediately. Her hair and makeup were perfect. She didn't look at all like she had been roused from a passionate embrace only to be told that she was being taken from a handsome and vigorous young lover and given to an ancient, nearly decrepit one. Javerri explained what she must have already learned from listening through the paper walls.

"I apologize, Ladylord," Safia said, bowing, "but I had no wish at all to journey to the land of the Burning Mountains. I am entirely happy to learn that I will become one of First Lord's ladies." She lowered her gaze modestly. "Perhaps I can find a way to make him young again, for a while, ei?"

"If such a thing is possible, you can do it." Javerri looked at the young woman, suddenly enjoying the sight of her as the exquisite creation she was. Much taller and more full-bodied than Javerri, she nevertheless gave an impression of doll-like fragility. Javerri wondered how anyone could look so perfect under such circumstances.

"You are too kind, Ladylord."

"Kind, no," Javerri said, full of new-found respect for the courtesan and her arts, "but you could very well make First Lord forget many cares and worries while we are away."

"I understand perfectly," Safia said. She bowed, went to the door to the corridor, and bowed again in farewell to Ivo before going to her own small chamber. He returned the bow. From this moment, the courtesan belonged to Yassai; therefore, it would be unthinkable for her to continue to share Ivo's bed.

Javerri looked at Ivo. "I apologize for disturbing the

arrangements our peculiar position has made necessary," she said.

"It is done and forgotten already." He kissed her hands and her forehead, but as a favored courtier and not as a lover. "Please sleep now. The quicker we begin our journey the quicker we can return, and the more secure you will be in Third Province."

"Thank you," she said. "Thank you. When I asked and you agreed to be my friend, I didn't realize how much that would require—from each of us." Then, as quietly as Safia had done, she slipped out into the corridor where Chimoko waited, and returned to her lonely bed.

ii

The following morning, Javerri's entourage, the palanquins and bearers, soldiers and servants all waited in an outer courtyard for the first rays of the sun to signal their departure. Their breaths showed white in the morning's chill and there was much stamping of feet and beating of hands as they sought to keep themselves warm. While they waited, she set Ivo and Michu to selecting which of her soldiers and other retinue would go south with them and which would return to Third Province with the news of where the Ladylord had gone, and the nature of her errand. Chakei huddled near her palanquin, unhappiness radiating from his entire body. He hated the cold. Yassai's men stood watch on the walls above the courtyard. Their red uniforms made a brave show, belying the discomfort they must be feeling; up there a cold wind blew that didn't reach the courtyard below.

Safia waited nearby amid more of Javerri's Greens, swathed in a warm silk mantle. For a while Javerri feared she would have to leave the courtesan in the care of one of the many stewards or even with the captain of the Residence guard. But Wande-hari predicted that Yassai would come and see them off himself.

"He won't be able to resist," the old magician said. "And he may try to detain you, just to make things even more uncomfortable for us all. It is rumored that executions of felons take place only one day a week in order that the Sublime Ruler can be present. He enjoys watching the discomfort of others."

"He keeps close watch over every detail of his fief," Javerri said, mindful of the Red guard captain who approached within earshot. "Yes, Captain? Is it time to open the gates?"

"My Lord Yassai wishes to bid you farewell," the man said, bowing, "and to wish you good luck in your endeavor."

Then he straightened up so quickly he stumbled, brushing against her and jostling her a little. Apologizing profusely, he turned and saluted just as Yassai himself entered the courtyard, flanked by his personal Reds, many mages, and the ever-present physicians. It was the first time she had seen the Sublime Ruler standing; he was so small and stooped with age he looked like an elderly child in the midst of his retainers. He moved slowly; his limbs must also have been stiff with the morning's chill. But his eyes twinkled with malice and a little smile lay in the corners of his mouth.

"Ah, Ladylord Javere," he said. "How happy I am to have found you before you departed! I must offer an apology. It seems that one of my officials took it upon himself to issue an order denying you or your people access to goods or supplies you will surely need on your journey. I had the man executed at once—" He shrugged. "But what good is that to you now? Let me make up this grievous error. Stay here with me a while longer."

She bowed. "No, Sire," she said. "Your orders were most specific. I am ready to leave now. It would be very unlucky for me to turn back at the very gate, ei?"

"Still, I regret your leaving unprepared for what may lie ahead." Lord Yassai's manner was bland as boiled milk; obviously he regretted nothing whatsoever.

"I am glad, however, that you honored me by your presence at my departure," Javerri continued. At her gesture Safia came forward from where she had been nearly hidden by

Javerri's soldiers. The woman let her mantle drop and everyone got a good look at her for the first time. In place of the
heavily veiled figure she had presented while on the road,
now the courtesan displayed herself in her full beauty. She
dazzled the eye. Her underdress of deep green matched precisely the delicate embroidery on her peach-colored overdress; hair, makeup, and nails all were perfection itself. She
seemed not to notice the chill of the morning. Around her and
extending even to those watching from the walls, Javerri
sensed men drawing themselves up in tribute as the sun's first
rays touched Safia and made her glow like the jewel she was.
Javerri took Safia by the hand and led her to Lord Yassai. "In
token of my gratitude at your having given me the chance to
prove myself gloriously in your service, allow me to present
you with this exquisite lady. Her name is Safia and her reputation in Third Province is very great. Of course," Javerri
added deferentially, "she must seem to you very poor indeed
compared to the ladies in First Province—"

"Not at all, not at all!" Yassai said. He motioned Safia to
come closer and held out a hand. Gracefully she took it in
both her own, holding it from the sides so that she did not
touch the jeweled nail guards. She bowed, touching her forehead to his hand.

"It is my pleasure to serve you in any way that I can, Sire,"
she said in her prettiest voice.

The faintest scraping noise from overhead caught Javerri's
attention. She looked up just in time to glimpse someone
pulling back from an open window. Lady Seniz-Nan, she
thought. She wouldn't miss the show this morning, either.

"This is a fine gift, indeed," Lord Yassai said. He turned
toward Javerri, still allowing Safia to hold his hand, his surprise plain. His other hand wandered, half-seen, toward the
courtesan's delectable body. She bent closer to Yassai, letting
the neck of her garments fall away slightly so he could peer
down at her breasts. Her perfume wafted out onto the morning air, and he absentmindedly patted her bottom. "But surely
your generosity is too great—"

"Please. I insist."

"You have my undying gratitude." He scanned Javerri's ranks with a keen eye. "But it seems that even though you leave one of your followers behind there is still the same number as before. How can that be, Ladylord?"

"It is just another mage," Javerri said lightly, "a newcomer of slight ability, an apprentice the good Wande-hari asked me to engage, to help him with his duties."

"I see. Another mage." Yassai grimaced. "Wande-hari is old. It is commendable for you to seek help for him."

"Thank you, Sire. Until I return victoriously." With a final bow, before he could detain her with any further conversation, she gave the signal to start. "When we are outside, my picked company will turn south," she announced in a voice calculated to reach Yassai, "and the remainder will return to Third Province."

She made no move as yet to enter her conveyance. Properly, the empty palanquins brought up the rear. Her nerves singing, she mounted it at last though she did not draw the curtains. As the procession wound through the gate she allowed herself a glance backward in Yassai's direction just long enough to see the scowl on his face and the flush the Sublime Ruler couldn't keep from suffusing his cheeks. He must be deeply annoyed, she thought with satisfaction. That made up, just a little, for her shame at the way First Lord had gulled her so easily the day before.

I'm glad to be out of here, she thought. No wonder Father came to First City as seldom as possible. I hope Safia will prove valuable to me here.

She kept her fist closed tightly on the tiny square of paper the captain of the guard had slipped into her hand when everyone's attention was diverted by Lord Yassai's entrance into the courtyard. As soon as they were out of Yassai's sight, she dismounted from the palanquin. Then she opened the paper and read the message it contained.

"Bad news? Are we betrayed again, Ladylord?"

Javerri look up and met Ivo's gaze. "No," she said, folding the note and tucking it away in her bosom. "Not this time.

At least, I hope not. This tells me how I will recognize the man Lady Seniz-Nan sends after us, and he me."

iii

They had journeyed many *ri,* nearly through the narrow arm of Fourth Province that separated Monserria from Fogestria, before Seniz-Nan's representative approached them. To conserve their strength, they always spent the night at roadside inns if such accommodations were available when daylight ran out and they had to stop. As Javerri climbed the steps of the inn they had chosen on this particular evening, a man arose from where he had been waiting on the veranda and came toward her. He had the look of one who hires his services to the highest bidder. Nothing in his bearing or his rather shabby road-stained clothing suggested First City or Lady Seniz-Nan. In fact, the puckered scars over one side of his face and neck gave him a distinctly brigand's look. Javerri stopped nevertheless, instinctively certain that he was that lady's emissary. Chakei immediately stiffened beside her, while on her other side both Ivo and Michu put hands to weapons.

"Wait," she said to them. "Who are you, and what do you want?"

"My name is Ezzat. The snow lies deep on the Burning Mountains this year."

It was the first phrase of recognition on the scrap of paper she had been given. "And yet the fires within keep winter's touch too light to notice."

"And those who dare greatly will surely discover eternal spring."

"It is well," she told her companions. "This man is one I have been waiting for—in fact, one we have all awaited most eagerly. I believe you have some things for us, Ezzat?"

"Yes, Ladylord. They lie hidden in the buildings behind the inn, well guarded."

"Thank you, Ezzat."

"I was instructed to say also by—by the person who sent me, that your gift is most generous and gratefully appreciated by everyone concerned. This gift has touched several lives and won you the loyal friendship of a certain lady above all."

"Then I am glad for it."

"The person who sent me said also that I was to place myself at your complete disposal. I have spent many years traveling through the region to the south, and I might prove useful."

"Thank you again. Come inside with us. Let us talk later."

When Javerri had rested a little, she called Ivo, Michu, Wande-hari, and Halit to her room to meet with Ezzat and share a light meal prepared under Chimoko's supervision and served by her personally. Then Chimoko retired outside to wait until Javerri might need her again; later, when the meeting was finished, the inn's servants would be allowed to clear away, again under Chimoko's watchful eye, so Javerri could sleep. The physician Lek sat in the room as well, not officially one of her counselors but there to inspect each morsel of food and drop of drink the Ladylord touched. Chakei crouched outside the one door, and Michu stationed guards all around the inn as well, to ensure their privacy. Reassured, Ezzat spoke freely as they began to eat.

"There are a few places that ooze fire between here and the spot you seek, but they are only dying foothills that give shelter to brigands and murderers. Still, we must go through them, past Fogestria, and beyond the Great Desert," Ezzat said. Self-consciously, he tried to imitate the table manners of those around him. "The desert holds even more dangers than the hills. If we survive this journey, we will have to breach the Long Wall, for that is where the true Burning Mountains lie."

"The Long Wall!" Ivo exclaimed. "Surely there's no such thing. It is just a story made up to impress the ignorant."

"Oh, it exists, Lord Ivo. I've seen it myself. The Wall still stands untouched, except by the occasional seeker of Dragon-warrior eggs."

Javerri and her companions thought about this in silence.

The Wall, it was said, had been built back in the beginnings of time to keep dragons within their boundaries. When the dragons stopped troubling the lands of men, men gradually stopped believing in them, Dragon-warriors notwithstanding. And through the long years, the Wall itself entered the realm of fable, its very existence doubted in the lands to the north. Javerri was shocked to discover that this part of the fable, at least, was true.

"May I further suggest traveling with only a few people, Ladylord," Ezzat continued. It was more of an instruction than a question. "The Fogestrians will never let you past the border with such a company as you now possess."

"And why not?" Michu said. He set aside his bowl and puffed out his chest indignantly. "Who are the Fogestrians to tell Third Lord how many retainers she may or may not travel with?"

"They think themselves the rulers in their own land, General. I am sorry to say this, but it is true. The ways of Fogestria are beneath your notice, of course, but part of my duty is to know these things. Therefore, if you will permit my impertinence, I advise you to leave most of your followers behind. Take only the most trusted with you, and as few of those as possible. Pretend to be pilgrims and you will go virtually unnoticed."

"The suggestion has merit, Ladylord," Halit said. "During my sojourn in Fogestria I saw many such groups on the roads. Always they were ignored by everyone else."

"I'm not certain that I want to hide behind a pilgrim's robe," Javerri said.

"It is not very dignified," Ivo said. He stared at Ezzat. Javerri knew he was wondering whether or not the man could be trusted. So, for that matter, was she, though she couldn't say why.

"There are rumors back in First City that Lord Yassai wants the Third Province even more than he wants a new Dragon-warrior. He may be plotting that some calamity befall you on your way." Ezzat bowed his head humbly.

"Are your sources reliable?" Javerri asked.

"Yes, Ladylord. The most reliable."

She nodded. **Wande-hari? I can't speak beneath with Ezzat, nor look into his mind.**

I know. Nor should thou before thou dost learn more of the art. I will look for thee and be thy guide. Try to see through my eyes.

Following the ancient mage's lead, she caught a quick glimpse of Ezzat's thoughts. He was an earnest man, a serious one, seldom smiling, long in the employ of Lady Seniz-Nan, whose father had given him an honorable position after a youth spent in less than honest pursuits. With Wande-hari, she looked deeper, finding memories each as clear and vivid as a painted wall panel. Mountains brushing the sky, sending up red and black clouds that rained fire. A terror-filled night crouching at the foot of an impossibly huge wall, hiding in a niche made when a stone split and half vanished down the ravine on the edge of which the Wall was perched. Something enormous flew on silent bat wings. Then the mountain spoke and the fire came thundering down—

He was after Dragon-warrior eggs! she exclaimed. **He was a trader!**

Nay, he was but a boy at the time. They left him to watch.

And to die. Those scars— How can he bear to return?

Wande-hari frowned slightly as he sought the answer to her question. **I know he is under strict orders. But there is more. Perhaps he seeks to regain the courage he lost that night. In any case, I believe we can trust him, Ladylord.**

And I likewise. I thank thee. The magician gently withdrew from both her mind and Ezzat's, leaving her alone again.

"Dignified or not," she said aloud to the men around her, "it may be our best hope to call no great attention to ourselves. We will take Ezzat's advice and become pilgrims visiting Fogestria's shrines, our goal some new holy place beyond the Great Desert. I will dress as a boy. I am small enough, and that will attract even less attention than if I went as a woman in the midst of a company of men." Javerri smiled suddenly, a second plan unfolding in her mind. Chimoko would be scandalized no less at being left at the border than at what she would be asked to do there. "Ivo, you and Michu decide who will go with us, besides those in this room." She nodded at the physician, who bowed in return.

"No more than six additional soldiers," Ezzat said. "I regret to suggest that you leave your Dragon-warrior behind. He'll be virtually impossible to get through Fogestria undetected."

Javerri shuddered unaccountably. "Let it be so," she said. "Now leave me, please."

The men rose obediently; Ezzat hesitated at the door. "I beg for one moment of your time in privacy."

"One moment, then," Javerri said reluctantly. Chimoko was, unaccountably, nowhere in sight.

When they were alone, Ezzat took a carefully double-wrapped packet out from under his shirt. With grave ceremony he unfolded it until a piece of painted silk lay on the table. "This is what the dragons you seek look like," he said. "I thought you should see it, but not the others."

Javerri bent to examine the painting, two crimson dragons in a misty dreamscape. In the far distance, its color soft in contrast to that of the dragons, lay a blue-shadowed mountain; in the foreground, a few economical brushstrokes indicated a grassy plain. One dragon crouched as if examining something hidden in the grass while the other stood warily erect, its long, tapering tail held straight out as if poised for flight, its head up, as if sniffing the wind for danger. The underbody lightened in color to a pinkish cream. A frothy-leafed tree grew nearby, intended to give an idea of the size of the dragons, but as Javerri didn't know how tall this tree grew, it meant little to her.

She looked closer. The heads were adorned with the same kind of crest as Chakei's except that these creatures also bore a huge horn in the center of their foreheads; the standing dragon had his crest ruffled to full height while the crouching one did not. Despite the massive appearance of their hindquarters, they looked agile. Most likely, she thought, the dragons ran down their prey. She looked intently at the lipless mouths, the rows of needle-sharp teeth, the clawed five-digit forepaws, and repressed a shudder.

"Thank you," she said. "You showed wisdom in not revealing this to anyone but me. Soon enough the others will learn what we face. I would not frighten them before it is necessary."

He bowed, re-folded the painting in its coverings, and left just as Chimoko came scurrying in. As the maid hastened about putting the rooms to right and setting out the sleeping mats, Javerri forced herself to consider the implications of what she had seen. Then, firmly, she put it away in a compartment of her mind for consideration at the proper time.

But despite her best efforts, the danger ahead pressed in on her. When her company split again at Fogestria's borders, she would be truly alone. There would be no messengers to spare to take news of her whereabouts to those who waited anxiously. She couldn't even afford to carry panniers of pigeons with her. And Wande-hari would be far beyond the range where he could speak *beneath* with anyone in First City, let alone in the Third Province. Nor did she have her father's example to guide her, not in this unprecedented situation. She wondered why she was not more afraid. Instead, all she felt was an immense loneliness, as if she stood on a precipice somewhere with all roads behind her blocked. She wished with all her heart that she could seek comfort in Ivo's arms, but knew it to be impossible.

Later, when everyone had gone to bed, she sent Chimoko to Lek the physician for a sleeping draught.

iv

The next morning, Javerri told Chimoko of her plans. "Tomorrow, at the border, we will separate. You will stay behind and pretend to be me," she said, "dressed in my clothing and riding in my palanquin." To her surprise, the maid did not raise the protest Javerri expected.

"One favor, please."

"Name it."

"Leave Len-ti with me and I'll be a Ladylord these Fogestrians won't soon forget!" Chimoko declared with some satisfaction.

So that was why Chimoko had been late in returning the previous night. She decided to tease Chimoko a little. "But Len-ti is an excellent soldier. I had planned on his going with me."

"It is a lifetime favor, and I will never ask another."

Javerri smiled. "Then your request is granted, of course. Remember that I am under Lord Yassai's orders. The guards will almost certainly try to stop you. You must make them let you cross the borders with all your guards. All of them. Remember that."

"Yes, Lady," Chimoko said. "I understand completely. These dung-eating Fogestrians will know they've met their match in me."

"Exercise restraint," Javerri said. "Try to act as I would in all situations."

"My performance will be flawless. I promise it."

That part of her plan in place, Javerri turned to the problem of getting herself and those few with her into Fogestria unnoticed. Again, to her surprise, this proved unexpectedly easy. She and her small group of companions arrived at the guard station about half an hour later than the larger portion of her party. Her small entourage—pilgrims perhaps richer than most, but pilgrims nonetheless—slipped across the Fogestrian border almost unnoticed in the flurry of commotion being raised by the "Ladylord" of Third Province. Being denied passage by Fogestrian guards while brown-clad Fourth Province guards looked on without comment, Chimoko nevertheless demanded unconditional and immediate entrance in a performance Javerri would have liked to have lingered to enjoy.

As she and her companions made their way deeper into Fogestria, she allowed herself to consider the differences between the countries. The people of Monserria lived in comfortable balance with their gods. They revered the forces of nature—sun, moon, the six winds, and many lesser manifestations—but politely declined to bother them with incessant prayers and petitions. Instead, in times of stress, they tended to turn to the Ancestor Spirit. The Ancestor, so the reasoning went, was made up of the spirits of all the world's men and women who had gone before. They melted and blended into the eternal whole, entering and leaving as life's cycles demanded. Thus, the Ancestor changed constantly while it nonetheless remained the same. Being so much a part of life itself, it certainly could understand what being mortal meant, and wouldn't mind being prayed to. If need be, the Ancestor could always petition an appropriate higher power on a supplicant's behalf. So the people of Monserria went about their daily concerns, living with honor when they could, by what means as were available when they could not, dying and being reborn until their spirits could escape this wheel of life and ascend to the next higher plane.

By contrast, Fogestrians were a god-ridden people. Malevolent deities lurked at every corner, behind every bush, along every road, waiting to pounce on the unwary. Every sensible Fogestrian spent most of his life trying to placate these entities, truly more demons than gods, and every man, woman, and child was required at least once in his or her life to go on pilgrimage. Shrines of various sorts dotted the land, and all roads bore their groups of pious travelers going from this holy place to that, all seeking expiation from whatever terrible sin had caused them to be beset by such gods.

Perhaps because of this national preoccupation, Fogestria looked dirty, unkempt, and neglected to Monserrian eyes. What with all the traffic, people on foot and riding donkeys or horses or in ox-carts and wagons, the roads were in shocking condition. When the winter rains came, they would become knee-deep quagmires, impossible to negotiate. The villages were mere clusters of ramshackle buildings huddled around the local shrine. Javerri couldn't help noticing that the only people in Fogestria who didn't go about with fear in their eyes were the priests and keepers of these shrines. No wonder this country regularly rose in arms against Monserria.

Fear such as this inevitably spilled over into action against enemies the people could see and confront. And also with such fear there would be envy for Monserria's more stable existence. She longed for the cleanness and orderliness of her homeland, and wondered how Chimoko was faring.

Javerri had had much poorer luck with Chakei when it came time to tell him that he must leave her and go with her substitute. The Dragon-warrior's reaction was simple, and final.

no

But Chakei, this is what I want thee to do. I insist, I order—

no

How could I hide thee or explain the presence of a Dragon-warrior in the company of humble pilgrims? You must leave me.

no

In the end, she capitulated, unable to get past his stubbornness. Ezzat had donkeys for them all to ride and he had also purchased one of the despised ox carts. Perhaps they could hide Chakei in it.

Now Javerri perched atop the cart, dressed in boy's rough clothing, all makeup scrubbed from her face, her hair in a braid down her back. She was getting used to the cart, though the first night on the road she had been rendered so stiff and sore by the jolting that she could scarcely move.

Unexpectedly, Lek the physician came to her aid. "Let me help you, Ladylord," he said. "I know the art of *t'champu.*" *T'champu* was the manipulation of joints and muscles, an unparalleled technique for relieving all manner of aches and pains, not to mention setting to rights any dislocations, major or minor, particularly in the spine. With quick efficiency, Lek placed her just so, applied a bit of pressure, and then smiled in satisfaction as nearly every one of her vertebrae cracked loudly.

"That's marvelous, Lek!" she exclaimed, sitting up and moving, instantly pain free. "But who treats you?"

"Some adepts learn to adjust themselves, Ladylord," he

replied. He craned his neck to demonstrate, setting his fingertips to his jaw and moving his head so that his neck popped nearly as loudly as her back had. "I am fortunate to have learned to do so."

"We are fortunate to have you to help us."

He had bowed his thanks and gone to minister to the others.

There was really not much to occupy her. Their camps were safe enough, as Wande-hari cast a Circle of Protection around them that no ordinary enemy could cross. To amuse her in the evenings, Halit created wonderful singing butterflies that seemed made of silver or gold or copper that glowed red in the firelight. Most of her sense of danger receded as she allowed herself to experience the freedom the situation offered her. The roomy clothing she wore—trousers and loose tunic—proved unexpectedly comfortable as well as practical, and she made up her mind to adapt the style for future use when she returned to Third Province. In the daytime she pretended to drive, although the oxen plodded along so placidly that all she had to do was hold the reins. To her relief, Chakei agreed to curl up and stay hidden in the bottom of the vehicle, under a quilt. Taking their cue from other pilgrims, they had loaded their extra belongings into the cart—food, cooking utensils, spare clothing. Unlike other pilgrims, they had their weapons hidden under the floorboards of the cart in a specially prepared compartment. To hide Steel Fury's gold hilt, and also in case she had to join battle personally, she had, unable to find rawhide, wrapped it herself in leather strips.

Though the oxen accepted Chakei's presence with indifference, the donkeys shied away and had to be kept in close check until, eventually, they settled down and accepted the situation. She had objected to the donkeys at first, thinking to supply her company with horses, but those would have been completely unmanageable around the Dragon-warrior. Horses always were, except for those few back in Third Province that had been painstakingly trained to accept him.

Javerri glanced at Chakei. The quilt had slipped off him

and he appeared to be dozing. His skin was beginning to darken, a sure sign of approaching winter. The jolting cart couldn't have provided him any comfort, yet he made no protest either in irritable hissing, or the speech *beneath*. She reached back and pulled the quilt back over him again.

Thou'rt more trouble than thou art worth, she grumbled.

stay with ladylord i His thought was heavy with sleep.

Yes, Chakei, I know. I thank thee for it.

"Someone approaching." Ivo reined in beside the cart. She gave the oxen the signal to stop. They looked longingly at a patch of rank grass off to the side of the road and she loosened the reins so they could begin to crop.

"Enemies?"

"They don't look like pilgrims. Nor do they look like any other honest travelers we've seen so far." Unobtrusively Ivo opened the slot at the back of the cart and stood so that nobody else could see into it. Bow, arrows, swords, and drastically shortened pikes lay ready to hand. "Dismount and pretend to inspect a wheel. Let's see who we're facing."

Immediately she slid down from her seat, blessing the sturdy pilgrim's garb. She could move as freely as the boy she pretended to be. The others in her company likewise dismounted, coming close to the vehicle as she inspected the "faulty" wheel. Michu moved to her side, trying to be inconspicuous and guard her at the same time.

"Having trouble, ei?"

They looked up. A man on horseback stared down at them. There were perhaps a dozen others with him, all mounted and all clad in bits of armor. Their weapons, if any, were hidden under loose cloaks. "I said, are you having trouble?" the man repeated.

"Oh, just a little." Ezzat acted as their spokesman; only he and Halit spoke the Fogestrian dialect with no accent. "It is nothing. But you are kind to stop and ask."

The man didn't move, though his horse shuffled and stamped. So did the other horses behind him, and Javerri knew it was the Dragonwarrior's presence making the animals nervous. She hoped Chakei would have sense enough to stay hidden.

"You look a cut above the usual pilgrim," the man said, reining in his mount sharply. "Let's see what you've got hidden in that cart for tribute."

A couple of his men dismounted and strode forward, drawing swords from their places of concealment. A third followed carrying a large saddle bag.

"Bandits!" Michu shouted in fury. "They're nothing but filthy bandits!" He snatched his sword from the cart. Faster than thought he unsheathed it and struck. The man he attacked, caught off-guard, appeared simply to stand there meekly while Michu cut through his body, taking off his head, plus an arm and a shoulder.

Chakei erupted from the bottom of the cart, roaring a challenge. He launched himself at the nearest man, the one who had first spoken to them. Both man and horse went down under the big Dragon-warrior's onslaught. The horse, obviously terrified out of its wits, screamed and struggled to get to its feet, knocking down and crushing a bandit who got in its way. Both sides in the conflict edged away from the hideous creature who ripped to shreds anyone he caught. The other horses, panicked in their turn, began throwing their riders and galloping off, out of control. Javerri pulled Steel Fury out of the bottom of the cart, holding the scabbard in one hand, gripping the hilt with the other. The leather wrapping felt good under her hand.

She knew better than to draw sword and join this free-for-all at once; she had been trained in formal combat only, according to strict rules, and these enemies fought by no rules other than their own. She would have perished in an instant. But the mages needed protecting, and that she could do. Though mages are allowed to make various engines and materials of war, they are, by their own law, forbidden to kill directly. Only in the most extraordinary circumstances can one do so without risking the loss of his powers, if not his own life.

"Stay here, close beside me!" she cried, and Wande-hari and

Halit obeyed at once. They braced themselves against the cart. Halit moved as if to stand between her and danger and she waved him back.

Javerri's soldiers scrambled for weapons. Michu rushed forward, sword high. A bandit clambered to his feet and swung at him from behind. Ivo cut him down with one of the shortened pikes. A man slipped past the line of fighters, intent on the three who pressed against the side of the cart. Steel Fury sang as Javerri slid him out of the sheath. She blocked the man's downward blow, her arm going a little numb from the shock. He caught her answering blow on his blade. She saw his eyes widen a little with surprise. That was the opening she needed. She pressed the attack, getting inside the other's guard. Her cheek stung a little, and then the man was down, his blood pumping out onto the ground.

She looked up, unexpectedly eager for the next. But the battle was already over, the bandits dead or mortally wounded. Fen-ha lay writhing on the ground, dying fast; his sword lay shattered beside him.

"Farewell," he gasped. Then, sparing his comrades the unpleasant task of doing what was necessary, he picked up a fragment of the blade and carefully slit his throat with it.

Michu came and knelt at Javerri's feet. "I formally request permission to join Fen-ha in the Ancestor Spirit," he said. "You had to draw sword to defend yourself in battle. I have failed you."

"Permission denied," Javerri said. "You failed no one. I wish to hear no more about it."

Michu bowed his head, then got to his feet again. Under his direction the men finished off the wounded enemy with quick efficiency and dragged the corpses off the road, even Fen-ha's. They threw the bodies into a weed-grown ditch a quarter of a *ri* off the road. Ugly red-beaked *aa* birds were already circling.

"Looks like they learned to follow the bandits in order to feed off the bodies of unlucky pilgrims," Michu commented sourly. "They'll have to find other means of eating regularly now."

"The birds aren't to blame," Ivo said. "But I'm glad the country is minus one band of outlaws."

"There'll be others to take their place, Sire." Ezzat grinned at him, wiping the blood of an enemy from his forehead. "I told you the road wouldn't be easy, even for pilgrims. Have you bidden your men to search the bodies, go find the horses? Not all of those saddle bags were empty—"

Ivo looked at Ezzat, frowning. "We will let the horses go," he said finally. "But go and tell the men to look for anything that might give us word of—of the Ladylord, back at the border." Javerri's orders forbade referring to herself by that title here, even in privacy.

Ezzat bowed. "Yes, Sire," he said, and ran to obey.

Ivo hurried to Javerri's side, appalled to discover Lek the physician ministering to her.

"It is nothing, just a little cut," she said.

"Alas, this—this lad will never again be the perfect flower he once was, but he will live," Lek said. He dabbed the cut on Javerri's left cheekbone with a compound that stanched the flow of blood almost at once. "But a hand span lower and it would have touched the throat—"

"If only I'd been there," Ivo said. "I could have protected you."

"Oh, no, not you, too!" Javerri exclaimed. "I've already had to forbid Michu from turning his sword on himself! Lady Moon and Ancestor, don't you think I knew what the dangers were when we came here with so few people with us?" Then, realizing that she had spoken very sharply, she relented. "But I thank you for your concern." She smiled at him.

He managed to return her smile. "Thou wilt look like a brigand thyself with that scar," he said.

"The better to frighten our enemies, ei?" Her heart soared with pride that the two of them could joke together so soon after their close brush with disaster. He helped her to her feet.

Lek moved on, treating the other wounded. They had been lucky in losing only one of their number. Apart from a few cuts and slashes, they had come out of the engagement remarkably well. The physician examined the man who appeared hurt the worst. By the way he held his arm it was almost certain that it was dislocated.

"I won't know until we can stop somewhere safe and I can apply *t'champu,*" the physician said. "You look as if you could benefit by a treatment as well, young sir, if you don't mind my saying so," he added to Javerri.

She looked at him and nodded agreement. "We'll stop as soon as we can," she said. "In the meantime, the injured man will take my place on the cart, and I will ride his animal."

They loaded the soldier, Tal, onto the cart and hastened from the ambush site. Javerri glanced at the dust in the road; the spilled blood would soon be trodden away, leaving scarcely a trace. Except for the bodies lying in the weeds and the circling birds, they had left no evidence that anything untoward had even taken place.

5

i

*S*igon the Strategist passed through the garden of the Ladylord's Residence in Yonarin Castle, making one of many rounds of inspection while she was absent. He nodded his pleasure at the perfection he found.

Not beautiful, Yonarin Castle was nevertheless the strongest in all of Monserria. When Lord Yon had been building his stronghold, he had taken advantage of a curious ripple in the surface of the land and the castle he had constructed was almost impregnable. On three sides, a close scattering of immense rocks erupted from the level ground around, sheltering a bowl-like space within. Yon had his masons fill in any gaps in these rocks until they became solid walls, and atop these he built even higher walls. On the fourth side, he built from the ground up until the new fortifications blended with the rest of the masonwork and the bowl was complete. Here Yon had placed the tunnel-like gateway to Yonarin Castle, an opening that dwarfed those who used it, yet looked as insignificant as the stopper on a barrel when compared to the immensity of the stonework, both natural and man-made, that towered over it. Inside the gateway, one went up a low ramp to a terrace ringed with shops, servants' houses, and soldiers' quarters. Another steeper ramp led directly to a guard house and an inner gate. Above this stretched the long flight of stairs and the short one, with a lightly covered greeting area at the landing between them. At the apex one must then cross the garden containing the Ancestor Stone to reach the great Audience Hall; lesser castle buildings clustered on terraces still higher on the flanking sides. From the moment he emerged from the tunnel, supposing he lived long enough to do so, an invader would face defending fire from all directions.

The Residence building itself, at the heart of the ancient fort, stood walled-off and hidden behind the Audience Hall in the shelter of the strongest of the natural fortifications. Here, virtually isolated from the rest of the castle, the ruling lord's privacy was assured. Painted and carved double doors, twins to those of the building where Lord Qai had breathed his last, opened onto a garden. Inside, all was simple, rustic, uncomplicated to the casual or unknowing eye. Sigon knew the garden to be an ingenious fortification in its own right. Every rock, every bush in the carefully manicured garden had been designed to form a dense refuge into which the defenders might retire at need. A little stream, pleasant to look upon, meandered through the garden, crossed by delicate bridges that would collapse under the weight of a man in armor. Beneath its bubbling surface, sharpened stakes had been positioned cunningly in its bed to skewer anybody who fell in or tried to wade across. Yonarin Castle had seen hard fighting more than once through the years, but never had its defenders had to resort to this last bastion. Still, it was kept ready in case of need.

Sigon was content with his reputation as a thinking general rather than a warrior like Michu. He didn't even envy Michu his higher birth, though once he had. If one went by appearances these days, it was Michu who had been born with dung between his toes, not he. Still, Sigon had always been grateful that the old lord had never been one to put much stock in positions of birth. Long ago, Jinku qa Hyasti, the late Lord Qai's father, had seen the potential in a certain gangling peasant lad, and had elevated him to leader of his squad of foot soldiers. From there, under Lord Jinku's watchful eye, Sigon had advanced rapidly, eventually becoming one of Lord Jinku's most trusted advisors when it came to war and the planning of war. Michu, the leader of Jinku's pikemen, he treated likewise, though Michu was always one to relish being where the fighting was hottest. A lord who was well-served could, it was said, walk through a raging battle with his generals beside him, signaling orders by the flashing of his fan, and never be called upon to draw a weapon. And if the generals in turn could go with swords sheathed, then the lord they served was counted truly great. Neither Michu nor Sigon had had cause to defend themselves personally for years. Only Michu had minded.

Lord Jinku's son Qai had held the position of General of Archers under his father. The three men, working so closely together, therefore knew extraordinarily well one another's minds and the caliber of leadership they all represented.

When Lord Jinku died, Qai had not replaced himself; there was at that time nobody old enough or well qualified enough among his archers for the post. Young Ivo qa Gilad was the most promising, but he was still a boy then. And there seemed to be so much time, before Lord Qai was cut down in his prime by that mysterious illness.

Sigon well remembered the journey years ago to First City after Lord Jinku's death, when Lord Qai had gone seeking confirmation of his inheritance. Even then, the Sublime Ruler Yassai had been one to whom a wise man did not show his unprotected back. He had kept his new Third Lord waiting so long that Qai had very nearly lost his temper and only the certain knowledge that the other three lords would join Yassai against him kept him from declaring open rebellion then and there. That, and Sigon's own repeated assurances that Yassai was trying to goad him into just such a rash move. Then Yassai would have had the excuse he sought to annex the rice bowl that was the Third Province. If the rice crop was bountiful in Third Province, nobody went hungry; if it failed, the country depended on stores set by in better times. This knowledge lent every Third Lord a certain independence of spirit, bitterly resented by every First Lord. Yassai in particular wanted power over the control of such an important part of Monserria's food supply. But delay as he might, he had to confirm Lord Qai at last; there were no legal grounds for delaying as long as he had. The subsequent ratification of the other lords took far less time.

Sigon knew that the young Ladylord was in a much more precarious position than her father had occupied. Still, she was the heir. Yassai could do little but try to get her out of the way on some rash errand or other while he probed Third Province for weak spots he could turn to his advantage. Therefore, Sigon waited patiently in Yonarin Castle, sure that Lord Yassai would make a move.

Sigon estimated that the Ladylord and her company had been in First City less than a month. Though it was too soon to look for her return, still a messenger should have arrived long before now with such news as could be garnered. He had stationed lookouts three *ri* from the castle. And today a man had hurried in with the news of a visitor approaching.

"The guards bear the sigil of First Lord Yassai," Khen reported. "I got close enough to hear the name Lutfu."

"First Lord's favorite nephew," Sigon said. Favorite because he was so completely Yassai's creature. If Yassai turned a corner too quickly, a current joke had it, Lutfu's nose would be broken before he could dislodge it from its accustomed resting place between Yassai's nether cheeks. The only question had been whether Lutfu or Quang was coming. Quang, it was said, was the more brutal of the two, Lutfu the more cunning. But where were the messengers from the Ladylord? And why send Lutfu here now? Surely he would be more useful to Yassai in First City. Sigon thought briefly of Lord Ivo, and assassins. But that would not be Yassai's way, not yet. "Thank you, Khen."

Sigon immediately summoned Hanu, his personal steward whom he had elevated to the temporary status of head servant in the castle, and began issuing orders. It would not do to have such an illustrious guest as Lutfu arrive and find no preparations made for his coming, no matter that his visit was unexpected.

"It is First Lord's nephew after all. We must not shame the Ladylord in her absence," Sigon said.

"All will be ready, Sire," Hanu said deferentially. "Rely on me."

"See to it," Sigon said, scowling. Secretly he was pleased that the steward outwardly treated Lutfu's arrival as of no more importance than that of any other traveler. He hoped the rest of his people could maintain a similar aplomb.

His mind at ease, Sigon went to the stairway from the great Audience Hall to the sheltered area below. He wanted to be waiting when Lutfu arrived, wanted to greet him in the shadow of the Ancestor Stone. He found the Lady Nao-Pei already there.

"I just now sent a servant to tell you that Lord Lutfu qa Masfa was expected any moment," she said. "But I see your people were more efficient than I anticipated."

"Lady," he said, bowing. Now how in the name of the Ancestor had she known of Lutfu's visit to Third City? She had no spies that he was aware of, other than the insignificant gossips every lady maintained. It must have been Sakano—

—who was not in his accustomed place at Nao-Pei's side. His nose, Sigon thought, was in as great peril as Lutfu's except that in Sakano's case he kept it tucked into Nao-Pei's notorious back passage rather than Yassai's. Sakano had come back to Yonarin Castle the day after Ladylord Javere departed, and he and Nao-Pei had been more inseparable than ever, if such a thing were possible. Until today. Curious, he thought. And interesting.

"Unfortunately, the Baron Sakano was called back to his

home on pressing business just this morning," Nao-Pei said, thus relieving Sigon of the necessity of asking. "He will be sorry to miss Lord Lutfu."

"It is unthinkable that he not know of the Illustrious Nephew's visit," Sigon said politely. "I will send a messenger to him right away." Nao-Pei's cheeks colored, and Sigon hid a smile.

There was a scheme here, and no mistake. But what? It must involve Lord Lutfu, and also be something that Sakano doesn't particularly like. All at once Sigon saw the plan clearly. His inward smile deepened. Yassai was even more subtle than Sigon anticipated. Sigon knew it was unthinkable that Yassai hadn't already put Lutfu forward as the Ladylord's husband. After all, hadn't both he and Wande-hari anticipated such an obvious move by the First Lord? But now, he thought with satisfaction, Yassai had shown himself a worthy opponent by doing the unexpected: He has sent Lutfu to Third City as a suitor for Nao-Pei's hand. And what was Sakano's part in all this? Becoming Nao-Pei's lover fully, at last? More lands? The headsman's ax? All three? Eeeei, how very interesting.

He watched Lutfu as he came through the tunnel into the compound below. It was easy to pick him out of the crowd of servants and red-uniformed soldiers because of the deferential treatment they accorded him. Otherwise, his appearance was not in the least remarkable. He was a short, bowlegged man, very strong and very ugly. He also looked more than a little stupid. Careful, Sigon warned himself. He was rumored to be the intelligent one. Sigon, above all others, shouldn't let appearances deceive him. He went down the short flight of stairs, timing it so he knelt and bowed to the ground as Lutfu climbed the last few steps of the grand stairway. "In the absence of Javere, Lord of the Third Province, I welcome you to Yonarin Castle, Lord Lutfu. I hope our poor accommodations will not distress the Illustrious Nephew unduly."

"Thank you," Lutfu said, bowing in turn. "But I am just a

poor traveler who must impose on your hospitality. Anywhere you allow me to stay will be more than satisfactory." He glanced up and Sigon knew what he was seeing, what every person who stood in the greeting area saw, the Ancestor Stone rearing high and erect above them. Too bad Nao-Pei had picked just this spot to be seen by Lutfu for the first time.

Sigon got up, continuing the meaningless courtesies required in such a situation as long as he dared. "May I present the Lady Nao-Pei qa Hyasti?" he said at last, when good manners had been more than satisfied. She came forward and bowed.

"Who has not heard of the Lady Nao-Pei?" Lutfu said, bowing in return. "She is, after all, the highest-ranked lady in Third Province, ei?"

Nao-Pei smiled and blushed, holding up her hand demurely, pretending to ward off the compliments. "You honor me too much."

Sigon raised his eyebrows. An obvious trap, but one Lutfu looked incapable of, on his own. Nao-Pei was all but simpering. "Indeed, Lady Nao-Pei is second only to our Ladylord," Sigon said. He watched the smile fade from Nao-Pei's face.

"Ah, yes, the Ladylord," Lutfu said. "Neither the one nor, properly, the other. Well, there's no doubt that this lady is highest-ranked here in Third Province at the moment. And the most beautiful."

Hanu the steward hovered at Sigon's elbow, waiting to show Lutfu to Yonarin's guest apartments, up another set of stairs and to the right.

"Will my lord wish to visit the bath now, or later?" Hanu inquired.

"Bath first," Lutfu said. A little smile hovered at the corner of his mouth; Sigon realized what really lay on Lutfu's face. What he had at first thought mere stupidity was in fact self-satisfaction tinged with cruelty. The Illustrious Nephew was entitled to order anyone below a certain rank beaten, imprisoned, or executed at his whim, and Sigon knew that Lutfu had done just that, more than once. Sigon hoped Hanu's preparations were perfect.

ii

That evening, Sigon and Lutfu sat drinking together after the meal. Two of Madam Farhat's best ladies were with them, seeing that their wine cups were always full. Maidservants hovered nearby, ready with fresh flasks when needed. One of the tiny cups, scarcely touched, rested before each lady. From time to time they pretended to drink. Two of Lutfu's red-uniformed bodyguards knelt impassively just inside the door, and others waited outside.

Sigon was pleased to see that Hanu had had wit enough to provide Lutfu with double-distilled heated wine, the one with the eleven-petaled flower design painted on the flask. He was even more pleased that Hanu, without asking, served Sigon from the seven-petaled flask, the one generally given to women and old men. Ordinarily, both would have been drinking from nine-petaled flasks. Lutfu, obviously an experienced drinker, might have noticed if Hanu had given Sigon the five-petaled wine, the one only a little stronger than water. He made a note to himself to increase Hanu's salary. Lutfu's excuse for coming to Yonarin Castle was mere subterfuge; with the strong wine, Sigon hoped the Illustrious Nephew's tongue would become sufficiently loose that he could be persuaded to tell the real reason.

First, Lutfu was happy to tell Sigon about Javere's interview with the First Lord. "She vowed she was honored to go and get a Dragon-warrior egg," he concluded.

"She is a worthy successor to Lord Qai," Sigon said. "But even I am impressed with such bravery." Also he was impressed that Javere had been admitted to an audience with Yassai so quickly. Lord Qai had waited nearly three months.

Lutfu shrugged. "It is easy to be brave when one has no choice."

"I had hoped to hear this news before your arrival, and not trouble you for it."

"My apologies, General. I forgot to tell you that your Lady-lord's soldiers had to be detained in First City shortly after she departed. Something about their passes not being in order. So of course you would have been without news." Lutfu smiled in sympathy. Then, abruptly, he changed the subject. "My uncle has ordered me to marry again," he said. "My first wife is recently dead in childbirth, as you may have heard, and it is unseemly for me not to have a wife of high status."

Sigon nodded. All Monserria had known about Lutfu's marriage to the Lady Ra-lan, years his senior and very rich. Many indecent jokes had been made about the bridegroom's poverty, matched only by his reluctance; Ra-lan was no beauty at best, and an ill-natured shrew to boot. The Illustrious Nephew, it was said, far preferred to frequent the shabbiest sort of Hyacinth Shadow World houses. It was said also that he liked best to have two courtesans to watch and a boy to caress in order to reach his keenest pleasure. And he spoke openly of how little he cared for his wife's embraces. But somehow, Lutfu managed to overcome his repugnance toward his wife long enough to do his duty and impregnate the lady. There were jokes about that, too. But with the lady's death, all joking had ceased and the Lady Ra-lan immediately assumed every virtue of youth, beauty, and sweetness of disposition.

"The message from Lady Nao-Pei must have been balm to your grieving heart," Sigon said politely. Lutfu nodded and Sigon knew that his guess had been accurate; furthermore, Lutfu had not even noticed that he had not informed Sigon of his and Nao-Pei's plans.

"I was gratified that she would even consider me," Lutfu said.

"Of course, First Lord could have ordered her to marry you and she would have obeyed without question. However, I think it is a good sign that the lady herself shows such interest. It bodes better for your, ah, mutual happiness."

"I wish to marry her without delay."

"Even in the absence of Third Lord?" Sigon held his breath; he was on dangerous ground. But Lutfu merely shrugged.

"Let us speak freely," he said, slurring his words a little. "Officially, there is no Third Lord at present, nor will there be until Javere returns from my uncle's errand." Lutfu smiled. "And perhaps not even then. My uncle is quite perplexed about how to solve this unusual situation."

Sigon nodded wisely. Such a lie should make the entire castle stink, he thought. "I'm sure he will soon find the best answer, in his wisdom," he said.

"But in the meantime, there's no official ruler here. Nobody to give permission or deny it. I will marry Nao-Pei tomorrow." Lutfu brushed aside the tiny wine cup the courtesan offered him. "This thing is too small! Bring me something bigger!" A maid immediately offered the lady a teacup, brimming full, and she gave it to Lutfu. He drained it in one swallow.

"But the preparations—"

"Bah! Who cares about fancy gowns and face paint?" Lutfu nudged Sigon in the ribs. "It's what's under 'em that counts, don't you agree?" He ran one hand over the courtesan sitting next to him. Then he loosened the neck of her dress and slipped his hand inside. Both women smiled fixedly and Sigon knew they were as embarrassed as he was at Lutfu's appalling manners. Couldn't the man wait until he was alone with the woman?

"I was only thinking of the Lady Nao-Pei," Sigon said.

Lutfu took his hand out of the courtesan's dress. "Yes, women do set store by such things. But her reward later will be enough to make up for haste now, ei?"

"I suppose that would depend on the nature of the reward, Lord Lutfu," Sigon said carefully.

Lutfu stared at Sigon out of reddened eyes. Sigon looked back with all the blandness within his command. A very long moment passed. Then the Illustrious Nephew grinned. "She'll be happy over the bargain, I promise."

"And will you be taking your new wife back with you to First City?"

"Back with me? Surely, General Sigon, you've guessed already. My uncle has ordered me to stay here at Yonarin Castle while Javere, whatever she calls herself, is away."

"I scarcely dared hope," Sigon said. Eeeei, this was worse than he'd dared imagine! He bowed, partly to hide any expression on his face that might give away his feelings. "First Lord honors us exceedingly."

"Thank you. Of course, you shall continue as Javere ordered. After all, I'll need some time to acquaint myself with how matters stand in Third Province."

"Of course," Sigon said, his mind racing. Where was the Ladylord and what trap had Yassai set for her, that he dared establish Lutfu in her place even before word came back of her death? "Third Lord will be very grateful for your help in her absence."

Lutfu opened his mouth, closed it, opened it again. Sigon knew that if the Illustrious Nephew was ever to speak incautiously, now was the moment when he would do it.

"Her absence?" he said, his voice very thick. "Her *permanent* absence you mean. Javere's never coming back."

"Ah," Sigon said gently. "But she has the best people with her—"

"Means nothing. Nothing. My uncle—" Lutfu leaned closer, smiling slyly, gusting wine-heavy breath in Sigon's face. He hiccupped. "My uncle has someone with her as well, someone who will see to it that she doesn't come back. Believe me, your Ladylord is as good as dead."

Then he pitched forward, unconscious. Wine cups, flasks, delicate dishes broke under his head. Miraculously, he wasn't hurt; indeed, he began snoring at once. Lutfu's men came forward. With the ease of long practice, they picked him up and carried him off to bed.

"Go now," Sigon told the courtesans. "You have heard nothing here."

The women got to their feet and fled, pausing only for a hasty bow at the door.

Eeeei, he thought, if there were only a way to get word of this to Ladylord Javere! But once she had left First City, she was as good as vanished from the land unless she was able to send a messenger back herself. Sigon could only hope that the Ancestor Spirit would see fit to watch over her. Who was this traitor with her? Or was that just something Lutfu made up, to cause needless worry? All at once he was grateful that Javere had chosen Michu to go with her. She knew Sigon's distaste for First City and the Sublime Ruler. Though he had taught her everything she knew of courtier's skills, she had thought to spare him, choosing Michu instead despite his chaffing at the inanities of court behavior he would have to endure. Sigon had wondered at the wisdom of such a choice at the time. Now, as it turned out, the Ladylord's greatest need was for her fearless warrior general, and not him. His first duty now was to Yonarin Castle, to keep it for her until she returned to her province. And she had to return. She had taken a number of good men with her; Michu had picked them personally. She would need them in her struggle with First Lord Yassai. He hoped they would fight and die bravely.

The maids hovered outside, not daring to enter. The lamps burned low while Sigon continued to stare into the mess of smashed cups and wine flasks.

iii

Naturally, Madam Farhat had known of Lutfu's arrival even before the castle dwellers did. The news spread like smoke on the air; she had hastened to prepare her best ladies for service that night, knowing that Sigon would want to entertain his guest in the finest possible fashion. Likewise, she could expect a good business with her lesser ladies, from Lutfu's retainers.

"You, and you," she said, indicating Gyacho and Le-wha. "Your manners are perfect, and you know how to entertain or become one with the wall screens at need. Le-wha, wear your best dress—the lavender with the gold thread. The launderer has it? Eeeei, then your second best! Yes, Gyacho? Oh, the peach by all means, to bring out the bloom in your cheeks—"

The girls fluttered around her like so many bright butterflies, excited by the prospect of attending such a highborn guest.

"Ah, but Mother Farhat," Le-wha said shyly, "are you certain? In any case, I've heard it said that Lord Lutfu's tastes are, ah, somewhat lower than our rank suggests."

"Of course I'm certain," Farhat said sternly. "And Lutfu has never known anything better than First City whorehouses without a proper first-class courtesan among them. If the stories are true and he requires a boy, there'll be one waiting. But I doubt that he will, with the two of you to serve him. How could he learn to be discriminating in the Hyacinth Shadow World, with no real quality available? Just be careful when it comes to Sigon, that's all. Flirt a little, but not too much. The general is a widower, very strict, very proper, and has never been known to enjoy a woman other than his one wife."

Gyacho stifled a giggle with her hand. "And yet he was ready to marry the Ladylord."

"Merely a polite gesture," Farhat said. "And certainly not meant to be taken seriously."

And so it hadn't, Farhat thought. Lord Ivo had been the one chosen, just as everyone knew he would be, in order to keep the Ladylord out of the clutches of just such a malformed toad as Lutfu. Or worse, Quang. But that was old news, nothing to think about just now. Where was Safia? What had happened to her? Safia was extremely valuable, one of Farhat's very best, trained by her own hand. She had picked Safia most carefully, had allowed Safia to go to First City only on the hope that Lord Ivo would buy the girl's contract.

Now, as the hour grew late, she struck fire to an oil-nut

berry, not wishing to rouse her maid. If need be, she was prepared to wait until dawn if necessary for her ladies to return. There was bound to be a great deal of extremely interesting information to be gotten from such an evening, and the fewer people who knew of it, the better.

She couldn't hide her astonishment at Gyacho and Le-wha's story when the ladies came back early to the house. She prepared warm wine for them with her own hands; clearly, they had both suffered a shock. As they drank, they related what had transpired in General Sigon's dining hall.

"What of Safia?" she said.

"Nothing was mentioned, Mother," Gyacho said.

"We think the Ladylord must have taken her along," Le-wha added. "Lord Lutfu did not say she was with the soldiers detained in First City."

"Are you certain?" she said, eyes narrowed. "You must be absolutely sure."

"We are, Mother," Gyacho said. "But General Sigon ordered us to forget everything we'd heard—"

"And not to tell anyone," Le-wha added.

"And that was a very sound order, and one you must obey," she said. "Never tell a soul about anything you've seen and heard, except for me, of course. I must know everything, or how can I protect you, ei?"

"Thank you, Mother," Gyacho said, and both ladies bowed. "We knew you would know what to do next."

"Go to bed now," Farhat said soothingly. "You are only lucky you could return here, and not have to endure that vile Lutfu. Your services were engaged for the entire night, but I think I won't have to refund any money, considering the circumstances."

Le-wha shuddered. "Lord Lutfu is worse than the stories say he is! He has the manners of a dung eater. I thought I'd die of embarrassment when he put his hand inside my dress. I can still feel his dreadful touch. And General Sigon was embarrassed, too, I could tell."

"The shame will fade in time. I promise you that the next

man who enjoys your exquisite company will know how to behave."

The ladies bowed again and hurried off to bed, happy to have placed their problems where they belonged, on wiser, more experienced shoulders. The two of them would, Madam Farhat knew, now find it easier to ignore this evening's occurrences, if not to forget. Too bad General Sigon, for all his shrewdness, didn't understand women. These blossoms were too delicate to carry the kind of burden he had placed upon them.

The news about Safia was as alarming as the other items the ladies reported. Drag that fragile beauty out into the country on some stupid errand? She would be ruined. Ruined! Farhat rocked back and forth, the loss of the courtesan and the silver she represented creating a dreadful ache inside her. She longed for some strong heated wine.

Well, nothing could be done about it now. Farhat turned her thoughts to other matters closer to home. Lutfu and Nao-Pei! Farhat laughed silently through her nose. If it hadn't presented such a potential danger to Third Province, it would be funny indeed. Eeeei, those two richly deserved each other, if the stories she'd heard about both were true. But to have them here in Third Province, in Yonarin Castle! The trouble clouds were already boiling.

Of course it would be war. And war was always good for business, with men seeking one last glimpse of immortality before going out to die. Prices would rise of course, for everything. Most of all for her women. But where would the war start, and between whom? And on which side would it be wise to place her loyalties? The Ladylord, though young and lacking in experience, looked to grow into a tolerant and competent ruler who would let Farhat alone to run her business as she saw fit. Farhat had been agreeably impressed with the way she had handled the matter of her father's women. But she might not live through another week, if Lutfu's story was the truth.

Abruptly, she got up, opened the sliding screen, and roused the maid sleeping outside on the floor. "Hot wine," she said.

"The strong one." Nothing like strong wine to help one think, at least until one began to grow muddled.

"Yes, mistress," the little girl mumbled, rubbing her eyes. She wandered off sleepily to do Farhat's bidding.

Farhat silently bemoaned the fact that she couldn't really expect a better disciplined household, considering the business she was in. She waited what seemed a very long time before the child returned with the wine.

"Go back to bed," Farhat ordered, and the little girl obediently tumbled into the quilt, asleep before her head touched. Farhat stood a moment, enjoying the sight of the girl. She was perhaps six years old. Her complexion was moist, her skin fragrant and blooming with health, and her eyelashes lay like butterfly wings on her cheeks. Untouched by makeup, the length and thickness of these lashes already made every other lady in Farhat's house envious. She supposed she should be lenient. She had gotten the girl as an infant from the House of Children, recognizing a potential beauty, and had had her ever since. She must start her training immediately; the child was far too precious to waste as a mere maidservant. Also there were rich men who would pay much for her youth, beyond the exorbitant sum she planned to extract for the girl's virginity.

The wine helped clear her head. So war approached. That was nothing new, but from what quarter? Not from First Province. Not yet anyway, she amended. Only if the Ladylord returned and Lutfu pressed his claim through Nao-Pei. Then Lord Yassai would march against Javere. Farhat wondered how the Ladylord had been trapped into going on such a hazardous mission. Eeeei, but she was glad she had only the Hyacinth Shadow World to contend with. That was hard enough, for sometimes a girl grew despondent and ended her life. It always threw a pall over the others. Farhat poured more wine.

It had to be Baron Sakano. Either he would move against Lutfu in earnest, seeking Nao-Pei openly at last, or he would pretend to do so, in league with Nao-Pei and her highborn husband. With such a rebellion facing them, they could easily claim that it was Third Province's lack of a true ruler that was at fault. And from there it was only a short step to having Lutfu declared Third Lord.

Or even— Farhat sat bolt upright, her wine cup forgotten in her hand. She gasped, astonished at the subtlety and complexity of the pattern that now unrolled before her. She blessed the heated wine that helped memory's processes so agreeably.

One of Nao-Pei's maids had a highborn lover who fancied her as a change now and then from Kitsu, his favorite among Farhat's ladies. The maid had overheard Nao-Pei and Sakano when they thought they were alone, speaking of how in war many innocent people might die, including his wife and the husband she might some day have to marry. Then they could be together at last. The maid had told her lover, who mentioned it to Kitsu, who told Farhat. Farhat, thinking it just thoughtless lovers' prattle, had filed the information away and nearly forgotten it.

Eeeei, so that was it! Farhat sat back, astonished. Where was her best profit from this information? Should she tell General Sigon? He was impotent for the moment. Should she hint to Nao-Pei that she knew? No, she thought, shuddering. That would only earn her a slow, disgusting death. Better to wait and see, to do absolutely nothing, at least for the moment.

Slowly, she undressed and got into her bed. The puzzle was solved to her satisfaction, and required no immediate action on her part. She could sleep. The wine fumes buzzed pleasantly in her head.

Perhaps the maid had misunderstood. Perhaps neither Sakano nor Yassai would begin a war. Perhaps Lord Lutfu and Nao-Pei would find theirs a suitable match after all and Sakano would resign himself to a simple life on his huge estate with his plain-featured wife.

Or perhaps the Ladylord would return in time to save Third Province from whatever lay ahead. But that, she knew, was the most remote possibility of all.

iv

In the castle, Lady Nao-Pei lay alone in her bed staring at the ceiling, her body moving restlessly. Ancestor! she thought. Why did she find Lord Lutfu so attractive? The man was downright ugly. But there was also a vitality about him that brought her close to fainting when she imagined his weight on her, his Jade Stalk impaling her, his essence spurting hot between her legs.

She went over the scheme once more. She would marry Lutfu and, in time, take Third Province. That ridiculous prophecy that had kept her virgin so long, while she waited for her father to choose her as heir? She didn't give a snap of her fingers for it. It was only chance that Sakano had been called back to his estates by some problem with his curd-faced wife before they had had the opportunity to make love completely, chance that brought Lutfu to Yonarin Castle to marry her. She hadn't had any idea either he or First Lord would take her letter seriously. She had been on the very edge of giving herself to her lover. And what a mistake that would have been! Lutfu would be properly impressed to get a virgin. Men always were, she had heard. Stupid Javere. She should have leaped to marry Lutfu or even Quang rather than ally herself with that moneyless archer. She must have alienated First Lord completely with that action alone. But Nao-Pei wasn't so slow to recognize an opportunity. She could even turn Javere's elevation into her own advantage. Her official rank might now be lower than Javere's, but that only meant that the other province lords wouldn't be tempted to rise and remove her forcibly from the powerful position to which she aspired—and once she was married to Lutfu they wouldn't dare. Jealousy among all the province lords was all that kept Monserria from dissolving into anarchy. Among them, the four lesser lords could muster enough manpower to keep First Lord in check should his despotism grow too oppressive; they could also be counted on to unite and keep any one of them from growing much stronger than his neighbor. By carefully advancing now this one, now that one, administering rewards and punishments as needed, First Lord skillfully kept them all from flying at one another's throats. Nao-Pei doubted that Javere grasped this political fact of life.

Just as she hadn't grasped the implications of her marrying Lord Ivo and then substituting one of Madam Farhat's courtesans in his bed. All of Third City knew about this, discreet as she thought she had been.

Eeeei, Nao-Pei thought, it was no marriage at all. Would it have been better if she had fled immediately to First City and denounced her half sister to Lord Yassai? This sham marriage would have been dissolved on the spot and Javere married to Lutfu instead, even though this meant confirmation for Javere's claim. This would have pleased both First Lord and his nephew. Javere could have been set aside without much trouble and they would thus have come to control Third Province much more quickly than by waiting for her to be destroyed on this fool's errand she had allowed herself to be forced into undertaking. But would it then have caused the other lesser lords to rise up against them? Perhaps. Well, that was a lost opportunity, and no sense mourning it now.

Should she continue with the present scheme and marry Lutfu? Sakano waited only her word to begin a rebellion; Lutfu would be sure to perish, one way or another, and Sakano's idiotic wife as well. And she would be the logical one to assume the seat of power with Sakano beside her.

Lutfu. Ancestor, how extraordinarily attractive she found him! Marrying him would not be merely the means of relieving herself at last of her hateful maidenhead, as she and Sakano had planned to do. In fact— Her body moved again. She knew very well the pleasures a man's body could bring; only her Heavenly Pavilion remained uninvaded. Frequently, when Sakano caressed her in certain ways, she knew the Moment of Clouds and Rain. Lutfu's carnal urges would find their match in hers.

She began to smile, as still another scheme dawned in her head. What if there were no rebellion after all? she thought. That would just weaken Third Province, leave it open to intervention from its neighboring provinces, or even from Lord Yassai. After all, Lutfu was said to be his favorite nephew, and he was bound to be greatly displeased if Lutfu died during some minor noble's rising against his lawful lord.

The smile deepened and a soft laugh escaped her.

"Lady?" her maid said sleepily, rousing at once.

"Nothing," she said. "Go back to sleep."

Accustomed to sleeping through much more than this—or at least pretending to, the maid obediently turned over and lay still.

Eeeei, that was it! Nao-Pei thought. Third Province would remain at peace, its riches undisturbed. Lutfu would be her husband. And Sakano her lover, fully and completely. This would compensate him for staying in his present marriage. Of course, there was the possibility he had been scheming on his own to gain power in Third Province through marrying her. If this was the case, better to know it when she had enough authority of her own to do something about it, ei?

The only obstacle now was Javere. But if the tale Lutfu told was to be believed, she was as good as dead. Nao-Pei hadn't had to lift a hand to encompass her destruction. Still, she would be wise to tread softly until she had proof of Javere's death.

And even if by some miracle Javere survived and returned to Third Province, she and Lutfu would have become so entrenched in their positions that Javere wouldn't be able to oust them. She would be virtually alone, while Nao-Pei would have Baron Sakano's men plus the might of First Lord behind her. By the time she returned, if she returned, Javere would be seen as the would-be usurper, and Nao-Pei the rightful heir to Lord Qai.

She examined and re-examined the possibilities, unable to find a flaw. Whatever road was taken the end remained the same: She would have the power her father had denied her, she would have Lutfu and an unshakable alliance with First Lord, and she would have Sakano as well.

A new thought made her smile in the darkness. What if Sakano had become so accustomed to their peculiar practices that, when they could finally indulge themselves properly he became, ah, unable? Even in that unlikely event, she would take pleasure in helping him discover the full pleasures that waited in her depths.

She stretched and yawned, running her hands over her body. Very soon she would begin putting it to the full use for which it had been designed.

Eeeei! Life was indeed good! Smiling, she fell asleep.

6

i

*N*either Wande-hari nor Halit had ever been on a battlefield unprotected, or so close to the prospect of killing, as they had been in the brush with the bandits. Both were severely shaken by the experience. With trembling fingers Halit fumbled in his belongings until he found a certain parcel. He filled a pipe with crushed leaves, managed a spark from the end of his finger after several attempts, and soon lost himself in a cloud of *abaythim* smoke. Wande-hari drew his quilted pilgrim's coat closer and huddled on the saddle atop his donkey, focused on something the other travelers could not see. His face looked drained of blood. Javerri kept a watchful eye on him as they traveled, worrying that he might decide to stop his breath and wondering what she could do to prevent it. If he were determined enough, he would do it. It was an ability mages possessed, to slip out of this life when they thought it suitable to do so. They simply stopped breathing, went limp, and died.

Only the creaking of the oxcart and the *clip clop* of the donkeys' hooves broke the silence of their passage. Even the soldiers kept quiet, sensing Javerri's mood. Two *ri* or more separated them from the scene of carnage they had left behind before the elderly mage roused himself enough to contact Javerri *beneath*.

I failed thee.

With an effort Javerri kept herself from exploding joyfully into his mind. She had been on edge, hoping—no, *willing*—him to make just such a contact. She strove for just the right degree of severity in the tone of her reply. ****Thou didst no such thing. Thou'rt as foolish as Michu.****

A spark of interest showed. ****Michu?****

He would have joined the Ancestor Spirit if I hadn't forbidden it, and all because of a little cut Tcha! Two of my oldest and wisest friends act too foolishly to be believed. I suppose thou hast been thinking of journeying Beyond as well?

The idea had occurred to me. The old man's thoughts took on a decidedly sheepish tone.

She made her anger flare higher than what she really felt. ****Thou wouldst leave me alone in this wild land while thou fled to safety? Eeeei! No lord of any of the Five Provinces has ever been so poorly served as I! Thou'rt expressly forbidden to do it! If anyone is to go Beyond, I should, out of shame for having such miserable vassals around me—****

Now, now, my dear Javere—Ladylord—Javerri, I mean, dear nephew—

No more! Be still!

They rode along in silence for a while until Javerri judged it was safe for her to relent. ****Anyway, thou had no time in which to work thy spells, ei, Uncle?****

The Circle of Protection I cast every night when we camp takes time to construct. Nevertheless, I should have been able to do something. Thy face—

—is nothing, she broke in harshly. ****A little higher and I would have lost an eye. A little lower, and I would be dead and you would have to seek another master, one more lenient than I toward an old man's foolishness. Don't you think I would gladly trade every scrap of beauty I possess, if I can keep Third Province safe?****

But thou must live. Wande-hari lifted his head as an idea occurred to him. **I know what I can do! Eeeei, why didn't I think of this before? Once I tried making a movable Circle of Protection for Lord Qai but he ordered me to stop before I had discovered how to do it.** He smiled and a little color came back into his face. **Halit can help me, when he comes out of his dream. We'll make ourselves useful instead of being excess baggage, you'll see!**

He broke the contact and Javerri drew a sigh of relief. Successful or not, this new project of Wande-hari's would keep his mind occupied, his spirit active. She needed Wande-hari far more at this time for his sage counsel than for his magic-making.

ii

The road was a dusty brown ribbon cutting through nodding fields of a crop strange to Monserrian eyes. This was not rice in its proper watery paddies, but a yellowish grain that grew in dry ground. On the horizon, a few small mountains loomed, some leaking smoke. Javerri felt very vulnerable; conceivably, pursuit could come from any direction except for the damage to the fields. And they were traveling more slowly than she liked, because of the wounds most of them had suffered. For the next few days, Javerri watched from all sides, half expecting someone to come after them, whether more bandits seeking vengeance for their comrades, or priestly authorities with inconvenient questions to ask. But they met only other groups of pilgrims such as they pretended to be.

"More likely we'd be troubled by the priests," Ezzat said when she confided her concern to him. "But if they haven't found us by now, chances are they won't."

Thanks to Lek's skill, Tal's arm was almost usable once the physician put the shoulder back in its socket. Until it finished healing, however, Lek bound the arm close to Tal's body and forbade him to move it. As for the others, the physician's salves and potions helped their various injuries mend. But not even his best efforts could keep the wicked cut on Javerri's cheekbone from leaving a scar.

"Your skin is too delicate," Lek said as he fussed over her. "The edges of the cut keep pulling apart."

Javerri stoically endured the pain of the wound and the equally hurtful treatments, knowing that Lek was using every skill at his command to shrink the scar. When at last he declared that he could do no more, it was no more than two finger joints in length and little wider than the blade that had caused it. And, to the physician's satisfaction, it was flat, white and shiny.

"That's good," Lek said. "I was fearful of a hard and ropy lump you'd have difficulty hiding with makeup."

Halit lingered nearby, watching. "Never mind," he told her comfortingly. "You are still the prettiest *boy* I've ever seen. Please forgive my impertinence in saying so."

She smiled, liking him. His willingness to put himself in danger for her sake had touched her as much as this attempt to console her for her damaged beauty touched her now. All things considered, she thought Wande-hari had chosen well.

Their days on the road settled into their former routine, to put as much distance as they comfortably could between one camping and the next, while avoiding any unnecessary contact with anyone else. Visit the shrines, pay the tribute, receive the amulets, wait while some of them patronized the local pleasure house. These establishments were always located next door to the shrines, dedicated to the love god who must be propitiated as much as any other. Each pilgrim received an amulet in token of his devotion to duty. With this, he could visit the pleasure house; anyone seeking admission without the proper token was summarily beaten and thrown into the street. Javerri dutifully collected her tokens like the rest. By now everyone had a respectable string of the things. Each shrine had its own symbol, and a pilgrim could be judged on his piety by the number of amulets he could boast. Now Javerri understood why the most humble pilgrims carried as much silver as they could. The priests were as ruthless as Madam Farhat about extracting every possible silver piece from their patrons. No wonder bandits flourished to prey on them. While they had dawdled on the road, recuperating, she had seen other groups of pilgrims, better dressed and equipped than most, who carried weapons in defiance of custom. Now, by her orders, they all went openly armed as well. Anyone who might entertain thoughts of robbery certainly must think twice, seeing travelers who could fight back; they had not been troubled since that first time.

Now that she could turn her attention elsewhere, Javerri found herself more and more concerned about Ivo. He had not complained even once about the loss of Safia nor had he visited any of the pleasure houses. Sensibly, she instructed all the men to do so as often as they felt they could afford to. It would not do to have any of them suffering from constriction of the pelvic organs. That would lead to wandering thoughts, and for everyone's safety in this country a man must keep his mind on his business.

"You must go also," she had said to Michu.

"When I feel the need," he had answered.

The physician and Halit needed no urging, nor did Ezzat; as for her five remaining soldiers, they took to the custom with great enthusiasm. Wande-hari professed himself far beyond such matters. She spoke to the elderly magician about her concern for Ivo.

"Leave him alone, Nephew," Wande-hari advised. "He is no commoner to tumble into any bed at the first opportunity."

She nodded. For a moment she wondered why she had never asked the old mage to help her see into Ivo's mind, as he had with others. Then she realized that she didn't want to enter his most private sanctuary, didn't want to examine all his intimate thoughts and feelings. Not even with his permission.

She wouldn't hesitate with anyone else. Why with him? Could it be that she did not want to see certain memories, didn't want to know how he compared other ladies so well-trained in erotic skills with the virgin wife who denied him access to her body? Firmly, she put away these thoughts.

Their last night in Fogestria they made an early camp. The stream nearby was just a trickle with standing pools that bred swarms of biting insects, but there was plenty of green wood to burn. Halit added a few ingredients from his pouch and said a few words over the fire; the resulting wall of smoke kept all but the most determined gnats from feasting on them. Once it grew dark they could see the glow of lights on the horizon, against the clouds. According to both Ezzat and Halit, they could have reached Fanthore, the large city on the southern border, but night would have fallen by then, and prudence dictated they enter this place in full light.

Javerri had initially hoped to avoid the place entirely. "Isn't there another way we can go?"

"No, young sir, I'm sorry," Ezzat said. "The Fogestrian Mountains lie ahead. This is the border, and Fanthore is located at the one spot where any traffic can get through. Here the range dips to its lowest point, and its narrowest."

"Surely there is another way through the mountains?" she asked.

"There are a few paths," Ezzat admitted, "but, excuse me, it is no place for you. Nor can we take the oxcart. The paths are too dangerous this time of year even for a man on foot. It's more important to get through the Great Desert safely than to avoid Fanthore. We will be crossing just a narrow arm, to be sure, but I want to buy heavier quilted coats for the journey. Fanthore's tailors make the warmest."

"Can't we make do with the garments we have?"

"We'll be three days or more and nights are colder than you can imagine there and in the mountains. I want to buy more water skins as well. It's easy to lose your way out there."

"Fanthore is where I once lived and studied with the magician Anselme," Halit said. "If you will allow me to advise you, young sir. . . ."

Javerri looked questioningly at Ezzat.

"The mage knows more than I do about Fanthore's ways and customs," Ezzat said. "I—I never stayed long."

"Then please guide us," she said to Halit.

"We must visit Fanthore's shrine and pay lavish tribute if we're to buy clothing and water skins," he said. He touched the string of amulets that each of them now wore around their necks. "If we don't, no merchant in the city will deal with us, not just the pleasure houses. The designs on the tokens are changed regularly, to discourage anyone but the shrine from dealing in them. It will cost us dearly, I'm afraid. What the priests don't extort, the merchants will take. And we'll still have to get out of the city."

Javerri nodded, unsurprised, and not yet willing to think about how they would get back through the city. "I will rely on you to decide how much silver we must donate."

"Naturally, it would be most unwise to go armed inside the city. Let us hide some of our coins with our weapons when we put them away. If necessary, I will cast a spell to make everyone forget the weapons and silver even exist, in case we are questioned."

"That is a good idea."

"Once we are past the city, we will be in virtually unknown territory. Unknown to me, that is," Halit said, nodding to Ezzat.

"And there I will take up my duty again," Ezzat said. "If we're lucky we'll fall in with a caravan of desert dwellers who'll guide us to the far side. If not, well, the Ancestor waits for us all, ei?"

Michu set his four soldiers at equal points around the camp as he always did, unwilling to trust Wande-hari's Circle of Protection. It sparkled faintly in the moonlight and could have been mistaken for a snail's track if one didn't know better. Another smaller Circle, almost complete, glimmered inside the camp area. Javerri stepped through the small opening in the Circle and Wande-hari closed it behind her.

"Try it, nephew," he said.

Obediently, she went to the edge. The first time she had tested the movable Circle she couldn't budge it at all. It was as if she pressed against an invisible wall. She had learned great respect for the spell, realizing how frustrating it would be to an enemy, not to mention the one inside the Circle who would have his blood up, wanting to join the fight. Nothing got in or out of the cylinder that stretched higher than she could reach. Someone like her father naturally scorned such protection as cowardly. No wonder he relied upon the skill of his generals and the fierceness of his army to protect him. But he had had great numbers at his disposal, and she did not. She pushed; the wall yielded slightly, and then moved. She took a step, then another, each step costing her enormous effort. She stopped, panting. The ancient mage made a disgusted sound.

"But it's much better than it was last time," she told him reassuringly, glad that he was working on this, occupying his mind. "You'll get it perfect before long, I'm sure."

"I hope so. Sleep now." He dissolved the Circle.

More fatigued than she wanted to admit to Wande-hari, she lay down on her bedroll, arranged herself for sleep, and dozed off. A few hours later, something—she didn't know what—woke her. The fire had burned low. One of the oxen stamped sleepily, and in the distance a night bird called. She shifted the hard bundle under her head. She'd lost count of the times she had cursed Madam Farhat who had given her the box of pleasure instruments, and Chimoko who had secretly put the box with Javerri's belongings when the company had separated. Time and again she had tried to throw the wretched thing away. Once, Chakei had brought it back to her. Another time, Michu, checking the area of their camp for forgotten belongings, retrieved it. Cheeks flaming, she accepted the box and put it out of sight. Finally, rather than call so much attention that its contents would be discovered, Javerri kept it with her at all times, even to using it as a pillow.

Not for the first time, she wondered what was happening with Chimoko. If things went as Javerri planned, the maid would still be dawdling at the border, safe if infuriated at her "failure" to aid her mistress. Ah, but that is precisely where I want thee to be, Chimoko, she thought. I want thee very annoyed and very visible. Yassai's spies will carry back the tale that the Ladylord's arrogance bars her from even entering into Fogestria, not even close to fulfilling her errand.

Chakei lay between her and the fire, unconsciously crowding against her and seeking her warmth on his other side. The deepening cold made him miserable, and she didn't grudge his seeking comfort where he could. Actually, the nearness of the Dragon-warrior brought her great comfort these days. She hoped Halit could talk them safely through Fanthore. If mere money were all that were needed, she felt confident they could manage. Her great fear was that Chakei's presence would be discovered. She wondered how any desert dwellers might react to him.

She turned her head on her uncomfortable pillow. Ivo lay nearby, sleeping lightly. Ah, if she could lie in his arms, she would be content. But that was impossible. She allowed herself one more look at Ivo's handsome face, then snuggled more closely against Chakei. The Dragon-warrior sighed in his sleep. She sighed also.

iii

The little band of "pilgrims," weapons securely hidden once more, struggled through the crowded streets of Fanthore. These were more like alleys than real streets; five- and six-storied buildings that appeared to be slapped together from whatever came to hand loomed on either side. Javerri glanced up nervously, expecting to see one come sliding down on them at any moment. But perhaps each building borrowed stability from its neighbor with the ropes and lines strung from every projection, each bearing a colorful assortment of garments and pieces of fabric in every stage of wetness. The dust from the streets rose high enough that the articles must have been almost as soiled after they dried as they had been before being washed.

Halit kept tight to the oxen's yoke while the men moved in the wake the cart left. They didn't slip into a stream of traffic because there wasn't any; the inhabitants of Fanthore darted in every possible direction as fast as they could go, every man jostling his neighbor, cursing and being cursed for getting in the way. From her vantage point on the cart's seat, Javerri stared, appalled and a little sickened, at the people who swarmed through the narrow streets, filling them to overflowing from one side to the other. Smells—cooking, unwashed bodies, sewage, flowers, freshly dyed wool—filled the air. She wondered if the lines of laundry were ever taken down to be worn. Though all of her people had on their oldest clothes, trying to avoid paying any more tribute than they had to, they were as clean as they could manage, under the circumstances. The inhabitants of Fanthore all looked dirty; the noise of the place hit her like a blow.

"Can we—can we get through?" She had to shout to make herself heard.

"Don't worry, my boy!" Halit shouted back. "The main shrine is just ahead!"

She bent to make sure Chakei was well-hidden in the depths of the cart. When she looked up again, they had rounded a corner and the shrine gleamed in the morning light at the far side of a crowded square. Though dwarfed by the ramshackle buildings surrounding it, the shrine nevertheless proclaimed its own importance by the excellence and rich materials of its construction. Crimson-painted pillars flanked its entrance, and lavish gold and silver inlays made the doors shine. The walls of dressed and polished stone gave the place an air of permanence and finality. It sat, serene and aloof, in the center of Fanthore, and would continue to do so long after the frantic bustle of the city had vanished into its own dust.

Their progress grew a little easier; a stream of worshipers coming and going at the shrine created a slight flow in the traffic. Halit maneuvered them closer until they reached a backwater where a cluster of carts much like their own awaited the return of their owners. In the relative quiet among the carts Javerri realized that she had developed a headache.

"We'll go in groups," Halit said. "Somebody must stay with

the cart at all times." Inside, Chakei shifted and the cart swayed.

"Then you go first, magician," Michu said. "We need to have you available in case someone happens by with a mouthful of questions."

Halit nodded his assent. "Has everybody got their silver ready? Then let's go." Three of the soldiers and the physician followed him as he joined the line awaiting admission to the shrine. Javerri knew that they couldn't hope to get this part of their errand over with quickly, and her head ached even more as the waiting grew longer. She all but held her breath until the five emerged safely at last, from the door on the other side from where they had entered. She climbed down from the cart, and, flanked by Ivo and Michu, took her place in line.

It was cool and dark inside, and her head would have felt better had the air not been so heavy with incense. Light from braziers and torches flickered off jeweled walls. At the far end of the room, priests waited for the faithful. They were the first clean-looking people Javerri had seen in the city. She kept her eyes lowered, lest their unusual color bring her unwanted attention. But the priests cared about nothing save the money the people dropped into the cauldron. The one she faced merely snapped his fingers impatiently when she didn't move quickly enough to suit him.

The Fogestrian language was similar in some respects to Monserrian; she could frequently catch the gist of what people were saying by intonation though she didn't dare try to speak.

"Is that all you can spare?"

She nodded, very humbly, and opened her hands to indicate that she had given all she had.

The priest snapped his fingers again in irritation. Then he took a trinket from the heap of similar ones in the vessel beside him and all but threw it at her. "Move along, move along," he ordered brusquely. "Don't take all day."

She didn't examine the amulet until she was outside the shrine once more. It was as cheaply made as one from any of the roadside shrines they had visited, representing the same outlandish Fogestrian god. This current design, she realized, looking at it more closely, depicted him attending simultaneously to the needs of five smiling, round-breasted females clustered about him. Tongue, fingers, Jade Stalk, even the big toe on the god's left foot, all were occupied in this enterprise. She couldn't suppress her laughter at the absurdity.

"They certainly think much of themselves and their god," Michu said sourly, gazing at his amulet.

Ivo laughed in turn. "Surely a deity can do anything," he said, "especially on a work of, er, art. We've got what we came for, ei? Let's be gone from here."

They strung their amulets with the others, making sure the Fanthorian one showed prominently. Then, armed with the proof that they had performed their most important duty, the travelers shoved their way into the Street of the Garment Sellers. They selected a stall where the merchant displayed a brightly colored, outsized coat draped over a large wooden image to attract the attention of prospective customers. Ezzat selected heavy, warm garments for all of them, letting Halit do the actual haggling. Then, glancing at Javerri, the magician took the large coat off the stand and added it to the pile already purchased.

Javerri held her breath. Then she relaxed, realizing what Halit was about. The magician put his hands behind his back. He murmured a few words and made some gestures. As Javerri watched, the merchant grew vague and distracted, his mind wandering in some private realm; if Halit hadn't spoken up, he would have given them the display garment.

"Ah, no, my friend, we won't cheat you," Halit said kindly. He dropped a couple more coins into the man's hand. "Thank you for your courtesy. We'll recommend you to all our friends."

Javerri hoped Halit had kept the shopkeeper from noticing that none of Halit's companions were of a size to need such an item. She had no idea whether she could convince Chakei to wear the coat, but she was glad they had made the effort.

They needed no magical persuasion in the Street of the Shoemakers when they bought fur-lined boots for all but one. The quilted coat might or might not get past the Dragon-warrior's temper, but they still had to buy food, and the available money supply was getting low. Chakei got no boots.

It was late afternoon before they approached the gateway in Fanthore's southern wall. Beyond the gate, there was only a short distance and a little slope to the ground before the mountains sprang almost straight upward, and the city walls towered high and forbidding. The enormous wooden doors, like those at the gate through which they had entered, were five layers thick, each layer having its grain in a different direction. One of the doors stood a little open, the thick bar pushed back, indicating that passage through here was at least possible. The way the city wall appeared to grow out of the mountains behind it reminded Javerri poignantly of home. She exchanged glances with Ivo and Michu, and knew that they were thinking the same thing.

They had put three guards here, where a crippled old man with a walking stick could hold off an army. The captain had a badge of office pinned to his felt hat. His strident voice cut across Javerri's moment of homesickness. But why only three guards? The fewer to share the bribes, she thought.

"Here now, what d'you think you're about? Nobody leaves the city, not through this gate."

They had agreed on a story beforehand; Halit and Ezzat went up and spoke with the man. The lad with them—Javerri—was the son of a rich merchant from somewhere beyond the Great Desert. The boy, spoiled and petulant, had run away from home. Wasn't he fortunate to fall in with honest Fogestrians and not unscrupulous foreigners who might sell him into slavery, or even kill him for the sheer wickedness of it, ei? We want to take him back home and have put him to work driving the cart for the good of his soul. And if there should be a reward, then we will bring it back to the High Shrine of Fanthore straightaway.

The captain listened, visibly unimpressed. Lazily, he checked to see if they were wearing the proper amulets, grunting when he saw that they had. Javerri thought he looked disappointed; perhaps the wrong amulets would have meant they'd have to pay a bigger bribe. Halit handed him the pouch containing almost all of their remaining money. The captain, unsatisfied, rubbed thumb and fingers together; Halit stepped back a pace, his lips moving. Ezzat reached into his sleeve for the pouch with the last silver pieces in it and gave it to the guard. He still appeared unsatisfied. The three of them spoke at some length, and Javerri could tell that Ezzat's temper was beginning to fray. He stalked back in her direction.

"This son of a diseased dog demands more. We've given him all we possess and it still isn't enough," he told her, frowning. "Fogestria hates to have anybody pass its borders. Difficult as it is to get in, it's even harder to get out." He spoke with utter sincerity; Javerri went cold, thinking he was going to ask for the coins they had put away. Then she realized that Halit's spell had made Ezzat forget the very existence of the pouch hidden with the weapons in the cart.

Michu's hand reached for his sword and found nothing; his own scowl deepened. "Say the word, boy. I'll open the bottom of the cart and we'll fight our way out."

"No need, my friend," Wande-hari said placidly. He pulled his left hand from his sleeve. Without haste, he removed his golden nail guards one by one and handed them to Ezzat. "Will this satisfy the man?"

Ezzat took the jewel-studded guards. "If not, then it can't be done. Thank you, Wande-hari."

As Javerri watched, aghast, Wande-hari carefully snapped his nails off short, wincing a little with each one, and put the pieces into his sleeve pocket. "We're going into rough and dangerous country," he said in explanation. "It's been all well and good to let the youngster shoulder the burden here in the city, but I may have to use magic with both my hands before we are back home again, and I may as well start now."

"I thank you also," Javerri said. "I know what a sacrifice this was."

"Nothing that time won't cure, I assure you. The nails will grow again."

The guard captain, who had been watching wide-eyed, shouted harshly at Ezzat, then all but snatched the gold out of his hand. He said something further in a slightly milder tone, then turned and ordered his men to open the gate wide enough for them to pass. Halit gestured and whispered frantically.

"Hurry, now!" Ezzat shouted in Fogestrian. Javerri lashed the oxen and the cart rumbled through the gate. Someone yelled behind them, but they were through. The gate slammed and the bolt dropped. Ezzat nudged his donkey closer to the cart.

"That was close. He called me—well, never mind what he called me—and said we had been trying to cheat him. Then he said that he was going to search us individually and our cart as well but since we had turned out to be so generous we could go and he wouldn't bother this time. I thought it best we move quickly, and then he shouted for us to stop. But we were already through the gate by then."

Halit sagged with exhaustion. "I know. I kept up the spell as long as I could—"

"You?" Ezzat turned in surprise. "You did that?"

Javerri nodded. "Ei, that was close indeed!"

Ezzat gave her a crooked smile. "I remember what we've got hidden now. It's not much. In a way it's too bad our story was false. We could have used the reward for returning you to your 'home'!" He laughed.

"We'll make out," Ivo said proudly. He had ridden up on the other side. "We can sell these animals, and the cart as well."

"We need the cart for supplies and then to transport the eggs if we find them, when we find them—we'll have to take more than one. But it's good to have it and the animals to fall back on, if we can find anybody who'll want to buy 'em."

"In the meantime, let's put as much distance as we can between us and the city gates," Javerri said. "We'll have to spend the night in these mountains, won't we?"

"Not if we hurry and if the road hasn't been washed out.

The pass is fairly easy. And there won't be any traffic, this late in the year."

"Less talk then, and more speed." Javerri lashed the oxen again. The stolid beasts increased their pace fractionally. Chakei stirred in the bottom of the cart.

come now out i

As soon as we round this next bend. It won't be much longer, I promise.

rags heavy not so warm as sun

When we are clear of the city thou won't have to hide under the—the rags, not for a long time.

good is

Thou hast been most patient and I'm grateful to thee.

He rumbled and hissed a little. When they were safely out of sight of the city walls, she pulled the cart to a stop. Chakei scrambled out, stretching luxuriously.

run i now come back soon

The road lay in the hollow of a steep rift in the mountains. Chakei went up the slope on all fours as smoothly as a man could race on the flat. He skimmed along the ridge above them and Javerri had to start moving again or lose sight of him. From time to time, as the company hurried along, he would come down part way, hiss at them agreeably, then rush back up again.

"Poor fellow, he must be half-mad with relief to be out of that cart at last!" Michu still rode, though two of his men had dismounted. The road was cluttered with rocks fallen from the heights, signs of winter abandonment. Though the donkeys picked their way with no difficulty, the men had to clear the road for the cart. "Here, shove that boulder down the ravine, Nali."

"Chakei is as relieved as I am to be past Fogestria," Ivo said. "Have you noticed? He stays in the sunlight. I believe he's missed it sorely."

Javerri watched the dark-scaled figure of the Dragon-warrior darting across a cliff face that looked unclimbable from her vantage point below. Pebbles rattled down with his passage. ***Be careful!***

most glad i careful too

The cart lurched sharply as the wheels caught in a deep rut in the road and she had to clutch the seat to keep from being thrown off.

careful you Chakei sounded almost amused.

What canst thou see from up there? How near are we to being through the pass and off this dreadful road?

soon soon

The road rounded a spur of the mountainside and the lands beyond lay clear before them. As Ezzat had said, this section of mountains was narrow, and peaks reared threateningly on both sides of the notch through which they traveled. As the walls of Fanthore had nestled immediately against them on the one side, waves of sand had washed almost to the base of the mountains on this side. A narrow fringe of greenery made a kind of shore between rock and desolation. Other than this verdant strip, she could see no sign of life.

"So that's the Great Desert," Javerri said. She stood up to see better. The grayish-brown land became blue in the distance, and there was no distinguishable line to mark the horizon. "That's what we have to cross."

"We'll fill every vessel and skin with water down there," Ezzat said, indicating the green border. "Then, tomorrow, we'll start across. It's not too bad, traveling by day this time of year. But we'll freeze at night if we're not careful. We'll have to carry our own firewood and ration it carefully. There's very little to burn, once we're out on the sand."

"Then how do the desert people survive?"

He shook his head. "I don't know. But they do."

She took a deep breath, then urged the oxen forward, starting the descent toward the frightening expanse of wilderness in front of them. Her worries increased tenfold. Had they brought enough fodder for the animals? Enough food for themselves? How could they carry what they needed to sustain themselves through the days it would take to get across that wasteland? And how, she thought with a fresh pang, would they keep their bearings, know where they were heading? With approaching winter, both days and nights were mostly overcast.

that way know i

She looked up. Chakei, half-hidden in the rocks above, pointed south and west of the way they were now going. Of course. He had told her he knew. Some instinct of his race must speak to him as he got closer to the place he must, in some dim way, think of as home.

Night was falling by the time they found a suitable spot and made camp. By the way Ezzat directed their actions, Javerri realized he had used this place many times before. A grove of slender trees provided shelter on three sides, and in another season a small grove of berry bushes would have contributed to evening and morning meals. A little stream of water tumbled off a cliff edge nearby, made a pool, flowed into a thread of a brook half a *ri* long, then vanished as the sand soaked it up thirstily.

"Don't go near where the sand and water meet," Ezzat warned. "That's quicksand and they say it'll swallow you before you can cry out for help."

"Are there desert sharks in it?" one of the soldiers asked worriedly. His name was Fen-mu; his brother had been the one killed by the bandits.

"Not here," Ezzat said. "They swim in dry sand. I have seen it."

They all shuddered. Halit reached for his *abaythim*.

"Must you do that now?" Javerri asked, frowning in irritation.

"I apologize, my boy. If I promise not to smoke any until we are safely past the desert and into the dangers of the Burning Mountains beyond, will you allow this indulgence now?"

"No."

As she spoke, Wande-hari called to her. His voice was full of excitement and pleasure.

"I have something to show you," he said. Unconsciously he flexed his left hand. "I do believe that I've allowed myself to grow lazy and too fond of luxuries in my advancing years. Come and see."

She acquiesced gladly. He had another small Circle prepared for her, and she was amazed at how rapidly he had woven it. She stepped inside, let it close behind her, and leaned her shoulder against the invisible wall.

To her astonishment, it floated with her so easily she nearly stumbled and fell. "This is wonderful!" she said.

"It is an entirely new principle," he said proudly. "Instead of using whatever light is available, this one is plaited of strands of three different kinds—sun, moon, and star. It takes both hands to do it. I don't know why I didn't think of this before."

"But all three aren't seen at once! And the clouds—"

He patted his sleeve. "Never fear, I have some threads stored in here. They last a few days. Have I pleased you, nephew?"

"More than I can say, best of uncles!"

Pleased, he dissolved the spell. She went on her nightly inspection of the campsite, only to find Halit deep in his *abaythim* dream, despite her refusal. She scowled at the soldier standing nearby. "Why is this man in this condition when I expressly forbade it?"

"He had a pipe half-smoked when I saw him, La— I mean, sir," Nali said. "I thought you had refused him, but he convinced me I must have misunderstood. I apologize for my stupidity."

"You need not apologize. It wasn't your fault," she said. She walked back to Wande-hari, the frown still on her face. "Please punish your apprentice when he is in a condition to know what is happening to him."

"Abaythim again?"

"Yes. I will not have him with his faculties impaired for the remainder of our journey, is that understood? When we reach Third Province once more, what indulgences you do or do not allow him will be your business. But until then—"

"I understand. In fact, I'll do something about it at once." The old man drew out the pieces of fingernail from his sleeve. "I need to burn these. *Abaythim* in the fire will only make it burn brighter."

"See to it," she said sourly. She made a quick meal, glad to be using eating sticks again. The Fogestrians had the disgusting habit of eating with knives or fingers. She cleaned the sticks and put them away; if she had still been in Monserria, she would have discarded them and gotten fresh ones from the nearest oil-nut tree. But now none of them took even this simple luxury for granted.

"I'm going to bathe," she said to Michu. "Keep everyone away unless I call for help."

She made her way to the little pool a short distance away. The water, falling directly from the mountain, was breathtakingly cold; nevertheless, she bathed thoroughly, cleaning her teeth and washing her hair. There was no way to tell when she would have the opportunity again. The air, when she emerged, felt quite warm and so did she. Returning to camp, she lay down, trying to sleep. Her pleasure in the movable Circle of Protection was ruined, thanks to Halit. She stared at the cloudy sky for a long time, listening while Halit murmured and sang to himself, snatches of bawdy tunes comingled with sentimental ballads. At last he subsided. Eventually she fell into an uneasy slumber, waking to discover that Chakei had finally joined them and lay in his accustomed place, between her and the fire.

iv

Though Ezzat had tried his best, the company was unprepared for the realities of the desert. Only parts of it were coarse sand; most was dry hard crust through which many sharp rocks and an occasional spiny plant emerged. And there was life—strange creatures that could have come from drug-induced nightmares. The lizards and scorpions and sand spiders were bad, but most of all Javerri hated the jumping renders, vicious creatures about the size of a squirrel. Renders possessed long hind legs and a whiplike muscular tail that propelled them incredible distances. They traveled in packs, waiting in shadows to launch themselves fearlessly at passing prey. They were capable of leaping high enough to fasten on a donkey's ear, or an ox's neck. Before long, most of the men bore marks of their needle-sharp teeth and despite Lek's best efforts, the bites made festering sores that stank and ran. And every day at least one of the creatures would come flying into the cart, ready to scramble over the firewood and food sacks to get to Javerri. Chakei's scaly hide baffled them, however, and he merely shook them off.

Another animal, the fan-tailed luctor, charmed Javerri. It was slightly larger than a render and very shy.

"Naturally they're timid," Ezzat told her. "The renders feed on 'em mainly."

"That's when they can't get Monserrians to eat," Michu grumbled, scratching at a bite on his leg.

Javerri could sometimes catch a glimpse of several luctors standing on an outcropping of rock, holding their curved tails aloft to catch any breeze that might be had, looking for all the world like ladies with sunshades. But when they caught sight of the travelers, the luctors would immediately dash for cover, tails streaming behind them. She wanted to catch one and tame it for a pet, but despaired of ever being able to do so.

The travelers' pace was fairly steady as they avoided areas of sand as much as they could. When they had to cross these sections, their progress slowed greatly and if there was life in these areas, it stayed hidden.

They plodded painfully through the loose sand, each step heavy going. On the upward slopes the men had to get behind the cart and push. The cart wheels sank in the uncertain surface, making the oxen work harder than they were accustomed to doing. Their laments filled the air, and the travelers were forced to stop often to let them rest. During the midpart of the day they must stop anyway, whatever the terrain, for the heat sapped all their energy while the dry air parched skins and throats. All any of them wanted to do was lie in the shade of the cart and drink water without pause. Ezzat rationed the water strictly. Too much at once would simply run through, doing the person no good at all. Drinking a sip at a time allowed the body to absorb the water instead.

For four days they struggled on like this, and the only one who fared at all well was Chakei. Except for the nighttime when the cold descended and he suffered by the fire, he went lightly over the same sand and rocks that hampered the others, his big splayed feet giving him all the purchase he needed. He found the quilted coat bought for him back in Fanthore unexpectedly useful; though he generated virtually no heat himself, he discovered that the garment could trap warmth from the fire if he sat close and draped it around himself. **good is** he told Javerri. **thank you i**

Worry lines etched themselves more and more deeply into Ezzat's face. The morning of the fifth day, he approached Javerri. "We should have been past the desert by the fourth day at latest," he said. "We should be heading due south. Every dawn I take the direction as best I can despite the clouds. Every evening I feel that we've strayed farther west. I'm afraid we've gone off course and instead of crossing the narrow way, we've started down the length of this arm of the desert."

"But Chakei—" Javerri stopped in midsentence. Chakei frequently skimmed across the sand ahead of them, bored with their slow progress. And naturally, they had followed. Could it be that he had misled them? "I will speak with you again in a moment," she told Ezzat, and moved off a short distance.

Chakei?
here i ladylord
I fear we are going the wrong way.
going right way show i
But we have been in the desert too long
She felt his mental shrug. **going right way.**
Straight across the desert?
not straight but right way
She broke the connection *beneath* before he could sense her dismay. He had pointed to the southwest when she asked him, while they were still in the mountains. They would cer-

tainly have turned in that direction once they were past the desert. But Chakei knew nothing of this. Innocently, he had led them at an angle, directly toward their destination. He had no idea that he had put them all in jeopardy.

Ezzat didn't seem as surprised as he might have when she explained what had happened. "I should have known this. How could I have let myself be misled so easily? It's as if—" He blinked and shook his head, then took a deep breath, addressing the situation directly. "Our supplies are low," he said. "The animals must go for food. I told you once before that we'd be very lucky if we found a band of desert dwellers." He fingered the string of amulets he still wore around his neck. "Well, we'd all better pray hard now to the Ancestor, to Lady Moon, to the Six Winds, to those heathen gods we gave our coins to, and to whatever or whoever else can hear us. The desert dwellers have to find us now, or all of us, even your Dragon-warrior, may die."

Before she could reply, Fen-mu came running toward them, stumbling, waving his arms, and shouting in panic. "Desert sharks! Desert sharks!"

He would have run past unheeding but she grabbed him by the arm, swung him around, and slapped his face sharply. "Get control of yourself!" she ordered. "What desert sharks? Where?"

A little of the glazed look left his eyes. He gulped and shuddered, pulling himself together with a visible effort. "Out where the animals are tethered," he said, beginning to weep. "They snatched one of the donkeys. Peng went to investigate, and they got him, too. General Michu went after them— Oh, no, Ladylord, you mustn't go! You'll-be killed!"

But she was already running toward the cluster of men and animals at the far edge of the camp. She caught a glimpse of Ivo as he too ran toward them, responding to the emergency. And then he disappeared.

i

*C*himoko awoke, stretching luxuriously. She snuggled closer to Len-ti who lay sleeping beside her. Len-ti was now captain of the guards the Ladylord had been forced to leave behind at the Fogestrian border, and it had been an easy task to persuade him to impersonate the Ladylord's husband. Tall and slender, he even resembled Lord Ivo a little, if one didn't look too closely. She'd had her eye on him for months now, and was glad she had arranged for him to be included with the soldiers the Ladylord took with her. It was only natural that he be in her company when she left First City. Chimoko's heart had nearly stopped when Ladylord had at first refused her request, wanting him to go on into Fogestria when the company divided here at the border. Chimoko smiled; too bad if Ladylord hadn't taken advantage of her opportunity with Ivo as she had done with Len-ti, from their first evening together as soon as Ladylord was asleep and she could go outside to meet him. She stayed always within earshot, of course, in case Ladylord roused and needed her. Her absence could have been explained easily by a trip to the midden. It had been very pleasurable being with Len-ti, better each night thereafter, best when they could be together all night long. Last night had been very satisfactory indeed, for both of them, perhaps the best of all.

Ah, Len-ti, she thought contentedly, thou'rt warm and comforting in bed and I like thee much more than is good for thee to know. If I believed in love, I would say that I love thee. But I believe only in pleasure. And thou hast brought me much pleasure indeed. Has Ladylord discovered this warmth yet, with Ivo? Well, no matter. She has the box of pleasure instruments to keep her company, however much she pretended to be angry with me for bringing them. It was all well and good for her to be so circumspect before the old lord died, but now she is Third Lord, ei? In every respect but confirmation by that self-important old tyrant. Anyone could see the old man was impotent too, and probably jealous of the Ladylord and her husband. No reason to deny herself any longer, prophecy or no prophecy.

She nudged Len-ti. "Wake up," she said.

Len-ti stirred and, still asleep, put his arms around her. "Stay here a while longer," he mumbled.

"I wish I could. But I must go and face the border guards again."

He sighed and let her go. Both of them left the warmth of the bed reluctantly. They dressed in silence, she in the Ladylord's rose-colored dress with the dark green underdress, he in his green uniform. One of the maids at the inn where they were staying brought them food.

Every morning since Ladylord had gone, Chimoko had presented herself at the border with her demands; and every morning, the guards had denied her passage. It had almost become a ritual by now, both sides speaking their parts without paying much attention.

Eeeei, she thought. How clever of Ladylord to have her maid impersonate her. Naturally, she knew Chimoko would never be allowed to pass the border, acting in the manner in which she'd been instructed. But it gave her the chance to slip over, undetected. And Chimoko knew the longer she delayed, the safer Ladylord would be from pursuit.

A small village composed of inns and, of course, whorehouses because this was Fourth Province, had sprung up there at the border, catering to travelers detained on both sides. Many of these establishments had gardens. The inn Chimoko had chosen had a particularly well-tended garden, and every morning someone put a few late-blooming flowers in a vase in their room while they still slept, to glow in the sunlight. The ones this morning were particularly beautiful—or perhaps she was looking on them with pleasure because of the preceding night. She and Len-ti emerged from the inn. The soldiers were already waiting.

The morning was fine and cool, holding more than a hint of winter, making the air remarkably clear; the distant mountains looked much closer than they actually were. A few leaves, brilliantly colored, swirled around Chimoko's feet as she walked toward the guard house. The usual barricade lay across the road, the usual armed soldiers in their brown uniforms stood here and there. Once they had scowled when she approached; eventually indifference had set in. Now, however, the back of Chimoko's neck prickled with danger, for the soldiers were scowling again. Something had changed, but what? She could see nothing. . . .

Half a dozen red-uniformed soldiers stepped out into the road from behind an inn where they had been hidden and confronted her. They stood between her and the guard house, blocking the road. The border captain hovered in the background behind them; he looked frightened. Now she realized what had changed. The Fogestrian border guards were nowhere to be seen.

One of the Reds walked forward, his hand on his sword hilt. "Stop, woman!" he ordered. His tone was harsh and unforgivably rude.

Chimoko allowed herself to glance over her shoulder at the Greens following her, grateful that she had always made a practice of appearing with her soldiers as if ready to go into Fogestria the minute permission was granted. "To whom are you referring?" she retorted haughtily. "I do not see who you are addressing. I am Javere qa Hyasti, son of Qai qa Hyasti, and Lord of the Third Province. Stand aside! How dare you hinder me?"

"You are not Third Lord, but only a peasant with dung between your toes, dressed up in clothing too fine for you. I was in the courtyard the morning the real Javere qa Hyasti left First City and got a good look at the lady. You are not her. Where are your magicians? Where is your Dragon-warrior? Ei? I order you to stop. You are under arrest."

Chimoko's heart thumped and she gritted her teeth, willing herself not to faint. "I say that I am Third Lord, and that you are the mannerless peasant without the authority to arrest me. Now stand aside, or do I have to order you killed?"

He raised his hand. Immediately more red-uniformed men trotted out from their hiding place behind the building, from a grove of trees nearby, out of other inns at the border. There must have been five hundred of the Reds. They outnumbered the entire company of Greens slightly more than ten to one.

"I say that I do have the authority to arrest an imposter and take her back to First City with me." The Red soldier smiled; some of his teeth were rotten.

Without hesitation she turned to Len-ti. "This man threatens me," she said. "He stands between me and fulfilling my duty to my sworn lord. Please kill him for me."

"Pardon me, Lady," Len-ti said, "but that will accomplish nothing. There are ten of them for every one of us."

"Your duty—"

"Your duty is to live," he said gently. "My duty is to preserve your life if I can."

She paused, thinking rapidly. Of course he was correct. "Please advise me," she said.

He stared for a moment at the man in the uniform of First Lord. "Let me speak to your commander," he ordered abruptly.

"M-my commander?" The man betrayed his low status by his hesitation.

"Yes!" Chimoko said, pressing the advantage. "I will not deal with underlings!"

"You'll come with me, at once!" The soldier reached for her, put his hand on her arm—

Faster than thought, Len-ti's sword was out. Though the Red captain must have been expecting the attack, he was a heartbeat slower than Len-ti. Len-ti's sword flashed just as the other man's cleared its sheath. The blow caught the Red in the neck. The head bounced in the dust before the body crumpled.

Len-ti wiped the blade carefully, turned back to her, and bowed, his sword still in his hand. "He has paid for his presumption, Ladylord," he said.

"Thank you," she said, very proud of him.

A Red stepped forward, taking the fallen captain's place. Nine more Reds fell in behind him. Immediately ten Greens detached themselves from the column and moved out in front of Chimoko. Both sides stared, tense, waiting.

"No," Len-ti said. "We must go back, retreat—"

"Never!" one of the men muttered under his breath.

"You, to the back rank! The rest of you, fall in! Defensive square!"

The man Len-ti had shamed marched back as ordered. The rest snapped into formation, pikes ready, hands itching to draw sword and fall on the enemy then and there.

"When we get to the inn, find a horse and ride away at once," Len-ti said to her quietly. "It's you First Lord wants, whatever his reason. We can hold out a long time, behind those walls around the inn."

Incongruously, she thought that she wasn't even dressed for riding, had no gloves, no parasol—"I won't leave you!"

"It is your duty to go. And mine to stay."

They got no more than five paces before the Reds attacked and the killing began. Pikes flashed and the morning air rang with the sound of pike blade upon sword, sword upon sword, sword upon flesh. One of the Reds screamed, staggering back. His belly gaped open and he tangled his feet in his own intestines. The Green fighting him hesitated and paid for it with his life. Dust rose under their feet. The thick smell of blood filled the air, acrid with fear and rage. And with it came the unmistakable smell of battle, of excrement as blades sliced through men's bodies, of urine dribbling into the dust, the smell of charnel houses.

Border guards, innkeepers, servants, and a scattering of guests watched wide-eyed around doors, through windows, and from behind walls. This was a fight they would make songs of, that First Lord would send his soldiers after Third Lord and try to kill her.

A dozen Greens fell before they reached the comparative safety of the garden walls surrounding the inn. But for each Green left lying in the blood-soaked dust, four or five Reds lay with him.

"Quick!" Len-ti cried, shoving Chimoko toward the stables. "Get away! Hide! You mustn't be caught! If they don't have you, they've got nothing!"

The battle raged around them. She looked once into his eyes. He was bleeding but still strong on his feet. "I—I love thee," she said. Her words were lost even as they left her lips. She turned and ran.

In the short time it took to reach the stable she realized what was happening. The Greens took positions behind every wall, every tree, every rock suitable for defense, and let the Reds hurl themselves onto their pikes and swords. Eventually the Red commander, wherever he was, would realize that direct assault was too costly and would call for archers. Here and there a Green fell, and another unhesitatingly took the place of his fallen comrade. But as the ranks of Greens thinned, there would be no more replacements to take their places. When the arrows began they wouldn't last long. It would be sheer slaughter. The Reds would, inevitably, win.

Inside the stable, the horses stamped and whinnied nervously. She grabbed the bridle of the nearest one, hitched up her skirts, and scrambled onto its back. Clinging desperately to its mane, she dug her heels into its side and galloped out onto the road. Someone had anticipated this move. Dimly, she saw men moving to intercept her. She lashed the horse viciously. It redoubled its efforts. The men scattered under the horse's hooves. She was on the road. Keeping low, not daring to look at the carnage behind her, she urged the animal onward.

She rounded a bend in the road. They were waiting for her.

A man leaped for the reins. The horse shied away, rearing. Chimoko couldn't keep her seat and fell heavily into the dust, stunned.

A red-uniformed man grasped Chimoko by the arm and

hauled her to her feet. "I apologize, Lady, but I cannot permit you to go any farther."

She drew herself up as haughtily as she could, despite the pain in her back and shoulder and her inward quaking. "How dare you!" she said. "When my sworn lord hears of this—"

"My orders are directly from First Lord Yassai. He is the sworn lord you mean, of course?"

His manner was impeccably polite, yet she realized he knew she meant the Ladylord and the ruse that had worked considerably longer than she expected it to. She stared hatred at him. This had to be the real leader. He had known all along that the Greens wouldn't give up without a fight, that she would try to escape, even that she would keep to the road rather than take to the open country— She cursed herself for a fool.

Who betrayed me? she thought. Or perhaps one of the border guards sent word back to First City about this woman who made such a commotion every day. Or maybe First Lord sent these men after the Ladylord, to kill or capture her, or simply to make certain of her whereabouts. Or maybe their deception had just run its course. Whatever the answer, it was bad luck for her, and worse luck for the men who had died on both sides.

Chimoko wished she had taken up a sword and joined the battle. Surely she could have provoked someone into killing her then and there rather than endure the shame of being taken prisoner. But that moment had passed. If she drew her dagger and tried to stab herself, she knew she wouldn't be able to move fast enough for the new Red leader not to stop her in her last act of defiance.

The Reds surrounded her, taking her back the way she had come. The battle was over, quiet echoing through the garden. A handful of Greens stood shamefaced, surrounded by Reds. She forced herself to look for Len-ti's body. He lay with a Red soldier's dagger in his neck, his sword still through his enemy's body. Eeeei, she thought, thou wert a great comfort to me, in my bed, and at my side. Even spoiled as it was, thou had a better death than I can expect now. I apologize that too many *ri* separate us from our own Ancestor Stone. Cast thy soul upon the Six Winds and wait for me.

The Reds hustled her up the steps of the inn. They made her wait while some of them went into her bedroom to gather a few belongings. A fresh wave of shouts and screams told her that the Reds had fallen upon the remaining Greens and were now slaughtering them, to the last man.

She turned on the Red captain. "What kind of treachery is this?" she shouted. "Those are my men! They had given up—"

"I apologize," the man said. "But my orders were most specific. If it was true that you were impersonating Javere qa Hyasti, I was to bring you back to First City and only you. No soldiers, no one else left behind here with you."

With an inarticulate cry, Chimoko launched herself at him. He caught her easily by the wrists, and she felt the bones bend under his grip. The world slipped out from under her. When she came back to herself someone was holding a cup to her lips. Before she could gather her wits, she swallowed. The taste was odd, bitter, and too late she realized she had been drugged.

ii

She lay numb and forgetful in the palanquin rigged between two horses that carried her back to First City and Lord Yassai; even the prospect of an interview with the fearsome First Lord couldn't rouse her. Her head felt as if it was filled with smoke, and consciousness drifted in and out. Now and then, when the next dose was delayed, her mind could function a little. At these times she could think of nothing but how she had failed in her duty, and how, as a result, so many of the Ladylord's best men had died for nothing. Now in shameful captivity, she knew that she could, if she was lucky, be executed out of hand for treason. Or, First Lord possessed the means to make her say anything he wished her to say against her beloved Ladylord. Oh, how she wished she had died in the battle. That would have thwarted any scheme he might be thinking of. But at the moment, constantly drugged as she was, even the desire for death had become something unreachable, unattainable.

She was never alone for a moment. The soldiers treated her with rough courtesy even when they had to help her with her most intimate bodily functions. Despite the fact that she could scarcely move by herself, everything that might be used to take her own life was carefully removed from her presence; the captain even had the curtains on the palanquin ripped away.

"You could strangle yourself with your hair, Lady," he said, "and my orders are to deliver you to First City alive."

When she let her food sit, uneaten, one soldier forced her mouth open while another put food into it. Once begun, she could chew and swallow; but it was beyond her to initiate the action.

Days and nights blended together. She would be roused from sleep, dressed, and put into the palanquin. The next time she blinked, it seemed, the day was over and it was time to sleep again. She barely noticed when the stark gray walls of Stendas Castle loomed in the distance. It looked like a rock with First City being the sea that washed against it. Some people stared as the red-uniformed soldiers and the uncurtained palanquin moved through the streets toward the castle gates. Most, noting the color and badge of Lord Yassai, studiously looked away. As she was carried through the streets she tried to rouse herself but couldn't. She fell back on the palanquin cushions, dizzy and stuporous.

She expected to be thrust into the prisons that were said to be located somewhere beneath the castle. Instead, the soldiers took her out of the palanquin and carried her up, very far up. The idea that she might really be mistaken for the Ladylord and was being taken to her guest rooms cut through the fog in her head, a little. By concentrating as hard as she could she counted flights of stairs. Dimly she realized she was being put in smaller, much less luxurious apartments two floors or more above the ones the Ladylord had occupied earlier. The soldiers turned her over to maidservants, saluted, and left.

And there she stayed, waiting, while the days passed.

The women seldom spoke to her. She didn't mind. These new jailers proved far less strict than the soldiers had been. Perhaps they felt there was nothing she could do about her situation now. The drug dosage decreased; she was given only enough now to keep her slightly befuddled and easy to control. She learned how to recognize its characteristic bitter taste. The smaller dosage let her detect it; on the road, she had been kept so deeply drugged she couldn't taste anything. She expected to have the noxious mixture forced down her, but as long as she remained compliant, no one insisted on anything but occasional doses. Sometimes it appeared in her food, other times in her tea. When she could, she avoided it though this meant that she sometimes went hungry or thirsty. But the meals she was given were of such indifferent quality that she didn't mind. Gratefully, she began to come back to herself a little, though her thoughts remained muddled, confused, an aftereffect of the drug. She found it hard to concentrate on anything for long.

Why hasn't First Lord interrogated me, or had me questioned by someone skilled in making even the most reluctant prisoner speak? she thought over and over. He cares as little for me as I care about the insects crawling on my plate, except I will crush them and he won't take the trouble. I think that he very much wants me alive, for now at least. Am I to be his proof, when he needs it, that the Ladylord still lives? Or am I to demonstrate, somehow, that she is dead? What is it he wants to force me to say?

But she couldn't clear the mist in her head sufficiently to find any answers to her questions.

Whatever Lord Yassai's motives—if, indeed, he hadn't forgotten about her entirely—Chimoko discovered that First Lord's desire that she live was enough in itself to strengthen her desire for an honorable death. But that, she knew, would be denied her, once Yassai had finished with whatever obscure plan he had.

The days passed slowly, with nothing with which to occupy her mind other than waiting and dreading what lay ahead. Then one day, to her complete surprise, Lady Safia came to visit her.

Eeeei! Chimoko thought. She must have paid some extraordinary bribes to come. But why? Chimoko wasn't worth anything. There was more to this than appeared on the surface.

The courtesan had her own maid now, a woman of middle years with a stern manner and a sour expression. There was no warmth between them and Chimoko knew instinctively that the maid was one of Lord Yassai's creatures. But this scarcely mattered. She made Lady Safia as welcome as her resources allowed.

"I'm sorry that the room is so dim we must have lamps," Chimoko said. "You would think, being so high up as it is, that I would have plenty of light and air. But I don't."

"Please don't apologize," Safia said. She waved away the tea the serving maids offered, motioning to her own maid. The woman came forward reluctantly, uncovering a tray. Chimoko drew in her breath in surprise and pleasure. She had been a serving maid too long not to recognize what lay before her. Safia had brought fresh tea perfectly brewed and a generous plate of exquisite food—raw fish slivered and sprinkled with bean sauce, pickled vegetables, steaming noodles, rice.

"Seeing you is almost like being home in Third Province again!" Chimoko exclaimed in entirely unfeigned pleasure. Her mouth watered and her stomach cramped in anticipation. Though she wanted to fall upon the food and devour it all at once, she remembered the kind of manners she had always admired in the Ladylord and poured tea for the other woman. The peach-colored porcelain was so fragile the light from the lamps showed through.

"I have missed seeing familiar faces as well," Safia replied. She took her cup and breathed the fragrance. "Of course, my good fortune in belonging to my Lord Yassai is far beyond my most extravagant hope," she added carefully for the benefit of her maid and also any of First Lord's spies among the serving women. "He grows fonder of me by the day, I think. He can scarcely bear to have me out of his company."

Eeeei, thou hast kept him occupied and that might go far to explain why I haven't yet been put to the torture, Chimoko thought. "And are you happy in your new life?" she said. "But of course you are. It was foolish of me to ask. Your happiness is most evident."

Truly, Safia didn't look very happy. Signs of strain showed on the courtesan's face and in her manner. But it would have been very bad manners to say so.

"The Lady Seniz-Nan," Chimoko continued. "My Ladylord Javere remembers her fondly. Is she well?"

"She is near her time and very restless. But she bade me tell you that she also remembers Ladylord Javere with great fondness and prays for the successful completion of her task, as do I." With utter innocence, Safia glanced at a hovering maid and a smile touched her lips. "First Lord's Dragon-warrior grows weaker by the day, and will not last long. It is a pity."

Chimoko smiled in turn, pleased at Safia's cleverness. No one, not even Lord Yassai himself, could fault either lady on this reason for praying for the Ladylord.

- The two sat and chatted agreeably for the better part of an hour before Safia's maid indicated that the courtesan's visit was over.

"Forgive me, Lady," the woman said, "but Lord Yassai will be asking for you."

Safia got to her feet immediately. As if on impulse, and before any of the maidservants could move to prevent it, she embraced Chimoko, touching cheeks with her. The heady smell of Safia's perfume enveloped her. Immediately the lovely courtesan turned to confront the women who acted as jailers for Chimoko.

"This lady must have exercise," she said imperiously. "She grows weak and pale. Let her walk daily on the roof."

"But Lady—" one of the maids said.

"There are plenty of soldiers to guard this one weak woman, if you do not feel yourselves equal to the task." Safia's voice dripped contempt. "You act as if she were a prisoner. But I'm sure my Lord Yassai will not be pleased if his *honored guest* falls ill because she is so poorly treated."

"Yes, Lady, of course, Lady, we never meant—"

Safia brushed aside their protests. "Tomorrow morning, without fail. I will return personally to see that my country-woman is allowed some fresh air and sunshine, to bring a bloom back to her cheeks, ei? Until tomorrow, then, Chimoko."

And with that, she swept out, leaving a trail of perfume in her wake and maidservants terrified that Lord Yassai's favorite would report unfavorably to him, causing them to be punished for failing to heed a change in orders that somehow hadn't reached them. Chimoko could sense the change in atmosphere immediately.

Before anyone could remember that Lady Safia, exalted though her position was, commanded no real power, Chimoko went into the adjoining room and closed the screen in the face of the maid who followed.

"Your presence is as annoying as anything else in my captivity," she said vehemently. "This once, at least, I demand to relieve myself in privacy!" She made a point of rattling the lid on the jar, creating as much clatter as possible. She held her breath; the woman, intimidated perhaps, by this act of defiance coming so soon on Lady Safia's demands, didn't open the screen. She remained outside, as a matter of course; the sound of her breathing came through clearly to Chimoko. But that didn't matter. She had gained her immediate objective.

With the utmost care, making sure that not even the least rustle of the thin rice paper betrayed her, Chimoko unfolded the note Safia had slipped into her hand during their brief embrace. The writing was cramped, crowded on the small square.

"A lady salutes you. A man will see you tomorrow. Time is short. A lady knows your dishonor. This paper is treated with an antidote for what you have been given. She would do more to aid you, but cannot. She apologizes."

Chimoko stared at the note, thinking rapidly. The message was plain; tomorrow, the torture would begin. Nevertheless, hope sprang up in her once more. Tomorrow. It was little enough time to form a plan, but more than she would have had if Safia—and Lady Seniz-Nan as well—hadn't contrived to get word to her. And the antidote. May the Ancestor Spirit bless them both for that.

Without hesitation she put the bit of paper in her mouth, chewed, and swallowed. Then, because her bladder truly had been close to bursting, she finished her errand and opened the screen.

"Thank you," she told the maid courteously. "There are times when even the best service becomes oppressive. I promise I will not cause you any more trouble after this."

iii

Just after dawn the following morning, Chimoko went outside for the first time since she had entered Stendas Castle. It scarcely mattered to her that she was surrounded by red-uniformed guards and frowning maids. Her rooms were so high that the short stairway leading to the roof was located just at the end of the corridor. The day proved to be cold and blustery, and under other circumstances she would have been glad to have stayed inside. But to Chimoko the morning was extraordinarily beautiful.

She had refused to eat or drink anything since Safia's visit, not wanting to risk taking any more of the soporific even by accident. The mist in her head had evaporated entirely. It was like being reborn. She looked at the world with new eyes. Every detail shone clear, perfectly etched, a thing of rare beauty to be savored and enjoyed at leisure. A leaf blew past, and she drank in every detail—the veins, the faint tinge of green melting into gold, the dry brown of the stem. She looked at her hands, pleased. With her forced inactivity the skin had grown soft and white, the nails shapely. She had nice hands. She turned and let the breeze blow in her face, breathing the fresh, chilly air. She hadn't realized how much she had missed it. Because of the chill, she had been given a fur-lined robe that morning, a gift from Safia she was sure, and she relished the softness of the fur against her skin. Pulling the garment more closely about her, she began to walk along the rooftop. The Reds around her instantly became even more alert. But she kept close to the inner wall, pretending not to notice.

Eeeei, how wonderful life is! How you glare, you bastards! Every one of you guards his dagger the way most men guard their precious Jade Stalks. I think the stories I've heard are true. You pretend to hate women, but actually you're afraid— so afraid that you choose the back passages of your comrades rather than risk showing yourself indequate in a woman's bed. There was one, better than any of you, who looked at me with pleasure in bed and out. But thanks to such as you he no longer looks at anything.

The sound of a footstep at the door made everyone, including Chimoko, turn to see who it was.

Safia emerged into the pale light, coming to see for herself that her orders had been carried out as the maids had promised. Lady Seniz-Nan was with her, and red-uniformed guards wearing her personal insignia clustered nearby. Everyone on the rooftop bowed. Safia turned to Seniz-Nan.

"You see, Lady?" Safia said. "There was no need to trouble yourself."

"Indeed that is true," Seniz-Nan said. She was enormous by now and very pale; her breath wheezed in her throat. "Nevertheless I wanted to see for myself. I could scarcely believe it when you told me of this lady's mistreatment."

A man pushed his way up the stairs and through Seniz-Nan's guards. He wore Yassai's insignia. "I have orders that the woman Chimoko, lately calling herself Ladylord of the Third Province, shall be brought before First Lord without delay." His voice was harsh, his manner brusque. "Why is she here, and not inside under strict guard where she is safe?"

He's the one who will take me to the torturer, Chimoko thought. A moment of panic seized her. Eeeei, our plans are for nothing. Now what shall I do?

Safia turned her best smile on the messenger; it was enough

to make even a woman-hater think again. "But this lady is under the strictest possible guard," she said. "And as you can see, she is perfectly safe—"

At that moment, Seniz-Nan clutched her belly, moaned, and sagged into an astonished soldier's arms. For a heartbeat, all attention centered on the lady who carried the heir to First Province in her womb. Chimoko knew herself to be forgotten.

Slipping out of the fur-lined coat, she raced across the roof to the unguarded edge. No labor ever was so timely! she thought. Therefore, it must be a ruse, to give me a chance. Oh, thank you, thank you, she thought, Lady Seniz-Nan and Lady Safia!

Without a pause she leapt atop the low wall at the edge of the roof. Out of the corner of her eye she caught a glimpse of one of the Reds, quicker than the others, running toward her. But he would never make it in time.

Ah, Len-ti! she thought. Unless the Six Winds blew straight and swift thy soul must surely have fallen into the grasp of demons for thou wast ever too proud to join an Ancestor closer to hand. I give myself also to the Six Winds and if thy soul rests with demons, so will mine!

She leaned outward. Then she was flying, flying, with the wind in her hair. . . .

iv

Sigon stared distastefully at the messenger from First Lord. The man uncovered the head on its presentation spike, set it in front of the general and respectfully withdrew a pace.

"And what is this supposed to mean?" Sigon said. Beside him, Lutfu stirred and Nao-Pei drew in her breath. Breathe deep, Lady, Sigon thought. They'd washed it in salt and honey, but it was beginning to rot nonetheless.

"First Lord regrets to inform you that the whereabouts of Javere qa Hyasti qa Gilad, pretended heir of Qai qa Hyasti, late Lord of the Third Province, are unknown and she must be presumed dead." The messenger bowed. "He sends you this token in sadness."

Sigon stared at the head. Think, he told himself. Try to understand. Yassai wants Third Province for himself, or for his nephew, which amounts to the same thing. But how did Chimoko figure in this, and why send her to the headsman? He looked closer. Ei, but this was clumsy work! A Fourth Province alley murderer would have done it better. The neck, that ragged edge. Eeeei! That's no clean cut, it wasn't done with a headman's sword! This head was taken after the woman had already died. They couldn't even cover up the cuts and bruises there, where the skull was smashed in. Torture? I don't think so. Only a fall would do that sort of damage, I believe, caving in the skull and abrading the flesh. But how? My guess is that she jumped or was thrown from a great height. They would not have thrown her to her death. Certainly she jumped, and I think it happened at Stendas Castle. Otherwise, how did First Lord come to possess her head? If Yassai had captured the Ladylord and her company, Chimoko would never have left Javerri's side. And if Yassai had moved against his new Third Lord, he would have sent her head forthwith, with some excuse about treason. Therefore Chimoko killed herself. And why?

Because he didn't have Javerri!

And further, he had no way now to drum up a charge of treason against her with no Chimoko to torture into a false betrayal. Sigon almost gave away the excitement he felt. Eeeei, the ranks of Yassai's guards must be thin this day! He would not have been pleased by such blundering on their part. But Chimoko! Who would have thought it, that she could have outwitted them all like this?

"This proves nothing except that Third Lord's maid is dead," he said brusquely.

"But First Lord has had no word from my sister, General Sigon." Nao-Pei leaned forward. "I fear that she has perished. We would not be looking at this dreadful token if Javere were still alive. She was very loyal to my sister. My late sister."

"I agree," Lutfu said. "It is regrettable, very, but we must face facts." He stared hard into Sigon's eyes.

"I am understandably reluctant to think that the Ladylord Javere is gone," Sigon said.

"I commend your loyalty. Still, we must now think of Third Province. Surely we can't let it languish because there's no strong ruler, ei?"

"Ladylord Javere left me in command."

"And, as I said, your loyalty serves as an example to us all. I hope you will be as loyal to me in turn." Lutfu turned to the messenger. "Have you brought anything from my uncle?"

"Yes, Sire. He ordered me to give you this." The messenger pulled a sealed letter from his sleeve pocket and handed it to Lutfu.

It was First Lord's private chop imprinted in the wax. Lutfu bowed, then opened the letter. As he read, a smile began to spread over his face. Beside him, Nao-Pei fidgeted, scarcely able to conceal her impatience. At last he looked up at her. "My uncle has named me Governor for Third Province through you, in the absence of Lady Javere or another qualified claimant. He orders us to marry at once, if we have not done so already."

"I am very happy that we anticipated his order, my husband, and even more happy that you have the knowledge and experience to carry out this regency with skill and honor." Nao-Pei lowered her eyes demurely, but the corners of her mouth quivered. Sigon was sure that if it hadn't been for his presence in the room she would have leapt up, exulting aloud. He had no trouble imagining her gathering her skirts and dancing in an undignified manner.

His shoulders slumped a little.

"Keeping Third Province at its best and most productive is a goal we both share, General," Lutfu said. "I know you must grieve for Javere qa Hyasti, and want to express that grief in private. Go, by all means. Your sentiments are very much to your credit, my friend. Before you go, however, you will please give me the keys to the treasury."

Sigon stared at him, hating him. Slowly he took the keys from where they had been hanging by a cord around his neck, ever since Javerri had left for First City. "Please remember," he said, "that you are only a governor here. There is no real evidence of Third Lord's death. I will believe that she is gone when I see her head on a spike, not her maid's, or when I hear it reported by someone who saw it happen. I am sorry to be so blunt, but I am after all only a soldier." His hand went almost unconsciously to his sword hilt.

Lutfu returned the stare, and the cruel cast of the man's features intensified. "A soldier, yes, but one known for his deft maneuverings, both on the battlefield and off. You are very near death yourself, General." He brandished the letter. "This makes me Third Lord in all but name. I have only to give the word, and your own most loyal men will cut you down where you stand."

Sigon released his sword, forcing a calm appearance he didn't feel. He made a formal bow. "Please forgive me, Lord Lutfu, and Lady Nao-Pei. I—I am not quite in command of myself at the moment."

Lutfu is right, he thought. He had no business blustering about like Michu. Eeeei, it would not do the Ladylord any good to provoke this ill-tempered bastard and die for it however much he longed to take his head and put it on the spike in place of Chimoko's. He had to swallow his bile and live, even though the mere thought of Lutfu and Nao-Pei was enough to permanently sour his stomach.

How much faith dared he put in that ancient prophecy? Wande-hari believed in it utterly and that was the only reason Lutfu's wife had a maidenhead to breach. And when Lutfu pierced her he rendered her ineligible to succeed Javerri. If the prophecy is to be believed, and I hope the prophecy is to be believed, he thought earnestly, it must also somehow be true. Else what hope is there?

He wondered if Lutfu knew his devoted wife had secretly sent for Sakano to return to Third City? Or if she knew he had already arranged to pay Madam Farhat first-class prices for fifth-class whores? He wondered if either of them cared.

Lutfu relaxed. Nao-Pei held out a hand to Sigon. "You are forgiven, General Sigon," she said. "I think my husband does not fully understand your feelings. Go, by all means, and return only when your grief has passed."

"Thank you, Lady," Sigon said, and bowed again. "I will not require much time." He gazed at the two of them. If they had been his opponents before, now they were his bitter, implacable foes. He didn't know how he could manage to keep them from solidifying their power. He might have more than he could do, just to keep his own head on his shoulders. Glancing once more at the grisly trophy on the presentation spike, he turned and left the room. Nao-Pei's laughter floated after him.

8

i

Javerri reached the cart, her heart soaring with relief when she caught sight of Ivo. He had disappeared from her view only because he bent to string his bow. Steel Fury sang as she drew him from the sheath tucked in her belt and ran to aid Michu. She and Ivo exchanged grim glances as he sought a good vantage point from which to fire. He had an arrow nocked and ready. Lek was right behind him, carrying a length of rope. Ezzat pounded past, hurrying to help.

"Nephew! Wait!" It was Wande-hari. "Javerri!"

She paused briefly. The magician wouldn't have called to her without reason.

"What is it?" Even as she spoke he hastily finished braiding something that sparkled in his fingers—the threads of three different kinds of light.

"If thou must go, stand still only one moment— Ah, there! Now thou'rt protected. Go thou, my brave child—"

"I'll draw them off!" she shouted over her shoulder. The Circle of Protection, scarcely visible in the morning light, floated with her as she left the edge of the crust and got her first good look at what was happening in the loose sand beyond.

Desert sharks clustered around two forms, worrying them into a ghastly semblance of movement as the beasts gorged. They already had stripped the flesh from the donkey, leaving nothing but bones on which the sharks continued to chew. Peng's body still twitched, being dragged through the sand as if through sluggish water. The sand erupted here and there as more flat forms wriggled from their hiding places just beneath the surface.

Javerri's scalp prickled. Unless a shark moved, it blended into the sand so well someone could easily wander into danger unheeding. Nearly an arm's length from snout to rump with a whiplike tail even longer than the body, the sharks moved rapidly across the sand as if they swam, or flew. The tail thrust and recoiled powerfully, propelling them forward, and the two wide flukes rippled to steer them in the direction they wanted to go, leaving a distinctive triple track in their wake. A man could outrun them for a little distance but he'd tire quickly in the loose sand. And the sharks would take him.

Michu crouched at bay, a pike in his hands. He stabbed into the sand between him and the safety of the crust. Sand flew as a motionless shark leaped up. Dark blood gushed. "Ei!" he roared. "Got you, you whore bastard! C'mon, show yourselves!" Incredibly, he laughed. The shark flung itself into the air and flopped back onto the sand. It writhed violently, wounded but showing no sign of dying at once. More of the horrors surfaced. In moments the area between Javerri and where Michu was stranded was swarming with frenzied sharks. The general would have perished then and there if they had not begun to turn on their own kind, apparently excited by the blood. Sharks erupted in sandy showers and smashed onto the ground, teeth locked in one another's bodies. Michu laughed again, stabbing into the roiling confusion. "Go ahead, kill each other, you shit-filled buggers!"

Ivo's bow sang and a desert shark flopped twisting beside Michu, biting at the arrow. He leaped aside. Not all the sharks had joined the frenzy. One snapped at him. Michu stabbed again, missed.

"Try to catch the rope! We'll pull you back!" Lek tossed it over the sand. Unexpectedly, a shark bit at it, pulling it from Lek's grasp. Half a dozen more turned on that one, getting caught in the coils. Michu stumbled and went down. A shark had him by the foot. The bow sang again and Ivo's arrow quivered in the shark's side, but it wouldn't let go.

Javerri moved out over the sand, circling well away from the spot where most of the sharks still thrashed, entangled in the rope and in one another. Another shark tried for Michu and missed. One rippled toward Javerri and smashed against the Circle of Protection. She caught a flicker of movement out of the corner of her eye. Chakei, spiny ruff fully erect, appeared beside her. He snatched the shark off the sand before it could wriggle beneath the surface and bit just at the base of the skull. She heard a sharp *crack!* and the monster went limp. Chakei flung it away and scooped up another, bit, and cast it aside in turn. Understanding instantly, Ivo shifted his aim. His next arrow went into that spot on the shark attacking Michu. It died at once. Michu, leg bloody, kicked free and staggered to his feet.

"I'm coming!" Javerri cried. "Run, get to safety when they go after me!"

"No!" Michu shouted. "Get back where you belong!"

"Don't argue!"

A shout from behind made her turn. One of the soldiers had run out onto the sand. Sharks went rippling toward him at once and he retreated. Ivo took aim and fired. A wounded shark leaped the crust. Another soldier hacked it in two. Wande-hari spoke and a ball of fire landed amid the frenzied sharks still intent on devouring one another. Those that didn't die at once vanished into the sand with astonishing speed. The fireball flared, flickered, and went out.

A shark surfaced inside the Circle of Protection, next to Javerri's foot.

Instinct and training took over. She turned, screaming as she stabbed downward. Chakei whirled instantly, lunging for the shark. He crashed against the invisible barrier and nearly fell. Javerri's first blow only stunned the shark. Using both hands, she stabbed again. Bone grated under the tip of the blade. Then it slid into the vulnerable spot with a satisfying *snick!* and blood flew. She jumped away as quickly as she could through the deep sand before another shark, seeking the body, could figure out how to get inside the Circle as well. More were already rippling closer. For a moment she nearly panicked, thinking the Circle would drag the dead shark with it, but then she was clear. Chakei snatched another from the sand, bit, threw the body away.

She was tiring fast. **Get Michu!** she cried to him. **I'm all right, but he's hurt!**

save ladylord i save michu also

Michu first. Then me.

Reluctantly obeying, the Dragon-warrior loped toward Michu. The general was having trouble standing. His wounded foot wouldn't bear his weight. Chakei scooped Michu up in his great arms. Arrows began dotting the sand around him as Ivo kept up a steady fire, trying to cover his retreat.

The thin blare of a war horn sounded. Javerri looked up. Half a dozen strangers were advancing over the sand. More clustered behind them, dismounting from long-necked birds. They tossed the reins to a couple of their number and the rest joined the first group. They could barely be recognized as human. They were hugely tall, the smallest of them standing taller than Ivo. They wore loose, flowing garments girded high over inhumanly long legs, and their heads and faces were muffled to the eyes. Their lower limbs appeared to broaden from the knee, ending in enormous feet. They carried peculiar clublike weapons with two prongs on the end, and moved as rapidly over the sand as Chakei.

Wading into the midst of the churning mass of desert sharks without hesitation, they began wielding their twin-spiked weapons with devastating results. One of the strangers paused near Javerri. He smashed a shark that had surfaced near her and came closer. Javerri's hands tightened on Steel Fury's hilt.

"Ho-ho!" the man said. "Give hand, little boy! I take back to mama, veh!"

Javerri stepped back. The man dodged past her, killed a shark trying to attack from behind, and reached toward her. His hand crunched against the Circle of Protection.

"Yei!" he shouted, blowing on his fingers. "You got hard shell, little boy! Get back, get back, go to shelf with friends, veh. We got work to do. Talk later!"

Without argument, Javerri floundered through the sand toward the safety of the crust—the "shelf" edging the dangerous sand. Chakei had already put Michu down and started back toward her. ****I'm coming!**** she called to him.

As long as she kept moving she could avoid having other sharks swim under the bottom edge of the protective circle. She stumbled against the edge of the crust and nearly fell, utterly spent, and Wande-hari dissolved the circle quickly so she could be pulled to safety.

She hurried toward the cluster of men where Lek worked over Michu. The physician was tightening a bandage around the general's leg, slowing the blood that pumped out of the wound. Nearly half of Michu's foot was gone.

"We must stop the bleeding entirely," Lek muttered to no one in particular. "He's already lost far too much!"

"Can't you sear the wound?" Halit asked.

"No metal hot enough and no time for a fire, I'm afraid—"

"Try this." Halit pulled Michu's dagger from his belt, muttered a few words over it, and handed it to Lek. The physician took it gingerly by the hilt. The blade was already red hot; in moments it glowed white near the tip.

Without hesitation Lek laid the dagger against the wound where the blood still gushed. There was a sizzle, a stench of burned flesh, and Michu's scream. He slumped into the arms of the soldier who held him.

Javerri involuntarily took a step backward. Lek glanced up at her.

"He has a chance now, young sir," he said, "thanks to Halit. He may never walk properly again, but he'll most likely live."

"Thank you," she said. "Both of you." She looked back toward the sand. The strangely clad men were now working systematically among the sharks, moving almost unhampered through a threshing knot of sand-colored bodies. Their odd weapons suited their task precisely. Far from shrinking from the fearful jaws, the men actually encouraged attack. When a shark fastened onto one of them, its teeth caught for a fatal moment, allowing the man to strike with great accuracy. Rents appeared in the men's "feet," as the sharks tore pieces from the edges of them. Javerri realized the men were wearing special footgear that baffled the vicious predators they were slaughtering as well as lending them their unnatural height.

As the strangers killed sharks, they flung the bodies back toward their waiting companions before the diminishing number of live sharks could get at them. There, the waiting men quickly skinned and gutted the creatures. They threw the hides onto what looked like a sheet of shark skin, and put the carcasses into big net sacks. The offal went onto another sheet of shark skin. The clubbers quit only when the surviving sharks gave up the battle and wriggled away to the safety of deeper sand. The man who had come to Javerri's aid approached the watching Monserrians, unwrapping the cloth from his head and face.

"Great Ancestor, they're desert demons!" Fen-mu exclaimed. "Whoever saw such dark skin? Or hair that curls?"

"Desert demons? Not far off mark, veh," the man said. He sounded pleased. "How you like what we do, little boy?" He put his fists on his hips and grinned at Javerri. His teeth were very white against his swarthy face.

"You—you saved our lives, sir," Javerri said. "We are greatly in your debt."

"Save lives?" The man spat in the sand. "No. We hunting the *sarhandas*. You get in the way." He indicated the desert sharks his companions were skillfully preparing for transport. "But you learn how to kill *sarhandas*. That big fellow with you, he show you."

"Chakei?" Javerri said, startled.

"That what you call him, the *larac-vil?*"

"The Dragon-warrior, yes."

The man stood looking at her while the hot breeze ruffled his loose garments. "I am Vorsa," he said finally. "Leader of Walloh family of Kallait. Who are you? Who in charge of caravan?"

"I'm in—" Javerri began proudly, but Wande-hari interrupted.

"This is my nephew," the old man said. "He's the son of my brother's daughter. She married a merchant who lives somewhere across the Great Desert. I'm afraid the boy is spoiled and a little overbearing at times. He ran away and found me. We're taking him back home."

Vorsa's expression didn't change. "So. And other men, Uncle?"

"The—the gentleman who was wounded is the leader of the soldiers we hired to protect us." Wande-hari indicated the others in turn. "This is our physician. This—" Halit bowed—"is a friend. This—"

Ivo came and put his hands on Javerri's shoulders. "I am the boy's elder brother," he said.

"You man who shoot arrows with tall bow, standing. Not from back of *plandal,*" Vorsa said. "Is good trick, Elder Brother."

Another desert dweller had approached and now stood next to Vorsa. "My second, Yarif," Vorsa said. He turned to his lieutenant. "Go, see what to do for hurt man. You, Uncle, Elder Brother, and little boy, is Kallait custom in desert to invite to eat, drink, when meet with others."

Ezzat stepped into view. "And so we would, Shab Vorsa, if we had anything to offer. But our stores are almost exhausted."

Vorsa stared at Ezzat, blinking a little. "How you know proper title, leader of Kallait family?"

"I'm the, er, guide for these people. Not such a good one as it turns out. We should have been through the desert two days ago. But we got off course."

Vorsa's mouth twisted a little. "Ho, you bad guide because not real desert man!" He thought a moment. "You know, I think I see you once, though, long ago. You don't see me. You been out of desert too long, veh. Yarif, how is hurt man?"

Yarif said something in his own language. He had several teeth missing, and whistled when he spoke.

Vorsa nodded. "He say man will live. Need fannaberry poultice though." To Javerri's surprise, the desert leader laughed aloud. "You just lost *deklas,* like childs, understand? Stay out here, die soon. You not have food, water to share, we take you our place instead! That suit you, Uncle, Elder Brother? Little boy?"

Javerri and Wande-hari exchanged glances. ** *We are exhausted. Our water is nearly gone. The fight took too much of our strength* ** he said. ** *And Michu needs more help than Lek can be, out here.* **

** *Ezzat did say our hope was to run across some of these people. If Ezzat is to be trusted—* ** She frowned. A doubt had arisen about Ezzat, one she could not shake off.

** *Ezzat notwithstanding, the Kallait have a reputation for honesty, according to their own notions.* **

** *Then I'll risk it. We'll go with them.* **

"We're grateful for your kindness," Wande-hari said.

Vorsa turned and shouted something in his own tongue to his waiting men. They laughed and cheered in turn. "I tell them we take you home, join feast, dance, smoke holy herbs, let Lidian nurse little boy, veh! She like that," he added. "Last child have two childs of own now."

At once the waiting desert men came across the sand and entered the camp. They stripped off their unique footgear as soon as they reached the crust. Then they loosened their belts, letting their garments fall to normal length, covering them to the ankle. That done, they went to work with brisk efficiency. They repacked the wagon, making a bed of empty water skins for Michu to lie upon. Javerri watched anxiously while they placed him onto it, but Michu didn't stir. He seemed to be in a deep sleep. She looked a question at Halit.

"Yes, that's my doing," he said quietly.

Yarif, Vorsa's lieutenant, came up to Wande-hari. He understood their language a great deal better than he spoke it. With signs, gestures, mostly incomprehensible words—and, Javerri suspected, a little contact by Wande-hari *beneath*—the man indicated that although they had brought extra pack birds, they would like to load most of their catch of desert sharks onto the donkeys for transporting.

"Garry more san *plandals*, veh?" he said, whistling through the gaps in his teeth.

"Yes, they surely can carry more than your riding birds," the magician said. "This must have been an exceptionally good hunt."

Yarif nodded vigorously. "I see better hunt, but good veast!" he said. "*Sarhandas* good eat."

"So they actually eat the meat from these creatures," Javerri said disgustedly. Thoughts of the human flesh some of the sharks had devoured refused to leave her mind. She watched the sacks being loaded onto the donkeys. "Will we be expected to eat the awful things as well?"

A large, comradely hand dropped on her shoulder. "*Sarhandas* for desert people, little boy," Vorsa said. "Strangers not like, but good anyway. You eat for good manners, veh. Now, you think you can ride *plandal?*"

"I'll try."

"Good! Good!"

By this time the desert men had wrapped the offal from their catch, dug a shallow pit, and buried it. The traces of the Monserrian camp on the hard edge of the sand had all but vanished under the skilled hands of the desert people. All their gear was now repacked neatly, stowed in the wagon around Michu to cushion any jolting, or laden onto the backs of the donkeys. Most of her people were already mounted or in the process of getting into the saddles of the long-legged *plandals*. The men's uneasiness about their strange mounts communicated itself to the birds. The *plandals* skittered and squawked, nipping at fingers and knees. The desert men laughed, enjoying the spectacle.

"Men play joke. Those *plandals,* they just pack birds," Vorsa said. "Not so good for riding. You take Imroud's *plandal,* he drive wagon." He gave another order in his own language and, still laughing, some of the desert men dismounted and exchanged *plandals* with the Monserrians, showing them the trick of hauling sharply on the reins as they lifted themselves into the saddle so the *plandal* couldn't bite. The entourage grew more orderly almost at once, as the experienced riders, brooking no nonsense, brought their *plandals* into line. Except for a little nervousness here and there, the *plandals* accepted their new riders. Vorsa gave a signal, and they started off across the sand.

ii

"You dress all wrong for desert," Vorsa said. He rode with the Monserrians, keeping an eye on them lest they get in trouble with their riding birds and be unable to control them. "Wrap up face, head, keep sand out of nose, veh. Wear sand shoes."

Javerri stared curiously at the odd footgear each Kallait hunter now carried hanging from his saddle. Woven and framed of wood and covered with shark skin, the wide surface of the soles of the shoes gave good purchase in deep sand. Also, the shark-skin covering protected the wearer. She had seen more than one shark leap up trying to bite the smooth surface, and, baffled, slide off again. Vorsa noticed her scrutiny.

"Veh, little boy, sand shoes. Go fast like your *larac-vil.* Why he stay with you, I wonder, not Uncle Whitehair or Elder Brother?"

Chakei loped along beside Javerri, in part protectively, in part happy that she could match his pace at last. She felt entirely ridiculous on the back of the huge bird, but she had to admit their pace had picked up. The donkeys and oxcart lagged far behind now. Imroud, inexperienced in driving

oxen, shouted and cracked his whip but the oxen pulled un-
evenly, slowing their rate of travel even more. Lek struggled
with his *plandal,* staying near his patient. She concentrated
on keeping in her saddle, learning how to move with the unfamiliar gait. The riding bird's drab feathers smelled warm
and fusty and she was certain they were alive with sand fleas
and worse. The birds' heads were absurdly small for their
bodies, perched on long flexible necks, and their eyelashes
curled as frivolously as a first-class courtesan's. Their wings
were tiny, unable to sustain them in any sort of flight. But the
plandals' thick muscular legs pumped tirelessly, and their feet
were even better adapted for running over loose sand than
Chakei's. Also, the birds accepted his presence with supreme
indifference.

"You must know that Dragon-warriors attach themselves
where they will and not at another's command," Wande-hari
said. He sat his *plandal* with great dignity, not like Halit who
clutched saddle and reins as if terrified of falling off at any
moment. "There are some who say we went searching for
Chakei as much as for the runaway boy."

"Who have no name, but *larac-vil* have. Veh, honored
uncle? How he get scar on cheek? Be in fight? Never mind,
never mind. Vorsa knows you will tell when you want. He
meet people from over the mountain before. Very strange, but
not everybody lucky and live in desert."

"Tell us about the sand sharks," Javerri said hastily.

"I've been wondering about them also," Ivo said. "There
were so many— Do they always travel like that?"

"Ho, ho! *Sarhandas* go in small packs most times, not so
much trouble, except when is mating time, veh? Kallait hunt
then, when *sarhandas* have other things on mind. Drive together, kill many for feast, dry meat for later, for winter."

"Then the, the *sarhandas* aren't as dangerous as the stories
people tell about them."

Vorsa turned to Ivo. "Ho, you think that, you dead man
for sure, Elder Brother! You wonder why you don't see *aa*
birds, scavengers, out on sand, just nest in rocks? *Sarhandas*
not leave enough for *aa* chick to live. Eat renders, luctors,

scorpions, *plandals,* people, bones and all. We not be out hunting, you nothing left but cart rims when *sarhandas* get through!" Then the leader's attitude softened. "But you not have so many to fight if Vorsa's people not drive *sarhandas* your way. So we make up for this, take you home, care for you."

At dusk they found an outcropping of crust and camped for the night. The Kallait picketed their *plandals* some distance from the donkeys and oxen; if the birds accepted Chakei with equanimity, the same couldn't be said for their attitude toward the livestock. They swayed their long necks and whistled mournful complaints through open beaks whenever a donkey or the ox cart came near.

Some of the men spitted a desert shark and roasted it over the campfire. Others found a bag of Fogestrian grain the travelers hadn't touched, saving it for when everything else was gone. The desert men put this in a pot to boil together with dried vegetables from their own stores; as it cooked it began to smell unexpectedly savory. Vorsa slipped on his sand shoes, took his club, and left the camp, returning a while later carrying another shark by the tail. He flopped it down next to Javerri.

"Here, little boy," he said. "Take close look at *sarhandas* you fight today."

Tentatively, she poked at the thing, turned it over. The hairless, sand-colored skin was very smooth and tough. It would take a hard blow with a sharp object to penetrate it. Vorsa took his skinning tool from his belt where it rested next to his curved dagger. For the first time Javerri could see that the skinning tool was edged with *sarhandas* teeth. Briskly, Vorsa cut away the tail.

"Kallait make whip of this sometimes," he explained. "I make for you, veh?"

"I thought it would have legs," she said.

"No, *sarhandas* move on hard shelf but not fast, not easy. We stay on shelf, we safe enough." Vorsa opened the shark's mouth to show her the rows of teeth. He ran the back of his hand over the outer row; the light contact left a bloody line of scratches. "If I don't know better, I am in trouble now," he said. "They hide just under sand. Smell blood, feel when something walks nearby, jump and catch. But they bite sand shoes instead." And indeed, by now Vorsa's sand shoes hung in shreds, the shark-skin covering pierced and tattered, the woven surface gnawed inward almost as far as his boots. If the sand shoes had not been designed to keep his feet well above the surface he trod upon, he might have fared as badly as Michu.

Javerri shuddered, looking away from the monster. The pictures and drawings she had seen hadn't told the half of it. Even First Lord Yassai at his worst looked benign beside this creature.

"Not like looks, veh, *dekla?*" Laughing, he tossed the shark to the men at the cooking fire. They prepared it quickly and added it to the one already roasting. "You eat now, sleep. We be home tomorrow."

All of them were glad to have hot food in their bellies and the vegetable gruel was heartening. Javerri took out her eating sticks; when the desert men didn't laugh or jeer, the rest of her people did likewise. Michu slept on under Halit's spell, rousing just long enough to drink some water and take a little vegetable broth.

"He's better off for now," Lek said. He had stayed near the oxcart through the day's journey despite his *plandal's* strenuous objections, keeping a close eye on the general. "I'll try to rouse him in the morning, make him eat a cup of gruel." He lifted Michu's eyelid, pressed his cheek, checking for signs that his condition was deteriorating. But Michu seemed in tolerable shape despite the gravity of his injury. Lek removed the old bandages, replacing them with fresh ones. The wound was seared over completely. Bits of charred flesh came away with the soiled bandages. To Javerri's eyes, it looked more dreadful than ever. But the physician's demeanor indicated that he was well pleased with Michu's progress. He hummed tonelessly to himself as he worked.

"He'll be annoyed when he wakes up and discovers what I've done to his dagger," Halit said. "I'm not sure even my master can restore the edge."

Javerri looked over her shoulder. Halit smiled at her ruefully. "Surely it's a small price to pay for his life," she said.

"Still."

She walked on, checking her people as inconspicuously as possible. She noted the faint, shining track of Wande-hari's Circle of Protection around the camp. She saw Vorsa watching her, his gaze keen and speculative.

"All is well, little *dekla*," he said. "I call you that for name you won't say to me. I see is more to you and your people than you tell unless I miss guess. And Vorsa not wrong many times."

"We are very grateful to you for your kindness, Shab Vorsa."

"Sleep well, Dekla."

iii

At midafternoon the next day, they neared another tumbled outcropping of rock, this one larger than most. Javerri stared upward, wondering if they were going to climb it. Wisps of steam rose here and there, venting the earth's heat. Some of the stony spears and slabs leaned against one another, forming a gate—not by accident, she realized as they rode through it. Sentries on either side hailed Shab Vorsa with ululating cries that echoed from the close walls into the depths of the stronghold. The Kallait poured through a second, smaller cleft in the rocks, surrounding the incomers. A sturdy, large-limbed woman with her curly hair in tight pigtails that bounced on her ample breasts shoved her way through the crowd. Unlike Monserrian women who stayed modestly in the background, even when greeting husbands and relatives home after a long absence, this one—and the others as well, Javerri realized—conducted herself as a full equal to the man she addressed.

"Vorsa!" she shouted. Her voice was deep-toned and cut through the noise of the crowd. *"Weldas, weldas!"*

"Use trader speech, Lidian!" Vorsa shouted in return. "We got guests!"

"So I see! Where do you find them?"

"Getting eaten by *sarhandas!* I tell you all about, later, veh?"

The other Kallait women were already busy stripping the donkeys of their burdens. To Javerri the meat smelled quite rotten. But the women didn't seem to notice. By their exclamations of pleasure and the way they bantered with the returning hunters, it was plain that they anticipated a real treat.

"Uncle, you go inside, take your people, have nice hot bath. We get you real clothes, veh? Ready for feast tonight!"

Javerri stared at Vorsa, then at Wande-hari. A picture of how she looked formed in her mind. Her black hair was matted and filthy, its shine and color almost obscured by dust. Her skin had forgotten the touch of cosmetics. It was burned and where it was not peeling, it bore grime that ran with the tracks of her sweat and congealed in the creases of her neck. The scar across her cheek gleamed white, the only thing about her that looked clean, and she had a sudden suspicion that she smelled bad.

Ei, truly thou'rt as dirty a little boy as I ever saw. Thou wilt feel much better for a bath, nephew. Wande-hari's thoughts were tinged with more than a little amusement.

I long to be clean, she replied. **But how? I can't undress before the Kallait, and even less before our people.**

I'll find a way.

But as it turned out, Wande-hari had no time to intervene in the matter of her getting clean again. Lidian, Vorsa's wife, took her immediately under her protection and would not be gainsaid.

"Ho, such a nice little boy!" she exclaimed. She would have hugged Javerri if she hadn't ducked away in time. Javerri could imagine being pressed into enormous pillows, suffocating. "I take, wash good, veh? Behind ears and all! You think you too big because you wear pretty sword? Hard to tell, you not Kallait, but don't look more than ten, twelve years. Come with Lidian, we get acquainted, veh?"

"No—" Javerri said in protest. But it was trying to reason with a desert whirlwind. Vorsa stood watching them, hands on hips, laughing.

"I say I take you to mama Lidian, Dekla!" he exclaimed. "Vorsa man of his word. We see you later, veh?"

The second, smaller opening in the rocks led into a vast interior space. The emplacement was completely hidden from outside view, and would be virtually impregnable to attack. Javerri reached out to Chakei's mind.

Where art thou?
nice here, safe you ladylord
Chakei!—
safe you He broke the contact.

Puzzled by the Dragon-warrior's indifference but too breathless to think clearly, Javerri scarcely glimpsed the Kallait village. As Lidian whisked her over hard-packed ground through the cluster of thatched huts, enclosures of sheep and goats and *plandal* pens, she got only an impression of neatness and tidiness that would do even Third Province credit. Grass ringed the village, and tall trees with rough trunks and fringed leaves cast welcome shade. The big woman had hold of her hand in a grip that nearly paralyzed her, making Javerri trot helplessly at her heels. As they went, Lidian kept up a steady stream of complaints.

"What they think of, letting little *dekla* like you out of stronghold? You not big enough yet, no wonder *sarhandas* try to eat. Young and tender, veh, they use you for bait maybe? And so dirty!—"

Javerri thought they would have to scale the tumble of rocks her captor was headed for. But a path appeared, hidden behind a boulder. They climbed a little way, made a couple of turns. Javerri sensed the place before they rounded the final corner, caught the smell of brimstone.

Eeeei, she thought, are we going to be burned in magicians' fire? Then she gasped in pleasure. They had come upon a small rift in the rocks that formed a natural bathhouse, as efficient as any back in Monserria. The canyon walls nearly met overhead and here the air was heavy with moisture. A series of pools, fed by a boiling spring high above, dotted the slope ahead of them. Each pool spilled its overflow into the one below it, cooling a little in the process. Soap plants and other vegetation grew in every pocket of loose soil. Lidian, still grumbling, dragged Javerri up a well-worn path to a pool where the water steamed in the hot, humid air.

"—let you go off with careless friends, you dab a little, call it clean, good for you Lidian here now—" Javerri tried to fend her off, to no effect. With brusque efficiency, Lidian knelt down and hauled Javerri's tunic out of her belt and over her head, not bothering to undo it. Then, astonished, she sat back on her heels, staring. "You not little boy at all!"

Javerri clutched futilely at herself, then gave up the effort to hide. She stared into the woman's face and decided to risk all in a single cast. "No, Lidian, I'm not," she said. "I'm— I'm going disguised, you understand? I didn't think it was wise for a woman to travel in this country, even with guards—"

Lidian's eyebrows rose and the corners of her mouth turned down as she adjusted to this unexpected turn of events. "Not wise, you right about that." Then she laughed aloud. "Lucky for you Kallait have different places for men and women, and Lidian such a good mama she take you where little *deklas* go with mamas, veh? Not even call another woman to help. Go ahead, go ahead, little boy-woman. I keep quiet. You wash self, I get clothes. You want woman clothes or boy clothes?"

"Boy, please. And thank you for keeping my secret."

Lidian shrugged. "Not Lidian's business. I go get now."

Javerri took Steel Fury from her belt and laid him nearby. Then she finished undressing and climbed into the steaming pool. It was wonderful! she thought blissfully. She hoped the others had a place even half as good as this. Probably they did. The rocks seemed to be full of hot springs. The water smelled foul, but at that moment she didn't care.

She unbraided her hair, pulled a handful of soap plant,

crushed the stems, and worked up a lather. When she had scrubbed herself from head to foot, she lay back to soak. The water falling from the pool above kept the one she was in at a constant temperature, and also washed the dirty water into the next pool down. Eventually the lowest pool emptied into a crack in the rock. A short time after she had finished her bath, all would be clean again. It was such an efficient arrangement she wished there was one like it at Third City. Perhaps in the rocky outcrop Third City nestled against, where nobody ever bothered to go—

Someone was coming up the path. Javerri pulled herself from the pool and reached for Steel Fury. Drawing him halfway from his scabbard, she crouched down until she saw it was Lidian, returning. The Kallait woman carried brightly colored clothing over her arm.

"Here, Dekla," she said. "These belong to my son when he was little boy, like you." She laughed. "Now he bigger than Vorsa almost." Proudly, she laid out the garments, still creased from being packed away. Woven in stripes of red and green and ocherous yellow, both tunic and trousers were heavily embroidered and sewn with bits of black, highly polished glass.

"This was his best, wasn't it?" Javerri held up the clothing admiringly. "Shouldn't it be saved, for your son's children?"

"You put on, you not dirty it much. These clothes for feast days, weddings. Go ahead, put on. Green coat look nice with your green eyes. Very pretty little boy-woman even with scar on face. Make you look strong, fierce. Lidian comb hair, so straight and black like fireglass, braid it neat like Kallait *dekla,* veh?"

Presently, wearing the borrowed finery and with her hair in two pigtails, Kallait-fashion, Javerri followed Lidian back down the canyon and into the village. The huts were arranged in rows and streets, now empty and deserted, leading toward an open area in the center. Lidian took her in this direction where a larger hut, obviously a guest house, waited.

"I go look over *sarhandas* now," Lidian said. "Some women, they put too much spice. Give Vorsa—" She fumbled for the word, thumped herself on the breastbone, pantomiming indigestion. "You stay here, with friends. You be all right now?"

"Yes, thank you, Lidian. My, er, friends all understand what I am about."

"I see you at feast tonight, we sit together, veh? Tell you what is happening."

Before Javerri could thank her again the Kallait woman turned and strode off toward the spot where rising smoke, shimmering air, and the smell of roasting flesh marked the cooking pits. Javerri ducked into the hut through the low door.

Inside, her people were busy laying out bedrolls and setting their few personal belongings neatly here and there. Ivo and Halit worked putting up a curtain to give Javerri even more privacy than she had had in their open camps. Her own bundle of things lay near her bedroll behind the curtain.

"Where's Michu?" she asked.

"Yarif took him and Lek to their doctor," Ivo said. "There was some mention of a poultice."

She nodded.

"You look very fine, nephew," Wande-hari said. "Did you fare well?"

Javerri nodded. **Lidian knows my secret but she said she won't tell.**

If she promised, you can rely on her. As I told you, the Kallait are people of their word, if you can get them to give it.

"Where is Chakei?" she asked aloud.

"The Kallait children have him," Ezzat said. "They caught him as he started after you and that formidable lady. I think he was pleased that they wanted to play with him."

Javerri nodded again. Now that she could think about it, she realized that the Dragon-warrior sensed the same confidence about the Kallait and their stronghold that she did. Otherwise he would never have allowed himself to be diverted from her side when she had been dragged away by Lidian. Rough, coarse, and crude of manner though the Kallait were, she felt more comfortable here among them than she had since leaving Third Province. She was a little surprised, however, that the *deklas* had taken to him so thoroughly. Most children, unless they had been brought up around the breed, tended to run from Chakei in terror. He liked children and this reaction had always saddened him. No wonder he had gone off to play with them now. "And the Kallait men we came in with? The village was practically deserted when I returned."

"They've gone to sleep. Vorsa recommended that we do the same. Apparently a *sarhandas* feast lasts all night."

It did seem like an excellent idea. Beyond the curtain, Hali had already lain down and begun to snore. Wande-hari's eyelids drooped and even Ivo stifled a yawn when he thought she wasn't looking. The strain of the past few days had taken it toll on all of them. Javerri pulled the curtain closed and lay down.

Why dost thou always call me nephew? she said just before she drifted off. **I have wondered.**

Because I am truly thy uncle, Wande-hari replied drowsily. ** Thy mother Shantar was the grandchild of my brother's daughter, even as I told our Kallait host.**

Oh. Then she fell into a deep sleep, rousing only when sounds of merriment from the village inhabitants gathering in the open area outside grew loud enough to wake her.

i

The Kallait stronghold was a place of long twilight. Only when the sun rose above one high stony ridge did dawn become day. Then the people took shelter from the merciless rays until the sun dropped below the opposite ridge and day became dusk.

By the time Javerri emerged from the hut, dusk had begun to deepen into nightfall. When she opened her eyes, the building was empty. The others had apparently arisen, dressed, and left her to wake on her own. She felt much better for the sleep.

Out in the open compound, torches cast flickering light on the women hurrying here and there, carrying trays of food and jugs of drink. The air was full of unexpectedly appetizing smells and Javerri's stomach growled hungrily in response. A large fire blazed in the center. The music of deep-toned flutes playing a simple but insistent melody drifted through the sound of chattering voices, and drums throbbed in a seductive rhythm. Already some of the younger women danced as they walked, hips swaying. Children appeared from nowhere and clustered around Javerri, staring at her in fascination, touching her straight dark braids. But wisely, they appeared to realize that, although she was only a little taller than they were, she was not one of them. To Javerri's delight, a little girl, smiling shyly, handed her a luctor; it wore a collar around its neck attached to a leash made of plaited grass. The luctor quivered in her hands, its heart racing. Javerri stroked the tiny creature until it stopped trembling, then gave the child's pet back to her.

"Ho, ho, little Dekla!" Vorsa came striding toward her, his teeth gleaming in the firelight. "You wake up at last! Mama Lidian do good job, veh?"

"Very good." Javerri touched the colorful tunic. "She gave me these clothes to wear."

"Hansa's. Look nice on little Dekla."

"Please, Shab Vorsa, where is—is the man who was hurt?"

"He with Kallait doctor, doctor of you. He feel much better with fannaberry poultice."

"May I go see for myself?"

"That way," he said, pointing.

If Lek hadn't called to her as she passed, she would have missed the place entirely. The Kallait healer's hut was no larger than any of the others, not specially set off in any way; perhaps these people scorned sickness or injury and didn't regard their healers as worthy of more than ordinary notice.

"In here, young sir!" the physician said. He sounded pleased.

When Javerri ducked through the low door and saw Michu, she realized why. The general was sitting up, hungrily attacking a platter of food.

"Well," she said humorously, "it's plain to see that I was worried for nothing!"

"About that?" Michu indicated his bandaged foot and kept eating. "Just a little inconvenience, that's all. Give me a limp. Keep me away from the feast and the girls."

"I hope you aren't eating *sarhandas.*"

"And if I am, so what?" The general shrugged. "This fellow here explained it to me." He beamed at the Kallait doctor. "Feras says desert sharks eat them, so they eat the sharks. Take some of their own back, so to speak. Anyway, this is delicious, whatever it is. And the grain boiled with vinegar. I've never had such a roaring appetite!"

The physician adjusted Michu's bandage a little, making sure the poultice was where it would do the most good. He grinned at Javerri, bobbing his head. She moved closer; the clean bandages were beginning to show a green stain, but the smell—fruity and a little sharp—told her this was from the fannaberry poultice.

"I wanted to make sure you were all right—"

"Oh, I am, I am. Go back to the feast, boy. I'm in excellent hands!"

She touched Michu on the shoulder, liking him greatly, and ducked back out through the doorway. Lek followed her.

"I never thought to see him in such good humor," Lek said when they were out of convenient earshot. "Those fannaberries are wonderful medicine. He really began getting better when Feras gave him the juice to drink as well. If I could only take some back with me when we return, try to grow them—"

"By all means, get some seeds," she said. "Or arrange to take a seedling with us. Third Province should have this won-

derful medicine." Then she nodded to the physician and retraced her steps toward the compound. In her brief absence
even more people had gathered.

ii

As she came back into the firelight she saw Chakei surrounded by Kallait children, all dressed in their best and
jostling one another for the Dragon-warrior's attention as
they vied for which of them would hold his hands. They had
adorned their new friend for the festival; he wore brightly colored ribbons around his neck and limbs, and the children had
strung fireglass ornaments on a cord and decorated his ruff.

Thou looks very fine, she said to him.
fine i very, handsome also
Art thou well?
warm here more than sand

Javerri had also noticed that the night was considerably
more comfortable than she had expected. Perhaps the sun-
warmed rocks, riddled with thermal springs, had something
to do with that. ***I'm glad thou hast found new friends.***

new yes but always with ladylord i
I know and understand, and thank thee.

Ivo, Wande-hari, Ezzat, and her four remaining soldiers
stood with Vorsa, flagons in hands, watching the preparations. They, like her, wore borrowed finery and looked more
than a little self-conscious in it. Even Ivo seemed a little uneasy in the strange garments though he wore them well. The
Monserrians' skin glowed golden in the firelight; the blackness of their hair melted into the night. Even dressed as they
were they could never be mistaken for Kallait. But nobody
else seemed to mind; as she watched, Vorsa clasped Ivo's arm.

"Dekla!" the shab shouted. "Over here! I just tell Elder
Brother I want learn about bow you shoot from standing
up!"

Javerri made the decision she had been pondering, drawing upon the ability Wande-hari had developed in her that let her trust the feelings she got from other people. "I have something to tell you, Shab Vorsa—"

"Sure, sure, but drink first, veh?" He held two flagons; as he proffered one he drank deeply from the other. His eyes were bright and his hand not altogether steady. "Don't worry, Dekla, takes many of these for real drunk!"

Javerri accepted the flagon and tasted it cautiously. It wasn't proper wine. The liquid inside was cool, not hot, and entirely too sweet, almost to the point of being sickening, yet it burned agreeably going down. Perhaps she would get used to it as she drank. She took a larger swallow. Vorsa laughed.

"Good, veh? We make it from dates. Grow on these trees." He indicated the trees with feathery fronds for leaves that grew profusely inside the stronghold. "Dates also good for eating. Make very strong. All your people eat lots, fight *sarhandas* very good, veh? Give meat to Vorsa!"

Javerri laughed. Obviously this wasn't Vorsa's first flagon; and just as obviously, he was a man who grew happy and convivial when he drank. "It is good to have wine again," she said. She hadn't realized how much she had missed this small comfort, and how gratifying even this rather repugnant beverage could be. The Fogestrians forbade the use of alcohol, in any form. "Is there somewhere we can talk a moment?"

"Come, you sit with me," Vorsa said. Here and there, at the edges of the firelight, women were laying out cushions on embroidered ground cloths. He indicated a particularly large one, with tassels on the corners. "That shab's place for feast. We talk in—in—"

"Private?" Javerri said.

"Veh, private. Vorsa forgets words sometimes when he drinks." He took another enthusiastic pull at the flagon, emptying it, and got a refill from a jar carried by a passing woman before leading Javerri to the privileged area. Obviously he was intending to become gloriously drunk before the celebration was finished.

"We are from Monserria," Javerri explained, when they

were seated and she was certain nobody was trying to over-hear. "And I am not a little boy."

In economical phrases she described who they were and what the errand was that had brought them so close to dis-aster, out on the sands. Frequently she had to stop and re-explain something when Vorsa's knowledge of the language proved inadequate for his understanding. When she had fin-ished, the shab appeared considerably more sober than he had when she had begun. He nodded.

"Veh, veh, Vorsa knows from first there is more to you than you say. Dekla that carry sword with gold hilt? And hard shell, that not for ordinary little boy either." He smiled and flexed his fingers. "Damn near break hand on. And Vorsa see ball of fire also, come out of nowhere. You got mage, this Vorsa know, but not think you got two though."

The leather wrapping on the sword hilt had come loose, showing the ornate pierced goldwork. Javerri pulled it off and discarded it along with the pretense that they were merely travelers who had met with misfortune.

"We were that easy to see through?"

"Not for ordinary Kallait, other people likewise." He tapped himself on the chest. "But I Shab Vorsa. I not notice things like this, I not shab for long. So Elder Brother not brother at all, veh? And go for *larac-vil* egg. Much danger. I think just Lidian and me know real story of you, for now any-way. I tell her later." He looked at Javerri keenly, all traces of tipsiness vanished. "There is something more also I think. You got guide, you got *larac-vil*. How do you get lost so much? You can't see stars, see path of sun?"

"Ezzat said Chakei—the *larac-vil*—led him off course. And Chakei did veer to the southwest instead of heading due south."

"Hmmm. Can men of magic mix up heads, veh?"

"Yes. Halit was very useful in Fanthore, with the trading and again at the gate. Wande-hari—well, I think he's forgot-ten how much power he can command. But neither of them would mix—"

Even though they spoke in relative privacy he leaned closer to whisper. "But even if guide not true Kallait, he is in desert before many times, veh?"

"Yes, Shab Vorsa. I know what you're asking. Halit could have cast a spell on Ezzat so he wouldn't notice we were going off our course. Or Ezzat could have followed Chakei deliberately, so we would be lost. I don't know."

"Or maybe desert gods guide you to this place to laugh at us all." Vorsa grinned at her. Abruptly he flung the contents of his flagon onto the ground. "You throw away, too."

"B-but why?" she said, startled. If she found herself a little sickened by the heavy sweet beverage, she was at least beginning to enjoy its effects.

"Do. You see." Vorsa lifted his head. "You, Kendris! Bring jug, veh!"

Hastily, Javerri emptied out her flagon just as the Kallait girl reached them. She lifted the cup next to Vorsa's and Kendris filled both to the rim.

"Now," Vorsa said with satisfaction, "we make pledge from full hearts, with full cups. Vorsa and all his people now friends of Dekla and all his—her people. You let me still call you Dekla?"

"I am honored. And we are now friends of Vorsa and all his people in turn."

"You understand Vorsa speaks only for Walloh family, veh? Other Kallait, maybe not friends."

"I understand."

"Now drink all. Leave some in cup, then pledge not binds. Is Kallait thing to do."

Following his lead, she closed her eyes, tilted her head back, and allowed the sweet fiery liquid to flow down her throat, trying not to think about the taste. When she opened her eyes, Vorsa was looking at her, grinning.

"Good, good," he said. "Now we friends forever. Or until new pledge. Bring friends, sit, celebration start, veh?" He picked up a horn lying nearby and blew a note on it that cut through all the noise. Immediately a glad cry rose, and the drums began a new beat. Everyone scurried to his or her place. A young man Javerri hadn't noticed before sat down at the edge of the tasseled ground cloth, with but not a part of the shab's group. His skin was a little darker than the others', his clothes of a slightly different cut. Nobody introduced him.

Lidian appeared out of the darkness. She wedged herself between Javerri and Ivo.

"This good! Lidian with Dekla and Elder Brother at once, veh?" she said comfortably. She threw her arms around their shoulders and gave them a warm maternal hug. "Like have family again! Look, now comes *bifat,* then feast."

Young Kallait girls gave each of them a spadelike utensil, and a double platter, one side empty and the other heaped high with handsize flat cakes. Javerri had never seen anything like them. She picked up one of the cakes and looked at it uncomprehendingly.

"Bifat, you understand, veh? No? Watch." Lidian used her utensil to rake food from one of the serving plates onto the empty side of her platter. Then she showed them how to use the *bifat,* making a cup with it in the palm of her hand, filling it with meat and grain, then wrapping the cake neatly around the whole mess. "Now you eat, not spill on clothes, veh?"

Young women were already circulating, carrying trays of *sarhandas* meat prepared in every conceivable manner—roasted, boiled, fried, simmered in date and apricot sauce with spices, stewed in curdled milk. Shab Vorsa carefully chose from the trays and directed that they put generous servings on each of his guests' platters. Other girls carried pots of the boiled grain with vinegar Michu had found so savory.

"Eat, eat," he urged his guests. "Just a little, for good manners, veh?"

Javerri swallowed hard. Well, I ate what might have been poisoned meat in my interview with First Lord Yassai, she thought. Surely this can't be any worse. She looked around at her companions; all of them bore an expression of distaste, try though they might to conceal it. Tal was the only one of them who looked interested. The young man seated at the edge of the group regarded them all, a filled *bifat* halfway to his lips, a cynical smile touching the corners of his mouth. For some reason she couldn't explain, Javerri knew she'd shame both her people and Shab Vorsa's if this person observed the shab's guests making a poor show for themselves. "We have to do this," she said in a low voice. "It's expected."

But if I must, I'll do it my way, she thought. She picked up the *bifat,* holding it as if it were a rice bowl, and put a little meat cooked in date sauce on the cake. Then she took up her eating sticks. With an effort she kept her hands steady and her face impassive. Then she picked out a morsel, put it into her mouth and chewed. The rest followed suit, more or less reluctantly.

It was delicious. She had expected something foul, its rankness masked indifferently with the sweet sauce; but to her complete surprise she found the flavor quite good. She took another bite.

Shab Vorsa, watching her keenly, threw back his head and roared with laughter. "Good, good, little Dekla! You brave fellow! I see faces when we bring *sarhandas* in, think Kallait eat rotten meat but you do it now anyway for friendship!" He wiped his eyes. "Don't be afraid, Vorsa just playing little joke. You got nice mutton, like your friend in hut."

Lidian laughed with her husband. "Veh, I cook special for you, me, with these hands!"

Wande-hari began to chuckle. "If you had used bean sauce in the preparation as well, and added just a little ginger root—" he said around a mouthful.

Ivo smiled uncertainly; then he too joined the laughter as he tasted the strange concoction and found it good. Within moments the Monserrians were happily devouring the food they had regarded with abhorrence before.

"*Sarhandas* meat too wild taste if eat fresh," Vorsa explained. "Hunters do, veh, but that to show each other we strong, tough. Real desert men, understand? We eat little bit fresh meat for festival, veh, but mostly mutton. Let rest sit night, two night, wild taste not so much, prepare for real eating later. That what my fine Dekla smell, wild taste running out of *sarhandas* meat. Ho, ho, should see look on face when Vorsa make joke! Kallait love good jokes. Veh, Yanno?"

The stranger looked up. "Veh, Shab Vorsa."

"Yanno is son of shab of Yonal family of Kallait," Vorsa continued genially. He gave the young man a fond look. "Maybe Yanno and my son Inbar fight later. With knives!"

"Whatever for?" Javerri said, startled.

"Yonal family live three nights' journey from here," Lidian said. "Not so big as Walloh place, not so fine. Yonal family always send us a son for *sarhandas* feast, we send also. This year is Hansa, you wear his clothes. Walloh family take too many *sarhandas,* not leave enough for Yonal family. Yonal family take, Walloh family have too small feast. So we send sons watch, they come back and tell. Almost always fight also."

Yanno grinned and touched the curved dagger he had in his sash.

"That not till much later, when good and drunk," Vorsa said, dismissing the matter. "Enjoy first!"

While they ate, people from other groups came by and greeted the shab and his guests politely. Lidian kept up a running commentary in Javerri's ear. This one was a son with his wife and children, that merely one of the Walloh family, no kin but family nonetheless, you know Yarif, he has new young wife, here is son Inbar, not married but living alone, there a daughter, big-bellied for fifth time, veh. The names and faces quickly swam together in Javerri's mind. She nodded and smiled, forgetting who each person was almost at once.

As if at some prearranged signal the drumbeat changed to a rhythm even more seductive than the one Javerri had heard earlier, and the flutes began a new five-toned melody as fresh musicians took up the song. Older people moved their cushions back almost out of the light, smiling. Javerri became aware that the young women had disappeared.

"Girls go to make themselves fine for the dancing, for the young men," Lidian said. She glanced at her husband. "Remember, Vorsa, how I dance for you? Lidian slender like date palm in those days. We marry quick, veh."

"This is like courtship, then?" Ivo said, interested.

"Courtship, veh. You watch."

The music from the drums and deep flutes entered Javerri's blood, warmed by the food and the date wine, and she began swaying to the irresistible rhythm. So did the others in the shab's company. The throbbing beat ignited a spark that seemed to well up from her Jewel Terrace. She wondered if she were the only one affected. Young men scrambled for the best places in the circle of firelight, positioning themselves where they would be sure to be seen. They sat cross-legged, impatiently drumming fingers on knees, smiling with anticipation and peering back over their shoulders.

Girls came dancing from the shadows, slipping between the young men out into the open space. Their appearance was entirely different from the way they had looked when they were serving the food. Now they wore full skirts and brief jackets tight over swelling breasts, showing a great deal of warm brown skin. They circled the fire, light glittering from their many ornaments and the paint on eyelids and cheeks. Their hair fell in dark curling masses, released from the braids. They swooped and whirled, skirts belling outward to reveal colorful undertrousers. And they added to the music as they danced, with tiny finger cymbals and jingling anklets and bracelets. Now and then a girl would leave the circle and pause in front of a particular man, only to run laughing to rejoin the dance when he started to get up from his place. The men grinned and nudged one another, clapping their hands to the rhythm. And occasionally a girl waited before the man of her choice, still swaying, until he rose to his feet and the couple disappeared into the darkness.

The way Shab Vorsa's party was crowded on the ground cloth, they were all sitting much closer than they would have under ordinary circumstances. Without willing it, Javerri moved her hand toward Ivo only to discover his hand reaching for her. They looked at each other. Her breath caught in her throat, held there by the pounding of her pulse. Ivo stared at her, a world of longing in his eyes. Eeeei, had the Kallait put aphrodisiacs in their food? Weren't they married? Wasn't this proper between husband and wife? It would be so easy. She could leave quietly, go to the guest hut, and by the time he got there she would be naked, waiting for him in the dark—

Vorsa said something in his own language and a young woman Javerri recognized as one of his daughters-in-law brought him a box and a coal from the fire in a small pair of tongs. He opened it, filled a long-stemmed pipe, and put the coal to it. The bowl of the pipe was very small; two or three puffs would exhaust the contents. Vorsa drew in smoke and the unmistakable aroma of *abaythim* drifted onto the air. Javerri extricated her hand from Ivo's. Halit leaned forward.

"Holy herbs," the shab explained, "use at feast. You know these?"

"A little." Halit shifted on his cushion. "You don't get very much out of one bowlful."

"Just smoke little bit, too much make you silly, drunk. You want some?"

Halit glanced at Javerri, who frowned at him narrow-eyed. She shook her head. "Another time," he said to Vorsa.

"Good. You take girl instead, veh? Not proper do both in one night."

A blue-clad girl came up to Yanno, teasing him with her eyes. He smiled, eyebrows raised, and nodded. She let out a trilling laugh and raced back. Another girl approached Ivo. Javerri recognized Kendris and her temples throbbed. *If I had any sense I'd have taken Ivo into the guest hut before the shab brought out the* abaythim, *and let the spark that burns in both of us take fire,* she thought. *But I didn't. When I refused him then, how could Ivo resist her now?*

"How do you say, I already have a wife?" he asked Lidian quietly, not taking his eyes off Kendris. She was very beautiful.

Lidian turned to stare incredulously. *"Sandas ponessa ues,"* she told him. "But why? You want woman, Lidian can tell."

Ivo repeated the phrase. A brief look of disappointment crossed Kendris's face, then she too rejoined her sisters.

Another headed for Ezzat. *"Passan ues,"* he told her.

"Means, I'd be delighted," he added to his companions. "I know that much Kallait, anyway. If you want to say no, it's *ruggan ues.*"

"But who'd want to say no?" Fen-mu smiled up at the swaying girl before him. *"Passan ues,* you beauty."

All the Monserrians, even Wande-hari who declined politely, came in for their share of attention from the Kallait women. They were very different from the Fogestrian pleasure girls whose attitude was one of bored indifference. The Kallait exuded joy from every pore, a lusty innocence and promise of delights never before realized. Yanno got up and followed the blue-clad girl into the shadows. Fen-mu eagerly accepted the invitation of the lovely Kendris.

"But I thought this was for courtship, for marriage," Javerri said, puzzled.

Lidian laughed. "Is, is. But is good manners with guests too, veh? Sometimes get babies that way. Girl won't marry before she have baby, in belly at least." She was more than a little drunk, flushed with the wine. By now she too had indulged in a small pipe of *abaythim.* "Oh, music bring back fine times, veh." She glanced at Ivo, then bent to whisper in Javerri's ear. "Too bad elder brother say no because have wife. Is silly. Wife somewhere else, he here now, strong and ready. He make very handsome babies, I think."

Javerri jumped a little, then remembered that Lidian didn't yet know that the wife Ivo referred to was herself. Abruptly her mood darkened. Her body was tormenting her with desire and the throbbing in her head turned to pain. "I'm tired," she said.

"Is time for little Dekla to go to bed? Too bad alone. I ask Inbar go with you. He enjoy little boy sometimes." Lidian nudged Javerri in the ribs and giggled. "We give him big surprise, veh?"

"Thank you, no. I—I can't explain." True enough, she thought. Who would believe I burn for my husband and dare not enjoy his body, his most desirable body. . . .

Wande-hari's voice spoke in her mind. **Beware.**

She turned to glared at him. **My thoughts were private!**

Yes, but so strong I could sense them. And perhaps another as well He moved his head slightly. Halit, a woman swaying before him, was looking curiously in their direction.

I—I've drunk too much. My head hurts, the smoke makes me dizzy, I don't know what I'm thinking.

Then go to thy bed and sleep. I will help thee. All will be well.

Thank thee, uncle.

Halit had turned back to the woman. Javerri got up and, unexpectedly wobbly on her feet, finally found the right hut after almost entering the wrong doorway a couple of times. Passionate outcries and the sound of sweaty bodies rubbing together warned her away. She ducked into the guest hut, pulled back the curtain, and all but collapsed onto her bedroll. She automatically checked to see if the box was in its accustomed place and then, with the aid of Wande-hari's slumber spell and in spite of the nap she'd had that afternoon, she fell into a deep blessedly dreamless sleep.

iii

"Better you stay here seven nights, maybe more." In the bright morning Shab Vorsa, none the worse for the previous evening, walked with Javerri toward the place where Ivo had set up a target. A number of Kallait men watched as he displayed his skill with the bow. Ivo sent still another arrow into the center of the target. Vorsa grinned at Javerri. "Elder brother fine, but take longer for some of your people to recover, veh?"

She nodded ruefully. When the company had assembled earlier, more than one of the men was pleasantly exhausted and bore marks of nails and teeth. They had returned to the guest hut after the waking meal, to catch up on their sleep. Fen-mu and Ezzat were missing, presumably still with the women who had chosen them the night before. She remembered something. "That fight you mentioned, between—Inbar, was it?—and Yanno. Did it happen?"

"Veh, veh, little fight, you not miss much. They with your

fellow with half a foot now, all got fannaberry poultices. Little cuts, maybe not even scars later. Yanno go home soon, today."

Javerri caught sight of Halit. The mage was sitting comfortably in the morning sunlight. He had created one of his singing butterflies and a number of women and children now clustered around, oohing and aahing in delight. A handsome boy with just a shadow beginning to appear on his upper lip stood nearby. He was watching the magician, not the butterfly. Halit smiled. He made the butterfly disappear, then created another even more beautiful and nestled it in the boy's hair.

"I can't stay," Javerri said, "though I thank you. I must obey my lord's orders and return as quickly as I can. And I've no idea what's been going on in my own land while I've been gone."

"Is problem, I know," Vorsa said. "But you stay seven nights. Your man with half a foot, he take many more nights before he can travel."

"But he seemed so much improved when I looked in on him this morning—"

"That just fannaberries, make everybody feel better than they are, veh?"

"I apologize for my bad manners. But I have to leave today, even if Michu must stay behind. I'll get him on my way back."

Vorsa scowled, thinking deeply. He spoke as if to himself. "In seven nights, we know if Yonal family going to have war with Walloh family. Only have little fight between Inbar and Yanno, that tell Vorsa *sarhandas* hunt good enough for Walloh family they not care much so maybe not war. Inbar almost as good as Vorsa, he be shab one day. And he got Yarif, good second." The shab's face cleared. "Veh, I decide! You leave now, Vorsa go with!"

Javerri was having a little trouble following Vorsa. "You mean you want to go with me after Dragon-warrior eggs?"

"Long time since have *larac-vil*. Forget how nice they are, good in *sarhandas* hunt. You get one, two eggs. No trouble get another, veh?"

"Is it permitted for you to have a Dragon-warrior for your-self?"

"In long-ago times, Kallait learn secret of *larac-vil*, hunt together always. Other people learn, take eggs until *larac-vil* almost all gone. Kallait stop, find other ways to hunt *sarhan-das*. Now I think I get *larac-vil* again, just one."

So that must be how the custom of keeping Dragon-warriors had begun, Javerri thought. First among the desert people, then the egg hunters bringing their prizes where they would bring the most money. She smiled. "I am very grate-ful."

"That mean Vorsa go?"

"Oh, yes. I will be glad to have you with me."

"Good. That settled. I go tell Lidian now, she scold and cry. You watch, enjoy. Lidian make good show when she mad at husband. Children also, but best with Vorsa." He gave her a friendly slap on the shoulder that nearly knocked her over, then cut across the compound in a different direction from the one they had been taking, and disappeared.

She hurried toward the knot of men watching while Ivo showed one of them how to hold the bow. "Ivo!" she called. "Elder brother! I have news!"

He turned, then indicated to the men with him that the les-son was over for the moment. "What is it, little brother?"

"Michu is healing well, but it will be many days before he can travel. I want to go today, so we'll have to leave him with the Kallait. But Vorsa will be joining us." A woman's an-guished cry rose from the direction the shab had taken. "I think he's telling Lidian now."

"Of course I'll be glad to have an experienced desert man with us," Ivo said, "but whatever possessed him to make the offer?"

"He wants a Dragon-warrior of his own. I'll tell you all about it later. I have to go tell Michu of our plans. You find the rest of our people and get them ready."

Ivo's lips twitched. "Neither task will be easy, I fear."

"Michu is bound to object strenuously. And that music, the dancing—"

"It was very, ah, stimulating." He took a step toward her.

"Yes." The pulse quickened in her throat again. Then she turned away resolutely. "You forget yourself." She glanced back at him. "We forget ourselves," she added in a soft voice, and hurried toward the physician's hut to inform her general that he was being left behind in idleness. She didn't look forward to the interview.

iv

"No!" the general shouted. "I'll not have it!"

"You'll do as I tell you!" Javerri shouted in return. He lay on his bed and she stood over him, drawing herself up to her full height. "This is the man who had to be ordered not to kill himself because of a little cut on my face! Do you pick and choose which orders you will obey? You will stay here!"

"And let you go wandering off into the wilderness with nobody to guard you but a Dragon-warrior, that boy Ivo, and a couple of good-for-nothing mages? Never!"

"Don't forget that I'll be surrounded by your soldiers, and Lek, and Ezzat, and Shab Vorsa," she said with more than a trace of sarcasm. "I suppose you think Vorsa's not to be trusted as well."

"And why should I? What's he done—"

"He saved your life, for one thing," Javerri said harshly. "You'd be in some *sarhandas*'s stomach by now if it weren't for Shab Vorsa, and the rest of us as well, more than likely." She stared at him, fighting him for command, willing him to submit. Sweat popped out on her forehead. Michu had had many years of dominating others, and she had not. In addition to which she was a woman and in her world women did not command, not openly—

Unexpectedly, he laughed. "You're right. The *sarhandas* would have digested me long ago. But maybe the Ancestor Spirit didn't intend your old friend to end up as shark shit, ei?" He moved the bandaged stump of his foot. "Let's be reasonable, boy. I'm feeling as well as I've ever been in my life. I can ride, even if I can't run."

"You can't even walk yet," she said. She moved closer and sat down gratefully, hoping he wouldn't sense her relief. She could scarcely believe that her stern general, Michu the Pikeman, the one who made soldiers blanch if he but frowned, now adopted a cajoling tone with her. There had been a long moment of doubt when she had almost capitulated, certain she would not be able to impose her will upon him. "It's the fannaberries. They make you feel well, so you will heal more quickly. But you must have time. And I can't afford to wait for you."

He looked away, frowning. "It's difficult to admit, but you're right," he said in a low voice. "Sometimes, when the physician is a little late with the berry juice, I know that I am far from mended. But it's even more difficult to send you off alone, without me. My place is at your side."

"Of course I'll miss your strong presence," she said gently. "But your duty is done for now, old friend. I promise I'll hurry back in time to rescue you from the Kallait women."

"Did some of them really approach old Wande-hari?" Michu said. He attempted to smile. "I'd have liked to have seen that."

"You would have enjoyed the spectacle. Several of them danced for him, only to be turned away with great politeness. You should have them standing in line for your attentions by the time I return."

"Then perhaps I will find the waiting tolerable."

She squeezed his hand and took her leave of him, greatly pleased at the way she had been able to bend him to her will after all.

In her absence, Vorsa had arranged an entirely new order of travel. Instead of taking the donkeys and ox cart, they would travel on highly trained riding birds.

"We carry *larac-vil* eggs two to a *plandal*," Vorsa explained, indicating panniers lashed to the birds' backs. "Donkeys slow us down too much, with little feet. Not need cart until out of desert, start home on road. Road not good for *plandals*. We leave them at place I know, walk some when we get to mountains."

"Which way do we go?" she asked Ezzat.

"That way," he said, pointing due southwest. "Right, Shab Vorsa?"

"Veh, you not need me to tell you, follow *larac-vil*. Now we go!"

This time Javerri and her companions, muffled to the eyes in ordinary Kallait garb, rode with more confidence than they had previously. Even Halit fared a little better on his peculiar steed, though he didn't dare relax his vigil. For some reason, all the *plandals* seemed to take malicious pleasure in nipping at the younger magician's knees, and he was constantly swatting at them with the ends of his reins.

The birds kept up easily with Chakei's gait, and the travelers made excellent progress. By midmorning of the second day, they had definitely left the desert and were facing the foothills of the mountain range that loomed in the distance. It was an ominous sight, and even from here they could hear the rumblings as one peak spoke to another. Wisps of red-tinged smoke curled into the air and the ground trembled beneath their feet.

"Those are the Burning Mountains," Ezzat said, and they all stared with awe. "The Wall was built between that line of hills and the Mountains. The laying ground for Dragon-warrior eggs lies in a fiery cavern beneath one of those peaks."

Abruptly, the world shifted, taking Javerri with it. The Mountains dwindled, becoming unimaginably distant. She thought she stood alone and dizzy on a hilltop with cold mists lapping at her feet, and for the first time she doubted her ability to complete the task that had been assigned to her. She was so small, measured against these huge, fire-breathing mountains, so far away. And her company, so few in number, had vanished altogether. How had she dared think she could lead them, a woman named as Third Lord's son and masquerading in man's clothes, but a woman nonetheless. In the desolation a chill wind blew, echoing mournfully in her ears.

Something trembled just below the level of thought, seeking to erupt into her consciousness. She swallowed hard and put it aside. A presence brushed against her mind and she shivered. As she watched, one of the smoking peaks belched a fresh gout of smoke and the ground trembled anew. She touched Steel Fury's hilt, seeking reassurance from the comfort of his nearness, his reality. But Steel Fury lay indifferent under her hand. Did he think that her grasp could never equal that of his true owner, Lord Qai?

"But thou'rt mine now," she muttered under her breath. "And if I am not yet Third Lord by Yassai's confirmation, I am Third Lord by my own right! I am!" Her voice rose in defiance. Taking firm hold of the hilt, she half drew the blade, stopping only when she realized that the etiquette of the sword forbade drawing it when no enemy waited. Even more decisively, she slid Steel Fury back into his sheath and the blade sang under her hand. It could have been her imagination, but it seemed to her that the sword accepted her touch with better grace than he had a moment earlier.

And that, she realized, was because she truly was Third Lord—*Third Lord,* who only incidentally happened to be a woman! Doubts? Those were for others, not her! And now that she knew who she was, she could make others know it as well. She would let no one forget it. Michu was only the first! Every man and woman would bend to her will, when she returned to Monserria, she solemnly vowed to herself.

Eeeei, she'd never again be known merely as the Ladylord! Everyone—all would address her as Third Lord, Lord Javere; she'd insist on it, would execute anyone who refused. . . .

In her mind she rose up exultantly, shouting in silent triumph, the thrill of her own power sweeping through her. The presence brushed against her mind again, bringing an unwelcome admonition. Her newfound ability, the presence said, carried its own responsibility with it. She must never abuse this gift, never dominate for the sheer pleasure of it, but use it wisely—

She turned and stared at the magician standing on the hilltop with her. The wind pulled at his white hair and wispy beard. **Wande-hari, this was thy doing, this realization.**

No. Only a small nudge, to help what was already there break through so thou could see it plain, he replied. **It was in thee already, child of my brother's child, heir to the great Lord Qai.**

Thou didst put me here, in this lonely place.

No. This is thy doing. I but followed.

Thou looked upon me in my pride. Shall I be ashamed?

No, for that is a necessary part of what thou wast born to be.

But thou had to remind me of my responsibility.

And that also is part of why I am here. Think, my child. Thy father held all the power you know and more, and he did not despise to be called Old Vinegar-Piss. At least thy nickname is one that can be used to thy face.

The savage arrogance dissolved, leaving chilly realization in its wake. She shivered again. Eeeei, there was truly danger in power. She had been on the verge of carrying her newfound gift of dominance too far, of destroying the very affection she needed in order to be an effective ruler. Her mind and vision cleared abruptly and she was back into the ordinary world again, seated on a *plandal,* in the midst of her people. Perhaps she had never really left.

Now I know truly why my father bade you stay near me, Wande-hari. Thou'rt wise beyond measure.

She felt him bow to her, in his mind. **I thank thee, Lady-lord.**

The *plandal* she rode shuffled its feet impatiently and tossed its head. Javerri realized that all of them were looking at her.

"What is your command?" Ivo said.

She turned, surprised. To her astonishment, she realized she had almost forgotten him. His manner had changed subtly, become deferential. He had not looked and sounded this way since Lord Qai had died. She lifted her head, looked around at her company, and took a deep breath.

"Why do we waste time, just staring at the mountains?" she said. "Let's go."

10

i

*F*irst Lord Yassai's rage reverberated throughout Stendas Castle. Greater servants beat lesser servants; everyone crept about their duties on silent feet, trying to be invisible. Physicians and mages stayed in their quarters and busied themselves with their books. Red-uniformed guards, smarting under harsh discipline by their superiors, surged into the city streets where they took out their own anger on whoever was unlucky enough to get in their way. Few among them dared even wonder why so much importance had been put on the life of one servant, even though she had been personal maid to that unnatural woman who claimed to be Third Lord.

Yassai had been forced to act hastily, and he detested doing this. His most powerful mage and advisor couldn't be found when he was needed most. While Yassai had managed to avoid total disaster, reluctantly he had to admit his solution had lacked the suavity the Scorpion could have provided, the polish these things demanded. It was awkward. Now Yassai had to do something to redeem his pride and self-confidence.

There was a private room in Stendas Castle, a forgotten chamber closed off during a remodeling phase many years ago. Another ruler in subsequent years, First Lord Cheh-fu, moved perhaps by the same needs that now drove Yassai, had gained access to this room by ordering secret passages carved through thick stone walls. Afterward, he had had the workmen and stonemasons killed, leaving the very existence of the room known to very few. If Cheh-fu hadn't been a man obsessed with recording every detail of his otherwise insignificant life in personal journals, Yassai wouldn't have learned of it. However, unable to sleep one night, he had begun read-

ing some of these private documents, hoping to be bore
into slumber, and had come across notations detailing the en
tire operation.

Now only Yassai and one other knew of this room. Yassa
sent a message ordering the Scorpion to meet him there. If i
could be said that Yassai trusted anybody, it was the Scor
pion, and even him not entirely. But the man could always b
counted upon to deliver sound advice. Hadn't he suggeste
First Lord send Javere qa Hyasti on that fool's errand, thu
ridding himself of her presence with no effort on his part? Cu
rious how the Scorpion had stayed in the background durin
the interview with the woman, though. He had, he said
wanted to avoid Wande-hari even though Yassai assured hin
nobody ever brought a mage into his presence. Despite hi
lord's urging, the Scorpion stayed in the shadows. Yassai wa
willing to overlook these little peculiarities for he found th
man quite valuable.

He wearied quickly, for he had almost forgotten how t
walk unsupported. He was out of breath by the time he ar
rived, his forehead damp. The Scorpion was already waiting
He was a tall, spare man, appearing to be well into his mid
dle years. This, Yassai knew, was magicians' fakery; the mai
was ancient, though well-preserved. Some things couldn't b
entirely disguised. His dark hair showed white wings at eithe
temple. His hands were clasped and hidden in his long sleeves
as was his habit, to hide wrinkles and age spots. His eyes, how
ever, still burned in dark sockets as fiercely as a young man
would. At Yassai's approach, the mage bowed deferentiall
Grateful and panting, First Lord accepted his help in lower
ing himself to the cushion on the floor. Then the Scorpior
seated himself without waiting to be invited.

"So you've decided to make yourself available at last.
suppose you've heard about the botched-up business wit
the maid," Yassai said by way of greeting. His jeweled na
guards clashed as he brushed fretfully at the layer of dust or
the cushion.

"Yes," the Scorpion replied. "Most unfortunate."

"I merely wanted to keep the woman in my custody, just i

case. I wouldn't have harmed her. Not yet, anyway." Yassai frowned. Then his expression lightened a little. "Still, I was able to turn her death to some advantage despite your absence. Lutfu is now unquestionably Governor of Third Province."

"I doubt that the Excellent Strategist has been taken in by any of this."

Yassai frowned again. "If you'd worked a spell on the woman's head, the way I ordered you—"

"It would have been a waste of time and energy. Any spell would have dissolved long before your messenger got to Yonarin Castle. Surely the physicians were able to make the head presentable—"

"They did their best. Still, I think you could have done something if you'd chosen to."

The two men fell into an irritable silence. Sunlight filtered through the one cobwebbed window and dust motes danced in the air. The mage sat imperturbable, secure in his power. He could, Yassai knew, challenge even First Lord if he chose, and only Yassai's own inner defenses would save him. But for the moment at least, it was to their mutual advantage that they be allies. Yassai knew he would have to be the one to speak first, and this added to his irritation.

"I haven't heard anything from the man I sent with Javere qa Hyasti's party. I must have definite proof that the woman has perished. I can't take any more action in Third Province until then. Isn't there something you can do?"

"As I have told you, the distances are too far for any contact. But don't worry. Even if the woman Chimoko gave Javere enough time to get through Fogestria, the chances of her surviving the journey through the desert are slim indeed. The man had orders to lead them off-course so they would run out of food and water."

"And how is he supposed to get back and report?"

"Oh, he has resources," the Scorpion said. "And he is familiar with that country. If you will recall, you chose him for that very reason. And paid him well enough to dissolve any former, ah, loyalties."

"I know, I know," Yassai said impatiently. "But what if she manages to get to the Burning Mountains in spite of everything?"

The mage took his hands out of his sleeves and stared at them. He wore his nails short. Like his hands, they bore the marks of age, being yellowish and deeply ridged. "Have faith in your humble advisor," he said in a gentle voice. "It is far better that her death occur naturally, but if it appears that she might succeed the man has other instructions."

"What instructions?" Yassai leaned forward. "Will the Fogestrians waylay her on the journey back?"

"Ah, allow me to keep this one secret." The Scorpion, still looking at his hands, smiled tenderly and a cold ripple ran down Yassai's back. "Her ruse at the border is now exposed and the Fogestrians won't be duped into letting her back in. Wait until it happens, if it happens. Then I will tell you. You will enjoy it all the more for the delay."

Another long and brooding silence. "That wasn't why I called you here," Yassai said finally. "I wanted to discuss the Lady Seniz-Nan and the courtesan Safia with you. Safia swears she was merely being kind when she ordered that the maid should be allowed outside on the roof. Seniz-Nan swears her presence there was just happenstance that morning, and only bad luck that she fainted with false labor pains. I can't prove it, but I believe they arranged matters so the wretched woman could do away with herself."

"I know they did."

Yassai breathed hard through his nose. "Safia would never have had the audacity, so this had to be Seniz-Nan's doing. She defied me before, in the matter of Third Lord. She will pay," he said. The corners of his lips curved upward in the kind of smile that made courtiers cringe. "Both of them will."

"I think not. Lady Seniz-Nan has too many connections with powerful houses, including my own," the Scorpion said. His voice was curiously toneless. "Naturally you are angry that the woman ended her own life, and in a manner befitting one of a much higher class. And you want nothing more than to see both these women crushed before you, as broken as that maid's corpse. But Lady Seniz-Nan carries the heir. . . . "

Yassai glared at the magician. Of course he knew all this, but he was irritated that the Scorpion felt so free to speak these things aloud. And that droning voice. . . . He checked his mental defenses to make sure they were intact. This mage was far, far too clever. "After it is born, then."

"If the child is healthy and lives, most of all if it is a male, the Lady Seniz-Nan's position will be even stronger than before. You cannot move against her directly."

Yassai had hoped for other advice. But the Scorpion was right. If Seniz-Nan bore a male child and if she came to harm traceable back to him, it would be war from every quarter, even his own province. The Second, Fourth and Fifth Lords would join in gladly, and he would be overthrown. "But Safia doesn't enjoy any such protection," he said.

"Only Lady Seniz-Nan's patronage."

"It is a pity. She was a lovely woman."

The Scorpion shrugged. "She knew the risks."

Yassai allowed the man to help him to his feet. They left the room, pausing where the passageway branched. "Won't you tell me what is in store for Javere qa Hyasti, if she is still alive?"

"Eventually." The mage bowed and disappeared in the gloom.

Yassai stared after him. The Scorpion was entirely too arrogant for his own safety, he thought. When all this was over and he had the leisure, he'd have the man's Fruit on a golden tray.

ii

Early next morning, ten of Yassai's inmost elite guard brought Lady Safia to him in another room, just as private but far less secret, situated close by the prison. On this occasion, the First Lord kept only these most select guards around him. They were, he knew, utterly loyal.

Yassai allowed himself the luxury of a moment's regret when Safia entered the room. She looked so tall and elegant, yet so delicate in the midst of the guards surrounding her. And proud. Her hair and makeup were flawless, and by coincidence she wore the hyacinth-colored dress that had been First Lord's gift to her the morning after that first night. It had been wonderful. He hadn't been so hard in years.

She glanced from side to side. Yassai watched her composure falter momentarily as she recognized where she was, noted the absence of courtiers, mages, and physicians. Only two servants, the ones who usually supported him when he walked, stood behind his chair. Even the headsman was banished from this meeting. She walked forward and knelt before him. As always, the grace of her movements pleased him.

"Your messengers said you wished to see me, Lord," she said. "I obey."

"Do you know why I ordered you brought *here?*" The word hung ominously in the air.

She raised her head. "No," she said. But he could tell that she wasn't telling the truth. A thin sheen of perspiration showed on her forehead.

"You told me it was none of your doing that the maidservant Chimoko killed herself."

"Yes, Lord. As I said—"

"I know. Still, you earned my displeasure."

"I crave your forgiveness."

"And it will be granted. I had you brought here because I wanted to frighten you a little, that's all." He smiled and held out his hand. With a radiant smile she got to her feet and took a step toward him; a warning look from him stopped her. "You will be forgiven, yes. But you haven't even begun to be frightened yet." He motioned to his men. This was one of the best moments, when the accused thought the matter had been settled, only to discover that it had not. Guards grasped her arms. Safia went dead white under her makeup. If the guards hadn't been supporting her she would have fallen.

"B-but, Lord—"

He looked at his guards. They grinned eagerly in anticipation. "When you have finished," he told them, "and she has earned my forgiveness, throw her out onto the rubbish heap. She deserves no better."

Then he nodded to them to begin.

He watched only a few moments before turning away. "Now take me back to my Audience Hall," Yassai said to his servants. He didn't bother to look back, even when Safia began screaming.

When he had been ensconced on his dais once more he ordered the doors be opened to the people waiting outside. As they entered he allowed himself to smile benignly upon his courtiers, servants, mages, and lesser guards. A special look passed between him and the Scorpion as the mage moved silently into the room. A wave of relief, almost tangible, swept through the crowd at this indication of his improved mood. A messenger, one of his wife's maids, came forward.

"Lady Seniz-Nan is in her travail," the woman said timidly.

"Ah. Good. I will be there to watch the birth, of course. When is the birth expected?"

"It may be hours. She is young, and her passage is narrow."

"Good," he repeated. "Good." There was a symmetry here that pleased him very much. Both women were suffering at this very moment, though from different causes. He wished he could have dealt with Seniz-Nan as he had with the courtesan. Childbirth was so ordinary, something almost every woman went through sooner or later, and therefore it could not possibly be the agony they all pretended it to be. Some scholars went so far as to claim that women didn't feel pain at all, the way a man did, or they couldn't endure it. Yassai rejected that notion. He had seen both men and women under torture, and they were much the same in their reactions. Perhaps childbirth was something altogether different. Judging from the commotion many women made about it, he conceded that there was probably a degree of discomfort involved. Let Seniz-Nan howl and gnash her teeth all she liked. Perhaps she would die.

"Inform your mistress," he told the maidservant pleasantly, "that if she gives me a girl I will set aside one wing of the castle for the child's own. But if she gives me a boy, I will cause an entire section of First City to be razed and build him a Residence, and this will be known as Castle Seniz. It will be her memorial for countless years to come." He caught the Scorpion's warning glance from across the room and nodded very slightly. "Tell her also that regardless of whether the child is male or female, I will order Second, Fourth, and Fifth Lords and the Governor of Third Province to come to First City, to honor its naming day."

The maid knelt and bowed, touching her forehead to the floor. "Thank you, most noble and generous Lord," she said. "My mistress will be deeply touched and grateful when she learns what you have done."

iii

When Lutfu was formally named Governor over Third Province, he and Nao-Pei moved into the Residence. As a matter of course Lutfu took over Javerri's apartments. Nao-Pei had her belongings transferred into what had once been Ivo's quarters.

Tonight, as was his custom, Lutfu dined in his wife's company, in her rooms. They sat on silk cushions at a low table inlaid with costly woods and mother-of-pearl. Sliding doors in this room opened to the corridor that served this wing, another to the alcove where her bed mat waited, with still another hiding musicians in an alcove. A melancholy song drifted through the room, softly mourning the fading autumn while at the same time looking ahead to the return of spring. A vase of late-blooming flowers in the corner of the room flawlessly complemented the plaintive melody. Maids came and went silently and almost invisibly, bringing tea, rice, and platters of food as required and setting the dishes before Nao-Pei. The servants pleased her; she had been correct in dismissing her former personal maid and engaging Yuroko in her stead. Yuroko was better even than Chimoko

had been when it came to overseeing the staff. Certainly none
of Javerri's maids had ever reached this degree of perfection
in their training. But then Javerri had never cared much for
such niceties, even though it was attention to this sort of detail that made the difference between a well-run household
and one that was not. A maid rattled the cover on a dish, disturbing the mood. Nao-Pei merely glanced at her. The
woman, cheeks flaming, hastily set the dish down and backed
out of the room.

Nao-Pei sat very quietly on her cushion, moving only to
serve her husband at his meal. As was proper, she had eaten
beforehand so she could devote herself entirely to him. She
set aside the matter of the clumsy servant; later she would personally oversee the woman's punishment. She drifted in
peaceful reverie. A faint smile touched her lips, the smile she
had practiced in the mirror for so many hours, the one that
would not cause wrinkles.

Lutfu held out his bowl for her to refill. "You look very
happy tonight," he said.

A warning bell rang in her mind and she instantly became
alert. So far he had made no comment about what he must
surely have guessed—that she and Sakano were lovers, and
that he came to her bed almost every night. Ironically, she
now thanked Javerri for having remodeled Lord Ivo's apartment, the one she now occupied, so an outsider's comings and
goings could go unremarked. Did Lutfu know her smile was
really in anticipation of Sakano's visit tonight, anticipation
that made her grow moist between her legs? She had a surprise for Sakano, and thinking of it had caused her thoughts
to stray. . . .

She paused just long enough before answering, pretending
that Lutfu had merely disturbed the waking dream the music
and flowers had created. "Happy?" she said, and let her smile
deepen just a little. "Of course I'm happy. You rule Third
Province, and I am your wife."

"I rule Third Province as much because of my marriage to
you as by my uncle's orders."

There was no point in denying that obvious truth. "Yes," she said. "But you are a good governor, very stern. Much better than Javerri would have been."

Lutfu smiled in turn. "The treasury is growing full. Your late father was much too lenient in his taxation policies, and your sister hadn't had time to make any great reforms."

"My late sister."

"Of course."

"Has General Sigon been any more problem to you?"

"No." Lutfu shifted on his cushion and belched. "He is smart enough to know which way the wind is blowing."

"I am so glad we have been able to accomplish all this without fighting."

"And I, though war is a man's proper business. Still, a land at war can't be squeezed for extra taxes, ei?"

"How wise you are," Nao-Pei murmured.

Abruptly he got to his feet. "Good night, Lady," he said, bowing.

She rose in turn. "Good night, husband," she said affectionately. "Sleep well."

"Thank you. And you sleep well also."

She stood at her door and watched him go. His section of the Residence was not nearly as well arranged for discretion as hers; she caught a glimpse of one of Madam Farhat's courtesans being hurried through the corridor at the end of the one where she now stood. She pretended not to see.

Lutfu was far from the virile presence she had imagined when the thought of his body covering hers had almost been enough to bring on the Moment of Clouds and Rain. Nor was the truth about him anything so extraordinary as the rumors had it. He took his pleasure in the most ordinary way, without any great finesse but also without needing another woman in his bed. And as for the stories about a boy, nothing could have been further from the fact. Lutfu was simply one of those men who was almost incapable of functioning with a so-called "decent" woman, and this Nao-Pei demonstrably was, having brought him an intact maidenhead. So he approached her only on rare occasions, as duty demanded, and found relief in the embraces of low-class whores at other times.

Perhaps the certain knowledge of her liaison with Sakano would have made her more desirable in his eyes; more probably not. He was a possessive sort. The unspoken agreement between them that each would find pleasure as they liked, so long as both maintained the face they presented to the world to each other as well, was, she had to admit, more a product of her own wishful thinking than a matter of reality. She had no wish to test it. Therefore, she took no chances. The music had stopped and also the sounds of the musicians gathering their instruments; they always vanished the moment the Governor left. Behind her, the maids cleared away the remnants of the meal. With a last courteous bow in her direction, Lutfu disappeared around the corner.

"Thank you," Nao-Pei told the maidservant. "I am tired and wish to sleep now."

Yuroko hurried the servants out of the room, closing the screens behind them, and then discreetly opened Nao-Pei's private sleeping quarters. Behind one wall in the outer room lay a hidden alcove giving onto a corridor with a sheltered outside entrance. Sakano opened the screen, so cleverly hidden it seemed a part of the wall, and entered from where he had been waiting in this alcove. He brushed the back of her neck with his lips.

"Sleep?" he murmured. "Is it really sleep you want?"

She turned in his arms, moaning. Skillfully he loosened her clothing, ran his hands over her body. "He took so long before he left," she said. "I could hardly wait, I want you so much."

He lifted her in his arms and carried her to the sleeping mat in the next room. The door slid to behind them and Yuroko took up her post outside. She would die before allowing her mistress to be disturbed.

His hands, his hands. . . . "Ah. Ah! Yes, there!" Nao-Pei cried. She let his nearness drive her wild, and this wildness sparked an answering flame in him. He knew when this mood was on her she liked to be mounted at once, with violence. She welcomed him into her body, rippling her internal muscles and quickly milking him to completion.

He fell back, touching her breast. The nipple was hard under his hand; she hadn't finished. But she stopped him before he could move on top of her again.

"Why not, my beloved?" he said, panting.

"Have you ever heard of something called The Occasion of Four Elephants Meeting?"

He propped himself on one elbow and stared down at her. "I have heard of it, but I thought it was just one of those stories men tell each other. And how did you come to learn of this?"

"My husband isn't the only one who has occasional dealings with Madam Farhat," she replied demurely. "I am the one who pays her. And I was curious enough to visit her one day. I must be certain that, low class or not, the women she supplies him with are free of disease. She was most cordial, not at all what you'd expect. Some of her women passed by outside, speaking of the Four Elephants. I asked her about it. After just a little coaxing, she told me how to do it, and also supplied me with the necessary instruments."

"And is this what you want tonight?"

"Yes. Oh, yes. As I understand it, Four Elephants Meeting is primarily something that is done to the woman, so I wanted you to finish your pleasure first."

"Then I am impatient to accomplish yours."

She felt under the mat for the small plain box containing the things they would need. "Here," she said. Despite her efforts to be calm, perspiration beaded her forehead and her blood pounded so hard her hands and body shook.

"Are you sure?" he said, looking at the instruments dubiously. "This one looks like it might hurt."

"And so it would if I weren't fully prepared beforehand. I must be deeply stimulated, Madam Farhat said. Here, I will show you the places you must bite."

iv

Safia stirred and caught a ragged breath. She realized dimly that she lived. She had hoped she would die and be done with it.

Slowly, painfully, she began to get her bearings. She lay half-buried under a pile of refuse. If she had been able to breathe properly through her nose she was certain the stench would have stifled her. The putrid air cut through the sour aftertaste of blood from her split lips. Gingerly, not wanting to, she felt her nose. There was only a grotesquely swollen lump that hurt unbearably even under her most gentle touch.

The pain served to clear her head a little. She coughed, retched, and brought up more blood that she must have inhaled or swallowed. One side of her chest flamed; instinctively she knew that, in addition to her nose, some ribs must be broken. Because she had to, she checked the rest of her body for damage. Arms and legs seemed intact; one tooth was shattered. Her womanly parts were swollen and abraded, aching abominably. It could have been worse.

It could have been better; she could be dead.

She couldn't see; her eyes were swollen shut even if her lashes hadn't been stuck together. Choosing a direction at random, she dragged herself away from the place where they had thrown her when they were finished with her.

She struck a wall and fresh pain lanced through her head. She hitched herself up until she could lean against the surface. The action brought her close to fainting.

Conquer it, she told herself grimly. The Ancestor Spirit didn't want her yet, that was clear. Therefore, she must summon up as much strength as she could, get away from this place, find shelter, try to heal. Think about something else. She couldn't afford the luxury of being afraid, of mourning what had happened to her. She thought instead about Lord Yassai and how much she would enjoy seeing him helpless in the hands of his pet guards.

The idea of Yassai's wrinkled old body stretched out on the

raping bench while the guards took turns mounting him made the corners of Safia's mouth stretch in a ghastly travesty of a smile. The skin of her lips threatened to split anew. But the anger and hatred the thought of Lord Yassai kindled in her brought out a deep store of strength she hadn't known she possessed.

Water splashed somewhere close, making her realize how parched she was. She wondered which rubbish heap she had been thrown onto. Suddenly, she knew where she was. The stables, out beyond the prison. Horses stamped and whinnied and despite her useless nose, she knew the breeze carried the unmistakable aroma of manure. Somewhere there was a water trough and, she remembered, a small postern gate leading out into the alleys of First City.

Painfully she began pulling herself along the wall, toward the sound of the water. The wall ended. A little way farther she found the stone trough. Moss grew on the stone and the trickle of water from the pipe above moved the scum to the edges. She pushed it aside to get at the water. Nothing—no exquisitely blended, perfectly brewed tea, no heated wine from the most famous distillery—nothing had ever tasted so good. The coldness of the water hurt her broken tooth and she had to cover it as best she could with her tongue. When she had drunk enough she splashed a little water on her face, carefully cleaning away the worst of the crusted blood in her lashes, and discovered she could see a little out of one eye.

Yes, she was at the stables, in sight of the postern gate. Next to it was a small doorway that nobody in the castle ever touched. This was the gate the dung eaters used when they came daily to clean out the horse stalls and take away the rubbish. Dung eaters were the lowest of the low, cast out even by other pariahs. They carried away night soil, handled any task thought too menial or disgusting for ordinary people. By law they were too degraded for the honor of proper names, so they called themselves by words relating to their profession.

The Reds must have thrown her out for the dung eaters to dispose of, she thought. All she had to do was wait long enough and someone would come. She wondered how many more they had done away with like this. She leaned against the horse trough, shivering and sick. And how often, she thought, did they deliberately leave a woman half-dead so the dung eaters could enjoy her as well?

But no. She knew Yassai too well. Sometimes, when he had been absent a few hours, he would speak vaguely of having witnessed the "interrogation" of women prisoners. Then he had not needed the drugs or special caresses for his pathetic withered Jade Stalk to get hard. On his orders she would mount him.

"Am I not enormous?" he would say. "Is not my virility more than you can bear?"

"Eeeei, but thou'rt killing me, my lord!" she would cry. "Thou reachest my very heart!" She would contort her face in pretended pain and clutch herself as if he really were on the verge of piercing her heart from beneath, and he would pulse a little, in completion.

I think he intended me to die under the ministrations of his guards.

A noise behind her made her turn around. Two dung eaters were coming through the door. They saw her and stopped.

"Help me," Safia said weakly. She coughed. "Please, help me."

They came closer, full of caution and fear, staring at her. One of them glanced at the trail of bloodstains she had left as she dragged herself across the cobblestones. "Didn't quite kill you, ei?" he said. "The guards not always so careless."

"We get caught helping prisoner escape," the other one said. "They do worse to us. Leave her alone, Rag."

"Them dirty their hands on us?" Rag said scornfully. "This lady isn't ordinary prisoner or I miss my guess. She'll die if we don't help her." He crouched beside her. Automatically she flinched away from him. If she could have smelled his rank odor, it would have overpowered her. "What did you do, Lady?"

She squinted at him. There was no point in dissembling. She was almost as likely to die with help as without it. "Angered First Lord."

Rag sucked air with his tongue. Unexpectedly, he laughed, showing surprisingly good teeth, though some were missing. "Eeeei, and you live to tell? Good!"

"Rag—"

"Shut your mouth, Worm. Afraid he'll come out here with his pet mage and blast us to bug shit?" Rag turned back to Safia. "Any woman who can live through this gets *my* help, ei. Can't stay here. Where you want to go?"

Safia's head whirled. She hadn't thought that far. "Women's Precinct—" she mumbled.

Rag's expression cleared, as if a puzzle had just unraveled for him. "Eeeei!" he said. "Bad luck you're the one get sent for, when old Shit-Pizzle wants to see Reds diddle another woman to death. Old bastard. Women's District, ei." He grinned. "I got a brother takes out slop over there. But you don't go back to your own mama, ei? They find you too easy."

Worm shuffled his feet. He pulled his lips back in disapproval; his mouth was full of rotten stumps. "We got our own work to do," he said.

"Then go do it or let the great ones rake their own shit for a change. Kin-chao, she's the best, most powerful. Unless she's your mama, ei?"

Safia started to shake her head but the pain stopped her. "No," she said.

"Then I take you to Mama Kin-chao. You walk now?"

Safia realized Rag was trying to let her avoid his touch. She tried to get to her feet and failed. Rag scooped her up in his arms.

"Rag, stop!"

"Shut your dirty mouth, Worm," Rag said fiercely. "If you're worried, stay here. I'll take cart, be back before you clean one stall, slow as you work."

Despite his partner's protests, Rag pushed his way through the pariah gate and kicked it shut behind him. As gently as possible he laid Safia in the bottom of the cart, covered her with a pile of malodorous rags, and picked up the handles. "We'll be at Mama Kin-chao's house before you know it," he said.

Indeed, they did arrive before she knew it, but only because as the cart jounced over cobblestones Safia's broken ribs flared with fresh pain, and she fainted from the agony.

She regained consciousness to discover a man and two women working over her. She tried to speak.

"She's waking up," the older of the women said. "Sssh, Lady, don't try to talk just yet. Too bad you didn't finish with her nose before she came back to herself, ei, physician?"

The man nodded. He pulled on something. Safia's eyebrow stung and she realized he was closing a cut with stitches.

"Shall I give her the medicine now?" the younger woman said.

"Yes. It will make her sleep." The physician addressed Safia directly. "I have tended your injuries. You will live. Do you understand?"

"Yes," she whispered.

The young woman held a cup to her battered lips. She swallowed the bitter liquid gratefully and let the drug send her back into darkness. When she awoke again she found herself in bed, dressed in a clean sleeping garment. She had been bathed and her hair combed. She touched herself gingerly. Her lower chest was tightly bandaged and the ribs no longer pained her so much. Above this bandage she found several places where the physician had sewn her skin together. Feeling the stitches, she remembered one of the men prodding her experimentally with the point of his dagger all around her breast, not deeply, but enough to make her scream again when she thought she had passed beyond it. Continuing her inventory, she discovered that the sharp splinters of broken tooth were gone, leaving a hole in her gum. She could breathe through her nose after a fashion and discovered that someone had put a small cylinder of paper in each nostril to shape it. She opened her eyes as far as she was able. The room was dark except for a lighted oil-nut in a dish. The older woman who had been with her earlier sat by her bed.

"Good. You're awake. Do you want some tea?" the woman said. "The doctor said it would be all right."

"Yes. Thank you." She felt better, much stronger than she

would have dreamed possible. The woman helped Safia raise her head and held the cup to her lips. The tea, just pleasantly warm, strengthened her even more. "That's good. There was a man. He brought me here, helped me. His name was Rag—"

"He was paid for his trouble. Don't worry about him. I am Madam Kin-chao," the woman said.

"I'm afraid to tell you who I am. If you don't know my name you won't have to lie about me."

Kin-chao laughed. "Oh, I doubt if anybody will come around with questions, not in the condition you were in. And I am very powerful here in my section of the city. Still, keep your secret if it will make you feel better. . . . Drink some more tea. Sleep. Later, I will bring food and we will talk."

v

Nao-Pei, only half-awake, gazed at Sakano, asleep beside her. Madam Farhat had been right. The Occasion of Four Elephants Meeting wasn't something to be repeated more than once or twice in a decade, and after that one would be too old for it. She had never felt more utterly satisfied.

How lucky she was, she thought exultantly. Sakano belonged to her more fully than any man claimed by his lover before. Third Province belonged to her also, to rule through her husband. Lutfu belonged to her, for he needed her in order for him to stay in Third Province legally. Their marriage was good and there was peace between them for they each closed their eyes to the activities of the other. And she was a member of the First Lord Yassai's family, the most powerful in Monserria. What more could any woman want?

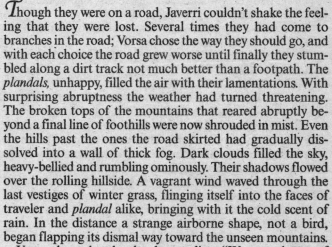

11

*T*hough they were on a road, Javerri couldn't shake the feeling that they were lost. Several times they had come to branches in the road; Vorsa chose the way they should go, and with each choice the road grew worse until finally they stumbled along a dirt track not much better than a footpath. The *plandals,* unhappy, filled the air with their lamentations. With surprising abruptness the weather had turned threatening. The broken tops of the mountains that reared abruptly beyond a final line of foothills were now shrouded in mist. Even the hills past the ones the road skirted had gradually dissolved into a wall of thick fog. Dark clouds filled the sky, heavy-bellied and rumbling ominously. Their shadows flowed over the rolling hillside. A vagrant wind waved through the last vestiges of winter grass, flinging itself into the faces of traveler and *plandal* alike, bringing with it the cold scent of rain. In the distance a strange airborne shape, not a bird, began flapping its dismal way toward the unseen mountains.

Vorsa glanced at the clouds, scowling. "We get to house of San-ji the herdsman or we get wet soon," he said.

Javerri willed her teeth not to chatter. Cold rain soaking their desert garments was not a pleasant prospect, and, if they didn't find shelter immediately, could be a disaster. Wet clothing meant they would be chilled to the bone and they could catch an ague that would end in their coughing their lungs out. To cover her concern she pretended scorn for Vorsa's statement. "Are you afraid of a little rain?" she said, frowning.

Vorsa thumped himself on the chest. "Afraid? No! I am desert man!" he said proudly. "Afraid of nothing! But I say when I put water on self, not damned sky that don't know Shab Vorsa from *larac-vil!"*

The wind whined past and through them, making them shiver. The *plandals* squonked plaintively, and Chakei clutched at Javerri's knee.

too much cold, not like i he said.

Javerri touched his crest sympathetically; she knew the depths of his misery. **** *We'll find shelter soon, I promise.*****

"Don't you know where this San-ji lives?" she shouted over the wind. A raindrop spattered on her cheek.

"Sure, sure, but maybe Vorsa forget a little one time to another. Think he's not much farther, veh!"

"He'd better not be much farther, or we'll have to stop and try to make camp!"

"No, no, Dekla, just a little way!"

Privately, Javerri felt that Vorsa was lost, going on bluff and bravado. Grimly, the little band of travelers toiled on. A flurry of raindrops splattered on them and Javerri began to consider ordering camp anyway. Surely they could manage to find a spot in the foothills that offered enough shelter so they could build a fire and keep warm. They came around a bend in the road and, to the relief of all the travelers, discovered a small settlement pressed hard against a steep hillside. Low barns surrounded by fenced-off pens lined either side of a narrow path leading toward a tiny house. The pens held many open-sided thatch-roofed shelters. Javerri was reminded, incongruously, of garden houses at home where one might take tea, only no garden back in Monserria had ever been so generously covered in manure as this. A trickle of smoke vented from somewhere behind the house, only to be swept away by the wind almost as soon as it emerged. The house itself was nearly hidden by the firewood stacked in anticipation of the coming winter. Only a few sheep wandered outside in the dimming light, looking very lost and very stupid; the rest, more intelligent than these stragglers, must have retreated into the barns, seeking shelter from the storm that threatened to break any moment. A couple of bedraggled dogs stood staring at the strangers with grave suspicion. One whuffed and sneezed. The other growled. Then both went into a perfect frenzy of barking.

"Ho, there it is!" Vorsa cried triumphantly. "See? I am not lost at all." He nudged his *plandal* closer. The other birds, sensing shelter, followed. Vorsa cupped his hands to his mouth. "San-ji!" he bellowed over the wind. "You got visitors!"

After a long moment the door to the house opened a crack, and a man peered out suspiciously. "Who is it?" he shouted over the racket. "What do you want?"

"Ho, you not recognize Shab Vorsa?"

"Vorsa?" The man opened the door wider and came outside. "Why you here? Little late in the year for you, isn't it?"

"Veh, veh, Vorsa tell you all about it if you don't make him and his friends stand out in the rain all night!"

"Oh!" The man started guiltily. He turned and called over his shoulder. "Dal! We got company! Take the *plandals*, stable 'em out of the weather, give 'em some of that mash they like!" He turned back to the visitors. "Well, come on then. Storm's about to break."

A boy emerged from the house and a gust of wind almost knocked him off his feet. He came toward them, slapping at the dogs. "Hush! Friends, friends!" The dogs slunk away and began waving their tails uncertainly. "Here, give me your reins! Hurry!"

Ivo had already dismounted. He handed the reins to Dal, and held up his arms for Javerri. More to feel his nearness than because she needed help, she let him lift her from her saddle. Dal took her reins as well.

"I'll bring your baggage later!" the boy shouted. "Get inside!"

Hunched against the wind that had now begun to howl in earnest, the travelers fought their way into the house and San-ji slammed the door behind them. The house was tiny, the entire structure only one ill-made room, and with all of them inside at once, too crowded. Oddly, a second door appeared to lead straight into the hillside. Despite the stacked wood outside, the wind tore through wide cracks in the walls, bringing with it dirt and debris. Only the roof looked serviceable. A thunderclap announced the onset of the rain in earnest and droplets of water, forced through the walls and roof by the wind, splattered the travelers.

"Well, now, what we got here?" San-ji exclaimed, peering at his guests.

"I think there is not enough room for us," Javerri said.

"Some of us can bed down with the *plandals*," Ezzat said.

San-ji looked at Vorsa and began to laugh heartily. "You don't tell these people what to expect?" he said. "Same old Vorsa, always making jokes."

Vorsa laughed in turn. "Well, we don't got much time for telling, damn storm come on so sudden." He turned to the others. "San-ji and Vorsa, we old friends, trade wool for *sarhandas* hides, dates, other things. San-ji got big place, plenty room for all."

San-ji, still chuckling, opened the door at the hillside wall of the room. Light from many oil lamps came flooding out through a short corridor just inside the opening. With the rest of her company, Javerri hurried through the corridor into the welcome warmth. She looked around. A short flight of steps led down into a spacious cavern, partly natural, partly dug out of the hillside. At the far end stood a mud plaster hearth with a fire burning in it, warming a small kettle. For a vent, San-ji or a former occupant had built a chimney whose pipe rose against the wall and through the arched ceiling, with plaster sealing the hole to the outside. The workmanship was neat if not highly skilled; despite the chimney, some smoke leaked out of the fireplace and hung in the air, making Javerri's eyes sting and her nose begin to run. She stifled a cough.

San-ji bustled about, making hospitable gestures without really accomplishing anything. "Nice and warm in here. You like that, ei?"

"Indeed we do," Javerri said gratefully. Chakei hurried past her down the stairs to the hearth and pushed the firehook aside. "No, Chakei!" she said as he climbed into the fireplace. "You'll put out the fire!"

careful i, not put out anyway

He filled the opening, crouching blissfully among the flames and blocking the chimney vent entirely. Smoke rolled into the cavern.

"You must get out!" she cried. "You're choking us!"

Regretful but obedient, he got out again. The flames leapt up higher than before, from his stirring the coals. **not enough deep in wall too bad, cramped i**

It's just as well. The rest of us want to get warm too, Chakei. And we are hungry. We couldn't cook anything with you in the way.

stay close i then but eat also

"That's an unusual, ah, pet you've got there," San-ji said politely.

She turned. San-ji was staring at Chakei, the corners of his mouth turned down and an extremely dubious look on his face. "My Dragon-warrior—my *larac-vil*—is no pet. He could kill us all if he chose. He suffers greatly in the cold."

"Ah, a *larac-vil*, is it! Never seen one of them." San-ji cautiously came a little closer, peering at Chakei. "Heard stories, though. So that's what they look like. Ugly creatures."

"We come to find more," Vorsa said. "Got to leave *plandals* with you, though. Damn birds don't fly over Wall. Don't even go on road good."

"Sure, sure, you can leave your birds with me as long as you like," San-ji said. "You really going over the Wall?"

Before anyone could answer, a wooden grate pushed open and Dal emerged from a hole in the floor. He carried a sack with him and his clothes were very dry for someone who had just come through the storm outside. The top of a rough ladder showed at the rim of the hole and Javerri surmised that there were underground passageways running from the cavern to the barns. The dogs followed, scrambling up the ladder after Dal. They growled again at the strangers, hushing at the boy's command, then went immediately to a pile of rags in a corner and settled down, eyeing the intruders warily and rumbling a little in their throats from time to time. Wisely, they gave Chakei a wide berth.

"Birds are sheltered and fed," Dal said. "Baggage is safe in the tunnel. I brought food for our guests." He went to a covered niche, got out a large pot, emptied the contents of the small one on the firehook into it, and ladled water from the jug nearby. Then he began adding food from his bag. Several of Javerri's people opened packets of provisions to make their own contributions to the meal. Halit and Wande-hari consulted briefly; then the younger mage, fingers sparkling, set off a spell that cleared the lingering smoke from the air, much to Javerri's relief.

San-ji sat down, indicating that his guests join him. "Now Vorsa can tell me who you are, what you want going over the Wall."

"Here is Javere qa Hyasti, in spite of being woman, great Third Lord of Monserria, hunter of *larac-vil* egg for more great First Lord! Uncle and Elder Brother call her Javerri or Ladylord, but to me, always little Dekla." Vorsa beamed at Javerri as proudly as if he'd done it all himself.

She frowned, her temper stirring at Vorsa's lack of caution. Then she reconsidered. They were long past Fogestria, where going in disguise had been a necessity. Vorsa could be considered almost her equal in rank. And he was most certainly her ally. If he called San-ji friend, she was not yet ready to call him enemy. She could not help smiling to herself. She had thought Vorsa too tipsy to remember the particulars of what they had spoken about privately, back at the desert man's stronghold.

"Ambitious, egg hunting," San-ji said doubtfully. "Also dangerous."

"Is the Wall near this place?" Javerri asked.

"Half a day, by foot."

"So close. Aren't you afraid of the dragons?" Ivo said.

San-ji shrugged. "They never have come through the wall." He indicated their surroundings. "If they do, I'll be inside here, out of sight, before they get close. Sometimes the flyers take a sheep now and then, but mostly they're just scavengers."

"Flyers," Javerri said.

"Big things, with nasty beaks and wings like leather. Saw one heading for home just before you got here. Maybe you saw it, too. Not many of 'em left these days. Me and my neighbors, we've mostly trained 'em to go looking for food the next valley over. That's where we take dead and dying animals and dump 'em. I don't have much trouble with thieves, either, this close to the Wall. It's a good place to live."

A faint rumble sounded and the cavern floor trembled a little under their feet. Javerri looked anxiously at the ceiling. "There's more than dragons to fear, I think."

"Not likely," San-ji said. "Roof's nice and rounded. It'll hold if dragons danced atop the hill. It's them flat-roofed caves you have to watch out for. Collapse on top of you at the first chance."

"We'll keep that in mind," Javerri said.

Dal came over to where they were sitting, bringing wooden bowls and crudely shaped spoons. "Food's ready," he said, handing them the implements. "Help yourselves. I'll feed the dogs."

ii

The storm continued to rumble outside. After dinner Dal went back through the tunnel to check and to bring up their baggage. "Won't let up for a couple of days by the signs," he reported when he climbed the ladder. "No weather to go hunting dragons in. Better settle yourselves to wait it out."

Javerri agreed. With the abrupt drop in temperature they needed their heavy quilted clothing and it was of use only in dry weather; wet, in addition to bringing on sickness, it would weigh them down, slowing their progress to a dangerous degree. The cavern offered plenty of room for them to disperse themselves and their belongings and still find privacy if they spread out into other smaller rooms San-ji and Dal did not use.

Gratefully, she sat down in a quiet corner of the main cavern with Wande-hari, her back against the wall. "This is the first time we've had more than a minute to ourselves," she said. "I've put aside something I wanted to talk with you about, and now we have time."

The elderly mage appeared in an agreeable mood, willing to talk. "Speak," he said.

"You must know I want to ask you about our kinship."

"Ah. Well then. I was born in Vornas, near Third Province's borders. My parents were minor nobility, connected by blood to the Vornian ruling house. They weren't pleased when I started making small spells at an early age. However, when it became clear that I was born to be a mage, they gave in." He dug in his sleeve pocket for a small knife and began to clean and pare his nails, carefully setting the fragments beside him for burning later.

"And then?" Javerri said.

"They sent me to the Vornian guild house for instruction and made it plain they would not be insulted if I changed my name. This is something mages do by habit anyway, I found. When I completed my training I wanted to stay in Vornas but my family wouldn't hear of it. Also I'd had the misfortune to make an enemy at school." The old man smiled reminiscently. "Feng-chu qa Chamvas, bastard son of a noblewoman and so entitled to her name at least. He and I hated each other on sight and our relations grew steadily worse during our years of training. He had a real talent for creating trouble, that one. The only reason I lived was that I knew his real name and he didn't know mine, so he had no power over me. Well, that's beside the point. I went into service with your grandfather, Lord Jinku qa Hyasti. When he died and Lord Qai came to rule, he decided, at my suggestion, to bind Vornas to Third Province diplomatically without obligating himself as well, and he welcomed my slight connections to the Vornian ruler. I was the one who arranged to have a Vornian concubine sent to him, though she had lived all her life in Hinstannod. This was my great-niece, your mother Shantar. The family was honored that she would go to Lord Qai, and I was careful to make sure she didn't know the degree of kinship between us.

If it ever became necessary, I would have told her at once. Nor did Lord Qai ever know."

"Did you foresee—*this?*" Javerri asked. *Beneath,* she made sure the old mage understood her to mean her birth, her upbringing, her inheritance.

"Of course not," he said. "At that time my first loyalties still lay with Vornas and I merely wanted someone close to Lord Qai that I could call on, someone I could trust, if need be. And also this gave me an excuse to keep in touch with my family at Vornas, you know, with news of Shantar's progress."

Wande-hari fell silent. "Then when I was born—" Javerri said cautiously.

"When you were born, one of so many girls, my hopes began. I knew your bloodlines, your potential. If I could train you personally, what couldn't we accomplish together!"

"I see. That explains a great deal. Also, through me you would accomplish your goal of a permanent alliance with Vornas as well. I had always wondered why you treated me as a favorite."

"I would have done more, except that Lord Qai was always interrupting with the sword instructor, or the bowman."

The two of them smiled at that, and Javerri's glance went involuntarily to where Ivo sat with the men. As if he sensed her gaze on him he looked up. Javerri sighed.

"You will be his wife in more than name some day, I promise," the mage said. "And speaking of what I would have done with your training, there is something I've been meaning to show you. Now that we're weatherbound, this seems a good enough time for it."

"What is it, Uncle?"

"It is a way to hide your thoughts, make them proof against another's probing."

Javerri sat up straighter, her interest piqued. "That must be something like what I ran up against when I tried to go into First Lord's mind!"

"Ei?"

"Yes! I felt as if I had bruised myself." She shuddered a little at the memory. "Most unpleasant. Still, it seemed a very useful ability to have."

"Well then, learning it requires a certain amount of peace and tranquility. This looks like the nearest thing we'll have for some time to come, so let us begin."

iii

The storm kept them in for a day and a half. During that time Ivo, falling naturally into the role of second-in-command, unobtrusively watched over their people. Satisfied that discipline was holding well, he sorted through his arrows, setting aside those that needed mending, and waxed and polished his bow until it shone. The men sharpened their pikes and tended their gear as well. When they could no longer make tasks for themselves, out of boredom, they fell to gambling to pass the time, using small stones as stakes. Chakei soaked up warmth, glad to be inside. He seldom spoke *beneath* with Javerri; still, she had the strong impression the Dragon-warrior trembled inside with anxiety, eager to be gone, to return to the place of his origins.

Once Ezzat had put his own belongings to rights, he sat silent for hours, wrapped in his own thoughts, the firelight flickering off his scarred face in the most sinister fashion. He never joined the men in their game. Halit took a spot close to the lamplight and worked quietly over his stock of magical ingredients, mixing things and muttering over the mixtures. He examined everything closely to make certain all was in order, then packed his gear again and again in some private order until it suited him. He made singing butterflies to amuse them all, especially Dal, though the boy was pointedly not interested. Halit went out of his way to be charming, but there was something a shade resentful in the way Dal treated the magician, as if Halit had somehow given offense.

Dal spent a lot of time with the dogs. He had trained them to an amazing degree of obedience and sometimes he made them do tricks to amuse the visitors. He went out frequently through the tunnels to see to the various animals in their pens, San-ji less often. Lek went out as well for lack of anything better to do, and found work tending a sick sheep. The dogs, when they were not sleeping or patrolling with Dal or San-ji, loitered near Vorsa. He made over them the way their masters never did, petting them and feeding them tidbits saved back from his bowl, threatening to spoil Dal's hard work in training them. Once or twice Javerri thought she smelled *abaythim* smoke. She asked Vorsa about it.

"Did you bring any of your—" she couldn't remember what he had called it "—your smoking leaf with you?"

"No, not me, little Dekla. You think Halit-mage has holy herbs?"

"I forbade it and destroyed what he had, long ago."

Vorsa shrugged. "What harm is little holy herb smoke? There is plenty of herbs at stronghold. Not hurt nothing."

"Perhaps it's just my imagination." But though she kept an eye on the mage she never caught him with any *abaythim*, nor did she smell it again after her conversation with Vorsa. It remained a mystery. She almost forgot about it, with her hard work trying to master the secret of the mental shield.

"I can't do it!" she exclaimed in exasperation. "Trying makes my head ache in the most horrible way!"

"You have been on the verge several times," Wande-hari retorted. "If you can find the way just once, then you can do it always. Here, look *beneath.*"

Tired and unwilling, she made the effort and did as he asked. **I can't see anything unusual.**

Exactly. Now try.

She recoiled and cried out involuntarily.

Do you see the difference?

"Of course I see the difference," she said aloud irritably, rubbing her head. "I always see the difference. But I still can't do it!"

"Your mind is not clearly focused," Wande-hari said, frowning. "You need to put everything out of your mind but erecting the shield."

"Then I can't learn it, not now." She shrugged in apology. "Perhaps when we return to Third City."

"I still think you could do it, if you just cleared your thoughts." But at her frown he stopped grumbling.

iv

At last the storm died away though the wind remained. The company emerged from the cavern and the shack covering its entrance into the wan light of an early winter day. The air smelled unexpectedly sweet, washed clean, and it was clear and cold.

"Better get your business over with soon," San-ji said. "This storm was just the first. You can expect more very soon, and colder, too."

Javerri squinted at the hills nearby as if she could hope to catch a glimpse of the Wall from this distance. Her breath puffed white in the frost-touched air. She and her followers had packed their desert garb and now were dressed in the heavy quilted garments they had bought in Fanthore. All, even she, bore backpacks laden with various belongings and food and water. Most of them had their weapons strapped to their backs as well. Chakei paced restlessly in his oversize coat. Shab Vorsa, scorning the quilted garments as a foreign affectation, maintained his desert robes, though San-ji and Dal weren't too proud to accept Javerri's gift of Peng's quilted coats and trousers. She explained what had happened to the unfortunate soldier, lest the herders have some superstition about wearing a dead man's clothing.

"Dead and eaten by *sarhandas,* ei? He won't be needing this then," San-ji said, pulling on a thick coat. "This'll keep us snug when we're going through the tunnels, right, Dal?"

"These clothes are like new!" the boy said, stroking the garments with pleasure. "Thank you, Lady!"

"It's not nearly enough to repay you for your hospitality." San-ji shrugged. "Maybe there's really jewels and gold hidden in the dragons' dens. Bring me a handful when you return for your *plandals*."

"Done!" Javerri laughed.

"There're no jewels beyond the Wall," Ezzat said.

"I said maybe," San-ji said. "Don't expect a thing."

Ezzat grinned nervously. "Then you won't be disappointed."

Javerri turned and looked at the guide Seniz-Nan had sent her. His fire-scarred face was pale, wan in the morning light. He shifted from foot to foot, not from the cold. Was he frightened, or merely tense with excitement?

Ivo, however, stood gazing at her calmly, his great compound bow ready in his hands, a filled quiver at his belt. She drew strength and confidence from his presence, longing to have the search over and done with, to place the First Lord's Dragon-warrior egg in his possession, to be officially confirmed as Third Lord, to have Ivo. . . . She forced herself to think only of the present, on the difficulties facing them now.

There were too many of them for safety, Javerri thought, and not enough. Only two or three should go in, or she should enter with an army, which she didn't have. There were just enough of them to slow them down when speed might be their greatest need. Absently, she fingered the scar on her cheek, trying to approach the problem as her father would. But who could she leave? Surely not Ivo, provided that he would allow her to go without him. Not Ezzat. Despite her misgivings about him, he was the most experienced of them in this undertaking. Nor Chakei. His presence was vital.

The Dragon-warrior was in a strange mood. He didn't even seem to notice the chill in the breeze this morning. The closer they got, the wilder he became. It was as if he was driven by an inner force stronger even than his attachment to her. She was afraid she'd have trouble controlling him, keeping him near once they were inside the Wall. Vorsa? His errand was almost the same as hers. Without him she would never have gotten this far. The physician? Suppose one of them were to be injured? Tal? Nali? Fen-mu? If so many of them went, they would need the soldiers. They were oversupplied with one thing, though. . . .

"Wande-hari, I think you should stay behind."

The elderly mage looked up in some surprise. "I? For what reason?"

"You are old, Uncle. You have done very well during this hard journey. But always before you have ridden, and now we all must walk. Rest while you can, because I fear our road back home will be no easier and you will need all your strength for it."

"It is true that I have let many years pile up on me and I have not bothered with a youth spell in too long, but being out in the world again has done me enormous good. Without using any magic at all I've grown younger and stronger daily, remembered spells and incantations that had gathered cobwebs in my mind, and my health is of the best. Old? I was old before I started on this adventure, half useless." He held up his left hand meaningfully.

It was true, she had to admit. He still looked ancient but the old man's step was springier, his cheeks infused with healthy color these days, his entire bearing one of a man enjoying his newly recovered physical powers. "I could order you to stay behind."

"So you could and I would obey. But before you do I beseech you, Third Lord of Monserria, to allow me to go with you. I have a feeling that you may need me."

"If only for the Circle of Protection that only my master knows how to cast," Halit said. "Please, Ladylord. Forgive my interference."

She sighed. She hadn't really wanted to leave Wande-hari in the first place, had only wanted to spare him. "Your request is granted. Let us be off."

They set off on foot at a good pace and soon rounded the toe of the foothills that sheltered San-ji's homestead. Ahead, they glimpsed the Wall at the summit of a long slope though they were too far away to get any idea of its real size or how it was made. Strangely enough, a layer of mist coiling up beyond the Wall shrouded the mountains from their sight de-

pite the brisk wind that still blew. It was as if the Wall held
he clouds as well as the dragons captive beyond its confines.

A little before midday they reached the foot of the Wall.
Awed, Javerri reached out and put her hand on its chilly sur-
ace, as if the physical touch would make her believe they had
reached it at last. The height of four men, each standing on
another's shoulders, it was made of roughly hewn blocks of
grayish stone, stained in spots with moss and lichens. It
looked entirely ordinary, even prosaic, not worth the legends
that had grown around it thicker than the mossy covering it
bore. The walls of Third City were far more impressive.
Though this structure looked formidable enough for most
purposes, it certainly didn't appear sturdy enough to discourage dragons. Javerri turned to Ezzat.

"Is this near the area you are, ah, familiar with?"

The man's hands were shaking and the burn scars showed
vividly on his face. "No, Ladylord. That place is many *ri* to
he south."

"Then perhaps we have come to the wrong part of the
Wall."

"Excuse me, I think not. The dragons we are seeking roam
all through the Burning Mountains. But farther south there
are no settlements, no people living near the Wall. Also, where
we are is a gentler area, a part of the Mountains where the
fire does not rain down as freely as elsewhere, though there
s always danger."

She nodded, understanding. She remembered the glimpse
she had had into his mind with Wande-hari's help—the red
and black clouds, the half-grown boy crouching in a niche in
he Wall, the enormous unknown thing flying on leathery
wings, the fire. . . .

"Shall I blast a hole in the Wall for you, Ladylord?" Halit
held a pebble in the palm of his hand. "This should do the
rick, with no noise. And no flash or smoke, either, Master,"
he added to Wande-hari. "At least, I hope so. I haven't yet
tested this mixture. It's one of the things I was working on,
during the storm."

Javerri frowned, thinking. An opening in the Wall would

perhaps be a very convenient thing, should they have to de
part in a hurry. On the other hand, a dragon might see thi
as a way to get through the barrier that had stopped it before

"As Ezzat reminded us, there are people living nearby," sh
said. "I believe they would not thank us for blowing the Wal
apart."

"There's a saying among hunters of dragon eggs that you
must put a hole through the inside of the Wall, not the out
side," Ezzat said. "But that's just a saying." He knelt and
opened his pack, taking out a folding grapnel and a very long
coil of knotted rope.

Javerri looked at the rope doubtfully. It seemed too frail to
sustain all of their weight, and far longer than they could pos
sibly need.

Ezzat busied himself unfolding the grapnel and tying it se
curely to the rope. "We go up one at a time, and then down
the other side. We'll leave one of our number at the top, in
case something comes to tamper with the rope from within
or someone comes to interfere from without. He'll pull the
rope back up from the other side of the Wall and wait for u
to return, or come to warn us of danger. That is how it is
done."

Javerri nodded. In displaying his expertise before the mag
the man appeared to be recovering a measure of self
confidence. "We will follow your instructions," she said
"Nali, you will stay behind."

Even though Nali conscientiously looked disappointed a
being left, Javerri could tell he was relieved at the order. He
saluted and stepped back. Ezzat swung the grapnel in a tigh
circle, preparatory to casting. It made a curious, low whistling
sound. The grapnel failed to catch on his first try, but the
second was successful. The grapnel soared over the edge be
tween two crenels; the hooks grated on stone, found pur
chase, and dug in. Ezzat tugged on the rope. It held fast. "I'
go up first," he said, "just in case."

He coiled the remainder of the rope at the base of the wal
and started up, using the knots as grips. The wind gusted
whipping the rope, and he nearly lost his footing against the

Wall. Tal rushed to put his weight on the rope and steady him.

now i ladylord Ignoring the rope, Chakei skittered up the face of the wall like an enormous cloaked lizard, his fingers and toes finding purchase in minute cracks in the rough stone. He disappeared over the parapet and Javerri's attempt to reach him *beneath* brought no response.

She watched while Tal followed Ezzat. Nali took Tal's place steadying the rope for him. One by one, the rest followed. Lek went clumsily, hampered by his small chest of medicines that proved awkward to manage. She held her breath as Wandehari ascended the rope slowly, pausing twice to rest, but he made it without mishap. Halit followed more quickly, but no more nimbly than anyone before him; his own magical burden got in his way.

Ivo bowed. "I'm next," he said. "Then you." Taking hold of the rope, he ascended with easy grace, clearly the best climber of any of them.

She started her own ascent. She hadn't realized how her thick quilted jacket and trousers would hamper her movements. Nali steadied the rope below and the men atop the wall waited with outstretched hands to pull her to safety. Knot by knot she pulled herself upward, finding the climb itself tiring and frightening but not as difficult as she had feared. As she reached the top, Ivo and Fen-mu helped her over the parapet and set her on the paved surface below.

"Thank you," she said calmly. Chakei was nowhere to be seen for the moment.

Surprisingly, the upper surface of the Wall looked very much like a garden gone to ruin, full of weeds, ragged shrubs, and even small trees. She hadn't seen this miniature forest from the ground; it had been hidden by the parapet. The Wall was much thicker than she imagined, and it had been built with a second crenelated parapet along the inner surface. Javerri hurried across and peered through one of the openings. The inside face of the Wall was more than four times the height of the other side, topping the rim of a vast ravine that separated the Wall from the bank of fog lying across from where she stood, a little lower than the level of her eyes. Water from the recent rains stood in pools atop the wall and in depressions below, and a little stream meandered along the bed of the ravine. A faint glow somewhere far off in the depths of the mist marked a spot where fire must ooze from the depths of the earth.

Now she understood the Wall's construction and Ezzat's comment about how a hole punched through from the outside would not have helped them, as well as the length of rope she had thought far too generous. Wide enough that horsemen could have comfortably ridden four abreast, the top surface and both inner and outer faces of the Wall were of stonework. This great trench, too regular to be natural, had to have been dug at the same time the Wall was built. The Wall's interior must be filled with the earth and rubble gouged from below and the surface had then been paved over with more stonework. Through the years, these paving stones had shifted in spots, some tilted almost on end, shifted by the trembling earth and also cracked and broken, moved aside by the shrubs and stunted trees whose seeds had taken root there. It had been a long time since soldiers had patrolled the Wall, if any ever had. It stretched as far as she could see in either direction, lying like a vast stone serpent undulating along the deep, rock-strewn moat between the hills and the towering line of fog shrouding the Burning Mountains beyond. The wind shrieked in her ears. Judging by the way the leafless bushes whipped back and forth in the ravine below, the wind must be sweeping through down there with near gale force.

Truly the first climb was nothing, Javerri thought. This was the most perilous part, that is, until they met a dragon. What if they were running for their lives when they left this place? She anticipated Chakei could steady the climbers, knew he wouldn't need a rope. And surely the dragons wouldn't harm him since he was such close kindred with them. But he'd become so wild he was almost useless. She didn't know if she could rely on him.

Now she wondered if the coil of rope she had thought excessive would be long enough to let them down the other side safely. Nali had ascended by now, and they were all atop the

Wall. Ezzat was already pulling the rope up after him, hand over hand. He gestured to their right.

"A little way to that direction the ditch doesn't look quite as deep as it does here," he said. "The land must have shifted. We'll go down at that spot."

They picked their way over the uncertain footing of the Wall "road" until they reached the most likely place for descent. Chakei reappeared, hissing and shifting impatiently from foot to foot, his attachment to Javerri appearing to be the only thing keeping him from swarming over the inner parapet, across the ravine, and vanishing through the fog beyond. Then he vanished once more.

"I hope we can find this place again," she told Ivo.

He nodded. "We must mark our path inside. And I will instruct Nali to keep a close watch."

Ezzat reset the grapnel. His face had gone tight again, his jaw clenched. Nevertheless, when he had cast the rope he prepared to be the first one to descend.

Ei, Javerri thought, it would be so easy to let him do this, take the most dangerous task. If he falls and dies, what is that to me? But we must have the best and most agile down first and up last for the safety of us all. She swallowed hard. "Let Ivo go first," she said.

Without a word, Ivo nodded, took the rope from Ezzat, and stepped over the edge. He descended much more slowly than he had climbed. The rope whipped sickeningly in the wind; the slightest misstep and he'd be flung against the face of the Wall, perhaps losing his grip and falling to his death. Javerri watched his progress anxiously. Her temples pounded, her mouth had gone dry, and she realized she had been holding her breath.

The rope proved long enough, barely. It didn't touch the ground, but didn't miss by far, either. Chakei appeared out of nowhere and scrambled over the parapet.

Wait!*—*** But it was no use. In moments he was on the ground below. He raced down the ravine, across the brook, and up the other side, inexplicably stopping just short of the line of fog. He began running back and forth in circles. Javerri gave up trying to contact him *beneath* for the time being.

She let Lek precede her, then swung herself out on the rope for the dizzying descent. Grimly she concentrated on finding each foothold against the face of the Wall, making sure she was secure before going on to the next. The rope quivered in her grasp as the wind tried to snatch it out of her hands. If the wind grew any stronger . . .

Steadily she let herself down, grateful for the knots in the thin line. Then she sensed she was near the bottom.

"Drop, Javerri," Ivo said. "I'll catch you."

She let go, and fell awkwardly into his arms. "Are you all right?" she said breathlessly.

"Yes. And you?"

"Undamaged."

He set her down. She adjusted her clothing and pack and checked to see that Steel Fury was safe in his sheath strapped to her back. While the next man began the nerve-racking descent she started toward Chakei, thinking to ease his anxiety with her presence. But he only ran back up the ravine. It was as if he were on an invisible leash of his own making; the closer she came, the farther he was allowed to go.

She returned to the foot of the ravine, Chakei following reluctantly. Wande-hari was climbing down now, his long white hair blowing in the wind. She found the sight unendurable and looked away until he was safely down. With two moments of weakness to compensate for, she made herself watch each man thereafter make his descent. Shab Vorsa's voluminous robes flapped wildly about him, making him look like a grotesque bird about to sail away in the wind. Finally the last man, Tal, reached the bottom. Nali waved from the top of the Wall and began hauling the rope up for safekeeping.

"We will rest a little while, and eat and drink a little," she said. "Then we will begin to hunt for dragons."

"It isn't quite that simple, Ladylord," Wande-hari said. He stared at the line of mist beyond where Chakei still skittered back and forth. He lifted his hands, made a few gestures, and his eyes abruptly flared orange. Tal sucked in his breath sharply and drew back, fear on his face.

"It is only Mage's Eyes my master is using," Halit told him, "to help us see what is meant to be hidden."

"What do you see, Uncle?" Javerri said.

The orange glare faded from Wande-hari's eyes and he turned to her. "Now I understand," he said. "There is a magical barrier at the top of the ravine. My suspicious were aroused when I saw how the mist lay, not falling into the ravine as it should. It also explains how a mere wall, something made by men, could keep dragons penned inside. But how is the magic powered? What is its source?" Wande-hari turned to Ezzat. "You mentioned a saying, something about a hole in the inside of the Wall, not the outside. This must be what the saying meant," he said. "And did you ever hear aught of passageways, of gaps, or rents in a curtain?"

Ezzat nodded slowly. "I have. But I thought it was just talk."

"That explains it," the mage said. "Mages must have pierced the boundary in places to the south." He glanced at Javerri, his smile nearly hidden in his beard. "I must do the same here, with Halit's help."

The younger mage had already shrugged his pack off his back. "This looks to be brute magic, force against force," he said. "Show me what to do, Master."

"We will labor side by side," Wande-hari said tranquilly. "Follow me."

As they climbed the slope, Chakei bounded away at their approach. The two mages edged along the rim of the ravine, patting the wall of fog as they went. Javerri realized they were testing the magical barrier for some area of weakness, a place where they might have a chance of opening it. Twice Halit indicated a spot only to have Wande-hari shake his head. Then the younger mage discovered a place agreeable to both of them.

The mages set themselves on either side of an invisible line in the invisible barrier. Wande-hari paused to give his apprentice a few last-minute instructions. Carefully placing their fingertips upon the fog, they chanted a few words in unison and began pulling in opposite directions. At Wande-hari's signal they paused, shaking and rubbing their hands. Then they began pulling again. Even from below, Javerri could see that both men were exerting extreme effort. A trickle of fog began oozing out and spilling from between their hands.

Wande-hari waved Halit aside, examining the small rent they had made in the magical barrier. Then he turned, smiling, and gestured to the company waiting below. "Come up now!" he called, his words almost lost in the wind.

Fen-mu picked up Halit's pack and the travelers started eagerly up the slope toward the old magician. He waited for them, motionless except for his hair and clothing blowing in the wind, conserving his energy. Javerri frowned as she got close enough to see the lines of strain in the old man's face and the shadows under his eyes. "You have fatigued yourself," she said.

"Only because I hadn't discovered what to do so we went about it the wrong way. Observe," he said proudly. "It is trivial, when one knows the secret."

He reached into his sleeve pocket and took out a strand of sunlight. He fashioned it into a glowing key and touched it to the small opening he and Halit had wrested by force. The rent widened easily, enough for them to enter one at a time. Moist heated air rolled through from inside, turning to fog and spilling past their feet, shredding instantly in the wind.

"I think the fires of the sun must be similar to the fires from the earth," the old mage said. "Therefore, that power which keeps the interior wall closed must also make a key to open a door in it. This is only temporary, of course. In time the rent will heal itself. But even if it closes before we return I can open it again." He bowed to Halit. "My thanks. Without your help I could never have opened even a small hole in the barrier so I could make it tell me its secret."

"Master." Halit bowed in turn, hand to heart.

Javerri stared, fascinated. "Tal, Fen-mu," she said. The soldiers ducked through the opening. The others followed cautiously. She stepped through in turn, wishing Chakei were with her. The misty wall was unexpectedly thin; it looked like a kind of membrane and the raw edges of the rent on either side of her glittered and sizzled. Though Wande-hari may have handled them with impunity she was careful not to touch. Damp tropical air washed over her. "We won't need our winter clothing," she called back over her shoulder. "It's summer in here!"

"It is!" Ivo was right beside her. "We can leave our heavy garments just outside and put them on again as we leave. Or we could take them with us."

"We need to have our movements as free as possible. We'll take the chance and leave them outside, at the opening." She was already slipping Steel Fury off her back, her fingers busy with the fastenings of the quilted coat.

"Is like home!" Vorsa exclaimed. "Only more wet." He took a deep breath and stepped forward, parting the underbrush just ahead of them. *"Veh!"*

Javerri whirled around at the surprise and shock in his voice. A creature born of nightmare crouched just beyond the brush, staring almost nose to nose with Vorsa. She had an impression of lizardlike features, enormous jaws filled with sharp teeth. Ludicrously, the dragon looked as startled as Vorsa at this unexpected encounter. Hysterical laughter bubbled up in her throat and she stifled an impulse to yield to it. The monster reared back and rose to its full height, uttering a sound between a bellow and a hiss. Appalled, she stared upward. The dragon stood higher than three tall men. Its thick tail lashed—in nervousness? Fear? Anger?

Two more dragons emerged from a stand of trees half a *ri* distant. They went on their hind legs, bodies leaning forward, tails erect and balancing them as they ran to their companion's aid.

Hand trembling and palms beginning to sweat, Javerri reached for Steel Fury, knowing as she did so that the gesture was futile. What use were any of their weapons against creatures like these?

i

*S*eniz-Nan screamed until she had no voice. Someone put a rope in her hands, giving her something to pull on in her frantic efforts to fight free of the pain tormenting her. Just when she had thought she would surely die, the midwife had given her a potion to drink. Afterward, though her body labored mightily, she herself hovered on a remote plane, detached and uninvolved, only a thread of awareness holding her to her own flesh. She was not concerned over much even when something hot and wet wriggled out, bringing relief to the stranger writhing on the bed below. Then she drifted down, down until she floated on a vast lake of quiet pain. Vaguely, she became aware of voices. She couldn't decide if she was bobbing in and out of consciousness or if the voices were advancing and receding. It didn't matter, and she was far too weary to think about it. But the sounds disturbed her. Perhaps, if she listened for a moment, she could make them go away. Mildly curious, she came closer. If she tried she could occasionally understand what was being said.

"It is a boy, Sire." That was the mage, the one they called the Scorpion, who dared treat First Lord as an equal.

"Really? Then I am pleased." First Lord himself. Husband.

"Remember your promise, Sire. The Residence. And the four other lords for the naming day. . . . "

"Yes, yes, I remember."

They were probably speaking of important matters, concerning her and her child. But Seniz-Nan was too tired to care. She gave herself over to the floating sensation and fell asleep.

Later, when she awoke, the midwife was ready with another potion. She gulped it gratefully, eager to return to the shadows.

"What is this?" she said in irritation. The potion was having the unwelcome effect of clearing her head, not sending her back into the mists as she desired. She frowned.

"You must wake up now. The child will be hungry."

"There's a wet nurse for that. I'm tired." Seniz-Nan shifted a little, and gasped. Her Celestial Chamber pained her, her back ached dreadfully, and her arms were so sore she could scarcely move them. "Go away, all of you."

"Nevertheless, you must suckle him, a few times anyway. It is to help your womb return to its proper place. Lord Yassai has already acknowledged the baby as the Sublime."

Eeeei! Memories of the past several hours came flooding back to Seniz-Nan. She cautiously put a hand on her belly. Though the skin was flaccid and bulged over the bandages wrapped around her middle, she was unmistakably rid of the burden that had weighed her down until it threatened to choke the breath out of her—"The Heir," she said. "My son."

"Lord Yassai seems quite pleased."

"Bring him to me. I want to see my son."

The midwife nodded and bowed. She gestured to a nearby maidservant and the woman hurried forward and placed the infant in Seniz-Nan's arms. In the manner of all new mothers, Seniz-Nan unwrapped the baby, examining each finger and toe, and most carefully of all, his features. The baby, still red from the birthing, screwed up his face and yowled.

Ei, cry lustily, she thought. Live and thrive. She thanked every god there was nothing on his countenance to show who his real father was. She knew she should have picked the one who resembled Yassai. But when the time had come to choose she couldn't do it. So she lay under someone young and strong and handsome instead.

Now that she was safe, she allowed herself the luxury of remembering what she had resolutely forgotten, had not dared even to think about for a moment. How frightened she had been! She had come to the prison, masked and disguised as a courtesan, her story ready.

"I've heard it said that a woman who lies with a condemned man knows the ultimate in pleasure," she said. "The shadow of death hanging over him prompts him to the peak performance of his life." She moved close to the guard, swaying under her veils, making certain that he could smell her perfume.

The guard stared at her, insolent and suspicious. She held her breath then; everything depended on his reaction.

"I've never heard such a story," he said finally. "But if you want to try it out and pay me well, it's all the same to me."

"Thank you," she said, flirting her eyelashes at him like the prostitute she pretended to be. "I live by pleasure and I very much desire to learn if this is true." She took out a purse and clinked its contents alluringly. The guard reached for it but she slipped it back into its hiding place. "Afterward."

The guard merely shrugged. She knew he knew she would not get out without paying, not that she intended to try.

The prisoners due to be executed soon were kept separately in barred pens. Their every activity was exposed to scrutiny, lest one of them manage to kill himself or, worse, kill a friend out of mercy and thus cheat the headsman. The men stood or sat up, gaping in openmouthed astonishment as she passed by. Some shouted filthy words; others whistled and pushed a finger through a circle made with thumb and forefinger on the other hand. One, a good-looking fellow, simply stared at her. Another, small and ugly, waggled his hips suggestively in her direction.

"This is quite a treat for them. They like you, Lady. Take this one here," the guard said, grinning as he led her down the path separating the pens. "Or that one. He still looks vigorous enough to do the job for you."

She hesitated outside the pen holding the ugly little man, but then she returned to the one who had been too overwhelmed to do anything but look. Something in his eyes, his face—Looking at him, she felt a definite twinge of desire. Surely, she thought, wanting him would allow her to conceive. With the ugly one, the opening of her womb would clamp shut and reject his seed. It was no wonder Yassai had never managed to impregnate a women. How could she—how could any woman ever be stirred by him?

"This one," she said. "Take him to a place where we can be alone."

The guard laughed. "This is no fancy house with your 'mother' watching the door and collecting the money, Lady. It's here and now with Yan-kwo the cutpurse, or resign yourself to never knowing the pleasure you came looking for."

She could have left then, errand unfinished, bribe unpaid. Perhaps she should have, but she didn't. She nodded assent. The guard opened the gate of the pen just enough to allow her to enter. Then he locked it behind her.

She lay down on the straw and Yan-kwo lay down with her. Now she was helpless, entirely at his mercy. Her loins tingled at the thought of what he could do to her if he wished and her blood pounded in her ears. She had never been more excited, and longed for his harsh touch on her body. But to her surprise he was shy, gentle, awe-filled. He acted as if Lady Moon herself had come to give him this last favor and hesitated to soil her with his caresses. Around them the other prisoners stared with hot eyes and made lewd remarks but she scarcely heard. Wild with lust, she brushed his hands aside and pulled him into her until he filled her to the brim and beyond. She could swear he penetrated her very womb, that it opened and sucked him inside. For the first time she knew fully the pleasure a virile male can bring a woman and she lay impaled, wanting more and still more until he loosed the boundaries of their bodies and melted into her entirely. The guard opened his garments and rubbed himself while he watched them do it. The lascivious stares of the prisoners around them excited her even more and Yan-kwo and she reached the Moment of Clouds and Rain together.

Warm with remembering, she must have stopped breathing for a while. She knew she returned to herself reluctantly, easing out from under him, pulling her nipple from his mouth. He groped for it blindly, then resigned himself to letting her go.

She thought the guard would claim his turn as payment.

But he had emptied himself and she escaped with the promise that she would return later. He was busy gloating over the purse, filled not with silver as he had thought, but with gold.

So who was harmed? For all she knew, her lover died happy; the guard never learned the "courtesan's" identity; the other prisoners doubtless sustained themselves with the hope that it would happen again, to them; and Lord Yassai finally got his heir.

She didn't—couldn't allow herself even to think about that day again. She convinced herself that the baby was Yassai's, so completely that she despised it as an unwelcome burden. But now—Now! He was here, healthy, and entirely hers. Yassai was old. Surely he couldn't live much longer. Together they'd rule, she and her son.

A baby didn't get its name until its soul was well fixed in its body, at least three months after it was born. But there was nothing wrong in the meantime with giving a child a nickname. It would be a two-part nickname, for her, she thought, and for the stranger Yan-kwo who sired him. Yassai would think she was honoring him and never be the wiser. She laughed.

"Sen-Ya," she said aloud. The child gnawed at its fist, crying. She loosened her garment, guided her nipple into the eager mouth, and the baby began to suck.

ii

After a week, Seniz-Nan found it preferable to forget how much agony Sen-Ya's birth had cost her. She was young and healthy. The wet nurse took over the baby's feeding entirely now so Seniz-Nan could devote herself to repairing the ravages of pregnancy and motherhood. She soaked in milk baths. Maids rubbed her body with perfumed oil, kneading and massaging her belly to encourage it to return to its former flatness and other maids worked over her hair, which had grown lusterless during the last months of her pregnancy. Still others tended her nails and complexion, and applied makeup with exquisite skill. She experimented with new perfumes and luxuriated in wearing extravagant new clothing which she changed completely several times a day. She drank hot wine freely, no longer constrained by the physicians' concerns for the child. She liked the haziness imbibing just enough wine induced; it softened the hard edges of life.

Now and then she wondered why Safia had not been to see her. She asked once, but the maids knew nothing. She never heard the courtesan's name mentioned in her hearing by any of Yassai's stewards or courtiers and by this she understood that Safia must be under some shadow. More than this she could not imagine; Yassai's absorption in the beautiful courtesan had long been a fact of life accepted by those who dwelled in Stendas Castle.

Though she seldom ventured outside her apartment, she knew from the maids' gossip that work had already begun on razing a section of the city preparatory to building the promised Residence. Stendas Castle had seldom seen such activity. Architects, so the maids reported, squabbled in the corridors, courtiers accompanied by bands of armed men glared at one another as they passed, lesser people came and went unremarked at all hours, foremen of work crews sought the architects to settle various questions as to what should be destroyed, what retained as a base on which to build. Also, stewards came daily to her apartment to inquire after the Sublime Heir who now had his own quarters next to hers. On those occasions when Lord Yassai himself came to see her and the child, she scarcely minded; she just drank a little more from the wine flask that was always close at hand.

Sen-Ya was nearly two weeks old when Seniz-Nan's maid Lin-ko brought word that a strange woman desired audience with her. A private audience.

"Did she give you her name?" Seniz-Nan said.

"No, Lady. But she told me to say to you that a certain lady who was not intended to die did so and another who should have died now lives."

Seniz-Nan raised her eyebrows. Curiosity piqued, she decided to see this mysterious stranger. "Bring the lady to see me at once," she said. She thought a moment. Surely this was nobody of importance. "Bring tea—no food, just tea. And more wine. Then leave us."

Lin-ko bowed and hurried to obey. When the heavily veiled woman came into the room, Seniz-Nan was certain she had never met the woman before. She limped and held one shoulder higher than the other, as if she were in pain. Nevertheless, Seniz-Nan gestured toward the cushion next to the one where she sat. The woman lowered herself onto it without grace. They waited in polite silence while Lin-ko brought the tea and wine flask.

"I have allowed you this audience because your message was very strange. It interested me," Seniz-Nan said when Lin-ko had closed the sliding doors behind her. "Who are you?"

The woman raised her veil.

Seniz-Nan stared at her, shocked, refusing at first to recognize the truth of what she was seeing. *"Safia!"*

She could not believe her own eyes. Surely this woman was someone else entirely. And in a way she was. So that was what the cryptic message had meant! Seniz-Nan looked at her closely. There was scarcely a trace remaining of Safia's beauty in the countenance of the woman who sat beside her. Deep bruises still ringed each eye, indicative of how dreadfully she had been beaten. Her nose, badly swollen, sat askew on her face. Automatically, Seniz-Nan offered tea.

"Thank you, Lady. Please. Do not look at me, I beg you. I am embarrassed to be stared at." When Safia spoke she revealed the empty space where one of her perfect teeth had been.

"I—I'm sorry. It's just that—"

"I know." With unhurried motions Safia unfastened her dress and dropped it from her shoulders, naked to the waist. Someone had stabbed her repeatedly, methodically, across one breast. The marks were well scabbed; they would leave terrible scars. A bandage circled Safia's ribcage; bones must have been broken and not yet healed. "There's more, but it's mainly inside." Safia refastened her dress and pulled the veil over her head once again, just enough to shield her features and still allow her to sip her tea.

"Yassai?" Seniz-Nan's lips had gone numb. Safia nodded. "But why?"

"It was because of Chimoko. Me he could dispose of with impunity. But you carried the Sublime Heir. Now you do not. And that puts you in great danger."

Hands trembling, Seniz-Nan dashed the contents of her teacup onto the floor and refilled it from the wine flask: "But I am—"

"—the Sublime Heir's mother?" Safia laughed softly and bitterly. "That's no shield, Lady. The Sublime Heir is born and thrives. Therefore, you are no longer necessary. There is an army of servants to bring up the Sublime Heir."

Seniz-Nan shook her head. "I cannot believe Yassai would harm me."

"Would you have believed he would do this to me?"

Seniz-Nan shook her head again. "No." She drank two cups of wine in quick succession. "What can I do?"

"I present you with a plan. It is very dangerous, and it may not work. But I believe it is better than waiting for Lord Yassai to send his men for you in the night."

"What is this plan?"

"First, the Sublime Heir must vanish."

"*What?*"

"He must appear to have been kidnapped. While his fate is in question, I do not believe Lord Yassai will move against you. After all, you are the only one of his women ever to bear a child. If there is a chance that the Sublime Heir should die, he would not dare harm you when you could have another."

Seniz-Nan shuddered. To have to go through that again—the fumbling, the failures, not to mention the pain of carrying and bearing a child. Another part of her mind leapt ahead in anticipation of a second venture into the palace prison. "What will happen to my son?"

She felt rather than saw Safia's smile. "Have no fear in that regard, Lady. He will be in my care, and that of some people

I know and trust. Have you ever heard of Third Province's House of Children?"

Seniz-Nan wondered if the dreadful beating Safia had undergone had affected her mind. "No. I haven't."

The courtesan shifted on her cushion. "The House of Children is a place where girls send unwanted babies rather than expose them and let them die. Sometimes parents are forced by poverty to send their children there, hoping to redeem them later. Sometimes childless couples will go to the House of Children to adopt a baby. Or someone will take a child for other purposes. I had my beginnings in the House of Children. Madam Farhat, who became my mother, found me there."

Seniz-Nan's head was reeling. "She became your mother? I don't understand."

"We of the Hyacinth Shadow World call the ladies who shelter us and who handle the business details for us our mothers. I was very lucky to have been found by Madam Farhat. She is very clever. I will take your son to the House of Children and Madam Farhat will find him in turn."

"And *that* will keep him safe?"

Again the unseen smile. "Can you think of a safer place, where Lord Yassai's men would be less likely to look, than a house of the Hyacinth Shadow World?"

"But Lord Yassai's nephew rules in Third Province."

"Even so. And his reputation makes it certain he must have regular dealings with Madam Farhat. It is said that the safest place to hide, when one is pursued by the tiger, is in the tiger's mouth."

Seniz-Nan shuddered. "I can scarcely bear the thought—"

Safia's voice turned harsh. "As you will, Lady. Remember that, while the guards are tying you to the raping bench." She made as if to rise.

"No! Please. What, what must I do?"

"I have no money. And it takes money to hire those who can enter Stendas Castle, do what must be done, and depart unseen."

Seniz-Nan went cold. She had only heard rumors of the caste of men for hire, called the Faceless Ones. It was said they had another name, a secret held strictly among themselves. These men, a highly trained brotherhood of warriors, were rumored to have the ability to become invisible at will and even to fly at need. It was said they could enter a brightly lit room where a lord sat guarded by a hundred men, cut off the sleeve of his garment, and slip out again undetected. They were selective about what they would and would not do and punished those who presented what they deemed inappropriate assignments; knowing this, it took a brave man even to engage their services, and a rich one. But once engaged, they were utterly trustworthy, and would unhesitatingly kill themselves before betraying their employer. So feared were they that even the most powerful lords were reluctant to speak of them except in the most guarded manner. This was the first time she had an inkling that their existence was not just a story. "As much as you require. More. But what will happen then? How will my son get to this House of Children?"

"Don't concern yourself. The less you know about that part, the better. But it is well for you to know about the ones who must be hired. In fact, you should put the blame on them at once, say that an enemy of Lord Yassai's must have hired them to kidnap the Sublime Heir. It won't be that far from the truth and will help to convince him."

"When will I see my son again?"

Safia turned somber. "When it is safe to do so, Lady. Beyond that, I do not know. As I said, this is a dangerous plan and it may not work. But it is certain that Lord Yassai will move against you if something does not distract him. And you will die in a more painful, humiliating manner than you could ever imagine."

"Then do what you think best." Seniz-Nan got up, rummaged through a chest until she found a handful of coins and some jewelry she seldom wore, earrings and finger rings, some set with semiprecious stones. She wrapped it all in a scarf and gave it to Safia who had also risen to her feet. "Will this be enough?"

"Perhaps. If not, someone will contact you some time later. You will know that person by the same words I used to identify myself to you." She bowed and went out the door, closing it silently behind her.

Seniz-Nan dropped back onto her cushion, reaching for the wine flask. She lifted it to her lips, not bothering with the cup. Her teeth rattled against the rim. She couldn't bear to think about what she had just heard, and to what she had just agreed. She drank greedily, seeking oblivion.

iii

The next two days and nights were torture for Seniz-Nan. She had to pretend to go about her usual activities as if nothing unusual had happened, was going to happen. She dared confide in no one, not even Lin-ko, who had helped her with her courtesan disguise not quite a year earlier. She even limited her wine consumption, lest her tongue grow loose and she betray herself unthinking. On the third night, Seniz-Nan woke from an uneasy slumber to the chilling sounds of men's voices shouting, the clash of metal against metal, and a woman screaming.

Surrounded by her maids, she ran outside, nearly stumbling over the body of a guard crumpled just outside her door. It looked as if a vicious war had been fought in the corridor. The body of another guard lay near the door to Sen-Ya's quarters. Two more sprawled facedown in the middle of the corridor, and another pile of bodies clustered near the back stairway. One of them was black-clad, contrasting starkly with the red of the guards' uniforms. The tension of the recent battle and the smell of blood still hung heavily in the air. "What is it?" she cried, panic-stricken. "What has happened?"

Another guard, holding his side while blood spilled over his hand, saluted her hastily. His face was pale, beaded with sweat, and his breath wheezed in his throat. He was dying where he stood; the Faceless Ones, it was said, always used poison on their weapons. "Forgive, Lady—The Sublime Heir—" He collapsed at her feet.

It took very little for her to pretend complete hysteria. She uttered a piercing scream and fell back into the arms of her maids. "Eeeei! My son, my son! He's dead!"

Another guard hastened toward her. "No, Lady," he said. "There's no sign, no proof—"

"Then bring him to me at once!"

"I regret I cannot. He—the Sublime Heir is missing."

"Missing!" She screamed again, even more loudly. Out of the corner of her eye she glimpsed red-uniformed guards rushing, too late, to make certain the area was safe before the Sublime Ruler entered. Then Yassai and his usual cluster of sleepy-eyed servants hurried along the corridor toward her, as fast as Yassai could manage. Still more people—courtiers, soldiers, servants—crowded in with every passing moment, craning their necks and whispering among themselves. Seniz-Nan could almost hear the rumors flying through the crowd. "Oh, gods, gods, where is my son!" she shrieked.

"Please, Lady. I regret— The nurse is dead. The Sublime Heir is nowhere to be found."

"Then you must search again— Husband, something has happened to our child!"

Yassai scowled, glaring at her in deep suspicion. She flung herself at his feet, hands clasped imploringly. "You must do something, husband! The child, the child—" She tore at her hair and scratched her cheeks in grief and agony.

"You, guard! What has happened to make this woman create such a disturbance?"

The man knelt in turn, head bowed, as pale as the dying guard had been. "Forgive me, First Lord. The Faceless Ones have come in the night and stolen the Sublime Heir. They killed the nurse, others who tried to stop them—"

Yassai raised both hands over his head. "Eeeei!" he cried, looking heavenward. He gestured abruptly to the headsman who had pushed through the crowd to stand next to him, great curved sword unsheathed and ready. The headsman brought the sword down. The guard's head bounced once and rolled while his body sagged to the floor, throbbing horribly. Some blood splashed on Seniz-Nan. She pulled her hair over her face.

"Oh, punish them all, husband! They failed to safeguard our son—"

He brushed past her. "I would see the heir's apartment. Perhaps there is something to be learned there."

Still sobbing, she dragged herself to her feet and stumbled after him. In contrast to the carnage outside, the rooms within appeared almost undisturbed. A maid—doubtless the one who had screamed—trembled and whimpered in the corner. In the inner chamber where the Sublime Heir had slept the nurse's bed was rumpled, as if she had risen hastily, aroused by something or someone. Her body lay in a puddle of blood where it had fallen. But the covers of the Sublime Heir's bed were turned back neatly, as if the child had been lifted out for some legitimate reason and would be returned at any moment.

The Scorpion insinuated himself close to Yassai. First Lord glanced at the magician. "Do you have any ideas?"

"Only the obvious, Sire. Some powerful enemy has struck at you in your most vulnerable area. You must set aside all your other plans—" he stared at Yassai, heavily emphasizing the words "—all the other plans you might have had, and concentrate your full powers on discovering who has done this, and on getting your son returned safely to you."

Yassai nodded slowly. "Yes." He held out his hands to the servants on either side of him. "I can no longer afford the luxury of idleness. Bring clippers and free me," he said.

Trembling, the servants began removing the jeweled gold nail guards. A body servant of the inner chamber came forward with a pair of clippers. He hesitated, hands shaking, until Yassai harshly repeated his order and the headsman took a step forward. Then the servant carefully snipped each yellowish nail off short. It was the strongest of declarations to the entire company watching that First Lord Yassai would work without ceasing until the mystery was solved.

He scowled balefully at the leaders of his guards and the men cowered under his anger. "If they've taken the child, what is to stop them from attacking the mother next? Double the guards around this lady, and if so much as a hair on her head is disturbed, you will all curse the whore who bore you before I am finished." He turned toward Seniz-Nan who still leaned heavily on her maids, overcome with grief. "You are more important to me now than ever. You must give me more sons."

She burst into fresh sobs, then managed to nod agreement. "You are wise beyond measure, O Sublime Ruler," she said in a small, broken voice. "I await your pleasure."

He grunted. Then he started toward the door. "Kill everyone who failed me this night—the maids, those of the Sublime Heir's guards still alive, the fools standing watch at the gates. I won't tolerate anyone who serves me so badly. You see to it," he said to the Scorpion.

"Depend on me, Sire," the magician said, bowing. "And be certain that if any of them knows anything at all, even to the least scrap of information, they will give it up gladly before they die."

Seniz-Nan repressed a shudder. Gathering her own frightened maids around her, she hurried back to her own apartment. At her orders they barred the door. Then and only then did she allow the terror and grief of the past two days, oddly mixed with gratitude, to overwhelm her and she gave way at last to genuine tears.

iv

"Of course the great lady's money is not enough," Kin-chao told Safia. She seemed almost amused. "She had no idea of what services like these cost. I'll make up the difference."

Though they were alone, they spoke in guarded terms. They could ill afford to relax their vigilance. Safia nodded. "You are generous," she said humbly.

Kin-chao laughed aloud. "Never fear, I'll be repaid very

generously later, when it is safe to contact her. Now, wait
here. Naturally I do not keep such sums on hand, so I must
pay a call or two before I know that all the arrangements are
made."

"I will take the place of the woman we spoke about, and
be ready to leave at once when the, ah, other person arrives."

"Alone? You wouldn't last ten *ri*. You need companions.
You look more like a servant someone has nearly beaten to
death than a woman who has just—" Kin-chao frowned
thoughtfully. Then her face cleared. "I know. *I* will be the
child's mother."

"You?"

"Who else is more trustworthy?"

Safia allowed herself to smile. "We will need a nurse. And
a husband, to protect us."

"Perfect. Who would suspect such a commonplace family
as we will be? You have a good head on your shoulders,
Safia."

"Madam Farhat taught me well."

"I know her, by reputation. I think a visit to her sounds
very attractive just now. I have been in First City too long.
Yes, it is decided." And with that, Kin-chao bustled out on
her errands to withdraw the money from its safe place and
start the roundabout process of hiring the Faceless Ones.

She was less enthusiastic when she discovered who Safia
had in mind to play the part of the father.

"Rag was the only one brave enough to defy First Lord and
bring me to you," Safia said. "He'll be brave enough to do this
as well. And in any case, he'll be so grateful to have the chance
to leave the ranks of the dung eaters, if only for a while, that
he would allow himself to be torn into pieces if it would save
us."

"Well, perhaps," Kin-chao said reluctantly. "We'll have to
see what he looks like once he's cleaned up."

It took two hot baths before the water wasn't black when
he emerged from it. Unaccountably modest, he insisted on
bathing himself and refused to be seen by anyone, even the
bath servants, without a cloth covering his private parts. Kin-

hao allowed him this peculiarity without protest, for after
two more scrubbings, followed by a massage with scented oil
and the ministrations of a barber, Rag began looking almost
presentable. Unable to do anything with the hacked-off,
louse-ridden mess of Rag's hair, the barber simply shaved
Rag's head. It transformed his appearance as much as the
baths had done, and also made him look more the part of the
middle-class tradesman he pretended to be. When Rag had
put on clean, sweet-smelling clothing that had been dried in
the sun, he took on a character entirely different from the
lowly dung eater who had rescued Safia. Now he carried himself with great dignity. Given the opportunity to eat good
wholesome food for once, he consumed so much that his
scrawny frame began to fill out virtually before the women's
eyes.

On the evening of the third day, Kin-chao moved the three
of them into a small house she owned under one of the names
she sometimes used, Ti-Mal. It was perfect for their purpose,
located on the edge of the tradesmen's district. There, according to instructions, they waited for the Faceless Ones.
They waited so long they began to doze. Then, a little before
midnight, Safia's hair stirred on the back of her neck when
she heard a baby crying from the next room. Marveling, she
realized they had entered the house, put the child into the crib
that had been prepared for him, and departed, all without the
least disturbance. A few minutes later, the wet nurse arrived
at the front door. Safia brought her inside.

"Well, you took your time getting here," Kin-chao said. She
was acting the part of Ti-Mal now and pretended to be
greatly annoyed. "The baby is hungry and crying."

"My instructions were to arrive at midnight," the woman
said imperturbably. She bustled off to feed the baby, loosen-
ing the neck of her garments as she went. "I am neither early
nor late."

"Ei? That was *your* doing," Ti-Mal said, rounding on the
hapless Rag. "You knew I wanted to return home as soon as
possible, and yet you arrange matters so you can delay another night in this wretched city. No doubt you want to visit

your Hyacinth Shadow Houses tomorrow for one more time!"

All this was for the benefit of the wet nurse, who could surely hear every word through the thin paper wall. She might be a spy. Neither Kin-chao nor Safia wanted to have to kill the woman; by their acting out this charade, they might be able to spare her life. In addition, it was good practice for the way they would all have to behave between here and Third City.

Rag, now called by the common name Nyo, played his part flawlessly. "Hyacinth Shadow Houses? I never even thought such a thing!"

"Oh, no? Don't you think I know what you've been doing while I was unable to accommodate you instead of attending to business? Business! All you want is to eat and sleep, and have your pleasure! You were born a peasant and that's all you'll ever be! If it hadn't been for my father's money, setting you up in that herb shop—"

"We leave tonight; now, if that will make you happy."

"Happiness and I are strangers. No wonder my milk has dried up, having to endure your presence. And if you think I'm going to let you come near me, after all the places where you've been poking your—"

To Safia's inner amusement, Ti-Mal, even while she railed and shouted her loudest, was busily putting the last of her things in order. She was packed and ready to go long before she finished her tirade at Nyo.

"Come on, you, nurse! You can feed the child as we go." The five of them—Ti-Mal, Nyo, the wet nurse, the baby, and Safia, now playing the part of Ti-Mal's luckless maid-servant—swept out of the house on the current of her words.

Ti-Mal had scarcely paused for breath by the time they reached an obscure gate, little used but convenient to the house where they had been staying.

"No guards," Nyo said mildly.

"They're like everything else in this cursed place. Not worth the sweat it took in bed to make them. *They're* probably off somewhere, enjoying themselves like somebody else I know.

Well, I don't propose to stand around and wait for them." She slid a glance at Safia.

Without being told, Safia understood that this had been the Faceless Ones' method of entry and exit from First City. The guards wouldn't be coming back. But the abduction must have been discovered by now, and soldiers would be swarming around the gate at any moment. Once again Safia marveled at the efficiency of these men and at the exquisite timing of their venture.

"We'll walk until dawn," Ti-Mal said imperiously. "I'm not the least bit tired now that we're actually on our way. Why I let you talk me into coming to First City with me so far along I'll never know, but without me you would doubtless have spent everything I've worked so hard for and left us as poor as you were when I married you. Well, are you going to stand here all night?"

"As you wish, wife."

The travelers slipped through the unguarded gate and into the night. The Lady Safia, in her servant's clothing, assumed the burden of the sleeping child and trudged along the dusty road in the wake of her "master" and "mistress." She was very contented. Nobody would ever suspect that this stooped figure carrying a baby on her back had once been First Lord Yassai's pampered concubine. With luck, anybody overhearing would pay no close attention to the lot of them, thinking Ti-Mal and Nyo were just another couple of a sort all too common—a decent quiet husband burdened with an overbearing wife. With a little more luck and some hard traveling, they would be near enough to the Third Province to seek shelter before the ones who sought the child with them thought to expand their search from First City outward, through Monserria.

i

Javerri slashed at the dragon. Vorsa scrambled back, drawing his own curved blade. The point of Steel Fury scored th
scaly hide. Blood gushed, but the monster paid less attention
to it than Javerri would have given a thorn scratch. The hil
slipped in her hand and she wished she had wrapped it in
something. Anything.

"Ladylord, get back!" Tal pushed ahead of her, brandishing his shortened spear. He jabbed at the beast.

Vorsa swung his sword, but was unable to find a vulnerable spot. The dragon shuffled nervously, crushing underfoo
masses of the ferns it had been eating when they disturbed it
It turned and, more by accident than by design, brushe
against Tal, knocking him sprawling.

"Vorsa, run!" Halit shouted. "Get away!"

A fist-size pebble flew past Javerri. At almost the same in
stant, the magician grabbed her and flung her to the side an
away from the dragon. A blinding flash erupted and a bubble of churning matter formed, encompassing Tal and mos
of the dragon. Its head, a portion of one back leg, and hal
its tail dropped, twitching, to the ground. Halit's weigh
pressed her hard against the jungle floor; then he rolled away
All she could think about for a moment was the pain in he
side where that accursed box of pleasure instruments in he
pack jabbed into her ribs.

"Get up, Lady!" Halit said. "Hurry! The whole thing wil
burst any moment—"

Spurred by the urgency in his voice, Javerri grabbed th
hand he offered, helping her to her feet. "Run, everybody ge
away!" she shouted. Even though Halit had knocked her ou

of the contained field of the explosion, she could feel the heat radiating from the gigantic churning ball and knew that it wouldn't be wise to be nearby when the bubble burst. . . .

They plunged into the rank growth of ferns that was impenetrable under ordinary circumstances. But that way was in the opposite direction from the other dragons, and fear lent them the necessary strength. Their heavy quilted garments hampered them. Sweating, Javerri struggled to follow the wake Halit made for her. She barely caught a glimpse of the others, but the sounds of them flailing their way through told her they were still more or less together. The ferns thinned unexpectedly. Halit stumbled a little, going through. He caught himself before he fell.

"This should be far enough for safety," he said, panting.

"Javerri!" Ivo fought his way through to the clearing. "Are you all right?"

"Unharmed," she said. A dull *boom!* sounded behind them. She looked back. Over the tops of the ferns a gout of steam billowed skyward as the bubble ruptured. Bits of matter began pattering down and a cloud of dust hung in the air.

"Remarkable," Wande-hari said. He wiped his forehead. "So that's the principle! Create a field to contain all the sound from the explosion; the water in the flesh overheats, goes into steam, and then the enormous sound vibrations bouncing back and forth literally pulverize—" He broke off. "I'm sorry, Ladylord. I forgot Tal was caught in it."

She set her jaw. "It couldn't be helped. Halit, you are not to blame. You did what you had to do." She wanted nothing more than to lose herself in Ivo's arms; she pushed the thought aside. She had to ascertain what damage had been done.

Somehow, she had kept Steel Fury with her, despite being knocked off her feet, and he had stayed in her hand during her headlong flight. She pried her fingers off the hilt. Then, with as much calmness as she could muster, she cleaned the blade on the sleeve of her quilted coat and put him in his sheath again. The box shifted, reminding her again of its presence. She had grown to loathe it. Ancestor and Lady

Moon knew she had become familiar with the box if not its contents, having carried it unwillingly for hundreds of *ri. . .*. Cautiously, the little band of adventurers retraced their steps.

The dragon—what was left of it—lay scattered and still smoking. Fangs of rock jutted from the half-melted ground where it had stood and where faint traces of steam now rose. The air was thick with the smells of dragon blood and brimstone, mingling oddly with the scent of freshly crushed ferns. There was no sign of the three dragons who had started toward them; presumably they had fled in terror.

"Tal," Javerri said. "Could there be any trace left of him?"

"Perhaps a few teeth—" Halit clamped his lips shut.

Javerri glanced around; Wande-hari's doorway in the wall of mist still sparkled behind them. "We must take off these heavy outer garments," she said decisively. "We were hampered and almost overcome by our own body heat. We will leave everything outside that we do not absolutely need. We cannot afford to be slowed down in the least degree, not if we will be fleeing from dragons again, which I suspect we will." At last, she thought, she could be rid of the accursed box, if only for a little while.

"Allow me, please, the task of carrying your encumbrances outside the misty wall and seeing to it that they are safe, Ladylord," Halit said humbly.

"Thank you. And everyone, make sure that you have a full skin of water." She sniffed the air. "I can't believe we'll find fresh pure water in here. And food. We must each have a packet of dried food."

Halit, Ivo, Ezzat, and Fen-mu vanished through the portal. Javerri waited nervously just inside with Wande-hari and Vorsa. Lek ducked out long enough to put his and Wande-hari's bulky outer clothing with the others'. Halit busied himself with taking their water skins, as many as he could carry at one time, clambering down the ravine and carefully filling them to capacity from the rain pools. Javerri, throat already dry from the sulphurous air, drank deeply before handing him hers to fill.

Wande-hari sat down and opened his pack full of magic

paraphernalia. He searched until he found a scrap of paper, ink, and writing instrument, and began scribbling notes, muttering to himself as he wrote. "—field of containment, strength proportional to the—"

Javerri frowned at him. As if he felt the force of her displeasure he fell silent, though he kept writing.

Somewhere, something moved in the underbrush. Javerri turned, instantly alert. It was too small to be another dragon—****Chakei?****

here i, ladylord, big light, too much hurt eyes

A plaintive note colored his thoughts. With an effort she kept herself from laughing with relief that he had allowed her to speak *beneath* with him. ****You must stay close to us. Please remember.****

stay close i, run free very much also

I know it's very difficult for you, being here, but you must help us— A certain lack of resonance made her realize that he had gone again, was no longer receiving her thoughts.

She frowned again. Ivo and Fen-mu should have returned by now. Surely it didn't take so long to put a few outer garments in a relatively safe place. "Please go and see what is keeping the others, Vorsa."

He nodded and went through the portal; in a moment he returned, a broad smile on his face. "Veh, Dekla, they just bringing other soldier down from Wall!" he said. "Vorsa thought we foolish to leave him. Who carries off rope from Wall if dragons inside mist? I think even Ezzat agree now, veh?"

The guide nodded, a little sheepishly. He took his freshly filled water skin from Halit and slung it on his belt.

Javerri nodded in turn; with Tai's death, they needed Nali more than ever. She wished she had Michu's entire army with her. Michu— How was he faring? Her brow furrowed and she rubbed the scar on her cheek.

Behind her, something screeched. She turned to see a small birdlike thing, not an *aa*, settling onto a fragment of the dragon's body. In a moment it was joined by two more. Busily, they began tearing at the flesh with sharp beaks, gulping down strips of fresh meat. She shuddered; who knew what other manner of scavengers lived in the depths of the jungle they faced?

Ivo, Fen-mu, and Nali came through the wall. "I found the Dragon-warrior's coat where he had left it outside the Wall, and brought it to put with our other garments," Nali told her.

"Thank you," Javerri said. "He will need it later."

Wande-hari put away his writing materials and got up, shrugging into his greatly reduced pack. Halit did likewise with his larger burden. He snapped his fingers in annoyance and handed Ezzat his own water skin. "Please," he said. "I was so busy with seeing the others had plenty to drink I forgot my own." Ezzat went at once to fill it.

"Can you leave that pack behind?" Javerri said. She was enjoying the feeling of freedom, of being in the open and unburdened for the first time since they had left Monserria.

"Forgive me, Ladylord," the younger mage said. "My master and I must have magical gear. But I am strong. I can carry enough for both of us."

She nodded, mind already busy elsewhere. Nali was, if anything, even paler than he had been when they left him atop the Wall. But to his credit, he hefted his short spear bravely and took his place with Fen-mu, on either side of Javerri.

Halit had proved he needed little if any protection, she thought. He had unhesitatingly saved her life, risking his own. And Wande-hari was certainly far from helpless.

"Ezzat," she said, "you have guided us well this far. We must rely completely on you now. You must find us a place where we can get our bearings. Then we must finish what we have come here to do."

ii

Leaving the jungle of ferns, they skirted the edge of a swamp full of quicksand and biting insects. They hacked their way through a barrier of thick brush growing man-high to find themselves at last out on a plain dotted with lace-leaf thorn trees and ringed with mountains. They went far enough to have an unencumbered view in every direction before pausing under one of these trees to rest. Everyone reached at once for the water skins they had on their belts and drank thirstily. The deeper they went in the land beyond the mists, the more sulphurous and unpleasant the air became. Even Chakei came close enough to lap from a water skin while they rested; then he skittered away once more.

"It is one of the Burning Mountains making the air bad," Ezzat said. "We can't avoid it; sorry. That's our goal, the place where the special dragons like to live."

"Then the dragons we encountered aren't the kind we are looking for." Ivo frowned thoughtfully and replaced the stopper in the neck of his water skin.

"No, Lord," Ezzat said. He glanced at Javerri. "Those were plant eaters. Not dangerous unless stirred up, as we discovered. The other dragons are smaller, much more dangerous." He took the grimy packet Javerri had seen once before out from under his shirt. As carefully as he had then, back in the inn at the southern border of Monserria, he opened it to show the square of painted silk and held it up so that everyone could see. "This is what we are searching for."

Javerri didn't need to look. The memory of the painting, put away so carefully in a compartment in her mind, sprang up as fresh as it had been that night—the two crimson dragons in their misty dreamscape. Now she herself was a part of the dreamscape. The same blue-shadowed mountain, or one very like it, dominated the horizon and they might have been resting beneath the same frothy-leafed thorn tree as in the painting.

Now, however, she knew how large the crimson dragons must be. While not of the immensity of the one Halit had killed, they must stand at least the height of two men.

"Eeeei!" Fen-mu and Nali exchanged dismayed glances.

Shab Vorsa nodded thoughtfully, stroking his lip with a hand that scarcely shook. He took another swallow of water.

"Veh, veh, that look like what old stories say fathers of *larac-vil* are."

Ezzat began folding the piece of silk and replacing it carefully in its wrappings.

"It is a lovely painting," Wande-hari said. "Exquisite technique."

"You are far calmer than I am, Master, at the sight of what we have to face," Halit said. His voice shook a little and his fingers twitched toward the pack of magical equipment he bore.

He longs for a pipe of *abaythim*, Javerri thought.

"Is an unknown enemy any less to be feared than one we can recognize?" Wande-hari shook his head. "Thank you, Ezzat. Though I must admit that I am glad you waited until we were here before showing us the dragons we must find."

"As to that," Lek said, "isn't it the wrong time of year to find dragon eggs? After all, it's nearly winter outside."

"Lek has put a nagging question of my own into words," Ivo said. "I would hate to think we have come this far, endured what we have endured, only to find empty nests—or whatever these creatures use."

"Oh, the crested dragons breed all year round," Ezzat said. "They lay clutches of two or three eggs at a time. Other dragons come and eat the eggs. Some of them breed all year as well, I think. Something to do with how warm it always is behind the Wall. There is only one season, you see."

Javerri glanced up; there was no sun, only a bright spot in the mists overhead. "I expect the flyers hew more closely to the natural order of things," she said. "Is the sun always hidden like this?"

"I think so, Ladylord," Ezzat said. "The, ah, ones who made the painting said it was very easy for them to lose their bearings for there was no real direction to their shadows. They were always careful to mark their path with secret signs, and then they erased their marks as they left."

Javerri nodded, glancing around the plain where they sat resting, small dots on the vast dreamscape of a giant's painting. If they were lost. . . . "We must do likewise, or we'll never find our way back."

"I have done so, Ladylord," Ezzat said. There was just a hint of reproach in his tone.

Javerri sighed. "Of course you would." Where, she thought, had this deep doubt about him come from? Ezzat had proved trustworthy up until now. But she found herself wondering what else he had kept hidden, or neglected to tell them. His hands shook nervously and his scarred face looked more sinister than ever in the misty light. "Do you know where these crimson dragons like to make their nests?"

"Yes, Ladylord. They prefer crevasses in the sides of those mountains with fire in their hearts, where an egg stealer doesn't like to go."

She squinted toward the mountain whose crest glowed fitfully in the dull, hazy light. "There perhaps?"

"I hope so. I think none of us want to carry a dragon's egg any farther than we have to."

"We'll carry it far enough before our errand is finished," she said a trifle sourly. "A *ri* or two either way won't make much difference."

iii

Though the company caught sight of more dragons of various types as they crossed the plain and neared the mountain, these dragons were the huge ones that moved sluggishly and were easy to avoid. It was the smaller, swiftly moving dragons, Ezzat said, the meat eaters, that were to be feared.

Chakei skittered in and out of sight. Now he popped through the brush ahead of them, now he paced them from the side. Perversely he danced far ahead of them for a while, only to lag behind again. Javerri despaired of reaching him *beneath* until they were back outside the misty Wall. If, she thought, he would follow her out.

They stopped again at noon, eating sparingly of the dry

food and using the trick they had learned in the desert of taking small sips so the water would be absorbed instead of being excreted almost immediately. Chakei crept close again for water, refusing the humans' food. An hour later, the travelers began straggling, strung out in a line along the broken ground that formed the shoulder of the mountain, instead of being grouped together. Javerri began to fall behind. Halit lagged even farther back. "Stop!" she cried.

Her throat and eyes burned. She longed for water, but refused to stop again to drink. Not yet, not until her thirst grew unbearable. Not until she was able to get her people to close ranks, not scattered like beads from a broken necklace. Frustrated, tired, her throat aching, she toiled up a slope after the others.

"Stop!" she shouted again. "Come back!"

The ground they traversed now was so scored it looked as if Halit had hurled his entire supply of exploding pebbles against it. Trees lay scattered, ripped up by the roots or leaning against one another at crazy angles. Great spears and slabs of rock reared upward, as if seeking a sky they had never seen, and the ground was littered with loose shale that created a slippery and treacherous footing. They all stumbled and fell often as they climbed up, and then down.

"Stop!" Javerri called tiredly. "We must stay together!" She might as well have been shouting at a tree stump for all the good it did.

Ivo and Ezzat led the way. Wande-hari followed closely with Vorsa. The two soldiers and Lek trailed at a little distance behind the mage and the desert man.

Frustrated at her inability either to force them to slow down or to catch up with them, Javerri fell back a few hundred feet. Halit had dropped entirely out of sight, even farther back than she. Now she discovered why. He had begun limping badly. A shadow flowed over the mage, swiftly approaching. She looked up, a chill raising gooseflesh despite the heat; one of the big leather-winged flyers soared past, as if surveying the creatures toiling along on the side of the mountain. She wondered if the cruelly curved beak had teeth. . . .

"Ladylord!" It was Halit. He sat on a downed tree trunk in the bottom of a rill, rocking back and forth and grasping his ankle, his pack on the ground beside him. She turned and began scrambling back down the slope toward him.

"What is it?" she said. "Are you hurt?"

"My ankle—twisted—" The mage bit his lip, grimacing.

She moved closer. "Do you need the physician?"

"No," he said. With a suddenness that caught her unprepared, he threw a glistening powdery substance into her face.

She recoiled instinctively—and discovered she could not move. Everything had gone numb. She could not feel her face. She wondered why she didn't fall.

Halit stood up. He scrambled up the slope far enough to see. "Good," he said, nodding. "They're all far ahead, past the next ridge. We have plenty of time before someone has enough wit to come back."

Muttering an incantation under his breath, he scooped up a handful of dirt. The powder had caused Javerri's eyes to water and tears had begun to run down her cheeks. Carefully, he wiped away the tears, mixing them with the soil. It became malleable clay almost at once.

"A little something, from here—and here—"

Appalled, she could do nothing to stop him. He plucked a few hairs from her head, an eyelash or two, and worked them into the clay. One of her nails had broken, the fragment barely hanging by a ragged edge, and he took this as well. He forced her mouth open and, despite the dryness of her mouth, scooped out a scant drop of spittle and added this to the mixture. Still chanting, he set the ball of clay on the ground. At once it began to grow and mold itself, borrowing more soil as required from where it stood, forming hollow feet, legs, a slender body, arms, a head. The clay closed over the top of the head and hair began to sprout, long, black and shining, covering the seam. Nails formed on fingers and toes. Moisture glinted in the eyes. Quickly, the skin took on nearly a natural shade. A nude woman stood there waiting.

It's me, Javerri thought, stunned. My shape, my likeness.

She felt herself being handled. She lost her balance and fell, or was thrown, to the ground. Halit knelt over her, none too gently stripping off her outer garments. She lay in whatever position he chose as he pulled off her desert garb. Then he dressed the clay doll, slung Steel Fury on its back, and turned it in the direction he wanted it to go. "Smile," he whispered into the doll's ear. "Go and find the others. You know how. Tell them I am resting and will catch up in a moment. But stay well back from the old man. He will see you for what you are."

The simulacrum smiled. As if it were possessed of intelligence, it turned at once and started up the slope. When it reached the crest, it paused and waved one arm, as if signaling those beyond that all was well. Then it disappeared down the other side.

Halit turned to Javerri. He also was smiling, and she closed her eyes at the sight. He rummaged in his pack and took out a length of thin rope. "The powder will wear off before long," he said. "I could give you more of it, but I want you to be fully alert for what comes next. And you will be. I saw to that."

Something in her look, her thought, must have communicated the question flooding through her; he laughed lightly.

"Why? Because my master—my real master—bids it." With deft, economical motions he bound her arms and feet. Sensation was returning. Distantly, she could sense the rope biting into her flesh. "Oh, my dear Third Lord, I am not going to kill you, though there are those who would wish it so. My master is far more subtle than that, more clever. Through me he will simply strip you of your right to Third Province and leave you to face the shame. Unless, of course, you choose an honorable death and open your throat with a dagger. Nobody will stop you from doing that, not even, I'll wager, your sham of a husband. Not when I'm done with you."

She managed to make a noise. With a nod of understanding, he turned to his pack again, opening it wide. He found a wad of rag which he stuffed into her mouth. She moaned with pain. He had caught a portion of her lower lip between her teeth and the gag and she was unable to free it. She tasted blood. He picked up his pack and hoisted Javerri over his shoulder.

"I've found a place just over there, through a crack in the rocks, a low cave. That will do admirably."

She could move, just a little. Sensation tingled back through her arms and legs. She shook her head, forcing a muffled sound of protest through the gag.

"Oh, Dekla, haven't you guessed how much I like little boys?" he said, crooning the words sardonically. "Haven't you guessed the effect you were having on me, in your boy's clothing?" He shifted her, setting her down for a moment. But it was only to squeeze the two of them through the narrow entrance to the cave. It was so cramped he couldn't stand erect. He tossed her carelessly on the ground and paused long enough to make a pebble glow and light the interior faintly before he finished stripping her. The sound of her silken undergarments tearing filled the cave.

"Yes, Dekla, I have waited for this moment for a long time. First, on my master's bidding, I shall take you as a man takes a woman. But then, for myself, I will take you as a man takes a boy." He paused, considering. He even smiled. "Then, I think there is time for some other amusing things for us to do."

Javerri's heart lurched. She had glimpsed the plain wooden box stowed in Halit's pack; he placed it in such a spot she knew he planned that she could see it. He must have taken it when they had divested themselves of everything cumbersome and he had carried her belongings outside. . . . No! she cried silently, I won't panic! She shut her eyelids tightly, concentrating.

Eeeei! Gathering her forces, she struck out at him with her mind, only to have him deflect the blow with careless skill.

"You should have listened to what that doddering old fool was trying to teach you, Javerri."

He laid his hands on her hips. Her very skin shrank from his touch. No—! **Wande-hari! Chakei! Help me!**

He laughed again. "They can't hear you. They're busy." He grasped her ankles, lifted her knees, and twisted the lower half of her body to one side. She was lying nearly facedown.

Accessible. Something within her contracted to a glowing point. Every sense sharpened, yet at the same time grew remote. She writhed away from him, screaming through the gag, trying to kick, struggling to turn over, to loosen the ropes, anything. No matter how she moved, he caught her. He fumbled at her flesh. Her teeth bit through her lip when he forced himself into her. He withdrew and forced himself into her again, even more painfully. She screamed again.

—agony white-hot, disgrace, one moment, only one little moment with Steel Fury in my hands, this bastard loses head, balls, and Stalk, oh yes, him and his whoreson master born when a diseased *sarhandas* pissed on a dungheap, his master who had to be Yassai, has always been Yassai, I'll take his head too and his Fruit, oh yes, I'll kill, kill—

Savage, unreasoning rage consumed her to the marrow of her bones. It shook free the glowing speck that was the essence of Javerri, sent it floating out into a vast limitless space. An unknown destination hovered somewhere beyond the darkness, but it eluded her, receding no matter how swiftly she pursued.

She fled toward the place she had sensed only to find a barrier looming ahead, more formidable than any she had ever encountered. Was there a way around it? Unaware of anything beyond her need to escape, she hurled the mote of her being against it.

She found a breach and slipped through so abruptly it would have taken her breath away had she had any.

This close to the barrier she could still feel, however dimly, what was happening to her on the other side. But here, all was mist. Nameless now, she left herself behind without regret and fled outward farther and still farther.

Many *ri* away, a madman abused a woman's body. He grunted and cried out, no, not yet, don't let it be over so soon, but he had finished. He withdrew, panting. Then he fumbled in the box and began using the pleasure objects, one by one, on the woman lying limp under his hands. But by that time the spark that had once been Javerri no longer knew or cared about anything happening to what she had once been.

iv

Ezzat uttered a cry of triumph. "Here it is! The nest of eggs!"

Wande-hari scrambled across the loose shale, following Ivo. "Is it from the correct species?" the old magician said, panting.

"The eggs are marked with crimson spots," Ivo said. He looked up. "Where is Javerri?"

"Javerri?" Wande-hari turned. Javerri topped a rise a distance behind them and waved. "There she is."

Ivo waved in return, gesturing to her to hurry. She nodded and began picking her way down the treacherous slope.

"She won't mind if we don't wait for her," the magician said. "How beautiful the eggs are!" He gazed with pleasure on the great oval eggs. The crimson spots glowed in the gloom.

"Yes, beautiful," Ivo said, fascinated.

The mountain rumbled. The ground trembled beneath their feet and sparks rained down on them. Ezzat crouched, pasty-faced with terror.

"Tell us what we must do next," Ivo said, "with these beautiful dragon eggs."

Ezzat cowered even more. "Forgive me, Lord, but I do not know!"

"What?" Startled, Wande-hari nearly lost the thread of the mind hold he had been keeping on Chakei ever since they had entered this terrible land.

"Forgive, I beg you! I—I don't know! I never did." He stared at the ground, shame written plainly on his face. "They always made me wait outside. I think there is something they do to the eggs but they would never tell me what it was."

Ivo raised his fist. Shab Vorsa hurried forward and grasped his arm before he could strike. "That not help, Dekla's husband."

Ivo stepped back reluctantly. "Yes. You are right. But—"

"You angry, Vorsa knows. But not know what to do to eggs." He looked at them, puzzled. "Always think they are red, like dragons and *larac-vil.*"

"But they are," Wande-hari said. "In spots."

"Oh. Yes. Vorsa not see at first. Sure, red spots."

Lek and the two soldiers neared the nest area. Ivo at once set Nali to watching for any signs of dragons returning to wreak vengeance on egg stealers, and sent Fen-mu back after Javerri.

Wande-hari pressed his hands over his eyes. He wasn't thinking right, not thinking quickly, too tired. This, then, was the reason for the uneasiness, the secretiveness that had lain over Ezzat like a cloud. He felt it clearly, yes and Javerri also; he picked up her concern. Where *was* she? She should have been here before now. Coming, but too slowly. And Halit. What a time for him to disappear. He must speak to him.

He stared at the red-speckled eggs, large and snug in their nest. They were so big! A man couldn't carry one unaided. Eeeei! What had to be done to them? *What?*

Something nudged his mind. ***i***

Chakei?

Wande-hari tried to conceal his surprise. It was the first time Chakei had ever spoken directly to him *beneath*, without Lord Qai or Javerri as intermediary.

sorry i for run away, too much memory

It wasn't the right word, but Wande-hari recognized the feeling Chakei was trying to convey, the headiness of wild recognition that had scrambled all his sense of devotion and duty and hurled him careening off, useless. ****I'm sure the Ladylord understands. Why don't you tell her?****

ladylord far away not listen

Out of range. ****Do you know what must be done now?****

find eggs, know i then, do also, none better

The old magician smothered a smile at the note of boasting in the Dragon-warrior's tone. **But we've found the eggs. Please, come and help us so that we may all take our Ladylord out of danger.**

no eggs, big rocks

Whatever are you talking about, Chakei, of course these are eggs—

rocks

Wande-hari's vision wavered for a moment. Lady Moon, but it *did* appear, just for a moment, as if the eggs had turned to boulders lying in a shallow depression in the ground! He pressed his hands against his eyes again. He looked, blinking, at the fabulously beautiful dragon eggs. Slowly they faded from his vision and the boulders took their place again, and stayed there.

He pulled himself up straight. Eeeei! What—? A faint acrid taste on the back of his tongue—he had thought it the bitterness of the air they breathed. He focused on the taste, noting an increase in his mental confusion as he did so. His mind was not obeying as it should. He must, he thought. He must. . . .

Grimly, he cleared away the cobwebs separating him from reality. That taste—in a flash of lucidity he recognized it! "Gods," he said aloud. "Lady Moon and Ancestor, we've all been drugged! The water, Halit put something in it! Javerri—"

Ivo still looked back along the path they had come. "She hasn't caught up with us yet," he said. "I am beginning to be worried about her."

The fog partially descended on Wande-hari again. "Then go and find her," he heard himself saying. "Take Nali. The rest of us will stay here. We'll be safe enough." He shook himself.

No, he thought. Don't alarm the others unnecessarily. He put his hand on Ivo's arm and made his tone unconcerned. "When you find Javerri, bring her to me."

Ivo was gone almost before the magician finished speaking. Wande-hari closed his eyes, and an instant later Ivo touched him on the shoulder. With a start, the elderly man realized he had dozed off. The drug, it had to be the drug making him so exhausted— Quickly, he re-established his contact with Chakei.

here i, not move The Dragon-warrior sounded almost his old self again. **feel very fine**

He drank the same water we did, Wande-hari thought. How strange that the drug that sent us wandering off like idiots, crazy men sharing a dream, brought him back to sanity.

Wande-hari sat up straight. "Javerri, did you find her?"

"Yes. She said Halit was resting and that he would catch up with us later."

"Ah." Wande-hari glanced at Javerri. At least she was all right, she was unharmed. She was smiling. He closed his eyes once more. Dreamily, he wondered why Halit had drugged them and then stopped to rest. Oh, I have never been so tired. . . .

"I thought she acted a little strange."

"Oh? In what way?"

"She smiled when she told me about Halit, when she should have been angry—"

Chakei whimpered a little, staring at the Ladylord.

Javerri stood a little distance away from them. She smiled.

Something was wrong. Wande-hari shook off his weariness. He knew of an antidote, something very simple, something every magician put in his kit as routinely as other men put on their shoes. If only he could remember what it was. . . .

Yes. A little charcoal, taken internally. And time. But they had no time to spare. He fumbled his pack open and took out the small wooden jar. He took a pinch between thumb and forefinger and put it on his tongue. Then he offered another pinch to Ivo. "Here," he said. "Swallow some of this."

The effect of the antidote was very quick; the drug must have been about to wear off anyway. Ivo's eyes seemed to come back into focus. He and Wande-hari stared at each other. "Give me your arm," Wande-hari said, "and help me up."

The archer raised his eyebrows, but offered the magician the support he required. The two of them started toward Javerri. She wandered away, smiling.

"Javerri!" Wande-hari said sharply.

The young woman paid no attention. The mage forced himself forward, joints creaking. Javerri, still smiling, glanced over her shoulder and began to run.

"Go after her, Ivo," the magician said. "Bring her back! Oh, gods and Lady Moon! I fear—"

Ivo caught her easily. She barely struggled. He carried her back toward Wande-hari, not the way a man carries a woman, but tucked under his arm the way one might carry an awkward bundle. The expression on Ivo's face told the magician that now he also recognized the essential *wrongness* of the thing that wore Javerri's likeness.

One close look was enough for the magician, now that his wits had returned. "Eeeei!" Wande-hari said. He drew a breath between his teeth. "A simulacrum! An image, designed to fool us!"

The two men stared at each other, appalled. The others watched in mild astonishment. Ivo raised his hand to shatter the counterfeit Javerri into the dust from which it had been made and Wande-hari caught his arm before the blow could fall.

"No," he told the archer. "We must keep it alive—or whatever passes for life within it."

"Why?"

"I do not know exactly. I only feel it must be thus."

"Then keep it out of my sight." He reached out and plucked Steel Fury, still in its sheath, from the clay doll's back, and removed Lady Impatience as well. He put the dagger in his belt. "At least I will keep these safe."

Shab Vorsa came back to himself first; a desert dweller accustomed to going without, he had drunk more sparingly than the rest and didn't need the antidote. "What is happening, Uncle?" he said in surprise. "And where is other mage?"

Wande-hari's gaze didn't leave Ivo's face. He had never

seen a man look more stricken, more bereft. "Are you all right?" he said.

"I am and must be, if we are to recover Javerri." The archer was pale and shaken, but he appeared more in command of himself than Wande-hari expected.

"Dekla? But here she stands."

Wande-hari turned to Vorsa. "It is not Javerri, but an image of her. I give it into your care. We must keep it alive. I don't know where the other mage is," he said. "But that he is somehow responsible for this, I have no doubt—" He staggered and would have fallen if Ivo hadn't caught him.

Chakei came and laid his clawed hand on Wande-hari's arm. **ladylord?** He sounded utterly bewildered. **not here but look like and wear clothes also**

Can you lend me your strength? We will search for her beneath.

yes and oh yes

Thank you.

"Let me sit," he said. "I must search for them while I am still physically able. Make me comfortable so I can save energy. I am exhausted. I am in no real danger, not yet, but the drug has taken its toll."

Lek suddenly snapped back into reality. "What's happened?" he said. "I think I was dreaming—"

Quickly, Ivo told him about the charcoal, and the physician began administering the antidote from his own medical supplies. "The drug is wearing off, to be sure, but we must avoid any lingering effects," Lek said. "Here, learned Wande-hari, take another dose."

With Chakei at his feet and the cleansing grains of charcoal on his tongue, Wande-hari closed his eyes and began to cast his thoughts the way a fisherman casts a net, in widening circles. Oh please, he thought, let her be within range. He spiraled up, projecting himself until he was seeing beyond the bounds of his body. There he was, there were his companions, there were the boulders they had mistaken for dragon eggs, the alien presence of dragons a few *ri* distant, somewhere the pulsating rage of a savage beast at bay. A faint sparkling of life nearby—aha! The real nest! The vision widened to include the ridges of the mountainside they had clambered over that afternoon, the edges of the grassy plain, the thorn trees. Too far. Come back.

He sensed Chakei searching also, in his own way.

Nothing. He began covering the area again. And again. But still he found nothing to indicate Javerri's presence.

No, he told himself, I will not believe that she is dead. I would have known. And Halit, Halit is hiding from me. I can sense him out there somewhere, like an unpleasant odor lingering in the air.

Ivo knelt anxiously at his side. "Can you find her?"

Wande-hari shook his head. "Nothing. Not yet. Just a hint of the mage's presence. I think he is fleeing, and with reason. If I ever—" He clenched his fist and, carefully, forced himself to relax. This kind of tenseness interfered with his search.

find hurt thing i

Wande-hari traced down the line of Chakei's thought. Yes. He had touched it earlier, that crouching beast at bay, throbbing redly with hate and mindless anger. It was so far removed from anything human he had passed it by. But he forced himself to examine it again. Chakei's perceptions were different. . . .

The distant scene superimposed itself on his surroundings, as it always did.

"What do you see, Wande-hari?" It was Ivo.

He shook his head. "I can sense nothing but Chakei, and our human companions. There are dragons nearby. I cannot yet make out what kind they are but the nest we seek is close. The dragons may be coming back to it to tend it or they may be another species wanting to feast on the eggs. I do not know. Farther away, I sense danger. There is an injured animal deep in a cave—"

His eyes flew open and he sat bolt upright, all fatigue forgotten. *"Oh, gods, gods!"* he gasped. *"That isn't an animal at all! It is Javerri!"*

i

The little "family" traveled all that night and well into the next day, despite the wet nurse's constant protests at being hurried along in such an undignified manner. She was proving to be a whiner and a complainer, always wanting to stop to rest.

"I can't keep up this pace," she said repeatedly. She clutched at her breasts. "My milk will surely curdle and dry up if we don't slow down! And my feet hurt!"

Safia gritted her teeth and kept silent, though her own scarcely healed injuries jolted pain through her at every step and the baby's weight on her back made her fractured ribs an agony. She didn't mind the complaints. The woman had no idea how lucky she was that she didn't have something real to complain about.

She and Kin-Chao had agreed privately that Safia would set the pace, according to her endurance. To keep herself going, she set goals to reach before giving one of their pre-arranged signals that she had to rest.

Just until they passed that grove of trees, she thought. That wasn't so bad. She'd wait until they were even with the hedge bordering this farm. Surely she could make it over that bridge. Then they'd stop.

In this way she coaxed herself to go on much farther than she would ordinarily have been able to before they rested.

But it was worth it, every pang, every ache. Eeeei! she thought exultantly, glancing back at the baby. Never did she dream of striking so hard at First Lord Yassai, Sublime Ruler of Monserria! Mama Kin-chao could have hired the Faceless Ones to kill Yassai as easily as she hired them to steal the child. She would have paid for it gladly. But this was better, much better. The dead were beyond suffering, and she very much wanted him to know pain though she didn't know how to do it alone. Now, with this child, they held his very stones.

Seniz-Nan had been the biggest unknown in the scheme that had sprung into Mama Kin-Chao's mind as soon as she was sure Safia wasn't going to die. But Safia was able to reassure her on that point. She had seen many like Seniz-Nan in the time since she had become Madam Farhat's most prized courtesan of the first rank. Too young for her years, too taken with her own cleverness. And, Safia added honestly, very easy to manage because of her fondness for the wine flask. The scheme between the two women involving Chimoko was proof enough of that. Reason alone said Yassai wouldn't move against Seniz-Nan, not yet. Oh, he might want to—Safia had no illusions that Yassai hadn't guessed or been told the truth about the role the two of them had played in helping Chimoko kill herself. He would have wanted to execute both of them then and there. But he wouldn't have dared risk his dynasty by killing the only one of his wives to bear a child, not before he had sired a houseful of little Yassais by her.

Safia smiled bitterly. How ironic. Too bad First Lord was incapable of realizing that the very prospect of such a fate would be a terrible punishment for any woman.

Always make a man think he is the best lover you have ever had, Madam Farhat had taught her. Men will deny it, but in their innermost hearts they all believe that they are superlative in bed. Though she only pretended to believe Farhat at the time, she came to know how wise the madam was in the ways of men. Yassai truly thought women fought for the privilege of being with him. Night after night when Safia wanted nothing more than to escape, even if it meant casting herself from the castle roof like Chimoko, she smiled and flirted, sang and danced with all the elegance she could muster, finally taking him by the hand and leading him to the bed as if she were overcome with desire and must cajole him into lying with her. How she hated kissing and caressing his dried-up old body into a shadow of potency, smelling his rotting teeth, sweating while she rode his half-limp Jade Stalk with all the skill she possessed, hoping he would be able to finish just this one time, oh please.

Seniz-Nan had far too many high-placed family connections to be in any great danger; she was the niece of the Lord of Fourth Province, it was said, and distantly related to First Lord himself. After his temper cooled she would be safe enough from Yassai for several years. And in that time, who knew what could happen? She was young. She could have more children. But she had agreed to this wild scheme now, that was the important thing. And here they were, on the road, going as fast as they were able toward Third Province.

The sun was halfway to its zenith when a mounted troop of Yassai's red-uniformed guards caught up with them. Safia recognized the leader's insignia of rank; he was a captain in Yassai's own guards. She made sure her veil covered her face, in case he had seen her in Stendas Castle.

"Halt!" the captain ordered brusquely. He swung down out of his saddle and strode toward them. "You are traveling away from First City and there is an infant with you. State your names and your business!"

Kin-chao, still calling herself Ti-Mal, reacted instantly with a bravado that bordered on recklessness. Sticking her chin out as if daring the world to gainsay her, she pulled herself up to her full height. She barely reached the leader's chin.

"How dare you interfere with peaceful honest citizens instead of chasing lawbreakers the way you should be?" Ti-Mal shouted indignantly. She turned on Nyo, who cringed from her wrath. "This is all your doing, I just know it! I wouldn't put it past you for a moment to arrange to have us all arrested and hauled back to First City so I'll be locked away somewhere and you can go off again and visit your fancy women—"

"Now, now, Mother," the captain said hastily, trying to soothe her. "We just wanted to ask a few questions—"

The two of them reminded Safia of nothing so much as a raucous little bird defending her nest from the startled cat who had blundered into it and now wished he had never developed a taste for eggs.

"Then ask your questions and be done."

"Your names—"

The men dismounted, holding their reins and watching the discomfiture of their leader with amusement. The nurse shuffled from foot to foot. The baby began to cry. She took him from Safia, moved to the side of the road, sat down heavily, and began to nurse him. Ti-Mal watched for a moment, the picture of a shrewd woman making sure she was getting her money's worth from a hired servant. She turned to the captain.

"If you must know, I am Ti-Mal," she said snappishly, "and this worthless worm here with me is my husband, Nyo. We own a shop near the Vornian border. I have to get back home and salvage what is left after my husband—" she glared at Nyo "—spent all our savings with such a lavish hand in First City! A pleasure trip!" She spat in Nyo's direction, and he dodged as if by long habit. "Pleasure for him. And now this!" Ti-Mal gazed upward, arms raised in supplication. "O Ancestor Spirit! How much more am I going to be called on to endure, I ask you?"

The red-uniformed troop leader moved back to confer in low tones with his second-in-command, both men glancing in Ti-Mal's direction and shaking their heads. Safia, crouching down to remove an imaginary pebble from her shoe, managed to stay just within earshot.

"Surely the ones we are searching for wouldn't behave in such a manner," the lieutenant said.

"I agree," the captain said. "I believe they are what they say they are, just a shopkeeper and his wife, traveling back to where they live."

"My sympathies to him. How glad I am that my wife stays home, where she belongs!"

The captain laughed. "She reminds me of my mother, curse her sharp tongue." He returned to Ti-Mal. "You and your husband may go on your way in peace," he said.

"Peace!" Ti-Mal spat again, this time into the dust beside

her. "You have to be looking for something or someone, or you wouldn't have stopped us. What's going to keep another lot of you from doing the same? And another after that? You'll delay us for a week! By the time I get home the business will be ruined—"

Clearly, the captain had not expected this response to his generosity. Behind him, a few of his men sniggered behind their hands. "I'll give you a pass," he said, rather more loudly than necessary. "Will that satisfy you?"

"I suppose so," Ti-Mal said grudgingly. "Are you sure other soldiers will know what it is?"

A muscle in the man's jaw twitched. Just as clearly, he was now wishing he had never accosted this little group of travelers in the first place. "Yes!" He made a visible effort to keep from losing his temper. "Yes," he said. "As one of First Lord's elite commanders, I have the authority to give out a few of the special passes. First Lord's chop is on the outside, in gold. *Now* are you satisfied?"

Safia held her breath. One of those prized passes would allow a person to go anywhere in Monserria, unchallenged by anyone below the rank of captain! She blessed the hour she had chosen Kin-chao to go with her, double-blessed Kin-chao for agreeing and thinking it was her idea, blessed her still again for her wonderful playacting and her ability to dominate even one of the dreaded commanders of First Lord's soldiers.

Ti-Mal plucked the folded red paper from the captain's hands and tucked it into her bodice as if she were doing the man a great favor. "Yes," she said, giving him a simpering smile. Then she frowned again. "But if this is a forgery, just another of my husband's tricks, I'll— You'd better give me your name."

"Never mind!" the captain shouted. Curtly, he gestured for them to move along, at the same time glaring at his men so furiously that they all wiped the smiles off their faces and became very busy remounting their horses.

Ti-Mal became Kin-chao again just long enough to shoot

Safia a glance that said as clearly as if she had spoken aloud,
You see, there are times when tactics other than sweetness and
compliancy are called for when dealing with men.

Greatly strengthened and encouraged by the way Kin-chao
had saved them all and by their unexpected luck in acquiring
one of the precious red documents, Safia got to her feet again,
eager to take the baby and walk on. By noon, they were near
the border of Third Province and had shown the red pass
twice to troops of guards, who let them proceed undisturbed.

"I think we can afford to rest a while," Ti-Mal said. "I
know I can use some sleep—alone," she added with a hard
look in Nyo's direction.

Safia's burst of energy had long since evaporated, and she
wanted nothing more than to have a hot bath and lie for
hours being massaged and cosseted by maids. She could only
hope that Kin-chao, still playing the part of an unpleasant
imperious matriarch, wouldn't require too much attention
before allowing Safia to collapse into exhausted sleep.

Once home, Safia could let Farhat and Kin-chao occupy
themselves with each other, each believing she had the upper
hand.

ii

When they reached a spot where the road branched, in sight
of Third City, Ti-Mal dismissed the wet nurse.

"B-but I thought we were going to the Vornian border," the
woman said. "You told the soldiers—"

"What has that got to do with anything?" Ti-Mal said. "I
started feeling my milk coming back after we stopped to sleep
at noon. It's a waste of money to pay you for doing what I
can do even better." She took the baby, cuddling him against
her in a vast display of motherly devotion.

"Lady, I don't think you can be sure—"

"I'll pay you half of what we agreed on."

"Half! You drag me out in the middle of the night, nearly

kill me rushing off at breakneck speed, then think you're going to cheat me out of my pay? I'll have my full pay plus half again as much for my trouble!"

"Three-quarters, and no more."

"Full pay plus a third."

Safia knew that the nurse had been counting on a lengthy well-paid term of employment; she had let slip as much while the two women were alone earlier. Ti-Mal's temperament and disposition were nothing to her; she had worked for scores just like her, so sour that their milk curdled in their children's stomachs. Also, Nyo was a nice-enough looking man, and might even be lured away from Ti-Mal if certain things went right—an observation that caused Safia to look at Nyo with different eyes. In the end, Kin-chao paid her the entire sum, minus the cost of the room at the inn, and the woman went away pleased with her bargain.

"I would have paid her ten times that if I thought she needed to be bribed to keep her mouth shut," Kin-chao told Safia. "But I am glad to have saved the money."

The baby stirred sleepily as Safia took him from Kin-chao. "I'll go to the House of Children. You and Nyo go ahead to Madam Farhat's. It's easy enough to find—just ask any passer-by."

Kin-chao nodded. Safia stood for a moment watching as she and Nyo walked on down the main branch of the road. In First City, the Hyacinth Shadow World was set off by a low wooden wall painted bluish purple, surrounding it and making it into a city within a city. There was no such division in Third City, but all such establishments did have the traditional blue-purple pillars flanking the front doors and Madam Farhat's were by far the largest and finest. Kin-chao and Nyo would have no trouble locating the place.

She sat down, felt in her sleeve pocket for a strand of scarlet silk she had put there before they had begun their journey. Carefully, she knotted it around the baby's left wrist. As a safeguard, she also braided a single strand with a few hairs behind his left ear, making certain that it was well hidden.

"If the stories are true, you aren't any more of Yassai's

blood than I am," she told the drowsy child. "But he's convinced you are, and that makes it so."

She got up, shifted the baby so his weight wouldn't make her ribs ache too much, and started down the branch of the road that led to the House of Children.

iii

Madam Farhat was all cordiality, all solicitude, as she made her guest comfortable. Her female guest, that is—the man Nyo she relegated to the kitchen as soon as Kin-chao had informed her of his origins. Though truly, the fellow did not look in the least like one of the dung eaters. . . .

No matter. Kin-chao was her problem, not the man. Farhat looked forward to dealing with her. She must be a veritable treasure of highly interesting information. Farhat anticipated that Kin-chao would not impart it willingly, but would attempt to keep the best portions to herself. Selfish of her, but expectable. Farhat relished the challenge. Generously, she provided plenty of strong hot wine, using the largest cups she dared and still stay within the bounds of propriety. Even though Kin-chao attacked a plate of food as if she had not had anything decent to eat since leaving First City, Farhat knew the wine would take effect before long. She appeared to match Kin-chao cup for cup but in reality was drinking sparingly. They ate and drank for the better part of an hour before she dismissed the servants and smoothly shifted from polite conversation to the serious matter that had brought these people from First City to her door.

"Now, my dear Kin-chao. I can hardly credit the story you bring me. The Sublime Heir stolen by Faceless Ones, taken who knows where. The First Lord prostrated with grief. Safia disfigured. Such a great loss. She was my finest daughter, clearly a courtesan of the first class anywhere, even in First City. She had no equal in all of Monserria."

"I would have been honored to have had her as one of my own," Kin-chao said, busy with her eating sticks. "These fried prawns are delicious. Tender crust and not at all greasy.

"I do pride myself on my kitchen. And you say there is, ah, now a baby to be taken from the House of Children?"

"A very important baby." Kin-chao laughed a little tipsily. "One might say, the most important baby in Third Province. Or even in First Province."

"I understand. Have some more vegetables."

"I couldn't eat another bite. Exquisite sauce. You must let your cook tell me his secret. More wine, though."

"Take the flask. There's plenty more. I can hardly wait to see Safia. She was always more like a real daughter than any of my other girls." Farhat sighed. Her mind was busy with balancing the price Ladylord had already paid for Safia's services against what she was entitled to ask now, particularly since Safia had come to grief in the Ladylord's service, so to speak, always providing Javere returned from the fool's errand she had gone on. . . . "The thought of such beauty ruined—"

"It's very depressing, I know. But don't be too sad. She could take your place one day, if you should ever retire. She'd need training, naturally, but Safia is very clever. It was she who persuaded a certain lady to give up her child for safekeeping. Of course, it was my idea." Kin-chao patted her stomach and belched delicately.

Farhat made sympathetic noises. "Another flask? I suppose you are right. Tell me more about this, ah, certain lady."

Kin-chao took the fresh flask of wine and filled her cup. "What more is there to tell? She bore a child, when no one before her had done so. Of course, there *is* a story—" She leaned forward, swaying a little; her features had taken on a soft and smudgy look.

"Really? Oh, you must share the story with me!"

"It is just pillow information, not to be relied upon. A maid told her lover, a minor official in the court, who told one of my girls, who told me. It seems that a certain lady went out one day disguised as a courtesan and visited the deep part of the prison where condemned prisoners are kept. Nobody knows for sure what happened down there, but nine months

ater—" Kin-chao sat up abruptly, snapping her fingers.
"What am I saying! That story was about another lady en-
irely! Where is my memory? What could I have been think-
ng of? My dear Farhat, your wine seems to have gone to my
head! I beg you to dismiss what I just said for the nonsense
t is!"

"I have forgotten it already. You are tired. You've been
hrough a shocking ordeal, being stopped on the road and not
knowing what moment was going to be your last."

"How understanding you are. If it hadn't been for this—"
Kin-chao pulled the red pass from her bodice, just enough to
show a flash of gold lettering.

In spite of herself, Farhat's eyes widened. What a valuable
hing— Certainly too valuable to leave in Kin-chao's hands!
Perhaps a stealthy visit in the night. . . .

A maidservant slipped through the door and whispered to
Farhat.

"Well, bring her in at once!" she exclaimed. She turned to
Kin-chao. "Safia has arrived—" But the other woman had
fallen asleep where she sat, a small bubble on her lips as she
snored gently. Farhat smiled to herself and poured another
cup of wine from her own flask—a much weaker beverage—
and drank it off to the honor and memory of Javere qa
Hyasti.

How fortunate that she learned that trick from the Ladylord, she thought, when she discovered herself offering to provide pillow information without even setting the price. She
hadn't noticed at the time they were drinking from flasks
with different designs.

She gently removed the red pass from Kin-chao's bodice,
putting it into her own for safekeeping. Then she rang for servants to come and carry Kin-chao off to prepare her for bed.
Then, after checking the doors and making certain that she
was alone, Farhat raised her skirts and performed a brief joy-
ous dance.

Now she knew an important part of what Kin-chao knew,
and she had the pass as well. Kin-chao must have lost it, too
bad. And she knew everything that went on in Third City,

which her guest would *not* get from her. Not easily, at any rat

Lutfu wallowed with the lowest-class women and babble freely to them about anything that came into his head. Ho fortunate she felt that she always maintained some girls that sort on her staff instead of snobbishly limiting he daughters to the upper classes alone, as too many Hyacint Shadow mothers do! Lutfu won't aid Yassai in his search, sh thought, not beyond what was required for show, for th coming of the Sublime Heir interfered with his own plans succeed to First Lordship himself.

But how could she best use the information? Perhaps Saf would provide a clue. Such a pity, such loveliness destroye forever. But take her own place? That light-minded creatur whose entire world was singing and dancing and pleasing man in bed? Hardly!

Still, she had to admit Safia was clever enough to have su vived where another would have perished. And someho she'd convinced Kin-chao that she was more clever than sh really was. And Farhat would be glad to see her again, in spi of what she must look like now.

Madam Farhat rearranged her clothing, sat down, an prepared herself to greet without flinching the ruined beaut who had once been her best courtesan.

iv

Sigon the Strategist paced back and forth in the garden, wai ing for Lutfu to emerge from the Residence. He discipline himself to make it appear that he walked for the sheer plea sure of the bright cloudless day, observing the beauty of th arrangement of trees, shrubs, rocks, graveled paths. Despit the nearly leafless condition of most of the vegetation, the e fect was not one of barrenness but rather one of quiescenc of sleep before the awakening in spring. At any other tim Sigon would have drawn peace and tranquility from the o dered perfection here. But now, peace and tranquility seeme destined to be strangers to the Third Province and all its inhabitants.

Strategist! he thought with savage mockery. He hadn't even been able to keep his Ladylord's holdings out of greedy grasping hands before she had a fair chance to legalize her inheritance. Lutfu and Nao-Pei grew more brazen, more arrogant with every day. She flaunted her lover openly, and he was wringing Third Province dry. No wonder people buried their meager savings lest Lutfu's tax collectors come and steal even the last scrap of copper. Silver grows scarce and there were no more gold coins to be found anywhere; they were all in his—in Third Lord's treasury. It was said the tax collectors spared no one, even to the lowest toiler in the rice fields.

Lutfu's soldiers and their severe treatment of any dissenter had caused the rumors of revolt to lessen for the moment, but that spark was far from extinguished. It just smoldered, waiting for the right moment to burst into flames. Also it was fortunate that Nao-Pei felt safe enough just now that she didn't think to overthrow Lutfu and take the Third Lordship for herself and Sakano. And why shouldn't she feel secure? She could leave the details of management to Lutfu while he milked every drop of wealth from the land, dally with her lover night and day, and then when she judged the time to be right, give Sakano a nudge in the right direction. She'd present herself as a lady more grievously wronged than any other person by the excesses of the hated Governor Lutfu of the Third Province, take the power—and the fortune Lutfu had considerably gathered for her—and she and Sakano together would surely make Third Province long for Lutfu back again.

And now the First Lord's red-uniformed guards had come, bringing news of fresh disaster with them like the wash of an evil tide. The Sublime Heir, stolen from his bed by the Faceless Ones! Only stiff military discipline kept Sigon from shuddering openly.

Yassai was an old man; at best the prospect of an underage heir brought with it the certainty of a regency. The panel of regents would be composed of the other four lords plus a

fifth member in case of a tied vote. This was infinitely to b
preferred to one of Yassai's nephews ascending to First Lord
ship. And Sigon knew which one would inherit. Lutfu, a
Governor of the Third Province, was now definitely the fron
runner, if the worst had befallen the Sublime Heir.

Sigon could not envision a worse fate for Monserria.

Therefore, the Sublime Heir must be found. And therefore
Lutfu would do everything in his power—short of ope
defiance—to make certain that the Sublime Heir was *no*
found, would never be found, would never be replaced by Yas
sai and that young girl he had married, about whom ther
were unsavory rumors. . . .

In Sigon's opinion, the Faceless Ones most likely had th
baby hidden away somewhere in the depths of First City, an
would be making ransom demands very soon. But with th
Faceless Ones nothing was ever certain. Hence the wide
spread search. Sigon's eyes narrowed in thought as a chillin
realization struck him. Third Province was the last place any
one would bring the missing Sublime Heir; therefore, Thir
Province was the most likely place to begin looking for him

"Sigon!" Lutfu, resplendently dressed, stepped out onto th
veranda surrounding the Residence. "No, stay there. I'll com
down and walk with you. It's a nice day, but we'll have snov
before too much longer. One of my knees tells me so." He de
scended the red-lacquered stairs, wincing a little and favor
ing his left leg. The painted Guardians on the doors behind
him seemed to glower threateningly at his back.

"I suppose you've heard the news?" he said. He and Sigo
followed the path through the garden, across the bridge span
ning the little stream. Lutfu paused a moment to admire a
bush with shiny dark green leaves. Unlike other plants, it wa
at its best in winter; soon it would blaze with scarlet berries

"Yes, Sire," Sigon said. "I couldn't believe what I heard."

"Well, it's true. The Sublime Heir is gone, vanished. The
hadn't heard a word from the abductors by the time the rid
ers started out for the provinces. So my uncle is widening th
search. His guards have scoured First Province from end to
end with no success."

"Am I to understand that you wish me to organize the search parties in Third Province?"

Lutfu glanced up at Sigon, eyes gleaming. A crafty smile hovered at the corners of his mouth. "I want you to lead the search, General," he said.

Sigon bowed. "And will you go with me, Governor?"

"Alas, no." Lutfu gestured at his left leg. "If only I could, I would start at once. My knee— But I am fortunate in having such an able assistant in Third Province's Admirable Strategist. You realize I don't believe for a moment the Faceless Ones would be stupid enough to bring the Sublime Heir here, where I rule. But if by some chance he should be located, my instructions to you are to bring him here, to me."

"But Governor—"

"To me." Lutfu's face set in an unpleasant expression. "If he is found in Third Province I will overcome my infirmity and return him to my uncle personally. I don't want anything to happen to him in the meantime."

Of course not, Sigon thought. Lutfu didn't want anything to happen to him that he himself had not personally arranged and overseen. . . . "As you wish," he said.

Lutfu cleared his throat. His expression lightened. "Do you have children, General?" he said.

"Yes," Sigon said, a little startled. "Three sons, several daughters, and five grandchildren."

"I rejoice for you. With all this unfortunate business about my uncle's son, and the abduction, it has come to me that it is time I had children of my own." The unpleasant expression settled on his face again. "I believe I shall begin that undertaking straightway."

"Yes, Governor," Sigon said politely, knowing exactly what Lutfu meant and wondering what else he had not yet said.

"Please search most carefully, General. Most carefully and thoroughly. I want you to scour every village, every farm, every baron's holding, even if it takes a long time to find them all. Take good men with you, men you can trust completely. And—" he laid his hand on Sigon's arm

"—please make the Baron Sakano qa Chava your second-
in-command."

Without allowing any expression at all to cross his face
Sigon nodded. "An excellent choice, Sire. The Baron Sakano
is well acquainted with the countryside. He has wide holdings
in Third Province, and goes out frequently to see to them."

"Not frequently enough of late. His estates need his attention. Surely you can carry on the search while he takes
care of all his business, ei?"

Sigon bowed. "Of course, Governor. With your permission, I will leave tomorrow.

"Today, within the hour if you can. And General—remember to take all the time you need."

v

Safia gazed at the sleeping infant. Yes, Madam Farhat had
chosen the right one. Though the thread of red silk had vanished from around his wrist the one hidden in the hair behind
his ear was still there, undiscovered.

She was glad she had thought of this little precaution.
There had been several other babies roughly the same age at
the House of Children, two of them boys, and moving such
an obvious mark from one child to another had been easy to
anticipate. Without the second bit of silk to signal which was
the correct one, the Sublime Heir to First Lordship might
have ended up being traded to some middle-class man and
wife with no sons and too many daughters, or coughing his
young life away in the rice fields while a peasant's brat lived
in luxury in Stendas Castle.

She glanced at Nyo. From the moment Madam Farhat
and her servant had brought the baby into the section of her
house reserved for pregnant ladies, ladies who had recently
given birth, and those children she was grooming for future
use, Nyo had appointed himself the child's guardian.

"Baby has full belly," Nyo said. "Big appetite, squalled and
sucked very strong. Very good, very healthy."

"He's really quite safe here, Nyo. You don't have to watch him every minute."

"I like to." He sat beside the bed. Every time the baby moved he made sure the covers were still in place, all snug and warm.

She looked at him speculatively. Ever since Kin-chao's servants had brought him enough hot water to scrub the accumulated grime of years from his hide and he had begun to eat good nourishing food, his appearance had improved steadily. Now he bathed every day, luxuriating in the hot water, and had become quite fastidious about the cleanliness of his person. Looking at him, no one would ever connect this faithful guardian with the dung eater who had found her, half-dead, and who had literally saved her life.

She steeled herself. She owed him a special debt and knew of only one way to repay it. Perhaps it would not be so bad. She had had to do worse in her time.

"Nyo," she said softly. He looked up. She smiled down at him.

Uncomprehending at first, he only stared. Then, as her meaning became clear, he grew flustered. "Is too much, wonderful lady," he said. "Also, I am ashamed because I cannot." Shyly, he opened his garments and showed her. Someone, not an expert, had made a eunuch of him, and he lacked both Fruit and much of the Night-Growing Mushroom as well.

"And you think the less of yourself because of this? No, you do not know how well you please me, just as you are. Come," she said. "Let us lie down together and share our warmth in friendliness." Oddly, his mutilation roused a faint spark of desire in her. There were many ways of satisfying desire, none involving the invasion she now loathed and detested. She could show him. . . .

Later, in her bed, he slept curled close to her, one arm thrown over her protectively, his hand resting on her breast.

Still awake, she idly stroked the stubble of hair that was beginning to grow back on his shaved skull. It was unexpectedly fine and soft. She hoped he believed her when she told him how much he pleased her and how grateful she was for him even in his impotent and incomplete state.

Especially in his impotent and incomplete state.

He would never know how much her gesture had cost her for she knew that she would never willingly give a man access to her body again for the rest of her life. Also, she was not a woman who found pleasure in another woman's embrace and despite everything, she did appreciate a man's warmth and presence. She would be content to remain with Nyo, both outcasts because of what life had dealt them. Perhaps together they could build a life of sorts.

15

i

*J*averri!" Ivo said, startled out of every trace of composure he was trying to show. "You have found her? What do you mean, wizard?"

Wande-hari shuddered, drawing back from the unclean touch of that snarling bestial mind. My sweet Javerri, gone feral and so dangerous she should be put in a cage? No, oh no. . . . Chakei crouched by his side, whimpering.

"I mean that something dreadful has happened to the Ladylord," he said heavily, laying his hand on Chakei's crest.

"What happens?" Vorsa demanded. "Has something to do with clay doll so like little Dekla, and mage with holy herbs, veh?"

"Alas, yes," Wande-hari said. "It's all my fault, I'm the one to blame—"

"Not you, sir," Ezzat said.

"I chose Halit to be my apprentice," the old magician said, his voice breaking on the word. "I knew there were dark areas in his mind, things hidden that he didn't want me to know about, but I thought I could control him. . . . "

"Let us not waste time in useless regrets," Ivo said. "We must find Javerri. Tell me where she is and I will go to her."

Wande-hari shook his head. "Alas, no, my friend. You must trust me when I tell you that she is safe enough for the moment where she is; indeed, she is safer than we are, in less peril for her life. We have more pressing matters to attend to. Halit is escaping—may be gone by now for all I know. He is hiding from me—his mind, which ordinarily I could locate—and it will take some effort on my part to find him." He put his trembling hand to his forehead. "Furthermore, when I cast my thoughts outward I discovered dragons on their way here. I know where the real nest is now, but I do not think we can do whatever we must do with the eggs before the dragons reach us."

"Then Ezzat, Fen-mu, Nali, and I will strive to divert the dragons from this spot." Ivo quickly checked his bowstring and arrows and Nali stepped forward to secure Steel Fury on Ivo's back.

Vorsa watched, hands on hips. Then he nodded, a decision reached. "Veh, I go fight dragons with good soldiers!" he said. "Elder Brother find naughty mage who does bad things to little Dekla and abuses holy herbs also. Hit him very hard in my name."

"Vorsa has a good idea," Wande-hari said. "Normally I would not like to split our forces, but I think we must. Let us hope you all are successful and come back quickly."

Ivo's eyebrows drew together in a frown. A muscle worked in his cheek. Then he nodded assent and without a word turned to retrace their steps. In this country, on this kind of rocky ground, finding the mage's trail would not be easy but Wande-hari knew the archer's eyes were keen. Also, he resolved to send as much aid and direction as he could spare in hopes that Ivo could receive it, to make his task easier.

"I will go with Shab Vorsa," Ezzat said. His voice trembled.

"Our plan of action becomes clear now," the mage said.

"Lek will continue to watch over the clay doll, and keep it from harm. Ezzat, you stay here with him instead of going with Vorsa for you are no warrior and will just get in the way. Chakei and I will deal with the eggs."

"Fighting dragons very much fun, almost like *sarhandas*," Vorsa said, grinning. "Also, I think hunting naughty and wicked mage very pleasant for Elder Brother when he finds him. Not so pleasant for mage, though. Come, brave soldiers. We go hunting now."

The shab strode off in the direction Wande-hari indicated. For a moment the mage watched him. Ivo had already disappeared from view. Such danger for such brave young men, he thought. Perhaps it is better for all that they do not know the full extent of it.

Come, Chakei he said. **Thou and I have work to do as well. The real nest of dragon eggs lies up there, hidden in the rocks.**

ladylord?

Later, I promise. We will find her

ii

Despite Wande-hari's best efforts, Chakei went wandering off again, up the side of the rumbling mountain, and Wande-hari had to locate the nest without him. Fortunately, the magician, having seen it clearly, was able to go directly to the spot which was obscured beneath a low overhang of shale. It contained three eggs.

Yes, these were the right ones—crimson-spotted, beginning to rock a little as the infant dragons inside knocked at the shell, seeking a way out. If Chakei did not return soon he might have to carry these eggs himself, Wande-hari thought. Just as the old man reached down to pick up an egg and judge for himself how heavy it was, Chakei came down into the nest area, bringing a hail of loosened stones with him. His winter-dark hide glowed dull scarlet in the uncertain light, and his crest was fully erect. Wande-hari was struck again at how closely he resembled the crimson dragons, and yet how far removed he was from them.

find fire cave i, bring eggs also i

Puzzled, Wande-hari laid his hand on the shell of the one for which he had been reaching. What did a fire cave have to do with the eggs? But then, surely the Dragon-warrior knew what he was doing. He had been the only one of them not to take a false step since they had entered the barrier of fog into this desolate land. The embryo, alarmed at its shell being touched, shifted violently. **Carry them as carefully as you can, trying not to disturb them any more than you have to,** he said. **It wouldn't do to have one of them break out prematurely.**

Chakei picked up the three eggs, cradling them in his huge arms and making the first sound other than hisses or roars Wande-hari had ever heard him utter—a kind of crooning buzz—until the occupants grew quieter. Then, he turned and started back up the mountainside. More slowly, Wande-hari followed Chakei's trail. It was easy to find, and not as difficult to climb as Wande-hari had feared. The Dragon-warrior had knocked most of the loose shale out of the way, leaving a fairly solid path.

The air burned in his throat, growing hotter and more stifling with every step he took upward. Here and there, fire danced on stray bits of tree branch. Wande-hari gathered his robe tightly about him, lest it burst into flame. The mountain rumbled again.

Chakei waited impatiently beside a rift in the side of the mountain. Light—fire?—radiated from within. **come inside little way, too much hot**

Without hesitation, he followed Chakei into the fire cave. Now more than ever he dared not relinquish the mind thread binding them together. Also, his curiosity aroused, he very much wanted to see what came next.

The walls gleamed in the red light. Shining strands hung from the ceiling—thread gold, leached out from the mountain's veins in an earlier time, when fire belched forth in earnest. A treasure fit to ransom the First Lord himself hung within arm's reach. What a display that must have been—not this feeble flicker at the heart of the cave, like a bed of embers on a gigantic scale. Even so, Wande-hari thought, the fire remaining was hot enough to singe his eyebrows where he stood. He wiped perspiration from his brow and leaned against the wall, conscious again of growing fatigue. The stone was hot enough to injure if he touched it too long. Wearily, he shoved himself upright again.

Chakei moved deep into the fire until he found a place he liked and set the eggs down into what might have been a puddle of molten rock. Then he crouched in the flames, unmindful of the heat, staring at them.

One of the eggs cracked and exploded. Its contents splattered, sizzling, in every direction, destroying the embryo in a gout of smoke. Chakei looked up.

was she-egg, too bad he said mournfully.

Another mystery solved, Wande-hari thought. Apparently only males could withstand the enormous heat required to anneal the embryos into Dragon-warriors. Therefore, no females among them. He nodded in understanding. ****Are you nearly done with this?**** he said. ****I can't stay here much longer.****

not done yet, go, bring i, yes

The mage retreated from the fire cave. The outside air, hot as it was, felt incredibly cool and refreshing to him by contrast. Wande-hari inhaled deeply. He slumped to the ground and leaned against a convenient boulder.

Summoning what strength remained to him, he cast his thoughts up and outward. Shab Vorsa and the soldiers—yes, they had found the dragons. They must do the best they could. He concentrated on Halit, and on Ivo.

Suddenly Halit came into focus for him and he had to draw back abruptly lest the other mage realize he had been found. With more caution, Wande-hari renewed the contact. Yes, it was as he suspected. Halit obviously thought himself beyond reach so he had dropped the mental shield that until now had hidden him from Wande-hari's vision. He located Ivo, noted gratefully that the archer was having no trouble following

Halit's trail. He must have thought himself safe from this avenue of approach as well. Ivo was moving rapidly, using what cover the land provided, a good hunter intent on his prey. Wande-hari closed his eyes. He was tired, so tired—

A noise, wakening him. He had not meant to doze. He wondered how long he had slept. Chakei emerged from the entrance to the cave, holding an egg in his arms. The red spots had now run together and the egg had become an even deep crimson. Wande-hari scrambled to his feet.

The Dragon-warrior placed the egg on the ground. It was smoking, and emitted cracking noises. Wande-hari expected to see it shatter in the relative coolness and groped in his sleeve pocket for a strand of sunlight to heat the spot where the egg lay. When it didn't split asunder at once, he relaxed cautiously. Chakei went back into the cave and returned with the other egg.

rest, must cool Chakei patted the eggs in what Wande-hari thought an unusually possessive manner. **take later when cool i** He began to buzz at them again.

A suspicion grew in the mage's mind. Dragon-warriors, always male, no direct way to propagate their line— **Those have become your sons, haven't they?**

Chakei looked up at the magician and his eyes were fathomless as pieces of obsidian. **yes**

Will you let them go to First Lord and to Shab Vorsa?
desert man yes, understand larac-vil
First Lord? We would not be here if he had not sent us.
not like i

Argument, Wande-hari knew, would be useless. He set the matter aside for the moment; he could only hope, when the time came, that the Dragon-warrior could be persuaded to give up his progeny so that Javerri could be confirmed in her lordship of Third Province.

If, that is, Javerri could be brought back from the horrible place she now inhabited. . . .

Come, Chakei, he said. **Let us return. We still have much to do, you and I.**

iii

"Ho-ho!" Shab Vorsa laughed aloud at the sight of four dark scarlet dragons lumbering toward him. "Now we have fun, veh! You, Nali, go that way—" he gestured to the right "—and Fen-mu go other way. We muddle up heads so they not know which one of us to bite!"

The two soldiers moved apart, hefting their short spears, and Vorsa tightened his grip on his sword. The scarlet dragons stopped, their heads swinging from right to left, looking at them. They began to whistle and hoot and one uttered a brief *whoop!* like a sneeze. Of a certainty, Vorsa thought in his own language, these most exquisite and very dangerous creatures cannot decide what to do about us. I would not like being caught in such sharp teeth but at least my ending would be quick. Let it be as the gods will decide.

He took a deep breath and, shouting a wordless cry of challenge, raced headlong toward the dragons, waving the sword over his head. As he had hoped, the big creatures skittered out of his way. They were not used to anything that does not run away at their approach, he thought. Now perhaps they would go away and forget why they returned to the nesting ground, at least long enough for us to escape from them. If the gods were pleased with Shab Vorsa. If not—

Purely by accident, two of the dragons turned in the direction of Fen-mu, so close they were nearly trampling him, and Vorsa shifted in midstride to rush to his aid. Nali, taking his cue from Vorsa, shouted and waved as he ran toward the other two dragons, brandishing his spear, and they turned back the way they had come, at least for the moment. Then he, too, ran to his companion's assistance.

"Ho!" Vorsa slashed at a dragon's hindquarters. It shuffled sideways, blundering into its companion, and turned to face its tormentor. Fen-mu jabbed at the dragon closest to him. The dragon gave a full-throated roar of pain and surprise, swatted him aside and plucked the spear from its hide with its five-fingered forepaw. Then it reached for Fen-mu.

A man's scream filled the air, more desperate than any
Shab Vorsa had ever heard, and then Fen-mu dangled limply
in the dragon's grasp. Vorsa slashed again, drawing blood,
and danced out of reach before the beast could catch him. He
heard a crunching sound, dared risk a glance upward and
wished he hadn't. Fen-mu's body lacked a head. The second
dragon turned and snatched at its companion's prize like a
child trying to take a sweetmeat away from another. In a moment they had torn Fen-mu's body to shreds and the two
dragons were roaring loudly enough to deafen as they fought
each other over the pieces. The stench of dragon blood smote
Vorsa, making him retch. Nali's spear suddenly appeared,
lodged in the eye of the dragon Vorsa had wounded. The
beast's roaring turned to a shriek and it staggered back, swatting uselessly at the spear. The other dragon moved forward.
Its jaws opened.

"Run, sir!" Nali shouted. "The others are coming!"

Through the dust kicked up by the fighting dragons, Vorsa
could dimly make out the first two that had initially been startled out of the way. Silent, predators on the hunt, they approached with a gliding speed that appalled him. Gods, he
thought, he must be finished. No one could outrun such a
creature. Protect Lidian and be with his sons!

To Vorsa's astonishment the dragons ignored both of the
insignificant humans, passing them by. It must be the smell
of the blood that attracts them, he thought, swallowing hard,
and the fact that between us, good Nali and he made scarcely
a mouthful. He thanked the gods that the dragons were not
above dining upon the flesh of their brothers and preferred
a good meal to a tidbit such as they were, and he promised
many offerings if they would but let him live to see his home
once more.

He and Nali fled gratefully, leaving the three dragons feasting on the body of the fourth. Perhaps this would occupy
them until his companions could regroup and leave the nesting ground area for good.

iv

Ivo peered from the inadequate concealment of a lace-leaf thorn tree. There! Halit was in sight, not hurrying. No doubt he thought himself safe by now, and the rest of his companions dead and being digested by dragons.

The archer nocked an arrow to the string. He would aim only to wound, to slow Halit down and capture him. It was a long shot from here, but Ivo knew he could make it if the Ancestor was with him. And if not, if he killed the mage by mistake, then no harm done— He drew the string to his cheek, then to his ear, sighted carefully, and released. The twanging of the bowstring resounded through the heavy air like a note from a deep-toned harp. Halit started, jerked around, and the arrow passed by him harmlessly.

He took a step toward Ivo, and smiled. "Well!" he called across the space separating them. "Ivo. Not dead yet?"

Ivo also moved forward. "No thanks to you and the drug you put in the water." He reached for another arrow.

"That won't be necessary," Halit said with a deprecatory gesture. "I am an intelligent man. You won't have to shoot me. Unless it is your intention to kill me, that is. I don't think your Ladylord would like that."

Ivo ground his teeth together. "What have you done to her? Wande-hari said—"

"Oh, so the old fool has discovered at last what I've been up to?"

"I think so, though he won't tell me the details. He did send me after you, though."

"I underestimated you both. That was always a failing of mine. Well, come ahead, Ladylord's husband."

Curious, the archer thought, the emphasis he put on the word husband. "I ask again, what have you done to her? I will not ask a third time."

"What will you do to me? Shoot me with an arrow? Not unless your aim improves. Ah, yes, I see you have her sword. I can see the glint of the haft over your shoulder. That means my little clay lady has been discovered for what she is. Will you behead me with her sword? You should have remained with the clay doll, archer. At least that one is still virginal."

Ivo's body shook and alternate waves of heat and cold passed through him. "Your lies do not help your chances of making it back to First Province alive."

"Lies? I do not lie." By now the magician had come close enough to Ivo that neither had to raise their voices to be heard. The magician chuckled, a chilling sound, and Ivo recognized the madness that had finally broken free in him. "Archer, I have just come from your Ladylord's embrace. I held her in my arms and ravished her thoroughly and with great pleasure. I think she enjoyed it as well for she quit fighting me soon after I had impaled her. My Jade Stalk was never so hard which was a good thing, for her maidenhead was very tough and I had to push hard to break it. Her nipples are exquisite, though. They taste very sweet, by the way. I suggest you plunge your Jade Stalk into her clay likeness if you want someone who is unbreached. Also, I wonder if you would find mud or dust inside the doll. You would ease my curiosity!" He tittered and a fleck of foamy saliva appeared at one corner of his mouth. "I leave her to you. A word from you and I will make the clay lady your willing slave."

"I will not kill you, madman, regardless of what you say." Ivo's voice sounded shaky and unconvincing, even in his own ears. He clutched the bow with both hands to keep himself from drawing Steel Fury and rushing forward to put an end to this prattling fool with his unendurable insults, once and for all.

"Alas, for I will not return to First Province with you, nor anywhere else. I have another journey in mind. You are close enough, however, for me to take you with me—"

Too late, Ivo realized what Halit's purpose had been in getting so close, recognized what he held in his hand. He turned away to flee just as the hand came down, hurling the pebble to explode at the magician's feet. . . .

V

Only Lek and the doll waited in the place where Wande-hari had left them. "Where is Ezzat?" Wande-hari said.

"Gone after Lord Ivo. He apologized but thought he might be of more help there than here. What now?" Lek asked.

"We will wait only long enough for Vorsa, Fen-mu, and Nali to return. Then we will leave this place and find Javerri. Lord Ivo will have taken Halit prisoner by that time. Or killed him." Wande-hari hoped his voice did not betray his doubt that any of them would live long enough to reach the fog barrier. "Now I am glad Ezzat went to his aid."

"Are those the Dragon-warrior eggs?"

"Yes, treated in the fire of the mountain. There were three but one broke."

"Well, two will make a balanced load on a *plandal* when we get back outside."

The clay simulacrum stirred. "Has your prisoner been giving you any trouble?" With the doll's movement Wande-hari could see that Lek had carefully tied it to a nearby tree.

"No, she's been very quiet. I daresay she needs your presence or Lord Ivo's to start her up again." Lek gazed past Wande-hari. "Shab Vorsa returns! But there is only one man with him—"

Wande-hari turned. Still too far away to see who was with him. Ah. Nali. Poor Fen-mu. "Untie the doll from the tree," he told the physician, "but keep good hold of the rope. We must leave this place at once and we must take her with us."

They started down the slope of the mountain and Vorsa and Nali veered from their course to join them. "Hurry, hurry, good Uncle!" Vorsa said, panting. "The dragons are eating each other but ones who are left be after us soon, veh!"

"This way!" Wande-hari said. He led them over the shale to the spot where Javerri—the real Javerri—had last been seen. "Now let me search again for her with my mind—"

The cave was closer than he had dared hope. How had Halit had the time to choose it with such care? This near, the

pulsating madness of the animal that had once been Javerri
throbbed so brightly the magician wondered that none of the
rest of them could sense it. Chakei raised his head, his crest
coming erect. Yes, of course Chakei would know.

ladylord?

Alas, yes, I fear so. I will need you with me.

The Dragon-warrior placed the eggs carefully on the
ground and started off at a lope. **here, here, find ladylord
i**

Wande-hari scrambled after him to the cave entrance, pausing inside to let his eyes adjust to the gloom. He stopped, too
stunned to move. He scarcely recognized the Ladylord,
Javerri, his beloved niece, in the wild thing that lay writhing
on the floor of the cave.

If Javerri had not been securely tied, she would surely have
attacked him. Her eyes reflected light the way a beast's eyes
do, and a red flame of madness danced in their depths. She
snarled and growled through the gag in her mouth, shaking
her head violently and straining against her bonds. She was
naked, Wande-hari thought numbly, but one did not notice.
She was, after all, just an animal. "Javerri—"

At the sound of his voice her struggles intensified. The
growling became a muffled howl and Wande-hari knew that
she would have mindlessly torn him apart if she could have
reached him. He shuddered; Shab Vorsa and the two soldiers
facing the dragons had been an easy task by comparison with
what confronted him now. Chakei crept close and laid his
great hand gently on Javerri's hair, crooning. To Wande-hari's
surprise she grew perceptibly calmer, staring at the Dragon-
warrior as if wondering where she could have seen his like before. This opportunity might not come again; the mage prepared the simplest of sleep spells and cast it. The red flame
in her eyes grew dim, and she relaxed into slumber. She began
to look more like herself, though pale and haggard. Even so,
he dared not try to look into her mind for fear of what he
might find there.

He gathered the pleasure instruments, not allowing himself
to wonder where they had come from or how they happened

to have come to Halit's hand that he made such use of them
accounted for all the niches in the box, and then set every
thing aside. To his relief, Javerri didn't seem to be badly dam
aged physically, though it would take some time before Lek
could come close enough to examine her. If ever, Wande
hari thought. He hoped his suspicions about the clay dol
were correct and that Javerri would not stay like this—a wild
animal never to be tamed—until she died.

Bring her outside, Chakei, while she is still sleeping.

The Dragon-warrior lifted Javerri's slight form and cradled
it in his arms as tenderly as he had held his egg children.

hurt

Wande-hari didn't know whether Chakei meant Javerri or
himself. **We will try to heal her.** He swallowed hard. **If
we cannot, I will make sure she never feels pain again.**

It was no more than anyone would do for any animal in
agony.

They made their way down the slope more slowly than
they had ascended. By sheer force of will, Wande-hari had re
gained most of his composure by the time they came in sight
of their companions. Vorsa, Lek, and Nali waited, anxious
and with growing fear and anger as Chakei carried Javerri to
ward them and they could begin to understand, if only a lit
tle, what Halit had done to her.

"Ho," Shab Vorsa exclaimed softly. "Ho. How much for
tunate Elder Brother goes ahead, does not see, veh."

"I daresay his reason might have come unhinged as well
and I can deal with only one case of madness at a time. I have
cast sleep upon her now, but I assure you if she were to wake
and find herself among so many men, these bonds would
prove inadequate to keep her from doing us—or herself—
great harm. Chakei, put her down, please, and then step aside
Guard your children—I mean, the eggs. Lek, bring the sim
ulacrum here."

The physician hurried to obey. Unresisting, the clay dol
followed like a pet on a leash. Vorsa and Nali watched, un
comprehending.

"Why you do this, Uncle? We waste time. Leave false Dekla, come away from this place."

"I must do this because Halit had to have used parts of Javerri herself to make the replica—hair, tears, whatever else he could take from her. These must be returned before we can hope to have her back with us."

Lek tried, without success; when the physician tugged at the rope, trying to bring it closer, the doll balked and struggled so hard Wande-hari bade him stop for fear it would damage itself. Once its "skin" was breached, its destruction would be inevitable—and rapid—and Javerri would be lost indeed. Lek could coax it only so close and no more.

"Now we are wasting valuable time," Wande-hari said, fuming. He spoke a word of summons and his eyelids began to burn. *"Look at me!"*

The doll, which heretofore had vacantly avoided giving anybody a direct glance, now gazed straight at him.

"Come here!"

The doll responded in a jerky, uncoordinated fashion, like a marionette with tangled strings. A tiny crack appeared at the corner of its left eye, but it took a step forward.

"Closer!"

Another step. The crack widened and a second one appeared at the corner of the doll's right eye. Wande-hari knew he was in a desperate race—could his strength hold out long enough to force the doll close enough before it broke his control by destroying itself with its own eyes? The doll's left cheek split and that eye fell out but not before it had taken a third step. Just a few moments, a little farther until the two could touch—

"Halt!" he cried.

The doll tottered on a step.

"Wait! Stop the doll, Shab Vorsa!" Wande-hari said urgently. "I suspect— I must do something first."

"Ho!" From behind Shab Vorsa grabbed the simulacrum and held it firmly. Where before it had seemed to resist moving toward Javerri, now it struggled to get to her.

Wande-hari closed his eyes, summoned what strength he had left, braced himself for the shock, and entered Javerri' mind. Sleeping, she might be reachable. Ignoring the anima part that was all that remained of her, he headed immediatel for the outer boundaries, the line beyond which it was unwis to go, then found what he was looking for—the breach in th wall. Outside, his physical body trembled and his brow damp ened with sweat. If he had succeeded in merging the simu lacrum with Javerri's physical body, this would have close that breach and Javerri would have been lost forever. So cun ning had her attacker been. . . .

He drew close to the opening. **Javerri, come back!**

Far, far away, he thought he saw something through th mists. Then a very faint, very tiny response.

Uncle?

Yes, it is thy uncle. Come back now. It is safe. I swear t thee on my head.

Thou has never lied to me.

And I do not lie now. Come back, please.

Perhaps. . . .

She wandered closer, a pale wraith in the mists of madnes:

Thou must return, Javerri. Only thou canst bring the re venge thou must desire above all other things of this world.

Yes. But I am tired. So tired.

Come back, he said gently. **There is no rest wher thou art. But here is rest and healing and safety and above al love for thee. Please, come back.**

Thou art a man.

Yes. But I am also thy friend. And thou hast other friend besides, who will never harm thee.

Wilt thou blast with wizard's fire any who tries?

Yes, and a thousand times yes! I swear this also!

Then I will believe thee.

To his infinite relief, she crossed the boundary though sh maintained a distance from him, even in mind speech. Well was that to be wondered at, then? Without leaving her mind guarding lest she panic and rush back across the breach again he directed his body to speak. "Let the doll go now, Vorsa, he heard himself say. The words echoed as if from a great distance. "Quickly. It must touch her."

He opened his physical eyes in time to see Vorsa release the simulacrum. It seemed to hesitate once more, but he gave it a hard shove, and it stumbled forward, falling onto Javerri where she lay on the shale.

Not even Wande-hari was prepared for the way the doll vanished the instant it touched Javerri's body. Its clothing—Javerri's clothing—along with a thick layer of dust settled onto her in a mockery of covering her nakedness. Wande-hari tarried inside Javerri's mind only long enough to determine that the melding of the two had also mended the breach in the boundary, and then he removed himself before his presence could cause her more pain.

Lek, to whom bare flesh was nothing, moved forward. He picked up the garments and began shaking the dust from them. Vorsa came to help and between them they dressed Javerri as if she had been a sleeping child.

Wande-hari sat down heavily before the black dots swarming in his vision ran together. Javerri was breathing more normally now and her color, when Lek had brushed some of the dust from her face, had improved. Before their eyes she was returning, physically at least, from the animal state to something more closely resembling human. He couldn't help but notice that Nali, cheeks flaming, studiously looked elsewhere as Lek and Vorsa covered the nakedness that had not affected any of them before. Cautiously, the mage sent a probe to touch the outlines of Javerri's mind and realized she was dreaming. He tried to pull back, but he had depleted his inadequate store of strength mastering the simulacrum and the dream caught him.

I, waiting waiting outside door to First Lord Yassai's hall (oh angry white hot). I, in green, color of Third Province. I love my coat, hides me pleases me, hangs so stiffly from my shoulders oh, it reaches the floor so beautiful covered with thick embroidery of seed pearls and jewels. Without green thread (silk sharp needles tired hands small drops of blood) would not know color.

Doors open. I go in. My loved coat hides feet, I glide down room. Ha! I look neither left nor right, still I see Second Province (yellow) Fourth Province (brown) Fifth Province (blue). Other lords will witness, good.

They buzz behind me surprised, I hear them (they will not stop me never anger bright so bright). I have all powers of righteous anger, unassailable, Yassai's people know it, know me, even headsman yes. They melt away, vanish entirely, look elsewhere. I am at dais in my loved coat.

"Yassai, First Lord of Monserria, I give you lawful challenge!" My voice rings through audience hall (echo hollowing earthdeep cavern).

He cowers on cushion where he sits. Somewhere he finds enough courage to answer. "Who are you to challenge me?"

He pretends to peer closer, pretends to recognize me (oh he knows told the other told tolled echoes for my mind). "Why, it's Qai qa Hyasti's get, the upstart who would be Third Lord. Go away, girl. You are an annoyance."

I am an annoyance. "I will not leave until you answer my challenge." I stand before dais, stern, never move from this spot no, feet apart, firmly based, someone taught me, prepared to wait forever (ever ever never burning feverish and rage).

Yassai looks from side to side, oh, wondering where have his people gone. He must do as I tell him. "Well then, I will fight you, as you insist. But I am not armed."

I am on dais yes, turn to watching crowd and open my coat. They see my dress, so beautiful plain green, shines clean, bright against the loved coat (I am clean am I clean will they know?). I have Steel Fury and Lady Impatience in scarlet sash (anger attack at last no not dagger in my throat). Everyone knows which weapon I use yes. They speak among themselves and I hold coat open so loved yes out with both hands. Many many weapons hanging from lining interior, I have magician's coat of cheap tricks (mages magic hatred bitter red bile). Swords, whips, flails, clubs hang waiting.

"Choose," I say.

He takes Kallait *sarhandas* club in his hands (anger both white and red). My coat vanishes, oh my loved coat. Steel Fury in my hands, singing from his sheath, I am in fighting stance.

Yassai lunges forward, ah, unexpected strength. I parry without effort. He attacks again. I block the blow. I can end it here and now but I see in his eyes, he knows choice of inferior weapon tarnishes my victory, no honor here. I must continue this mockery duel until I can kill kill kill him with honor (no honor from him oh no but I must must be clean). He can wear me down (down ground hurt oh anger pain). His attacks strong skillful.

Do I grow now to giant-size or does Yassai shrink? Doesn't matter, never, it is right, Yassai no bigger than worm he is. I could squash him with toe of my shoe.

I sit. My right leg over Yassai's cushion, I arrange my skirt with great care. Unclean where he sat, I will not touch. He knows what must do, what must be, begins climbing right foot (tiny hands like unclean insect on me) and cushion and folds of my dress. I balance Steel Fury on my knee oh careful. Living sword begins to spin, making whippa-whippa sound as it goes faster, faster.

Watch, interested. He must climb oh, close to my knee and slither in safety down my thigh (thigh between unthinkable don't good he is too small for it). But he isn't other other hated also, won't stay, must go on climb up my body and pierce my neck with twin spikes instead (no pleasure instrument this club). If he is careful, he can avoid blade of sword whippa-whippa. If he is oh so little careless. . . .

Whippa-whippa.

He toils up, up mountain slope of cushion and dress not touching sharp insect hands on me on my flesh. Almost I hope for him tender for him now, survive, make a fair fight but Steel Fury obstacle with life of its own.

Whippa-whippa.

Very near whirling blade now. Just a little farther before the safety of my thigh. I hold (hold hold could catch engulf him drown him oh never) my breath. Careful, Yassai—

Whippa-whippa.

Mist of red, droplets falling, falling, with tiny ruined thing once Yassai. Steel Fury vanishes, I go on knees regretting, except for honor should have pinched off sharp insect hands and head also not let ruined thing cast self onto sword whippa-whippa. Did he? Did he? Perhaps not, perhaps wanted to live yes but. Here is paper, blot red mist with it. I scoop mess onto paper, fold into neat packet, tie with scarlet ribbon, someone else will dispose of it.

Sleep (anger hot red soon oh very yes soon very).

Wande-hari shook himself. His spirit quailed. Lady Moon and Ancestor! he thought, appalled. She was more than animal now but she was still mad. Yet, she was dreaming, and no one is responsible for what happens or what they are when they sleep. He wondered if she would ever again be anything like the tender-hearted Javerri he once knew. He would have to keep her asleep as long as his strength held out, for her good and his own. He wondered who this woman would be when she woke up—

The dull boom of a distant explosion came rolling across the plain from the direction Ivo had taken.

Vorsa looked up from where he was fastening Javerri's jacket. "Veh!" he exclaimed. *"Now* what, revered Uncle?"

Even the shab, staunch desert man that he was, was close to having had enough. All of them were near their limit, or beyond. Painfully, Wande-hari hauled himself to his feet and wiped his faced with trembling hands. "I do not know, but knowing Halit's way with exploding pebbles, I now fear the worst."

16

i

Sigon was finding it more and more difficult to keep Baron Sakano in check. They had searched for a week, and then Sigon had suggested, according to Lutfu's command, that Sakano retire to his country home and attend to whatever matters awaited him there. Far from showing interest in any business he might have among his holdings, he insisted on accompanying the Strategist. Furthermore, he grew increasingly peevish the longer he was away from Third City. After three more days had passed, Sigon came to a decision. He waited until the company, half a dozen of his best and most trusted soldiers, had stopped to rest before he drew Sakano to one side, out of earshot of the rest.

"I know the thought of returning to your estates is irksome for a man of your undoubted courage and abilities," Sigon told him, "but now I must inform you it not my desire but Governor Lutfu's express command that you do so."

The disgruntled expression fell from Sakano's face as he turned to stare at Sigon. "Why did you not tell me this before?"

"Because in telling you this I must also tell you other things that you will not wish to hear." Sigon frowned. "I apologize, but this is true."

"What things, General?"

"Some things I know, and more I have guessed."

"Don't play games with me, Sigon!"

"The Governor has decided he will impregnate his wife. This I know, for he told me as much and also told me to be sure that you stayed gone from Third City for a good long while. From this knowledge comes the things I have guessed.

One, that the Governor knows of your involvement with the Lady Nao-Pei. Two, that he feels your continuing presence in Third City is not conducive to the happiness of his union with her. Three, that he is not yet determined to punish you for lying with his wife. I believe the penalty for this is harsh, even if Lutfu were not a member of First Lord's family. Four, that he may decide to kill both of you anyway."

"Yet," Sakano echoed faintly. "You said he will not punish us yet."

"Further," Sigon continued with a tranquil manner he did not in the least feel, "I have surmised that a certain—shall we say, unrest—lies with you and the Lady Nao-Pei as to who should actually rule in Third Province." Eeeei!, he thought exultantly, seeing the blood drain from Sakano's face. That hit squarely in the gold! "While I would be the first to admit that Lutfu is not the best governor for Third Province, still he is by First Lord's appointment and I would have to lead the fight against any rebellion that might arise."

Sakano struggled to regain his composure. "What you say is nonsense. We have been sent to look for the heir, supposing his abductors were stupid enough to bring him here of all places, not search for some rebellion that exists only in your mind."

"Where the heir is, I cannot say. But my guess is that the last thing Lutfu wants is to have the Sublime Heir found. Or, if he is found, that he should live for very long thereafter."

"Guesses!" Scorn fairly dripped from Sakano's tone. "Is that the best you have to offer? You are senile, General. Your enemies are all phantoms, like your imaginary revolution!"

"Be that as it may, I know that I am not senile and I know also that Governor Lutfu has commanded that you return home. Therefore, I tell you to obey this command. I tell you also to devote yourself entirely to your wife, and to the managing of your own affairs. I tell you to stop meddling in what is beyond you for this is the only way you will preserve your own life as well as the lives of your followers. I am prepared to enforce this command if it is necessary."

Sakano's face was like a thundercloud. "You will have to post guards to keep me from going where I will," he said, his voice low and threatening.

Sigon allowed himself a spare smile. Sakano was not questioning his embellishment of the orders. Good. "I do not think the Sublime Heir is anywhere we have been searching for him. Therefore, I will accept your hospitality for me and for my men. I believe another week, perhaps two, will be sufficient for the Governor to have accomplished his goal."

Sakano, furious, turned away. For the first time, Sigon thought, he realizes that none of the soldiers with them were his followers. And this, this thing would depose Lutfu! He wondered what Nao-Pei saw in him other than a slave to fill her bed and cater to her perversions. He also wondered if the stories about Four Elephants were true.

He turned to the soldiers who waited at a respectful distance. "We will set aside our search for now, and accompany Baron Sakano to his estates," he said.

Without a word they fell into line, prepared to carry out this change in orders without comment. Sigon returned to his line of speculation.

Baron Sakano had given in too easily; therefore, he was retreating today only so he would survive to advance tomorrow. Sigon wondered if Sakano, separated from Nao-Pei, would dwindle into no threat at all. He suspected Sakano was like a mage's exploding pebble—harmless until activated. Nao-Pei was, obviously, the key. Did pebbles ever explode by themselves? He couldn't take the chance. The Baron would bear watching from now on, and Sigon made a note to have a spy put into Sakano's household.

Nao-Pei and Sakano had long been the subject of obscene speculation regarding the nature of their pillow activities. He wondered with whom Sakano would now practice those delicate perversions he must have become accustomed to. His wife? No, he thought, if what he had learned about her was true, even Sakano would not dare attempt such a thing with the very strict and moral lady he had married.

For that matter, he wondered if the stories about Lutfu

were true. No, those he had verified even though they were servants' chatter. But then the story of Four Elephants was servants' chatter as well. He wondered if Lutfu would be able to make good his ambition to quicken Nao-Pei's womb.

He wondered what Nao-Pei thought about all this.

ii

Nao-Pei lay stunned, unable to move, not daring to try. Involuntarily, she shuddered and Lutfu struck her across the buttocks.

"Slut!" he said between clenched teeth. "Filthy slut!"

If Nao-Pei hadn't been so terrified, she might have reveled in Lutfu's massive virility. He was both harder and larger than she had ever seen him, large enough that if she hadn't been wet with excitement he might have ruptured her. First he had beaten her and then twice he had probed her to her inner limits and beyond, since confronting her with his suspicions of her infidelity, though the first time was very brief as he refused to let himself complete the act. The second time he had had his hands around her throat. Just as consciousness began to fade he emptied himself, perhaps involuntarily. That was when he ordered the frightened maids to fasten her to a special device he must have had made in secret and had hidden in his apartments where she did not go.

Now she lay on a crude platform with her arms tied down tightly, her legs hoisted and spread with her ankles fastened just as firmly to an overhead bar, the supporters of which formed a part of the platform. He had torn off most of her clothes and she was naked except for a forgotten ribbon in her hair. The platform was of such a height to make her easily accessible and Lutfu alternately hit her and worked away at her, bracing himself with both hands on the supports. He glared at her with such a malevolent expression of mingled lust and loathing that she would have closed her eyes if she had dared. "Slut!" he said again. He went limp and withdrew.

Grabbing a pillow, he shoved it under her hips so they were higher than her head.

She moaned.

"Go ahead, cry and plead for mercy," Lutfu said. "Cry like the whore you are. I had planned to pinch out your worthless life but I have changed my mind for now." He pressed her belly with his thumb, digging in cruelly. "Here. Right here is where I'll plant it, if I have to keep you tied while the seasons turn full circle, and then I'll kill you!"

Her nipples were hard as stones and ached for release. Her Celestial Chamber throbbed, engorged, and she knew it wouldn't take very much to trigger the Moment of Clouds and Rain. If only he weren't so quick. . . .

"My lord," she said timidly.

"Are you going to beg me to release you, whore?"

Suddenly everything snapped into clarity for Nao-Pei. He was uninterested in her pleasure or, it seemed to her, even his own. This was punishment, but of a sort that touched a streak of perversity deep inside her, one that Sakano had occasionally touched but never plumbed. A thrill went through her. He might be wavering about whether to kill her now or get a child from her first, but she had no illusions about how easily an "accident" could happen, pregnant or not. And Sakano would be his next victim. Crying and pleading might excite him, but she knew intuitively that meeting him on his own terms, matching perversion for perversion and even surpassing him, would excite him more. She had heard stories of the depravity of some of the practices of First City nobles. Well, she had both intelligence and imagination, plus the sharpness of mind that being so close to death brings. And was she not his better in things of this nature? Had she not developed a streak of delicately refined perversity that had both kept herself virginal and she and her lover satisfied for years, with certain practices Lutfu had never dreamed of? According to reports of what went on between him and Madam Farhat's ladies, his comportment with them was no more remarkable than it had been with her. This knowledge gave her power if she used it correctly, but she knew better than to rely on this alone to save her. She might be the skilled swordsman in this battle, but her opponent could still smash her to oblivion with a club.

She reached inside herself, searching for anything that would build his excitement, willing to say anything, do anything that would bind him to her long enough so she could find a way to live—

"No," she said in the same small voice. "Do not release me. I deserve all the punishment you give me. Keep me tied, my lord, and do to me what you will. Only one thing."

"What is it?" It seemed to her that his tone was a fraction less truculent.

"It is said that a woman's pleasure is necessary for conception. Observe. You have given me great pleasure already but I both want and need more, much more." It was true. Her nipples went even harder, contracting to points smaller than the end of her smallest finger, and her flesh shivered in anticipation of what he might do next. It could be mistaken for passion.

He looked at her incredulously. "You like this?"

"When you do it to me, I do."

"Would you let others do it? While I watch?"

"Yes," she said between her teeth. "Yes! Only get me with child first and then I will accept armies if that will please you!"

"Even Sakano?"

"If you desire it, my lord." Bolder now, she raised her head and looked at him directly. "Sakano is nothing! I had to tell him everything, arrange everything. But you—*you!*" Her blood pounded. His Jade Stalk was stirring again. "How you excite me! What you are doing drives me wild! I beg you, have another device such as this built—have many of them built and put them in every room of the Residence! Take me on them, one by one! Erect one in the garden where you and whomever you choose can take turns on me! I revel in it! Only command me for I am yours!"

"Is it true about Four Elephants?" he asked abruptly. "And Sakano?"

No sense in lying to him now. Her life depended on it. And Sakano's. "Yes."

"And was it pleasurable?"

"Yes."

"More so than this?"

"At the time. Now I long to see if it is even more pleasurable when you do it. I still have the instruments. I am eager to show you how to use them. You will be stronger than Sakano was."

"You are truly more debased than any whore," Lutfu said in an awed voice. "Any whore."

He took her breasts in his hands, kneading her nipples harshly between his fingers. Her back arched and to her surprise she began to spasm even before he could get inside her.

Ah, she thought somewhere in the depths of her mind, so the boundary between life and death was where real pleasure lay, not that between pleasure and pain. This must be something like what warriors talk about when they empty themselves as they kill an enemy. She must be careful now, for this was just the first skirmish. The real battle had yet to be fought. Eeeei, she thought, danger was truly a great spur to passion. Then she gave herself over entirely to physical sensation and thought ceased for a while.

Dimly, she was aware of Lutfu untying her and carrying her to a sleeping mat. They both fell asleep. Then it was morning and he lay beside her sleeping heavily, replete and snoring. She eased away from him enough so she could examine herself.

Nothing broken, she thought, and nothing even greatly bruised. He was hollow after all, her husband, despite his great show of power. But if it took pretending to be lower than any whore he has ever known to save her life and Sakano's, she'd do it. Sakano was his better in every way and she did love him.

She wondered how great a pretense it was. Those things she

said to stimulate him came so easily to her. Well, she'd think about it another time. He did perform well once she had begun to master him when he thought he was mastering her, and then she did enjoy it. If she was pregnant now, she'd take the medicine.

He stirred and reached for her. "Tea," he mumbled thickly.

She got out of bed at once and slid the door open a crack. Yuroko waited anxiously outside and without waiting to be told, scurried away at once to fetch both tea and food. Quicker than Nao-Pei thought possible, the maid returned with a tray.

"Give it to me and wait outside," Nao-Pei said so softly her lips barely moved. "Do nothing unless I call out." Yuroko nodded and settled down to wait, alert and ready to raise an alarm at Nao-Pei's signal. She had no doubt that Yuroko had already seen to it that green-uniformed guards loyal to the House of Hyasti and also to Nao-Pei were stationed close by. It stood to reason she couldn't afford to take any more chances. She carried the tray to the bed, set it down, and poured two cups of the scalding hot tea.

"Good," Lutfu said. He raised himself on one elbow and took a cup, blowing on it to cool it. "Nothing like hot tea first thing in the morning, ei?"

She poured a little sauce over a bowl of rice, the way he liked it, and set it in front of him. She didn't dare speak.

"We will never mention last night again. We both said and did things we did not mean." He began shoving food into his mouth.

"As you wish," she said. He was abashed, she thought, like a boy after his first time. He did not know what to say, what to do, and he's pretending that he does.

"It did serve to wipe out certain misunderstandings, though, and even a score between us. I will tell you what will happen now. We will forget the past and start anew. You will bear a child. There will be nothing of what we talked about, no armies of men taking turns with you, no coupling with two or more at once, none of that. It is not proper, not fitting. I will destroy the, the—"

The platform. "No," she said. She put her hand on his arm and allowed herself to smile. "Not that. I agree that some of what we spoke of should be between us only, perhaps to be taken out now and then like a pillow book to add to our pleasure, but do not destroy the platform."

"You mean you didn't object to being tied down?" he said in some surprise. The corners of his mouth turned down.

"I did not object." She lowered her eyelids modestly and sipped her tea. And actually, she had to admit to herself, it was the truth. She had greatly enjoyed the feeling of utter helplessness. Most of all she had enjoyed using this feeling against Lutfu, to blunt his anger and turn it into passion so he became helpless instead, though she was still bound. And if this could keep him enthralled with her, could save— No. She shouldn't think of Sakano, not yet. Perhaps not ever again. She must concentrate solely on Lutfu, on binding him to her completely. "Lying there like that, I felt more open than ever before in my life. Never had I wanted you more. I would not give up that feeling. Also, I think you found it pleasurable as well."

"It is not the sort of thing one does with one's wife!" Lutfu said.

She smiled again. "It is truly the sort of thing one does with me, and I am your wife! This morning is a time for truth. You did not think to ask before, whether I would like it as well. But now that we know we are a match for each other beyond all our hopes, we can truly begin anew, as you say."

He pondered this in silence. "When will you know that you are with child?"

The abrupt change in subject startled her. "Not for some time yet. We will have the opportunity to know each other very well before then. And when I am sure, I will return to my quarters and leave you in privacy here." To return to his former practices with Madam Farhat's lowest-class ladies, she added silently, and not without a certain pang, at least until she could take the medicine and pretend she had miscarried. But she must not confuse pleasure or expediency or power with love, she told herself. "I would ask a favor, though."

"What favor?"

"Let us not perform the Occasion of Four Elephants. While I am eager to experience everything with you, I spoke hastily, from passion. Now I request that we postpone certain, ah, extreme pleasures until well after our child is born. The reasons are obvious." Not for anything would she really allow Lutfu to do this to her, to spoil the plateau of ecstasy she had reached with, with someone she dared not think of by name. No, far better she satisfy that portion of her that reveled in baseness with Lutfu and leave more refined pleasures to some future time.

"That would be best," Lutfu said. His expression was unreadable. "Well, then. Let us go and bathe and refresh ourselves and then see what happens next. This is a new thing for me, the thought that a decent woman, that my wife—" He finished shoving the food into his mouth and washed it down with tea. "We will try it, this novelty. For a while."

"I will try not to disappoint you, my husband," Nao-Pei said, once more lowering her eyelids modestly. Inside, her mind was busier than ever before, making and remaking plans. First a bath, then a massage, then a visit to Madam Farhat. Perhaps the woman would have some advice—or, Nao-Pei thought with amusement she did not allow to show, she might teach Farhat a few things. And then, very cautiously, new plans for the future some time, when it was safe, when she could bring a certain person back to Yonarin Castle and her husband could discreetly and so conveniently die. . . .

iii

"How pleasant that you and your husband are so amiable together," Madam Farhat said. She poured heated wine. Nao-Pei tasted cautiously and then approved; she could tell strong wine from weak, and this was acceptable. It was a good sign that the woman wasn't trying to muddle her senses with a trick Nao-Pei had learned at her father's knee. At once her suspicions sharpened. What did Farhat want, other than the obvious?

"Yes," she said. "I regret that with this new amiability between us you will lose certain, ah, revenues, but I promise you I will make up the difference elsewhere."

"Please, do not give it a thought. But why did such a great lady as yourself come to tell me this in person? Surely you have servants who could be trusted with such an inconsequential matter."

"Because I wish to see this amiability continue and I hoped you might have some suggestions for me in this endeavor. I will pay you well."

Farhat's eyebrows rose and she fanned herself. "Suggestions?"

"Yes. It is said that you know certain secrets. . . . "

"No more than you, certainly, Lady."

Furious, Nao-Pei smiled at Madam Farhat. So there had been gossip after all! She sipped her wine and fanned herself in turn until she could master her temper. Farhat was smiling, waiting for her response. "Nevertheless," she said firmly.

"Well then, I will see what I can do. According to those daughters who have visited the Governor, he is a man of simple tastes and requirements. Therefore, I am at a loss as to what to suggest. Perhaps something new has occurred?"

"That is no concern of yours." Nao-Pei's mouth hurt from smiling.

"Come now, Lady, you must be frank with me. Otherwise I cannot help you." She spread her hands. "Truly. As I told your sister, the Ladylord Javere—"

"My late sister."

"Yes. Well, as I once told the Ladylord, the Hyacinth Shadow World holds many secrets. Yours will be just one of many that go no further than these walls."

What did it matter? She had not been entirely discreet with her liaison or Lutfu wouldn't have known about it, and Madam Farhat had been the one who had supplied the Four

Elephants instruments, after all. Nao-Pei shrugged, and told Farhat of the argument and of what happened later. Farhat asked many questions before she was satisfied.

"A platform he tied you to, you say. How interesting! Perhaps the Governor is not such a plain man as he has appeared."

"He was, well, quite abundant," Nao-Pei said. "As you can imagine, I now want to assure his continued interest." So he would not have time or inclination to think of more revenge, she thought, and fancied she could see echoes of this thought racing across Farhat's face as well.

"Are you sure this is wise? Your, ah, private life is one thing but the Governor is one of those men who see women as belonging to two classes only—pure and impure. I think it might be better if you came to him again with great modesty. You should apologize, say you were seized with a momentary madness—"

"Oh, no, I assure you he wishes me to continue ministering to his pleasure."

"And the child he wants you to have. Do you want this as well?"

"No. I thought, if the time came, to come to you for the medicine—"

"The medicine is a last resort. It is better to prevent it in the first place. I will show you how and the Governor will never know the difference." Farhat leaned forward and patted Nao-Pei on the knee. "Very well. Leave everything to me, Lady. You have shown much wisdom in coming here. Not many women would have been so clever."

Too shocked to protest the familiarity, Nao-Pei sat still as a stone.

"Though you have been lucky so far, you cannot trust this luck to continue forever. It is not too late to start taking proper precautions," the woman continued. "When was your last woman time?" Nao-Pei told her and Farhat counted on her fingers. "Close, very close. But perhaps we will be lucky again. Now, please stand up and let me examine you."

"Why?"

"So I will know how to proceed. The width of your hips, the shape of your Pavilion, all have a bearing on various acts you can perform in safety. It is only sensible. You do not want to allow lasting harm to come to you."

Grudgingly, Nao-Pei had to admit that the woman knew this part of her business better than she herself ever would. After all, despite her appetites she was an amateur who had known only two men, whereas Farhat and her ladies had known thousands. So she stood up and submitted to an examination that made her forget the unwarranted familiarity of the pat on her knee. But during the course of it, Farhat instructed her in matters she had, heretofore, only guessed at and so it was worth the humiliation. When Farhat was finished at last, she nodded with satisfaction.

"Admirable, entirely admirable," she said. "Forgive my saying so, but the Hyacinth Shadow World lost a treasure in you. I confess I wondered when I supplied you with certain items— That was some time ago. Has the Governor used them?"

How dare this impudent woman even make a glancing reference to her lover! "No," Nao-Pei answered coldly. "Nor did I intend that he should."

"They are almost as effective merely to look at," Farhat said. "Many ladies keep such things in secret and never take them from their box. Oh, yes, I know, for I have supplied a set to— Never mind. However, there are other items, less, ah, extravagant, that you can use with considerably less ceremony, if you are determined to pursue this course with the Governor. It will be my privilege to give them to you."

"I insist that you be paid."

Again Farhat demurred, and the two women sparred a little more before Nao-Pei finally took her leave, graciously allowing Farhat to win the argument. Nao-Pei had left a purse among the cushions when she disrobed for Farhat's examination and not retrieved it when she dressed again. Also, she suspected, Farhat had known about it all along.

iv

All that week and the next, Nao-Pei saw to it that Lutfu wallowed in pleasure with her only, both day and night. Cautiously, Nao-Pei would introduce this or that novelty, quick to withdraw it if it caused Lutfu to frown and smiling in feigned innocence when he accepted it—innocence that turned immediately to lust and pushed Lutfu to his limits. He took to eating foods known to strengthen sexual stamina, and all but gave up drinking. Nao-Pei spent much time bound to the platform, straining and writhing in real and pretended passion. She caused the platform to be padded to save her back, and also ordered thick silk straps installed in place of the rough ropes, to keep her skin from chafing. Now and then she wondered that Lutfu could bring her such pleasure, a man she no longer cared for, someone she had decided must die to clear the path for her to rule Third Province alone with the one whose name she must not think of by her side and in her bed. At such times she shut away such thoughts, concentrating only on the sensations flooding her, putting each new experience away carefully to be repeated—or not—later with the one she loved. A widow needed much consoling.

She secretly obtained a copy of the design for the platform from the craftsman who built it, and sent it to Madam Farhat. In return, she received another box of carved ivory and wood trinkets, a little more advanced than the first. This one contained pleasure rings and assorted sizes of beads as well.

Her Celestial Pavilion—indeed, her entire body—ached from the strain put on it, but she would not show any discomfort, not when playing for such high stakes. Following Farhat's instructions, she used astringent douches and exercised her internal muscles conscientiously to keep her intimate area from being stretched out of shape though, truth to tell, Lutfu's attention quickly seemed to wane and he seldom reached the massiveness he had exhibited at first. Nevertheless, she cared for herself scrupulously, maintaining the virginal tightness she knew intrigued and fascinated men. Now and then, when Lutfu had exhausted himself and his Jade Stalk would not rise no matter what they did to it, she would coax him into the unknown arts of bringing a woman pleasure for its own sake. Awkward though he was at such times, Nao-Pei nevertheless encouraged him with every evidence of delight at his fumbling efforts. The novelty of being tied, helpless, had worn off somewhat, so she devised new ways of bringing about that feeling of surrender by using what Madam Farhat had taught her. Sometimes, daring to play with his threat to kill her, she audaciously directed that he threaten her with his dagger, at her suggestion laying it across her breasts and balancing it on the hardness of her nipples; sometimes he used pleasure beads on her and pulled them out or left them in place as his whim directed. Sometimes he decked her body with jewels, and other times he stripped her bare. Once she put him on the platform, but that experiment was not a success, and they didn't repeat it.

The day General Sigon returned to First City her woman time also came upon her. Tearfully, she retired to her apartment to wait and to allow Lutfu to attend to various matters he had let slide. Let him think hers were tears of sorrow rather than relief. They could both use the rest.

v

"And is the Baron well?" Lutfu asked.

Sigon looked at him with curiosity he was careful to hide. The Governor looked more than a little tired, fined-down. Certainly, he thought with amusement, he must be taking seriously the task of impregnating Nao-Pei. He knew that he would learn the details sooner or later from Hanu, his steward, so he did not make any inquiries. "The Baron Sakano is both well and content now to remain at his country estates where he finds more than enough to occupy his time," he said. "He found many problems that must be resolved and craves your forgiveness for not returning to Third City."

"Forgiveness is granted. He may have to stay away for a

long while. My, ah, project is not proceeding as rapidly as I had hoped it would."

"Ah," Sigon said sympathetically. Some women preferred isolation when their time was upon them, though he hadn't noticed Nao-Pei's being of this sort before. Interesting. "I understand. I will send my greetings to Lady Nao-Pei by messenger until I can deliver them in person when she joins us once more."

"She will be glad to know of your return."

"Well then, despite this minor setback, I hope it is proving to be an agreeable task. For both of you."

"I find myself devoting every minute to it." Lutfu made an obscene gesture with his fingers, shoving one through a circle formed by the fingers of his other hand. Sigon thought he had seldom seen such an unpleasant expression on anyone's face, let alone seen a man make a gesture like that regarding his wife. "I believe you will have to take over more of the everyday details for me, at least for a while."

All at once Sigon recognized what was happening. He had seen that expression, or one close to it, once or twice before. Here, he thought, was a man caught in a war not only with an errant wife but also with himself. Now he reveled in a web of besotted sensuality, and the danger was that this sort of thing could drag a stupid weak man lower and lower until he fell. But Lutfu was neither stupid nor weak. When he left, Lutfu was ready to kill a faithless wife. How had Nao-Pei managed to turn Lutfu from the cold man intent on revenge to this coarse oaf who openly exists only to burrow his Stalk into her Pavilion one more time? It seemed obvious. Probably she was enjoying it all as shamelessly, as well. He really would have to find out, very discreetly, what had been going on in his absence.

"Count on me, sir," he said to Lutfu, bowing to the correct degree. "You need not trouble yourself to do anything you do not want to do."

Later, when Hanu had told him everything, not omitting the slightest detail, Sigon could only shake his head in disbelief. He revised his estimation of Nao-Pei. She had always been clever; more, she was diabolical. But was she clever enough now? Surely Nao-Pei knew that Lutfu could not change his nature. Surely she knew that when this present—and temporary—fascination with her body wore off Lutfu would remember her faithlessness and begin to think of punishment once more. He wondered if Lutfu knew how much closer he had come to death by allowing himself to become ensnared by a faithless wife's wiles rather than execute her as the law allowed. Surely Nao-Pei would not plunge Third Province into revolution for the sake of her pillow pleasures! But again—

All would be resolved once Javerri came back, if she came back, when she came back, oh please. Perhaps separating Nao-Pei from Sakano would work out for the best, if Lutfu could manage to stay alive until then. And if Lutfu could be persuaded not to kill Nao-Pei. Sigon knew he must guard both of them carefully, must exert every effort to keep Third Province safe for the Ladylord's eventual return. If not peace and tranquility, then surely a certain armed truce would suffice in the meantime.

7

i

If Ivo hadn't turned and run the instant he realized what Halit was doing, he would surely have been caught in the blast and perished. As it was, the dull heavy air rushed outward from the destructive force of the bubble and slammed into Ivo, hurling him just ahead of it. He redoubled his efforts, stumbled, and nearly fell. Unexpectedly, Ezzat popped up out of the undergrowth.

"Sir, sir, this way!" The guide cried. He pulled Ivo a few steps farther. The bubble exploded with a deafening boom, and Ezzat flung both of them to the ground, sheltering Ivo from the rain of scalding matter. Both men cradled their heads in their arms, trying to avoid being burned.

Ivo sat up gingerly, putting his hands over his ears. All he could hear was a kind of numb ringing, if numbness could be a sound.

"Are . . . right, sir?" Ezzat shook him gently. Ivo realized by the movement of his lips the guide was speaking to him though he could make out only a few words. Ezzat's voice echoed hollowly and seemed many *ri* distant from his body.

"Yes, I am unharmed." Ivo's own voice sounded distant to him. He shook his head, trying to clear it, and was rewarded by a stab of intense pain filling his skull. "What of the others? The eggs, the dragons. And the Ladylord, what of her?"

" . . . do not know, forgive me. . . . " He surveyed the steaming ruin behind them. " . . . danger . . . here."

Ivo turned and gazed in the direction Ezzat was looking, where Halit had once stood. Nothing remained but bare ground, still steaming. Halit had quite effectively blown himself to bits. Ivo shuddered. Furthermore, the magician had tried his best to take Ivo with him. What caused a man to hate with such venom?

"We must go back and find the others," he said. He tried to get up and fresh pain throbbed through his head. He reeled, dizzy and sick. "Can you walk?"

" . . . think . . . " But judging from Ezzat's grimace of pain when he got to his feet and the paleness of his face, Ivo judged Ezzat was in very bad shape. He looked like a man who had received a mortal wound. Blood was beginning to seep from one of his ears.

Fortunately, they did not have to backtrack very far. The rest of the company came hurrying after them, following the trail Ezzat had left. One of the soldiers—Fen-Mu—was missing, and Ivo didn't want to ask why.

"Javerri!" he said.

" . . . sleeps . . . Brother," Vorsa said. He cradled Javerri as if she were a baby.

"I cannot hear all your words. Please speak slowly so I can watch you saying it and help me understand."

"Veh, slow. Good uncle . . . Dekla into sleep . . . we . . . get her back to Mama Lidian . . . all is safe."

"Give her to me." Ivo stepped forward and in spite of the intense pain that threatened to burst his head apart, he took Javerri in his arms. "She is pale. What did Halit do to her?"

"We may never know," Wande-hari said. The magician's voice came through clearly to Ivo and he realized Wande-hari was speaking to him with means other than his voice.

"Surely you looked into her mind," Ivo said.

The elderly magician looked startled. "Yes, I— But how did you know?"

"You are doing it now, by habit, for I can hear you with other than my ears. Also, sometimes you and Javerri speak without saying a word. That can only mean you conversed mind to mind."

"I might have known the Ladylord would choose as consort a man of great discernment." Wande-hari bowed. "Now I ask also your understanding and patience. We must leave this terrible place at once and go where our various hurts can be healed. Vorsa and Nali and especially Fen-Mu bought us a little time with the scarlet dragons, but I think they might be following us now. We heard them behind us."

"Veh, Fen-Mu . . . big price. We hurry now."

"Lord Ivo . . . I . . . too close . . . explosion," Ezzat said. He wiped a streak of blood from his nose. " . . . something . . . broken inside . . . head."

Ivo tasted warm saltiness and realized that his nose must be bleeding as well. He shifted Javerri, holding her more closely. "Yes, we must leave immediately. Where is Chakei?"

"He has gone ahead, with his children."

Ivo frowned, trying to understand. Even this slight movement of his facial muscles brought with it a fresh stab of pain. "His children?"

"The eggs. He thinks of them as his now."

"I see there is much to tell, much to understand. It will occupy us on the way back to Monserria."

"Sir," Lek said, " . . . far from well. I understand why . . . want to carry . . . Ladylord but . . . allow . . . uninjured . . . take turns . . . burden."

"To me she is no burden." Ivo started off in the direction Halit had been going when he caught up with him. Surely the wall of fog lay in that direction, hidden by trees. Every step he took threatened to burst his skull anew and all he wanted to do was lie down with Javerri by his side and sleep for days.

They found the Dragon-warrior striding back and forth at the fog barrier. Something penetrated the numb ringing in Ivo's ears, a kind of buzz, as if a giant insect hovered nearby. "What is that sound?" he said.

"You must mean Chakei," Wande-hari said. "I think he is singing to his children, inside the eggs."

"You . . . hear it?" Lek appeared at Ivo's shoulder. "Perhaps . . . not permanently damaged after all. Can . . . hear it, too, Ezzat?"

"Nothing," the guide said. He touched his ears gingerly. " . . . trouble . . . if . . . not looking . . . you."

"Nevertheless . . . can hear a little. Perhaps . . . both . . . recover when . . . time to rest." It seemed to Ivo that more words were coming through to him than previously.

Wande-hari stepped forward, taking several strands of light from his sleeve pocket. He selected two, put the others back, and formed one into the shape of a dagger. With it he carefully slit a small hole in the barrier of fog. Before the hole could heal itself, he formed the second into a key and opened a doorway for them to go through. Cold outside air blew through the doorway. It acted as a great refresher for Ivo and for the rest as well, judging from the way they straightened up as if invisible burdens had been lifted from them.

Lek stepped through first, and scrambled down the hillside in search of fresh water. With it he quickly mixed a potion in a bottle and poured out doses in two cups for both Ivo and Ezzat. "This . . . not heal your ears, but . . . take away most of the pain," he said. "I regret . . . a temporary measure."

"Thank you, physician." Ivo put Javerri down outside the fog wall and accepted the cup gratefully. The bitterness of the potion made him gag but he got it all down. Perhaps it was his imagination, but it seemed to him that the pain began to lift at once. "We still have to find our belongings and then get over the great stone Wall. Only then can we think ourselves at all safe."

They had come out at a different spot from where they had entered, and nothing in their surroundings looked at all familiar.

"I think we . . . farther north than we went in," Nali said. "At least, it seems like north. I will go down that way . . . see if I can find anything." He pointed to a spot where the Wall made a slight bend to the left and disappeared behind fog.

"Veh, I think . . . right, but search other direction . . . in case," Vorsa said. "We come back . . . quick, not too far without everybody."

"Agreed," Wande-hari said. "Let the injured rest as much as they can."

Javerri shivered a little and Ivo lay down beside her, taking her in his arms to keep her warm. Definitely, his hearing was coming back. He discovered that he must have dozed off when Wande-hari laid his hand on Ivo's shoulder. He opened his eyes and found that he felt much better for even so little sleep.

ii

Ivo had benefitted greatly from the rest, Wande-hari thought, but he dared not let him sleep longer. "Nali was right," the magician said. "He spotted our pile of belongings a few *ri* beyond the bend. The climbing rope is still attached to the Wall. Even if we have to leave things behind, we must get over it the best way we can."

"Yes," Ivo said. "I understand. But someone else can carry

my bow, and still another can take Steel Fury and Lady Impatience. As to the rest, leave it if need be."

"Those items will go with us if nothing else does. I can carry a few things extra, you know."

For the first time in too long, Ivo smiled. Wande-hari knew without looking into his mind that the archer was amused at the absurd notion of Wande-hari carrying much more than himself, ascending and descending the Wall. But then, he thought, he really was stronger and healthier than he had been in years. Look at what he had accomplished, despite his fatigue. Perhaps his protestations when Javerri would have left him behind were true after all.

Ivo sighed and got up gingerly. "I expected my head to burst open," he said, "but I have only a small ache at the base of my skull."

"And your hearing?"

"If you are speaking only with your voice, it is better."

"I am trying to do so."

"Then the answer to your question is, yes, if you speak clearly and distinctly." Ivo picked up Javerri and started down the slope toward the spot where Nali had found their original entrance.

With Wande-hari's and Vorsa's help, he put Javerri's quilted garments on her. Her face began to look less pinched as her own body heat began to warm her. Then the others dressed themselves as well. Chakei put down the eggs and donned his outsize coat with every evidence of gratitude. Then he picked up the eggs again and crooned over them in a different note.

Wande-hari smiled. "He has figured out that he cannot climb the Wall carrying both eggs. He must leave one behind and get it later, and now cannot decide which one."

"Would be better if *larac-vil* take Dekla, let us worry with eggs, veh."

"He will not do that, regardless of his fondness for Javerri. He cannot."

"She is my wife, and she is hurt. I will get her over the Wall."

"Sir, you are not fit—"

"No, Lek, do not remonstrate with him," Wande-hari said softly, so Ivo would not hear. He sighed. "This may be the only way of getting both over the Wall alive. I believe that nothing in this world would deter our excellent archer from this task, even as nothing can sway Chakei."

"Veh, I think you right, Uncle," Vorsa said just as softly. "They both live or they both die together. But I think I follow little Dekla's husband close anyway. Maybe hand on bottom help him up if he too weak."

"No. If he falls, he will take you with him. If you would hold the rope steady, though—"

"Sure, sure, you right. Vorsa not think for minute. I do that."

"I am counting on you."

Fortunately the wind had died down, though occasional vicious gusts worried at the dangling rope and hurled a hint of snow into their faces. The little party of adventurers sorted through their belongings, making themselves ready for the dangerous ascent. First they emptied their water skins of the drugged potion Halit had given them, rinsed the receptacles thoroughly, and refilled them with water from the ditch. Though not as clean as water from a running stream would have been, still it would quench their thirst.

"Drink, but not too much," Lek said. "Just enough to get the taste of ashes out of your mouths."

"Don't drink much, just enough to clean your mouths," Ezzat said. Obviously he had not heard the physician's words. "A belly full of water isn't going to help you on the climb."

Wande-hari worried about him second only to his concerns over Javerri and Ivo. Ezzat's skin had a gray tinge to it and now blood was running from both ears. Lek's medicine had helped him, but not as much as it had Ivo.

Shadows swept over them and Wande-hari looked up. Three leather-winged flyers circled overhead.

"I think they smelling blood," Vorsa said. "Or know some of us hurt." He scowled.

"San-ji did say they had learned to take sick or injured sheep."

"We not sheep, but that don't matter, I think. We better get going, back to San-ji, get *plandals*, go to stronghold quick."

By the time Wande-hari had distributed Javerri's weapons and Ivo's bow among the others, Chakei had made two trips up the inside surface of the Wall and was preparing to descend the other side. Though he hated to do it, Wande-hari lashed Javerri's forearms together around Ivo's neck and likewise tied her feet firmly around his waist. "I hope her weight won't strangle you," he said worriedly.

"She is light, and I am strong enough. The distance is not very far."

Nali started to steady the rope for Ivo's ascent but Vorsa took his place. "I bigger than you and stronger, I think. If Elder Brother falls, I make better cushion, veh!" He laughed but Wande-hari could see the worry in the desert man's eyes.

Ivo began climbing carefully, hand over hand, stopping now and then to adjust Javerri's arms around his neck. At last he reached the top. Chakei was nowhere in sight.

"Now me," Vorsa said. "Too bad not more Vorsas with you, watch over you everywhere. But I think with Elder Brother best place. Then you, good uncle, and guide Ezzat, and then physician. Last comes brave soldier. Agreed?"

All nodded except Ezzat, who had to have the order of ascent explained to him by pointing to each man in turn.

"Can you help him any further?" Wande-hari asked Lek.

"Not here. I could give him more pain medicine, but it would not stop the bleeding. He needs rest and quiet, and even then I don't know. He said he felt like something was broken inside his head. I think he may have been right."

"Fannaberries," Vorsa said firmly. "Need fannaberries in medicine kit, veh. We see about taking seeds back or maybe little plants when you go home."

The shab grasped the rope and began climbing. This time the wind did not threaten to carry him away on the wings of his loose desert clothing and he reached the top quickly.

Wande-hari started his own ascent, pleased to discover that he, too, was climbing more easily than he had on the first journey over the Wall.

"Send Ezzat up now," he called to Lek and Nali below. But they seemed to be having an argument. The wind picked up briefly, taking their words with it. Then Lek ascended the rope.

"He is insisting that we should all go before him. Then he will tie the rope around himself and we can pull him up. Otherwise, he doesn't think he can make it."

Wande-hari glanced upward. There were now half a dozen or more of the leather-winged flyers hovering on air currents above them, waiting. "I do not think he intends to try."

Sure enough, when Nali had reached the top, Ezzat waved them on. "Go, go!" he shouted, and then covered his ears in pain. He shucked off his pack and his heavy clothing and started off down the ravine. He stumbled and fell, got up again, and staggered on.

Wande-hari glanced upward. The flyers, as if by accident rather than design, drifted after Ezzat. One of them dropped lower than the rest. Then a second followed. "He is a dead man, I fear," Wande-hari said.

"I think he knew it all along," Lek said. "And so did I, though I wouldn't admit it." He sighed heavily.

"So many deaths, just to save us and make sure Javerri succeeded though powerful enemies stood in her way. Lady Moon and Ancestor must approve of her." Wande-hari straightened. "I cannot abandon Ezzat to a painful and dishonorable death." He took a deep breath. *"Ezzat!"*

The others started at the immense power of his voice and to Wande-hari's chagrin, Ivo flinched. He had forgotten to warn him. Below, Ezzat turned and looked upward. Wande-hari took a thread of light from his sleeve and raised his hands. If only he could contact Ezzat through mind speech first; he dared not use his Wizard's Voice again, lest he injure Ivo even more. He had to try. **Dost thou want merciful oblivion now?**

"Yes!" Ezzat spread his arms wide and closed his eyes.

Wande-hari nodded. The thread of light sparkled and glowed, becoming a tiny pellet of orange flame. Then it left his hands and sped toward the guide. Ezzat's body glowed orange briefly, and then collapsed.

"Is he dead?" Lek stared, shocked, at the scene below.

Wande-hari glanced at him. "No," he said. "Wizards may not kill except in extraordinary circumstances. But I have put him into sleep so deep he will know nothing of what happens to him." He gazed down at Ezzat's limp body. "Go in peace," he said, "and may the Ancestor Spirit find you quickly and keep you safe." He turned to the others. "There is nothing more for us here. Let us go, and go quickly."

iii

They re-set the grapnel on the other side of the Long Wall and this time Nali went first, followed by Vorsa. Surprisingly, Chakei waited for them below.

Art thou well? Wande-hari sent to him.

very well i and children also

Good, he thought. If he has the eggs to look after, perhaps that will curb the wildness Javerri had to endure on the journey here. He looked worriedly at Javerri and Ivo as the archer prepared to descend the rope. Ivo was very pale though resolute, and if he trembled with fatigue he refused to show it.

"Come, come, brave Elder Brother!" Vorsa called from below. "Just a little farther and you and Dekla fall, I catch, veh!"

"I will not fall," Ivo said. He shifted Javerri's weight on his back, swung over the parapet, and began the descent on the other side.

"His hearing is improving," Lek said. "When we get back to the farm cave, I will apply warm compresses to his ears. And I will do what I can for the Ladylord." He shook his head. "I fear that her worst injuries are inside her mind, though."

"I agree." Yes, for I have been there, Wande-hari thought. If she can be healed of those hurts, it will not be a man's doing. Perhaps Lidian could help her.

"You go now, sir, and I will follow."

Despite his improved physical condition, Wande-hari was glad to get to the bottom and gladder still when Lek was on the ground as well. Vorsa had at last prevailed on Ivo to let him take Javerri; he had untied her arms and legs and now held her the way one does a sleeping child.

"We get to San-ji's place quick. Road always shorter going back."

He set off at a brisk pace. Several times they paused to shift Javerri from one to another; even Wande-hari had a brief turn carrying her. Despite her slight weight, she made a heavy burden because of the depth of her sleep. Nevertheless, Vorsa's prediction was correct; much sooner, it seemed, than they had arrived at the Wall, they reached the shack that was the entrance to San-ji's warm cave. Dal and the dogs came to meet them.

"Not so many now," he said. "Ladylord dead also?"

"No," Wande-hari said. "She is injured. She sleeps."

"Come inside, then." The boy led the way and the dogs, more curious than wary, followed as if herding the visitors. When all were safely in and getting settled with San-ji clucking over them, trying to help and succeeding only in getting in the way, the boy addressed Wande-hari again, a little too casually. "And the other mage? What of him?"

"Dead by his own hand. He tried to betray us all."

Dal nodded, expressionless. "Good," he said, and refused to comment beyond that one word.

Lek put his patients in a smaller room off the main cave, where it was less noisy, and made them as comfortable as possible. Ivo quickly fell into as profound a slumber as Javerri's and when he woke he proclaimed himself much better.

They rested as long as they dared, taking the time to finish cleansing themselves of any lingering effects of the drug Halit had put into their water, and replenishing the food they would need on their journey back to the Kallait stronghold.

From time to time, Wande-hari woke Javerri enough so she could eat and drink. He and Lek tended her as if she were an infant.

While their guests recuperated, Dal and San-ji put their heads together and then began constructing a litter made out of wicker, designed to be slung between two *plandals*. "This much easier than trying to make birds carry double, or keeping her in her saddle while she sleeps," San-ji explained.

"We got plenty extra *plandals* now, veh, with good men dead and one bad mage also," Vorsa said. He spat for emphasis. "Thank you. You clever fellow, San-ji!"

As soon as the litter was finished and lined so the wicker would not scrape Javerri's skin, the travelers set off once again for Vorsa's home. Wande-hari could not help but notice that the shab seemed deep in thought, occasionally smiling to himself. Once he chuckled out loud but declined to tell anybody what he had found amusing.

When the stony spires of the hollow mountain appeared on the horizon, Vorsa sent Nali ahead to notify his people of their return and in particular to tell Lidian of Javerri's condition. "With your permission, good uncle," he said.

"Granted, of course. Your wife must be worried about you."

"Lidian? Oh, she not worry much. But she make all ready for little Dekla, too much waiting already."

And sure enough, when the rest of the party reached the Stronghold, Lidian all but ignored Vorsa. She rushed to the litter where Javerri slept, startling the *plandals*, who skittered a few steps attempting to run in different directions and then stumbled, trying to keep their balance. "Oh, the poor little boy-woman!" she cried. "What have they done to you! Never mind, Mama Lidian fix." She scooped Javerri out of the litter and expertly hoisted her onto her well-padded shoulder. "You others, go rest, eat, sleep. Your house all ready for you."

"Can I go with you?" Ivo said.

"No, not now. This woman work, veh."

Wande-hari stroked Javerri's forehead, muttering a few

words. "She will awaken soon. I do not know what you will find when she does, Lidian."

The Kallait woman nodded and then strode off toward the path leading to the women's bathing area.

iv

Javerri swam upward into consciousness groggily. "Swim" was the right word, she thought. Someone had put her into a wonderfully warm bath. Oh, it felt so good, so soothing. But the smell— She recognized the odor of brimstone, and knew where she was.

"Veh, you wake up now. Uncle say you do." Lidian took one of Javerri's feet and began scrubbing it vigorously, working suds between the toes. "You not have good bath since you leave here! Not so dirty as first time Lidian wash you, but plenty dirty anyway."

"Dirty indeed." Without her willing it, tears began to slide down Javerri's cheeks. "I am soiled beyond what any bath can clean away."

"What is it, sweet Dekla? Your soldier tell us little bit what happens to you but he not know much, I think."

"No, he didn't know. How could anybody?" Javerri thought a moment. "Well, maybe Wande-hari. Oh, Lidian. That—that mage! He—he—"

Wet and covered with soap-plant suds as Javerri was, Lidian nevertheless gathered her and pillowed her against her vast bosom. "Tell if you want, Dekla. Is all right. Lidian think she know anyway."

Haltingly, and with many tears, Javerri managed to relate what had happened to her at the hands of Halit. "Some of it I barely remember," she said. "I had, well, gone away by then."

"Hmph," Lidian said. "Not like bad mage much anyway. What happens to him?"

"I don't know. I think he is dead. Some of them were talk-

ing about it once when Wande-hari woke me enough to fee
me."

"Good. Lucky mage, not to let Lidian get her hands on
She shows him what happens to wicked men who force littl
Dekla, veh!" She laughed and kissed Javerri resoundingly.

"He didn't just force me, he destroyed me. Now I am noth
ing, and less than nothing."

Lidian turned serious. "Look, little Dekla. You do noth
ing to wicked Halit-mage, it not your fault what he do, bu
he hurt you bad anyway. I can tell you stop hurt, but you no
listen to Lidian. I think he still have hold on you, veh."

"That's impossible. He is dead."

"Sure, sure, but he have hold anyway. One way to find out
get loose from him."

"What is that?"

"You smoke holy herbs, go into land beyond. Find mage
get rid of him once for all!"

"Holy herbs? You mean *abaythim?* No, I couldn't—"

"Can and must! You not like holy herbs, but that silly
Trust Mama Lidian!"

The Kallait woman hauled Javerri out of the pool. Despit
her protests, Lidian wrapped her in a towel as easily as if sh
had been a child and carried her farther up the mountainside
into a cave from which the hot sulphur-scented water origi
nated for the bathing area. She plopped Javerri down on a
benchlike shelf carved out of the stone wall. "Here," she said
"You need steam bath anyway. I go get herb jar and coal from
fire. You stay here or Lidian carry you with her down and
back again!"

Javerri wrapped herself more tightly in the towel and trie
to find a more comfortable place to sit. Only portions of the
interior of the cave were filled with steam, she discovered, and
these places showed signs of frequent visitation. An incense
pot such as the temple priests used in Fogestria sat in a niche
Someone had left behind a band of cloth that could only have
been used to tie back the owner's hair, and a couple of rather
soggy cushions. Despite the clouds of sulphurous steam, sh
could still catch the odor of *abaythim* coming from some

where nearby. Sweat began pouring from Javerri's skin. She wiped it away with a corner of the towel and discovered that, despite her bath, a deeper layer of grime had come pouring out with it. Now she understood that the Kallait women in addition to coming here to smoke their "holy herbs" also used the cave for really thorough cleansing of their skin. Perhaps they combined the two activities.

She considered leaving, but doubted that she could make it back down to where her clothing lay—provided it was still there and Lidian hadn't scooped it up and taken it with her—without being caught and hauled back to this spot again. Perhaps it would be better to pretend to do as Lidian wanted, and escape later.

The spring was not a steady one. When the unknown workmen had built the bathing pools below, they had also built a kind of reservoir for the spring water that erupted, rather than flowed, at fairly regular intervals in a manner reminiscent to Javerri of an overfull tea kettle boiling and spitting out its contents with the steam. The intervals of eruption were close enough that the water scarcely had time to cool before it spilled out over the edge to go precisely where the workmen had desired.

Lidian toiled back up the mountain path carrying a bundle and another towel. She opened the bundle, set some of the contents aside, and put two jars, one small and one large, on the floor in front of them. Without the least self-consciousness, she removed her garments and wrapped herself in the towel. "Now we both have nice steam bath together," she said companionably. "I know you not like holy herbs in pipe, so we do next best thing. I burn them in little jar with holes in lid and Dekla smell them, veh."

Humming to herself, Lidian took down the incense pot and measured what seemed to Javerri a very large amount of the dried leaves from the larger jar into the base of the incense burner. Lidian glanced at Javerri and smiled. "Got to use more than with pipe this way, veh. Pipe better but Dekla not used to pipe, not know how." Then she took a coal from the smaller jar and dropped it into the leaves, carefully scooping

them around and over the coal until the whole thing was
arranged and smoldering to suit her. She put the lid on the
pot and smoke immediately began rising from the three large
holes and as many smaller ones incised in it. It coiled itself
into a twisted concentrated rope and Javerri instinctively held
her breath.

"No, Dekla, this way." Lidian forced her forward until the
rope flowed into her nostrils. She had to take in air, she must
breathe. . . .

The sweetish *abaythim* smoke filled her lungs and, hot as
she already was in the steamy air, she grew warm with a different melting sensation. Then she grew cool again. The cave
drifted away and she found herself on the same cold hilltop
washed with mists she had visited briefly once before, when
she had claimed Steel Fury for her own and declared herself
the Lord of the Third Province. This time, however, she discovered Halit waiting for her. He had no choice; he was buried
upright in the earth, nearly to his chest. He had managed to
keep his hands above his head and he grasped a pole that had
been set into the ground. A red flag fixed to the top of the
pole lay limp with no breeze to lift it.

"Ah, so you've come at last," the magician said. He bowed
ironically, as far as his condition would allow. "But then, I
knew you couldn't resist searching for me, after all we enjoyed
together. Finally discovered the virtues of *abaythim*, have
you?"

"Why are you still persecuting me? You are dead! Haven't
you done enough? Leave me alone!"

"Forgive me. I forgot my manners." He didn't sound in the
least contrite. "You had to come. Dead I may be, but only you
have the power to release me."

"Oh?"

"Indeed. Only you can save me. When I first arrived here,
my feet were caught in the ground, and I only leaned against
the pole. Then I sank until I became as you see me now. I had
begun to despair that you would ever find me. But you have."
He smiled. "Remember, I was only doing as my lord instructed me."

Wande-hari?****

No answer. She tried again and again without results. Perhaps it is the *abaythim* keeping us apart, she thought. *******Can you hear me?*******

Nothing but silence answered her.

"Trying to confer with the old fellow?" Halit said. "He can't hear you. Nobody can. It's all up to you for once. You *must* help me."

"No," she said. She thought hard. What would Lord Qai do in a situation like this? "What I must do is make a choice. Obviously, you are lingering here before continuing to whatever punishment awaits you. I could help you. I could hurry you on your way."

"Then do it now and finish it. Don't leave me to suffer the fate of not knowing, or perishing by degrees." His face contorted. "Destroy me if you must, or save me! You have to!"

She hadn't realized she stood so close, or perhaps something moved her within his reach. He grasped her by the wrist and pulled himself upward a little. She shook him off, staggered, and caught at the flagpole for balance. It moved under her hands and Halit lost what he had gained as he sank once more. She realized that with only a little effort she could take the pole, snap it across her knee, use the pieces to shove him down until he was covered completely, and then send his lord's standard after him. Rage arose in her, darkening her vision. She wanted nothing more than to cast him into the blackness, to hurry him to damnation, to take revenge on him for what he had done to her—

With an effort, she mastered herself. She stepped back from the flagpole, striving to think once more. She was Lord Qai's son, and no dung-smeared peasant to think solely of revenge. "Even the lowest soldier is absolved from following the orders of a wicked leader." Her voice shook and she willed it steady. "If I save you, the Ancestor Spirit must think me kind but foolish to let you avoid the fate you have brought on yourself by your own actions. The Ancestor does not like fools and he would not help me when I face First Lord, and I would lose everything. If I destroy you—" Her heart lurched as she realized the implications of this course of action. "The Ancestor might not care for fools, but he despises those who try to interfere with what he has decreed, and what you now endure is surely your fate. If I destroyed you now, the Ancestor would stand against me when I face First Lord. And again I would lose everything—including my immortal soul!" She made a sound of utter loathing. "And there is the question of who put you here. If it was the Ancestor, I will do nothing to influence him, one way or another, for he is not to be bought. If it was you, you have traps lying at the end of either choice I make. Therefore, I, Third Lord of Monserria, will do nothing. Make the best of what death has brought you, magician."

"Third Lord of Monserria," Halit repeated scornfully. He began to sink at a rapid rate. In panic, he clutched at the pole. It sank with him. He was covered to his neck, his chin. "You think First Lord is your only enemy—" His voice was cut off as the ground covered his mouth and his eyes and then closed over his head. The flag lifted just long enough to display First Lord's sigil with another symbol superimposed on it, a strange eight-legged shape, and then it, too, mercifully vanished.

18

i

*J*averri opened her eyes. "Wait! I must go back! I didn't see the other symbol clearly!" she said.

"You speaking foolish," Lidian said. "But you speak even more foolish while in land of holy herbs. Maybe all foolish gone now, veh? Here, drink." She handed Javerri a bottle.

Her mouth and throat were parched, whether from the *abaythim* smoke or the brimstone fumes in the cave, and she drank eagerly, not caring what the bottle contained. It was only water after all, sweetened by something fruity. It was incredibly refreshing.

"Fannaberry water. Mage really dead now so he leaves you alone?"

Javerri thought a moment. "Yes, I think so. I saw him go under the ground. And I feel better. Thank you, Lidian."

The Kallait woman shrugged. "Is good. Better is not well, though. I think you need drink fannaberry for while yet. I get you plenty." She shook the ashes out of the incense pot and put it back in its niche. Then she reached for her clothing and tossed a bundle to Javerri. The clean scent of fresh, sun-dried Kallait garments rose as she opened it. Both women wiped themselves once more with the wet towels and began to dress.

"Lidian, do you know who I am, who I really am?"

"Sure, sure. You Dekla, good friend of Vorsa and me."

"I am more than that. Where I come from, the First Lord is the, the highest shab of all. I am the Third Lord, Third Shab. At least I would have been if First Lord had confirmed me while I was still untouched. In my province, Third Lord must come to it virgin. In my case, because I am a woman, that means with the Guardian of the Heavenly Pavilion intact."

To Javerri's astonishment, Lidian began to laugh. "Ho, ho! That all? You think virgin is in little tissue of private part?"

"Of course it is."

"Oh, silly. Virgin is in mind, is in want to, you understand? Body proof sometimes, but not every time. Always, always, is in mind!" She tapped Javerri's forehead meaningfully. "You are not wanting, like wanting husband, veh?"

"No. No!"

"Well, then. Still virgin of mind even if tissue gone. No matter at all. Silly custom, though, what you tell me. Your husband, he fine fellow. Lidian wonder why you not making much love with him all this time. Now all clear but silly custom of Third Province anyway, I think."

"He has endured much for my sake." The image of Safia, tall and beautiful, came into Javerri's mind and immediately she put the thought away as she belatedly remembered something else. "Michu! I had forgotten about Michu! How is he?"

"Oh, he nearly well now. He have couple Kallait girls in bed already." Lidian laughed heartily. "Hope if they get babies, babies not born with half a foot!"

In spite of herself, Javerri smiled. Between Lidian, with her earthy and no-nonsense approach to life in general, and the fannaberry drink, she suddenly felt much improved in mind, body, and spirit. If only the Kallait woman's novel ideas concerning virginity could be acceptable there might yet be hope. . . .

"Now you have decision to make," Lidian said. "You hold onto old hurt and make all suffer likewise, even good husband you not sleep with yet and maybe never, or you learn and become good shab to your people. And good wife to your husband, too."

"And what more is there to learn from this?"

"That all people not what they seem and some try to kill shab only for being shab. That way with Vorsa. And also that some are sick in minds like wicked mage. You have trust too much. Hmmm. You see mage making butterfly for children, making eyes also with Elhuas day you leave?"

Javerri searched her memory and recalled the morning they had set off for the Long Wall and the handsome boy on the outskirts of the crowd Halit had been amusing. "Yes."

"Well, Elhuas, he one who likes men only, you understand? But he say he never go with mage no matter what, and mage offer him many things many times while you are here. He tells Lidian mage is not good man. He can see what Dekla does not."

"Perhaps I should hire him as a counsellor."

"Veh! Maybe you ask more questions, listen to friends!" Lidian laughed again. "Well, not much chance when behind Wall and all friends silly from drinking mage water. Is over, is ended. Now heal. And go back for good wife and Third Shab in own country, veh!"

A little later, clean and refreshed and feeling quite well again, Javerri came back down the path and joined her com-anions. She was still a little weak from inaction and her long forced sleep and she moved slowly, but her step was steady enough. The smells of food cooking filled the air and she discovered she was hungry to the point of being ravenous. She thought about telling Wande-hari about the *abaythim* dream, and decided not to, not yet. They came crowding around her, marvelling at her recovery.

"I am healed," she assured them all. "Lidian has given me annaberry water. Later I will tell you about it but we have more important things to discuss. Ivo, Wande-hari, let us talk in private while we eat. Lek, please take my apologies to Shab Vorsa for any rudeness and arrange to have food brought to me. I know mealtimes are social occasions for the Kallait but I cannot afford that luxury just yet."

"I am sure the shab will understand. He has much to catch up with as well." The physician looked at her quizzically, but bowed and hurried off.

To her surprise, Javerri discovered Chakei inside the guest house. He crouched in the middle of the floor, guarding a single scarlet egg, and looked up at her when she entered. **lady-lord back now, good, very happy i and pleased also**

And I am happy to see thee back to thy old self again. I missed thee. Is that thy, thy child?

son It seemed to her that even his pebbled skin glowed with pride. **other son with desert man now, sorry i for lady-lord hurt, should have been with**

It is forgiven and couldn't be helped.

Two Kallait girls came into the house laden with trays and dishes. Javerri's mouth watered and her stomach cramped. She had been without real food for too long and the aroma threatened to overpower her. Without any ceremony, she seated herself on the cloth they spread on the floor and began to pile food on one of the *bifat* cakes, still hot from the oven. All proper eating utensils had vanished long ago so she folded it Kallait-style, ate it, and immediately began filling another before Ivo and Wande-hari had properly wrapped their first. She ate two more before telling them Lidian's ideas about what was and was not virginity. "This may be all well and

good among the Kallait, but what about Monserria in general, and Third Province in particular?"

"The matter deserves some thought," Wande-hari said, fas-
tidiously wiping his fingers. "And I will have to consult ancient books on the subject. It could be that the old warning
reflects nothing more than the obvious necessity for the ruling lord to devote himself—or in your case herself—to Third
Province first and foremost, and put private consideration
second. The rest may be simple custom that has grown around
this necessity, over the years. If it turns out all this violence
against you was for nothing. . . . Yes, it is an interesting
thought."

Javerri turned to Ivo. "Once you swore to be my friend,"
she said. "Now I must ask even more of you." She reached
out to him. On one level, it seemed the most natural of gestures. On another, she realized she should be feeling an uprush of revulsion at the idea of touching male flesh, any male
flesh, even his. . . . It must be the fannaberry water, allowing
her to behave normally. She took his face between her hands.
"I love thee. I have always loved thee even when I seemed not
to." Despite the strengthening draught, tears rose in her eyes
and she had to will her voice not to shake. "If Lady Moon
and the Ancestor Spirit decide, I will be Third Lord when we
return. If not, I will be nothing." The tears spilled over onto
her cheeks and she cursed herself for showing weakness.

Gently, Ivo brushed the tears from her face. "Then, if need
be, I will be nothing with thee and we will be together, for I
love thee more than thou hast ever known, and always will."

"I thank thee," she said, humbled. "Now I must go and visit
Michu. If he is well enough to travel, we must start back to
Monserria at once. We have a lot of unfinished business
there."

ii

She discovered Michu hobbling about the healer's dwelling.
He had a crutch under one arm and the other around the

waist of a giggling Kallait girl. "Ladylord!" he cried, flinging his arms wide. The crutch fell clattering to the ground and he staggered. The girl clutched him so he wouldn't fall and giggled harder. "Back so soon?"

The girl whispered something to him. "Oh, yes. I forgot. 've been in fannaberry dreamland ever since I got here." Michu grinned. "But I'm much better now."

Apparently, Javerri thought, a skilled physician can induce whatever level of oblivion he desires with these wonderful berries. Of course, I am taking only a diluted potion. Lek will be interested in this. "Are you well enough to return to Monserria?"

Vorsa appeared in the doorway. The Kallait girl helped Michu to sit down, and then slipped past Vorsa and disappeared. "Sure, sure, he fine now, ride *plandal*," Vorsa said genially. "They tell me he get in races even! But what you do when you get to Monserria, Dekla?"

She turned to face him. "Do? Why I shall—"

"Ha! You don't even think how you get through Fogestria first!" Vorsa laughed. Javerri recognized the gleam in his eye; the shab was getting ready to play one of his jokes.

"I will pass through Fogestria if the Ancestor Spirit wills it," she said. "And I will go to First City and confront First Lord—"

"With your army of one soldier and half-foot general?" Vorsa laughed again. "No, Dekla, your Ancestor not help you so much as Vorsa now. I already send word to Yonal family of Kallait and Oramin family also."

Javerri searched her memory again and found the young man who had been at the great *sarhandas* feast and who had fought a minor duel with one of Vorsa's sons. He had been of the Yonal family. But the other name she did not know. "Oramin family?"

"Veh. Walloh family and Yonal family not like each other much sometimes, and both not like Oramin family either. But we join together, drink pledge, make fine army for Dekla when she return to homeland! Fight very hard all on one side for once."

"I—I couldn't let you do that."

"We have great fun, veh! I like to see faces of Dekla's enemies when they see her and army riding on *plandals*."

In spite of herself, Javerri had to smile at the thought. She glanced at Michu. He was looking at her, the corners of his mouth twitching. "The best army," she said, echoing one of the pieces of military wisdom Michu had taught her, "is one that the lord never has to send into combat. Would your men be satisfied if there was no fighting after all?"

Vorsa shrugged. "Then we fight each other, same as we always have. Leave donkeys behind, leave cart. You not need now. March boldly with proud army behind you, veh!"

She turned to Michu. "What do you think of this?"

"I think it is a sign from the Ancestor Spirit, Ladylord. To be frank, I had wondered how we were going to get back, as many losses as we've had." He stared at the bandaged stump of his foot. "And I don't mean just this."

"General Half-foot still ride, still think, still good leader. Know own country very well. Vorsa command all of Kalla warriors, second only to General."

"That would suit me very well. As far as I'm concerned, it's settled, then," Michu said. "All we need is your approval, Ladylord."

Javerri closed her eyes, thinking. Then she looked at both of them and nodded. "You have it," she said. "And with it, my heartfelt thanks."

The air was already crackling with excitement among the Walloh men when Javerri emerged from the healer's hut. Vorsa translated snatches of their conversation for her as they walked back toward the guest house. Then Javerri knew the prospect of war was a welcome one; the fighters were arguing joyfully about which weapons would be superior, whether they should carry spears or bows but in any event their best swords, which tactics would surely be employed, what they could expect from their enemies in this strange foreign land to which they would be going. Within a day, Yonal warriors began arriving at the stronghold, and Yonal and Walloh shouted genially at one another over the same sub-

jects the Walloh had argued about among themselves. Within
another day, Oramin fighters began arriving as well and the
stronghold was filled with the sound of loud male voices
raised in strident quarreling, and the occasional clash of steel
as weapons were drawn and sometimes used. And yet, with
all this, there was a curious lack of real bloodshed. Javerri
began to understand that with the Kallait, war represented a
means of relieving the tedium of life in the desert. No wonder all of them looked upon this new adventure eagerly as an
opportunity unparalleled to generate stories for telling
around the fire for years to come.

No more than a week had gone by since they had arrived
at the stronghold, and all stood ready to ride out once again.

Vorsa handed Javerri a whip, the *sarhandas* tail, now cured
and fitted with a gold-trimmed handle. "I promise this to
Dekla when we first meet," he said, "and now is yours, veh."

She examined it curiously, then tucked it under her arm.
She laid her hand on the hilt of Steel Fury, now properly
wrapped for war. "Thank you, Shab Vorsa," she said.

Then Javerri mounted her *plandal* and at this signal, everyone else mounted their birds also. Michu had to have a little
help, but once in the saddle, he handled the bird expertly.

"We ride!" Vorsa bellowed. *"Waas fordan!"*

All the Kallait women lined the gateway or clung to the
rocks to watch as the army rode out. Javerri expected the
women to be wailing and screaming at the men's departure,
but even Lidian, who had complained so bitterly at Vorsa's
going off on the expedition to the Wall, shouted encourag-
ingly to the warriors as they passed. They beat on drums, applauded and whistled, or set up a shrill ululation that hurt
Javerri's ears and made Ivo wince as well. Apparently warfare was an activity even the women approved—or, perhaps,
it was something to get the men out from under foot for a
while once they had been in camp long enough for everyone
to get bored.

She pulled her *plandal* out of the column so she could re-
view the Kallait army as it passed. It was easy to tell Walloh
from Yonal, Yonal from Oramin by the colors and styles of

clothing they wore and the decorations on them. For herself
she had chosen the plainest of white garments with only a lit
tle ornamentation of gold embroidery. It would be easy to
pick her out of the crowd of brown and earth-yellow, red- and
green-striped garb the others wore, even her own people. Leb
brought up the end of the column, just ahead of the baggage
leading a pack *plandal* with panniers laden with fannaberry
plants in pots, and packets of seed as well. Chakei loped
along nearby, carrying his "son" with him.

And what wilt thou do with thy child if thou must fight?
Javerri asked with some amusement.

give son to ladylord, then fight i Chakei retorted, and
she knew he was amused as well.

Good. It spoke well that Chakei had lost the wildness that
had possessed him on their journey to this place. What he
would do if—when—he was faced with the prospect of turning over his progeny to First Lord, she did not want to consider just yet. For herself, she felt cheered to be doing some
thing, anything, without sensing that the whole world was
standing in her way. For the first time in a long while, she
began to have some real hope that she would live to return to
Monserria, where she would at last confront her enemies
Whether she would live through that encounter, only Lady
Moon and Ancestor knew.

She dug her heels into the *plandal's* side and rejoined Ivo
and Wande-hari at the head of the column.

iii

With Vorsa guiding them and by pushing hard, they crossed
the strip of desert between the Walloh stronghold and the Fogestria border in two days and two nights, arriving at the
spot where Javerri's little band of adventurers had passed
their last night before braving the wilderness. She recognized
the stand of trees, the stream trickling out to lose itself in the
sand. As if by habit, the Kallait warriors avoided the area:

where they were likely to be sucked down and drowned. By their ease in setting up camp and the way the different families sorted themselves out, no matter how they might have mixed on the journey, Javerri understood this was a well-known spot among them.

"Oh, sure," Vorsa said when she asked him about it. "We stay here always when go to Fogestria for trade. Plenty water, and here only good place for enter, understand?"

"Yes, I do."

"Little path that way," he added, pointing north, "but no good on *plandal* feet. If we not ride, maybe we go that way. But damn birds not able to go."

"I'd rather have the birds with us. We have many *ri* yet to travel. Have you ever been to the other side of Fogestria?"

"No! Vorsa not go farther than Fanthore city. Bad place anyway. Good trade, though."

"Fanthore is an evil place, to be sure. We barely made it outside the gate ourselves. We had to bribe the guards with nearly everything we had, even some, some jewels Wande-hari used to wear, and for a moment it seemed that wouldn't be enough for them."

Vorsa laughed. "You see guards be nice now, very good, very happy to please Dekla. No more bribe."

"I hope you're right."

"Vorsa right, you see."

They spent the night at the oasis, letting the birds rest. The following morning, they filled their water receptacles and began the climb up the steep path Javerri remembered descending all too well. They did not ride, however, but each warrior and baggage tender led his *plandal* while the birds picked their way with the dainty care of a lady who doesn't want to soil her shoes on the gravel path. Chakei didn't skitter along the top of the ridge, either, but stayed close to Javerri, the scarlet egg clutched in his arms. She moved a little way up the ridge, however, so she could watch over her army as it maneuvered through this hazardous slot in the mountains, rejoining it when all seemed to be going well. Better, in fact, than she had expected.

She was glad she happened to be at the head of the column and close to Vorsa when they rounded the last bend in the road and came to Fanthore's mountain gate. The look on the faces of the guards made her bite her cheeks hard to keep from laughing. Their mouths fell open and their eyes nearly started from their heads from sheer astonishment as, without any sign of acknowledgement on her part or that of any of her companions, she and her army rode majestically past them and into the city. She never even gestured toward the money pouch containing the remnants of the coins saved back the last time she and her companions had gone through these gates.

The *plandals* began to complain at once at the hardness of the pavement under their feet but neither Vorsa nor Javerri was inclined to pamper them. Looking neither left nor right she led the way through the narrow city streets, hoping she remembered the route to go, hoping that the tall and rickety buildings still festooned, it seemed, with the same loads of drying cloth strung on lines between them, would not fall down under their burdens. The inevitable noisy crowds parted like grass before them and even the worshippers paused and stared openly. She became aware that Ivo had caught up to her and now rode at her right hand.

"This way," he said in a low voice when they came to an intersection she did not remember. "The main gate is at the end of this street. When we were here before, we had to go to the temple rather than straight through the city."

Without hesitating, she turned in the direction he indicated and they rode through, to the other side of Fanthore. At Vorsa's command they all dismounted and the birds immediately began to ease their feet by lifting them one at a time and shaking them, as if they had been burned by the hard pavement they had just crossed. Javerri caught a deep breath for, it seemed, the first time since they had entered the mountain gate. She took a flask of concentrated juice from one of the panniers on her saddle, unfastened the water bottle at her pommel, and mixed a quick dose of diluted fannaberry water. Off to one side, Michu was doing the same.

"We did it." she said, unbelieving, to Ivo. "And nobody even challenged us."

"Nobody want to," Vorsa said. "We much too strong! Take more than priests with sweet-smelling smoke to stop Dekla's army."

"Shab Vorsa is right," Ivo said. "Fogestrians have never had much stomach for fighting, only bandits such as we encountered that one time, and even they were easily conquered. Easily except for this." He lightly touched the scar on Javerri's cheek.

She caught his hand; his touch was not as unwelcome as she had feared it would be. "It only makes me look fierce for what trials must lie ahead." She managed to smile.

"I think we go fast through Fogestria now," Vorsa said. "Fast as *plandals* take us without killing them, veh."

"First Lord will be there whenever we arrive," Javerri said. "I only wonder what has been happening in Third Province while I've been gone."

iv

With the capability now of riding beside the road rather than on it, along the verge separating the road from the fields of yellow grain, they made excellent time without laming the *plandals.* Nor were they troubled even once by bandits. The Kallait, growing bored, began to quarrel among themselves again, and Vorsa had his hands full to avoid warfare among them before they reached their destination. Only the hope of battle later kept them in check.

Javerri expected a similar reception at the Monserria border to the one they had received at the mountain gate of Fanthore, and she was not disappointed.

The Fourth Province guards, though openly astonished, were more skeptical than she had anticipated when she announced her identity. Behind her, the Kallait hooted and whistled in support and approval when she swung herself down from her saddle and faced the head of the border guards. She drew herself up to her full height, chagrined to note that she barely came to his shoulder. Well then, she thought, a small dog is the worst biter.

"I am Javere qa Hyasti, Lord of Third Province, and I demand that you allow me and my companions to pass."

"You, Lord of Third Province?" he said. "You are no lord. You're not even dressed like a woman! What kind of outlandish garb is that?"

"This clothing suits me to wear because I say it does. Now let the Lord of Third Province pass."

"What proof do you have that you are who you say you are?"

"Eeeei! Look around you!" She indicated her companions—Ivo, Wande-hari, Vorsa. By this time even Michu had dismounted and limped over to stand at her side. Chakei hovered in the background, still clutching the scarlet egg. As many of the Kallait as could crowded around to watch, still mounted on their *plandals*. They grinned in eager anticipation. "What sort of fool are you to demand proof from me? *Me!* Are you the idiot who allowed me to slip past you in the first place, while my maid pretended to be me? If so, I will kill you now and save your superior the bother. Then I will let my army loose against the rest of you and the village as well."

The man looked startled. "You—you know about that, about the maid?"

"Know about it? It was my idea! Where is my maid? Where is Chimoko? Bring her to me at once."

"I—I regret, Lady—I mean, Third Lord, I cannot obey. She is not here. They took her to First City when they discovered your, your clever ruse."

Javerri narrowed her eyes. "She had better be unharmed, for your sake."

"Please, Lord, I know nothing. All this happened before I was assigned here, though I heard about it, naturally. There was a battle—"

Javerri stared at the man, willing him to submit even more, willing him to abase himself. "The details," she said harshly. "Now."

"The maid Chimoko petitioned every day to be allowed to go into Fogestria, until soldiers came from First City who had seen the real Third Lord. They tried to stop her. She took her, your Greens through them, or tried to. The Greens fought valiantly but they were overcome. They captured Chimoko and took her away. That's all I know, Lord. Have mercy on me!"

"And you swear you took no part in this?"

"On my mother's head! By Lady Moon and the Ancestor Spirit, I swear!"

"If you swear by these, I must believe you. If you are lying, no forgiveness of mine will save you, even if by some miracle you escape my wrath."

The man dropped to his knees and groveled in the dirt. "Thank you, Lord!"

"Get up. You weary me." He complied at once and she regarded him almost fondly, now that she had dominated him. "You will send your fastest messengers to all four provinces— you did say the Third Province was now ruled by First Lord's nephew?"

"Yes, yes, Lord, at once, messengers to all, even Governor Lutfu!"

So that guess was correct. "And his wife?"

"The Lady Nao-Pei, all Monserria knows of her, of her great beauty—"

Of course. She stifled a smile. How easy it was to foresee that Nao-Pei would try to seize power the quickest, most expedient way possible. "Tell all three lords and the Governor and his wife that Third Lord rides with her army to First City and requests a meeting there. They will understand."

"It will be done at once, Lord, immediately—"

"Now prepare a place for my army and me and my companions. We have ridden hard and we would rest for a while before continuing on to First City." She turned to Vorsa. "And we can use the time to establish a little more discipline. Lord Yassai will not be impressed at a rag-tag gathering of desert men, even if they do come riding on *plandals!*"

"Veh, you right, Dekla. You see, Vorsa get them to make you proud, you see."

"Will you be wanting the services of a maid?" the guard asked respectfully. "And perhaps a dressmaker?"

She turned on him coldly. "Why are you still standing here? If I had wanted—or needed—a maid or a dressmaker I would have asked for them. Or is this the way you follow orders?"

"Excuse me, Lord, forgive me." He backed away hastily, then turned and ran.

"You do that as well as Old Vinegar-Piss ever did," Michu said. He laughed. "Let's not tarry here too long, though. I can hardly wait to see you face down First Lord himself!"

19

i

They stayed the better part of a week at the border. Javerri changed her mind, ordered a dressmaker brought to her, and when asked about the unexpected delay in their journey would reply only, "I stay here because it pleases me to do it." She borrowed the services of a maid but did not touch any of the contents of the mysterious bundle the dressmaker delivered to her, taking away the money pouch in return. She spent a lot of time gazing north, into the distance, an unreadable expression on her face.

Only Wande-hari dared venture a guess as to her motives for the delay. "I think you want to allow plenty of time for the other lords to arrive at First City, and the new Governor of Third Province also."

Javerri only shrugged noncommittally.

"Just be aware that the delay also gives your enemies time to strengthen themselves."

"Thank you for your concern, Uncle," she said. "I overlook nothing."

Vorsa took the waiting time as an opportunity to impose a stronger degree of discipline on his troops than they had exhibited heretofore. He separated them into companies and troops, and established subleaders for them—which followed, more or less, their own tribal leanings, but reinforced the concept of their being a cohesive force under Vorsa's command.

At last the entire company set out again on the road that led to First City. In contrast to the mad dash across Fogestria, this time Javerri led her entourage at a leisurely pace, not unduly tiring to man or *plandal*. One of the pack birds carried, in addition to its customary burden, the package she had received from the local dressmaker.

She rode a little apart, remote, alone, untouchable, as if living in a waking dream of her own devising, as if going willingly to her own sacrifice. Chakei loped along by her side, carrying his "child," and wrapped in the same kind of silence as she, for he seldom spoke to her. Little by little, the people gathered along the road to watch their progress. First one or two from the nearest field, and then entire villages turned out to see them ride by. The people stood silent and respectful and only a murmur of voices could be heard as they passed. It was as if the people recognized a solemn, even momentous occasion. Now and then someone held up a child and said quietly, "See and remember."

As Javerri and her entourage came ever nearer to First City, this feeling she radiated began to spread even through the desert men. Now they didn't need Vorsa's haranguing to discipline themselves. If Javerri rode toward sacrifice, they accompanied her as her respectful escorts.

Only Ivo dared approach her. "If you desire it, and the occasion arises when you must die by your own hand, I would be honored to act as your second," he said.

She turned to him, a faint smile on her face. "Yes," she said. "If it comes to that, I accept your offer. You do know that it would mean your death as well."

"We would be together. If you were gone I would rather not live without you."

"Whatever punishment Halit is receiving this moment, it is far too lenient." She reached out and almost touched Ivo, but then drew her hand back. As had become her habit, she was carrying the *sarhandas* whip in it.

Then she turned her face northward again, touched her heel to the *plandal's* side, and rode on toward the place where her fate awaited her.

ii

Lutfu stared, scowling, at the letter in his hand. Unconsciously, he crumpled the red ribbon that had been tied around it as his other hand formed a fist.

"What is the matter, husband?" Nao-Pei said. "Is it bad news?"

"The worst news. Javere qa Hyasti is alive."

"What!" Nao-Pei cried, startled out of any semblance of calm. "That's impossible! You said—"

"Everybody said. But nevertheless, she is alive and even now rides toward First City with an army at her back. An army!"

"But how?" Nao-Pei said. "Where could she have—"

"Some rag-tag lot, according to my uncle's informants," Lutfu said. His voice lowered to a growl. "If it's a fight she's come after, I'm the man—"

"No." Nao-Pei's tone was imperious and Lutfu turned to stare at his wife. "No, I say. If she has indeed come seeking a fight, after all this time and after she was thought dead, her quarrel isn't with you." Or with me, Nao-Pei added silently to herself. May the Ancestor be praised for that. "You said she rides to First City. Therefore, her quarrel is with First Lord. Obviously she has completed the task he set her before she could be confirmed, for otherwise she would not be returning at all. Now she will claim her province as her own."

"A province I was made governor over."

"You need not fear that she will think of you as a usurper. You were only following your uncle's instructions, and in fact my sister could even think that you have been doing her a service in her absence, safeguarding the Third Province until she should return. That is, she could be brought to think that."

"And you believe you are the one to do this?"

Nao-Pei nodded. "Yes, I know that I am."

"You have proven clever in the past," Lutfu said grudgingly. "Perhaps you will be so now as well."

"That letter is a summons, isn't it? You are bidden to go to First City to greet the new Third Lord returning in triumph, yes? Then take me with you. If I am correct, you will need me with you. Javerri would never harm me; we are sisters. It will not hurt to remind her that by marrying me you have become kindred with her as well."

"My uncle instructs me to bring General Sigon with me, with the customary honor guard. He does not expressly forbid you to come also. Therefore, I will allow you to make the journey as well, though I had hoped to go swiftly and not be slowed by a procession of servants and baggage."

Nao-Pei inclined her head. "Thank you. I believe that you will not regret this decision."

iii

Wha-Li qa Chula, Lord of Second Province, fingered his yellow fan. He gazed at his old friend and chief adviser, General Fong. "And what do you think this means," he said flatly. It was not really a question.

"Everything or nothing," Fong replied, shrugging. "You have stayed out of that rats' nest in First City this long. You should stay out of it now."

"I cannot ignore a summons from First Lord."

"Perhaps you have forgotten how Yassai betrayed your father Kwa-Fei and took First Province for himself! His own brother, and he betrayed him!"

"My father was not fit to rule Monserria in spite of the fact that he was the elder son. Yassai was the better choice."

"The speech of a weakling and a coward!" The thunder of Fong's words echoed in the private chamber of Second Castle. Wha-Li merely looked at Fong mildly. "I apologize, Sire. It is affection for you and how you were cheated of your rightful inheritance that angers me, and causes my tongue to run wild. I will leave your presence at once and never return."

"You will stay until I bid you go." Wha-Li allowed a frosty smile to touch the corners of his mouth. "I know where your heart and your loyalties lie. But now we have an interesting new question concerning First Lord, and the new Third Lord. Tell me what your spies have learned about this matter."

Fong bowed in acknowledgment. "Your mercy knows no bounds. I would have had the head off anyone within the hour for such impertinence. Well, it seems your uncle still has his streak of avarice. It must run in that side of the family. Yassai sent this youngster, Javere qa Hyasti, off on some fool's errand designed to kill him. Or her. I forget. There was some talk about how Old Vinegar-Piss never got anything but daughters. And Yassai finally got a son only to have him stolen. Anyway, at least your succession is secure. With the fledgling lord out of the way, or so Yassai thought, he installed one of his sister's sons in Third Province and now Javere has returned. That's why he's called the full Council."

"At the very least," Wha-Li said, "it should be interesting. I hope your information is reliable. I shall go because I must, and though I am permitted one companion at my side I ask that you stay here to keep Second Province safe in my absence. It is a request."

"And because my mouth, which I have never learned to control, might be the death of us both. I know, I know. Please, take my son Naka in my stead."

"If I cannot have you, I will happily take your son. He is very like you. Second Province may be looked down upon as only a poor place for merchants and traders, but I am rich in having a loyal friend like you. Also, Second Province brings in enough revenue that Yassai does not entirely despise it. Third Province, with its fertile fields and bulging granaries, is too rich. It attracted my uncle's attention." He smiled a little more warmly. "How lucky I am to be Second Province's lord, and to have you for my friend."

iv

The Lord of Fourth Province, Ka-jin qa Kallin, known as the Procurer, tapped his long fingernails on the letter from First Lord. Curiously, he picked a little at the brown wax seal on the second smaller letter enclosed with it before breaking the seal and opening it. The imprint in the wax was undoubtedly from Seniz-Nan's personal signet; he recognized the tiny flaw in the carving of the yoni symbol, the one he had expressly instructed the craftsman to incorporate in the chop before he had given it to his niece.

"This way you will be able to recognize at once whether a letter is from the lady herself, or is a forgery," the artist told him. "The flaw is one that only your eyes will recognize."

And yet, this did not mean that somebody could not have stolen Seniz-Nan's chop. Well, speculation was all well and good but he would not know that until he opened the letter and saw whether it contained one of the signal phrases they had agreed upon for their private correspondence. It might have been an unnecessary precaution, but Ka-jin had never found too many precautions to be anything but wise.

Yes, there it was. "A lady sends close greetings." He read the letter with interest, then folded it and put it into the fire of the nearby brazier. He watched until he was satisfied that it had been entirely destroyed. First Lord's letter he opened and read again. This one was not destined for the fire, oh no.

Eeeei, but what a coil Seniz-Nan had gotten herself embroiled in, he thought. Not that he had any doubt that the Sublime Heir was none of First Lord's getting. After all those years, all those women? At least Seniz-Nan had had sense enough to do what was necessary, what was required. But to have the child stolen?

He thought a moment. Then his mind cleared. Of course.

It was so simple. To have the child stolen indeed. He wondered where Seniz-Nan had put the Heir for safekeeping. Could she have had the audacity to hide him in First City? No. If she had, she would not have sent the note imploring him for his help when he arrived to witness the establishment of this new Third Lord.

The Third Lord was a woman, if his spies' information was accurate, and he took various steps to insure that it always was. No mama with her Hyacinth Shadow World garden of beauties was better informed than he as to what went on, not only in Fourth Province but in much of Monserria as well. Interesting. He would have to keep a closer eye on Third Province in the future. He had known when this Javere crossed his own province to get to Fogestria and, indeed, it was by his orders as given him by First Lord that she had been held at the border until First Lord grew suspicious and sent his soldiers. Interesting how the woman had managed to cross over into the land to the south. He would have liked to have interrogated that maid who impersonated her, but Yassai had eliminated that possibility. Too bad. There was much information beyond what he had managed to learn, considerable though that was.

And the Governor of Third Province! Ka-jin allowed himself to smile a little. How he wished he had had the providing of women for that one. What power he could have acquired over the man and, through him, over Yassai himself. Seniz-Nan, he dismissed from his thoughts. She had performed her role, had produced the Heir even though she found it expedient to remove him from First City to save her own neck. Ka-jin doubted that she could perform a second miracle and get herself pregnant again before her luck ran out. If it did run out before the Heir were found. . . .

And even if she could last until after the Sublime Heir was found, she was doomed. He had a granddaughter who was even more beautiful, even more resourceful. He picked up a phallus-shaped hammer and rang a small gong with it. A secretary appeared at once.

"Write a letter to First Lord and tell him that I will be hon-

ored to come to First City for the Gathering of the Lords,"
he told the man. "And a trusted companion of my own choosing as well, as he directs me."

And who could that possibly be, he thought, when there
was no one in this world whom he trusted?

v

Lord Lennai qa Rojan of Fifth Province straightened a
minute disarrangement of his blue robe and brushed an imaginary speck of lint from his sleeves. He placed First Lord's letter on the polished table in front of him and looked at the
council of scholars sitting around it, waiting.

"We have a question to consider today," he said. "First
Lord has summoned me to a full Council of the Lords."

"How long has it been?" Pei-lin qa Rojan, his sister and a
formidable expert on the law, always gave herself permission
to speak first in Council.

"I think this is the first complete gathering since Yassai
confirmed Lord Qai, the new lord's father," said Sheng. Despite his having been born a peasant, he had risen to become
the most learned historian in all of Fifth Province, and was
now in fact head of the historians' guild.

Pei-lin snorted through her nose, a habit Lennai had always
deplored as unfeminine. "A woman!" she exclaimed. "It is un-
heard of, a woman as a province lord!"

"No, not entirely." Sheng reached into his sleeve and drew
out a packet of notes. "I have done some research. Twice in
Monserria history a woman has ruled a province in that
province's heir's minority. Once, in Fourth Province—" a
hissed intake of breath greeted these words "—a woman
ruled for nearly forty years and established the Hyacinth
Shadow World as Monserria knows it. And countless other
times women have taken their lords' places when the country
was at war, not to mention those occasions when the lords
were simply occupied elsewhere. This includes the Third
Province."

"But never as ruler in law," Pei-lin said. She thumped her fist on the table for emphasis. "I have read the same books as you have. Never as ruler in law under any circumstances in the Third Province."

"No, not before now," Sheng said. "But you forget that Lord Qai declared her his son."

"As if that made any difference!" Pei-lin snorted again.

The other scholars at the table merely exchanged glances; this was old to everyone, the way Sheng and Pei-lin fought each other at the slightest provocation. Hana-ka the calligrapher cleared her throat. "Perhaps it is better to have a woman declared man to rule Third Province than have it fall into Yassai's greedy hands," she suggested mildly.

"Perhaps we should consider which of us should accompany Lennai," said Lu-wan, just as mildly. The head of the mages' guild traced a line of fire on the tabletop, watched it dance for a moment, and then extinguished it, leaving the surface undamaged.

"Not until the question of inheritance is settled!" Pei-lin said fiercely.

"I think not," Pau-qa the archivist said. "This matter has already been settled, at least partially. We have Lord Qai's original will stored safely, and a copy delivered to Yassai, as usual. In the will, Qai particularly declares Javere qa Hyast his son and his heir. I do not see any legal loophole to be used against him. Her. It was very neatly done."

"I recognized the hand of Wande-hari in this," Lu-wan said. "He and I were classmates together. I always said the law lost a good practitioner when he took up magic."

"Well, he or whoever else he had helping him created a nice muddle for us to straighten out. Yassai's meddling and trying to do away with Javere didn't help matters." Lennai smiled. "Did you know she is known as the Ladylord?"

"Well, that speaks for her audacity," Pei-lin said. "Very well, I will accompany you, brother. Let's be on our way quickly, so we can return and get back to our studies. I very much dislike having my research interrupted in this way."

Lennai declined to mention that Pei-lin had not been invited. He hoped he could find enough soldiers to make up a decent company of guards.

vi

In Third City, Madam Farhat withdrew into the privacy of her own room, leaving word that she was not to be disturbed until she came out again, for she had some thinking to do.

She poured hot strong wine and drank it quickly, eager for the liquid to start her mind working the way it always did. Just enough, and she could think clearly. Too much, and she tended to lose track of things these days. As the warmth spread through her she pondered how she could turn this latest piece of information to her best advantage.

Eeeei, but what a surprise to learn that the Ladylord still lived! It was, Farhat discovered to her mild astonishment, a welcome surprise at that for she had come to dislike Governor Lutfu intensely. Not that her dislike had anything to do with the way he ruled Third Province, which seemed competent enough if harsh. Oh, no, it was personal only and one did not allow personalities to get in the way of business. Also, with the new games Nao-Pei had discovered, Farhat knew that she held both of them in a web of power that waited only until she could figure out how best to use it. That platform, for example. Farhat knew what it was, even if Nao-Pei did not.

The Ladylord's miraculous return would disrupt all this careful maneuvering, to be sure, but then she owed Farhat a great deal as well and not the kind of debt that can be paid with a sack of coins. That is, Farhat thought as she poured herself more wine, if she lived through her confrontation with First Lord. Audacity was all well and good, but this was sheer foolhardiness if the rumors were true. The Ladylord was obviously riding toward First City to challenge Yassai—not that she hadn't reason, many times over—and one did not do this and expect to live.

Therefore, Farhat thought, she'd be in First City as well when this meeting took place, and in the very room if she could arrange it. The pass Kin-chao had "lost" would see to that. Farhat also had a few connections in First City, and some favors to call in. If Ladylord survived—and she couldn't think how she could survive—she'd be among the first to congratulate her. If she perished—and Farhat thought this far more likely—she'd be among the first to swear loyalty to the new Third Lord, Lutfu. And also she would not miss such a spectacle for anything in the world!

She wondered who else in her house had learned the news. Perhaps nobody, perhaps everybody. Well, it didn't matter. All would know soon enough.

vii

Javerri and her entourage met a small army of red-uniformed soldiers about five *ri* outside First City, close enough that the walls could just be seen as a smudge on the horizon. The sky had grown dark, signaling an approaching winter storm. The soldiers blocked the road and deployed on either side so no one could go through. Counting quickly, she reckoned that they outnumbered her forces by roughly half. Dismounting from her *plandal,* she stalked forward to speak with the commander of the soldiers. She put her hands on the hilts of Steel Fury and Lady Impatience, not defiantly, but as a show of firmness.

"Move aside," she said. "I have business in First City and you are in my way."

"Who are you and what business is that?" the commander said. He didn't have the bearing or the mien of someone used to command. Perhaps he had been very recently promoted and was not yet used to his status. "First Lord orders you to halt and wait here. My orders are to make sure you stay in this spot until you can produce proof of your identity."

Javerri smiled grimly. The man was a fool in addition to

being inexperienced. "Move aside," she repeated, "or I will move you." She tightened her grip on her weapons.

"No. Return to wherever you came from with your army of brigands and the unnatural creatures they—and you—ride."

Behind her, Javerri could hear the shuffling of *plandals* and the murmuring of the desert men as they dismounted. "My army and my mounts are none of your concern. I tell you for the third time, move aside, or I will destroy you."

"You wouldn't dare refuse to obey First Lord's order, or to fight First Lord's soldiers." The commander laughed. "But if it's a lesson you need—" He reached for his sword. Before he could clear it, Vorsa yelled something in his own speech that could have only been an order to attack. The shab raced forward, his own sword drawn, and hacked the man down where he stood.

"Ho!" Vorsa cried. "Now we see little fighting, veh!"

In a heartbeat the battle was joined. Amid shouts and the most blood-curdling of war cries, red-uniformed soldiers began falling wholesale under the weapons of the desert men. Here and there a desert dweller went down and did not rise again, but the sheer ferocity Javerri's men displayed more than made up for their inferiority of numbers. Apparently their long idleness had honed their appetite and spirit for fighting to a keen edge lacking in Yassai's hired troops.

Michu appeared at Javerri's side. "Now you're close to seeing a real battle!" he shouted. The din was so loud Javerri could scarcely hear him. "Even though these desert men don't know our customs, they can show you how a lord should be protected!" His weapons were undrawn, though his hands rested on the hilts.

At almost the same moment, Ivo took his place at Javerri's other side. "Now you are truly safe!" he told her.

Any reply Javerri might have thought of making would have been lost in the din. She glanced around, looking for Chakei and Wande-hari. To her relief she spotted the ancient mage and Lek close together. Wande-hari was holding the

Dragon-warrior's "child" while Chakei, roaring loudly
enough to be heard over the noise of battle, fought his way
toward her.

Guard thou the old one! she told him. **He needs it and
I do not!**

He didn't pause. **protect ladylord always i**

She turned to Michu and cupped her hand to her mouth,
shouting into his ear. "We must go to Wande-hari! Chakei
should be guarding him but he won't!"

Michu nodded. She turned to repeat her words to Ivo, but
he had already taken in the situation and understood it. He
put Javerri in front of him and motioned to Michu to go in
front of her. Then they picked their way across the space that
separated them from the old magician, matching themselves
to Michu's pace.

Wait, wait, I come to you! Javerri told Chakei. **Now
do as I command! Wande-hari holds your son, remember!**

Chakei wavered. **forget i, very bad**

A red-uniformed soldier rushed toward the mage, his sword
upraised. Lek flinched. Then, bravely, he set himself between
the soldier and Wande-hari. The attacker slammed into something unseen, and staggered backwards, dazed. A desert man
rushed past and cut him down instantly. Wande-hari and
Lek, she realized, were standing in a Circle of Protection.
No, thou art not bad, she told Chakei. **But thou art not
obedient when thou should be.**

obedient hard sometimes

Yes, I know. She sighed mentally.

They reached their companions and Wande-hari opened
the Circle just enough for them to slip inside. Chakei hesitated, and then stepped back. **fight i, too long not**

"Why doesn't he come inside?" Ivo said.

Chakei went roaring into the thick of the combat and
Javerri caught a sense of great delight in the way he scattered
the First Lord's soldiers before him. "He wants to enjoy himself like the others are doing," she said. "Apparently he had
been idle for too long."

"He'd better hurry," Michu said, laughing. "Maybe he can have his fun chasing the ones who are running away!"

And indeed, the battle—virtually a slaughter of Yassai's troops—had ended almost as quickly as it had begun. As they watched, reduniformed soldiers streamed in the direction of First City, running as fast as they could go. Vorsa reappeared, moving in Javerri's direction, and since there was no more danger in their immediate vicinity, Wande-hari dissolved the Circle before the shab could hurt himself on it the way he had the first time he and Javerri had met.

"Too soon over," Vorsa said, pleased. "Too easy. But men happy to have little fight at last!"

"They are running toward something no better there than here," Michu said sourly. "Yassai will not be pleased. His temper will not be any the sweeter for your having routed his troops."

"Veh, we teach him better lesson later!" He grinned, gesturing at the desert men who were even now running to mount their *plandals* the better to pursue the runaways.

Let him have his triumph, Javerri thought, and the desert men with him. Truly they deserved it. But Michu was right. Even if First Lord picked fools to command his troops, thinking that nobody would dare gainsay his least orders, the sheer numbers he had at muster could still overcome his enemies when they came too close to First City.

Strange that First Lord's soldiers had been vanquished so easily. If she had been in First Lord's place, especially considering the trials Yassai had put her to and how much trouble he had gone to, to ensure her death— She would never have allowed an enemy to get as far as she had, and certainly would have dealt with him in a more decisive way than Yassai had done.

However, in this as in so many other matters, she would follow her father's example. When all odds seemed against him, Wande-hari had told her, that was the time he raised his banners to their highest and blew the loudest war horns.

Think, Javerri, think! she told herself. Try to imagine what

Lord Qai would do in a situation such as this, supposing he were foolish enough to get himself into the position of opposing First Lord. She forced herself to a calmness she didn't really feel.

Only a coalition of the other lords would have a chance of forcing First Lord into an action or into abandoning an action he proposed to take—and now, with this battle almost at the walls of First City, Yassai had managed to make it appear that Javerri had come against him as a rebel. She had no illusions that the whole thing, and the sacrifice of the soldiers, had been deliberately contrived to present just such an appearance.

With a chill, she realized that Yassai had played yet another trick on her. If he had truly wanted to stop her, he would have sent an overwhelming force and not just enough to make the odds seem a little dangerous. And he would have sent crack troops. These men were probably the dregs, picked from among Yassai's worst, and dispatched with the express purpose of being killed by her army. Now, with just a little manipulation of the reports, she could be portrayed as being a traitor, of engaging in open rebellion against her sovereign lord rather than defending herself against his unwarranted attack on her. But she had no proof of what she instinctively felt to be true.

And she had no idea what any of the other lords of Monserria would think about it, if this were true and if the truth were known, or whose side they would ultimately wind up on. One thing was certain, though. If she took anything but a defensive posture they would not—could not—support her.

She turned to Vorsa. "Stop them," she said. "The men must not pursue First Lord's soldiers!" Mincing no words, she outlined her suspicions. "No matter how they—and I, for that matter—might enjoy it, running them down would damage my cause beyond repair!"

He nodded, understanding at once, and ran to stop his troops from slaughtering their opponents. Sounds of protest and quarreling began to rise at once as a result of this unwelcome order. Vorsa's voice rose even louder as he bellowed the men into submission.

She sent a mental message to Chakei as well, only to find that he was loping back toward her, having quickly grown bored with chasing the red-uniformed soldiers who would not turn and fight.

not fun, return i he said. ***son?***

Thy child is safe, she told him. ** *Wande-hari guarded him well.***

is good old man, sweet inside

** *Yes, very sweet—*** But Chakei had broken the connection.

Gradually the shouting died away and Vorsa returned. "Not happy with order, but they obey anyway." He grinned. "I think they a little afraid of Dekla as well, small woman with fierce soul and scar on face to boot."

"Thank you," she said. "We will ride to First City, but not in pursuit. I must leave the men encamped outside the walls. This is Lord Yassai's order, and the custom as well. Please choose trusted messengers to keep communications open in case we have to send for them."

"Veh," Vorsa said. "I leave Imroud in charge of camp and go inside city with you."

"Thank you," she said gratefully. "And Lek, where is Lek?"

"Already seeing to the wounded," Ivo said. "On both sides."

"Excellent. I will want him to stay outside and continue to look after those who were hurt."

"I will tell him."

Javerri turned to Wande-hari. "Do you still have paper and ink and writing implements?"

"I do have a little of all of these remaining."

"And my personal chop?"

"Yes, I have kept it safe with me. And green wax also."

"Then write a formal message from me to the First Lord. List all the crimes he has committed or attempted to commit against me, and say also that he has shown himself unfit for the position he holds. Say that I challenge him on behalf of all the other lords of Monserria and personally as well. Say that I demand a formal hearing before the full Council of Lords, that my demands for justice be heard." She handed Wande-hari the *sarhandas* whip. "Include this with the letter."

"Do you think this is wise, to send him such a challenge?" Ivo said. "Wouldn't the charges alone suffice?"

"I agree," Wande-hari said. "The personal challenge is unnecessary and may even injure your cause, which Lady Moon and Ancestor know is just!"

"Write it as I have instructed you," she said stubbornly. She put her hands on the hilts of her weapons and glared at each of her companions in turn. "It is a matter of honor."

"I believe this is what you really meant when you asked me to be your second," Ivo said.

"Yes. And I will hold you to your promise. All on one throw. If I win, I win and if not, I die. I must say that I do not believe Yassai will answer the challenge, though. Now, Uncle, will you obey me?"

Wande-hari bowed his head. "Yes, Ladylord."

"Good. Now, let us proceed to First City, but at a modest pace, not too eagerly and not dawdling on the way, but as people with a fair and legitimate reason for going there. We must give First Lord no cause to move against us again. Are you agreed?"

They all nodded. "Yes, Ladylord," Michu said. "And if I may say so, you grow more and more like Old Vinegar-Piss every day," he added. "I mean this as a compliment."

"And I take it as such." She led the way to where their *plandals* waited, mounted, and clicked her tongue at the bird to signal it to go forward. As she rode past the desert men, she saw some sullen faces in the crowd but most of them eyed her with something akin to respect.

"Chase cowards not for Walloh, Yonal, Oramin!" someone cried from the ranks. "We fight real men, veh!"

"Even if we fight each other!" someone else yelled.

That seemed to break the tension, and, laughing, the desert men fell in behind Javerri. They traveled the remaining distance to First City without further incident. She lingered outside only long enough to make sure that the company had picked a site to camp on that would be easily defended in case of treachery, and also one out of the wintry wind, protected as much as possible from the storm that would break soon. The desert men began putting up their tents, much less concerned than she. Lek went to work immediately, ministering to the wounded. Then she entered the city with Ivo, Wande-hari, Vorsa, Michu, Chakei—still carrying his "son"—and her one remaining Monserrian soldier, Nali, very proud to be put in charge of the Ladylord's honor guard of desert men.

As she expected, Red guards awaited her just inside the gate. "Send word to First Lord that Third Lord Javere qa Hyasti qa Gilad has returned and now requires that he should admit her at once into his presence."

"We have been instructed that you would soon return," the commander of the guard said, "and have orders to conduct you to a place where you can refresh yourself until Lord Yassai sends for you."

"In the meantime, please take this to him from me," Javerri said, handing him the parcel of her sealed letter wrapped around the *sarhandas* whip Wande-hari had prepared at her command. "Nali, please take three men with you and see with your own eyes that my letter is delivered properly. Then report to me."

"Yes, Ladylord," Nali said, very proud.

The commander glowered, but did not object. "Come this way," he told Nali.

"More waiting, cooling our heels," Michu muttered under his breath. Javerri shot him a warning look and he subsided though he scowled and turned the corners of his mouth down in disapproval. He exaggerated his limp as they followed an escort of Reds to a set of apartments, not the same as they had occupied before, inside Stendas Castle, where servants waited to minister to them.

Javerri closed herself inside her room, admitting no one, and emerging only for meals. She refused the services of all but one maid, though she did send for the mysterious bundle she had acquired at the border. The rest of her companions arranged themselves to wait as best they could, according to their temperaments, and Chakei crouched, as was his custom, just outside Javerri's door.

20

i

*T*he storm broke the next day, bringing with it rains mixed with snow and ice. The day after that, during breakfast, the summons came from Yassai. They were to appear in his Audience Hall at the hour before noon. In addition, there was a letter.

"Record time," Wande-hari said. He handed Javerri the letter and she broke the seal.

"He has already called the Council," she said, scanning rapidly, "for purposes of endorsing his confirming or not confirming me as Third Lord. He says nothing about answering my challenge. As for my charges against him, I must prove them. Nothing unexpected here. Ah. He will allow me four witnesses."

"Did he place any restrictions on who these witnesses can be?" Wande-hari asked.

"No, just that they be qualified to present evidence to support my claim."

"Good," the magician said with satisfaction. "I have quite a bit to say about the, the person First Lord arranged to have accompany us on our journey."

Javerri gazed at her companions. "Five total. You, Ivo, Michu, Vorsa. And Chakei, who will not testify. Among us, we can present the entire story." She took a deep breath. "The hour before noon, he said. I have some preparation, and I must dress appropriately. Please excuse me."

She returned to her room and the maid slid the door shut behind her.

Ivo watched her go, worry plain on his face. "I fear she will not live to see the day end," he said quietly.

"It is possible," Michu said. "But think, boy! She is pitting herself against the First Lord. He is a corrupt old bastard, but he is still the Supreme Ruler of all of Monserria. She may die but if she brings Yassai down with her, think of the songs and legends about her!" He smiled. "I admire her enormously. My own private nickname for her is going to be Young Lady Vinegar-Piss."

"Then you do not expect her to grow old," Ivo said. "If he kills her, I swear I will kill him myself before they get me."

"You decide too much too soon, Elder Brother, kill off little Dekla before fight even," Vorsa said. He stretched vigorously. "Me, I am glad for seeing this great First Lord, finally get out of rooms where we stay too long. Maybe we all have big fight after all, then go home or maybe someplace else."

"I hope it is all that simple, Vorsa," Wande-hari said, "but I wonder if any of us will be alive by sunset. Third Lord is right, however. If we are facing death and even if we aren't, it behooves each of us to dress our finest. First Lord's stewards are well-trained; they have provided us with suitable clothing. Let us follow Javerri's example and make ourselves as presentable as we can."

A little while later, freshly bathed and clad in green—even Vorsa, who looked very uncomfortable and out of place in Monserrian garb—the four men and Chakei waited for Javerri to emerge from her room. When she did, a little shock ran through all but Vorsa, who did not know what to expect.

Instead of being fashionably attired in a rich dress and even richer underdress, her hair immaculately coiled and her face made up to hide the scar on her cheek and enhance her natural beauty, Javerri presented a bizarre, even stark appearance. Her face was clean and shiny, shadows under her eyes, marks of strain apparent. She had clubbed her hair back in warrior fashion and tied a white band around her forehead. She wore a green coat of strange design, heavily embroidered with jewels on the collar, that hid her completely. Wande-hari gave a start of recognition.

"The coat in the dream—"

She just looked at him, her expression remote, as if she scarcely saw him. Without a word, she moved past him and Ivo took his place at her side, half a step behind her. Chakei loped to her other side, refusing to give way to anyone. The stiff green coat concealed her so well that she seemed to glide rather than walk. She nodded at the escort of Reds outside the apartment door, and followed them the short distance to Yassai's Audience Hall. Nali, now promoted to captain, fell in behind with his company of desert men.

The doors were already open, and their carved Guardians glowered at them. But they had never created such a stir as her appearance did among the men and women crowded inside. A buzz of comment and speculation from the onlookers immediately arose and, from the ranks of the courtiers on one side of the room, a tall and lean figure rose and came toward her. A woman's voice rose in protest from the front of the room, quickly silenced by a man telling her to be quiet. Javerri recognized Nao-Pei and Lutfu.

"Greetings, Ladylord Javere qa Hyasti qa Gilad. I am informed that Third Lord is allowed four witnesses in addition to herself at this proceeding," Sigon said. He bowed very low. "I beg you, please allow me to be one of them. I have much to say about how Third Province was treated in your absence."

Javerri turned her head slowly to look at him. "Greetings, General Sigon," she said. "Indeed, I think you may have much that is valuable to say. But that means that one of my present number of witnesses must remain behind."

"I will," Wande-hari said. "Lord Yassai has no love of mages, as we all know. But I will wait just outside the door with Nali, in case you need me."

"Thank you, Uncle." Then Javerri turned and the guards closed the doors behind her. She walked without haste, her companions following, toward the dais. There were no braziers; the heat of many bodies warmed the room. Because this was a full Council, all the lords had guards standing around the inside of the room—red, blue, green, yellow, brown. She wondered how many Greens were truly Greens, loyal to her. To the left of the cushion where Yassai sat, the other three lords of Monserria occupied cushions of honor, all clad in their province colors. Two of them, the Second and Fifth Lords, had companions with them but Fourth Lord sat alone. With them was Lutfu—dressed, Javerri noted, in green—and by his side, Nao-Pei. Only two other people besides Yassai occupied the dais—the customary headsman, and a shadowy figure dressed in black robes with orange embroidery on the sleeves. "Yassai, First Lord of Monserria!" Javerri said. "I have returned with the token you required to confirm me as Third Lord."

She turned to Chakei. **Place thy son at his feet.**
no
It will be well, I promise thee. It is only for a little while.
no But he sounded a little less adamant.
For me I ask thee. For me.
little while only

The Dragon-warrior, moving with great reluctance, set the scarlet egg on the corner of the dais as far from Yassai as he could and still obey. From somewhere in the room a baby whimpered as if in sympathy.

Javerri turned again to face First Lord. "Now I charge you with hindering me in the task you set for me, even to scheming for my death. I have brought witnesses to attest to the truth of these charges."

Yassai inclined his head formally. "I will hear them."

One by one, the witnesses stepped forward to tell their portions of the story while Javerri stood, motionless in her green coat, and everyone in the room leaned forward to listen. Michu spoke of the difficulties escaping across the border into Fogestria, and how they had nearly perished in the desert. Then Shab Vorsa took up the tale, to the point where they located the eggs beyond the Great Wall. Ivo then corroborated the preceding testimony and gave his account of Halit's death, after which Sigon related the state of affairs in Third Province under Governor Lutfu's rule, and how he had assumed from the first that the Ladylord had never even been expected to return. He hinted at, but did not elaborate upon, the possibility of revolt by a noble with close—very close—personal ties to a member of the ruling family. Then it was Javerri's turn to speak.

Not another sound could be heard anywhere in the room. Even the baby was silent, as, sparing nothing, she told of her rape by Halit. "And it is this," she said, her voice beginning to rise, "that constitutes the deepest crime of all. You know the custom in Third Province, that the lord must come to it virgin. Even if you could not kill me with all your scheming, you sought at least to bar me from my inheritance in this most cowardly fashion. And it is for this that I challenge you—not as First Lord, but you, Yassai qa Chula—to personal combat to wipe out this stain against my honor!"

A sound as of many held breaths being released went through the room and Yassai stirred for the first time since the testimony had begun. "I received your challenge in the letter you sent me," he said, "and believed you would think better of it once your head had cooled."

Javerri stared at him, unyielding. "Never."

Yassai sighed. "So be it. But I am an old man, feeble and scarcely fit to move. I have not used weapons for many years. You are a woman and, despite your many adventures, women can never be the equal of men in combat. Let us choose champions, therefore, and settle this score between us."

A courtier arose from where he had been sitting. "I will be the Third Lord's champion!" he said.

"No, I will!" cried another.

"Choose me!" The young man with Second Lord leapt to his feet. The headsman moved toward him, and Second Lord pulled him back down again before he could strike.

Throughout the room, men supposedly loyal to Yassai were risking certain death to oppose him. The baby began to wail in earnest. At almost the same instant, Michu, Sigon, and Vorsa all declared themselves ready to fight for Javerri.

"If any will be her champion, I claim that right." Ivo laid his hand on his sword but Javerri stopped him.

"I see that nobody proclaims himself your man and offers to go against me. You must order someone to fight for you, Yassai," she said. "If Lady Moon and Ancestor are on my side, I will prevail. But be sure that when I have vanquished your champion I will then kill you in turn."

"You would die for the very attempt," Yassai said flatly, "even for lifting a weapon in my direction."

"Just so."

Yassai turned, smiling. "I have my champion ready." He beckoned and the shadowy figure stepped forward. He was unarmed.

"What foolishness is this?" Javerri said. "You mock me. This is no fighter."

The man bowed. "I have weapons though they are not what you might recognize," he said. "I am the one known as the Scorpion, and you will face me or no one. Prepare yourself."

A magician. Ancestor knew what he would use against her. Would he throw tiny exploding pebbles at her? Smother her with singing butterflies? Well, nothing for it but to play out the charade, Javerri thought, and hope he doesn't use wizard's fire. She led her companions to the side of the dais opposite from the one occupied by the three lords and Lutfu. "Wait for me here," she said. "Whatever happens, do not interfere." She unfastened the jeweled collar of her coat and slipped it off, handing it to Michu. Another murmur arose from the onlookers as she stood revealed in the pure white trousers and tunic of the ceremonial warrior. She carried both Steel Fury and Lady Impatience in her sash. From the inside of the coat she took four daggers and slipped them into the headband she wore—sure sign, if any were needed, that she intended this fight to be to the death.

The people in the room were already hastily clearing a

space in front of the dais and she positioned herself carefully
sideways to First Lord. Steel Fury rang as she drew him full
from his sheath, and she assumed a fighting stance. Then she
stood, poised, waiting for the combat to begin.

The Scorpion did not step down from the dais. His hand
moved in curious gestures and his eyes glowed orange. His
face suddenly showed lines of strain. A rending noise came
from the back of the room, then another, and a woman
screamed. More shouts and outcries filled the room. The
Guardians tore themselves away from the doors and began
to stump forward on wooden legs. One man threw himself
against the nearest one and died for his trouble, swatted aside
as easily as a man might brush away a fly. Impossibly, the
crowd shrank back, making room for them. The reverbera-
tions of their footsteps shook the very walls. The rafters
trembled and the stink of fear filled the room. Chakei started
toward them.

No! I command thee! Stay back—

But he did not heed. Then, unaccountably, he halted and
stood motionless as the towering inhuman figures passed him
on their way toward Javerri. She spared a glance at the magician and realized, from the added lines in his face, that he
had immobilized the Dragon-warrior. Then she tightened
her grip on Steel Fury. One of the Guardians was almost
upon her. The Scorpion moved his hands as if he held a
weapon.

The Guardian struck at her. She dodged the blow easily
and attacked in turn. Wood chips flew as Steel Fury bit into
her opponent. The second Guardian attacked and she had to
parry, expecting to be crushed as easily as the dead man had
been. The blow was light, lighter by far than the one she
struck in return.

Thanks to Sigon's training, she recognized the strategy at
once. The carved wooden Guardians, slow and clumsy, were
probably unstoppable except by fire. Perhaps, given enough
time, she could hack them into small enough pieces to kill
them—if she lasted that long. Either of them could have
struck her down with a single blow but the Scorpion, con-

trolling their movements, chose not to allow them to do it. Therefore, she would have to fight them until she could no longer lift her weapon and then die ignominiously as they unleashed their immense strength at last.

With a scream of defiance, she attacked and, again, wood chips flew. Metal clanged against metal and sparks flew from the Guardian's breastplate. One of the Guardians tried to circle to her left and she turned quickly to block the blow that might have killed her. Beyond the Guardian, she caught a glimpse of Yassai leaning forward, intent on the battle. Suddenly aware of a movement behind her, she whirled just in time to see the second Guardian, sword held high, advancing on her, advancing toward First Lord.

Now! she thought. Ei, now! Ivo, Sigon, Michu, know thou what I do. She lowered Steel Fury, closed her eyes, and prepared to die.

"No!" The immense power of Wande-hari's voice cut across the din of battle. Javerri opened her eyes involuntarily. The mage fairly flew into the room, strands of light sparkling in his fingers. Before she could quite register the fact that he had entered through a hole in the door created by one of the Guardians tearing itself loose, he had launched a great fireball from each hand. The Guardians burst into flame. Javerri turned to see the Scorpion stagger back, clutching at his chest.

"Feng-chu qa Chamvas!" Wande-hari said. "Feng-chu, *come here!*"

The one known as the Scorpion took a step forward. Then another. And still another.

"Eeeei, my lifelong enemy met again at last. You! You are the Scorpion, and Anselme, and Feng-chu, and who knows how many other names you have gone by, but your true name commands you. It was you, as the Scorpion, who has corrupted First Lord beyond his natural inclination and nearly ruined Monserria in the doing. It was you, as Anselme, who trained Halit in his twisted ways until he was your creature entirely. Were you in his mind when he was raping Third Lord? *Tcha!"*

Orange fire gathered in Wande-hari's hands, shone from his eyes, lifted his hair wildly. He opened his mouth and the fire erupted in a great arrow that pierced the Scorpion's body. As the fire filled him, he swelled, glowing from every pore. Abruptly, with a *bang!* as air rushed in to replace the empty spot where he had stood, his robes collapsed. A scorpion scuttled out. Wande-hari stepped forward and crushed it underfoot.

He turned to Javerri. "I swore to thee that I would blast with wizard's fire any who would harm thee." He staggered and nearly fell. Ivo rushed forward to support the elderly mage. Chakei stirred a little.

Yassai raised his arms, fists clenched. "Guards!" he screeched. "Where are my guards! Headsman, do your duty!"

But everywhere, each red-uniformed man stood surrounded by Blues, Yellows, Browns, and a few Greens. Other Greens found themselves powerless as Nali and his guards blocked them. The headsman stepped forward, sword raised ready to take Javerri's head. Chakei, finally released from the spell binding him, leapt toward him and tore the man's arm off. As an afterthought, he tore off the other one as well and dropped the man to bleed to death, screaming, where he lay. Mercifully, he died very fast.

"Is there nobody who will obey their Sublime Ruler?" Yassai's rage looked fit to kill him where he sat. "This woman has defied me! Kill her! And kill the mage! He murdered my champion!"

Second Lord got to his feet. "I am Wha-Li qa Chula," he said, "nephew to Yassai qa Chula, being the son of his elder brother, and ruler of the Second Province. I say that I recognize what this lady has done today and salute her bravery. Also, I salute the magician." He tapped his yellow fan gracefully against his forearm, snapped it open, and brandished it.

"I agree," Fifth Lord Lennai qa Rojan said. "Extraordinary bravery." He applauded and snapped open his blue fan.

The woman beside him spoke up. "I am Pei-lin qa Rojan and no warrior, but I do know the law, including the laws of combat. This lady stood between your champion's creature and you, as it attacked—a clear and shocking act of dishonor. This lady showed the highest honor herself, willing to allow herself to be killed in protest. That she lives is due to the mage's action. Though mages may kill directly only in certain circumstances, I judge this to be a proper one. Strictly speaking, he killed an insect, not a man. In any case, they saved your life, First Lord."

"Your worthless life, that is," Fourth Lord Ka-jin qa Kallin said. He applauded with his fan. "Your actions would turn the stomach of the madam of the poorest house in all of Fourth Province."

Without anyone's willing it, all attention centered on Lutfu qa Masfa and also on Nao-Pei qa Hyasti qa Masfa. Slowly, as if all his joints hurt, he got to his feet and pulled Nao-Pei with him. "I must protest my loyalty to my uncle, while at the same time disapproving of, ah, certain of the things he has done."

"Well and cleverly put," Wha-Li said. He bowed with a good deal of irony. Then he turned to Javerri. "I don't think I have to ask any of my fellow lords whether or not they ratify you and at this point, Yassai's wishes are irrelevant. You deserved confirmation on the occasion of your first interview—ei, from the time your father drew his last breath. Therefore, I declare that your status was valid from that moment. Greetings, Javere qa Hyasti qa Gilad, rightful Lord of the Third Province!"

Emotions warred in Javerri's heart. So all had been for nothing—the perils, the journey, the rape, cheating her and Ivo out of their happiness. And yet, not for nothing. Yassai had been defeated, and it was something nearly everyone welcomed. At least she had accomplished that. Javerri managed to bow to them all. "Thank you," she said.

The entire room erupted in a frenzy of cheering. Second Lord moved to the front of the dais, raising his hands for silence. "Please, please!" he shouted. "This terrible business is ended. Please have the decency to leave us now."

At once, the guards began herding the reluctant crowd out through the ruined doors. They moved slowly, dragging their feet, watching the great ones still standing on or beside the dais.

"There remains the question of my uncle and his obvious unfitness for continuing as First Lord," Wha-Li said. He gestured, and two Yellows came and stationed themselves on either side of Yassai, though keeping a respectful distance. In a moment, obeying orders from the other lords, two Browns and two Blues joined them.

"You and you," Lutfu said, indicating the Greens. "And you two Reds over there. See to it that my uncle is guarded well."

Another four men joined the guard around Yassai. Wha-Li turned to the others. "This is but the first step. Now we must decide who will rule the First Province in the late First Lord's stead while we decide what, if anything, to do with him."

Lutfu actually took a step forward, brushing past Fourth Lord.

Pei-lin snorted through her nose. "Stand back, youngster," she said. "Yassai qa Chula usurped First Lordship from his elder brother, Kwa-Fei qa Chula, relegating him to Second Lordship. Wha-Li is Kwa-Fei's son. Therefore, in the absence of any direct heir of Yassai's body, the title of First Lord goes to Wha-Li."

"As Yassai's close kinsman I formally call for his removal from his high station and banishment from Monserria," Wha-Li said. "Vote!"

"Aye," Fifth Lord said promptly.

"Banishment?" Fourth Lord Ka-jin looked as if he wanted to spit. "I vote for execution!"

"That was not the option I offered," Wha-Li said mildly.

"Then banishment it is. I know of an island that will do. But it's far too good for him."

A veiled woman carrying a baby in her arms fought her way through the soldiers trying to remove the crowd from the room. Her companion, a man with close-cropped hair, struggled with the guard trying to stop her and she slipped past them. The veil covering her head fell off in the confusion.

"Safia!" Javerri exclaimed involuntarily. She scarcely recognized her. Behind her, Yassai gasped.

"You know this woman?" Wha-Li asked.

"Yes, yes—it is a long story!"

"Too long to tell any but the ending." The courtesan held up the infant. "First Lord thought I was dead, and I nearly was. But I lived. And here I am, bringing with me the new First Lord, son of Lady Seniz-Nan and Yassai."

"But the Sublime Heir was kidnapped," Fifth Lord said. "This could be anybody's child."

"Send for the Lady Seniz-Nan so she can identify him. We schemed together to hide him away safely," Safia said. "And to save her life as well. She had come under Lord Yassai's displeasure even as I did, and look at what he did to me."

"This will take a little time, that is clear." Wha-Li nodded to one of his Yellows and the man disappeared at once. The last of the crowd got herded out, guards closed the doors and stood outside blocking the interior from the curious, and the lords and their companions pulled cushions into a semicircle and sat down again. Gratefully, Javerri joined them. Her knees had, unaccountably, gone a little wobbly. She was struck by the remarkable informality the other lords accepted without question, but then this was truly a remarkable occasion.

While they waited, at Second Lord's direction Safia told them about the scheme that let Chimoko kill herself in honor, and its consequences. The lords shook their heads, gesturing and murmuring among themselves, believing and yet disbelieving. Javerri sat still, knowing Safia spoke the truth. And Lutfu, she noted. Lutfu didn't move. But then he knew his uncle.

The Yellow guard returned with Seniz-Nan. She took one look at the baby and all but wrested him out of Safia's arms.

"Sen-Ya, Sen-Ya," she crooned, tears beginning to run

down her cheeks. "I was afraid I would never see you again! Thank you," she said to Safia, "for keeping my son safe."

"Well," Wha-Li said a trifle wryly, "that settles the First Lordship." The question of Sen-Ya's dubious parentage hung delicately in the air. "That is, it does if Yassai officially recognized the child as his."

"He did, Sire. Before witnesses."

The question evaporated like smoke, never to be mentioned again. Wha-Li turned to Javerri. "It takes a unanimous vote of the other four lords to remove one of us," he said, "and you have not yet voted. Speak now."

Javerri arose, stalked over to Yassai and stared down at him. He had not moved from his cushion, mouth agape as if unable to believe what was happening to him. She still held Steel Fury. How easy it would be to lift the sword, bring it down on him— Her hands literally itched to do it, to end him once and for all.

"I want to kill him," she said, her voice low and shaking only a little. "I promised this to myself when I was fighting my way out of madness. It was to be my reward. I conjured the image of his head on a tray to help me go to sleep. I dreamed of smashing him into red haze like the miserable insect he is. I could do it now and nobody could move swiftly enough to stop me."

"That is true," Second Lord said.

"And it would be lawful and within your right, given his offenses against you," Pei-lin said.

"Yes. But I am only one of the three women he has offended so grievously, and I believe it is Lady Moon and Ancestor who has put us all in the same room with him at just this time. They also have a say in this, a vote in what I shall do with him."

"Kill him," Seniz-Nan said promptly. "I will help hold the sword while you do it."

"No," Safia said. "Would this restore my broken body, the Ladylord's virginity, Lady Seniz-Nan's youth and innocence? He is old. Let the Ancestor take him when it is his time."

"And again the deciding vote is mine," Javerri said. She

stood directly in front of Yassai, and watched him cringe. "Yes, I want you dead. I want to watch you dying. I wanted this very much while I was mad. But I am better now and a quick death is too good, too easy, and you would not suffer as you have made others suffer." She brought the blade close, indicating here, and here, and he shivered, his eyes darting back and forth, flecks of foam beginning to show at the corners of his mouth. "I want to cut off your ears. I want to cut the eyes and tongue from your head. I want to cut off your hands and then your feet, and I want to take your Jade Stalk as well and stuff it into your throat until you choke on it. Yes, you shall have a slow and very painful death indeed."

She raised Steel Fury and Yassai cried out in fear, raising both arms to ward off the blow. But she only checked the edge of the sword for any sign of damage incurred by the battle with the Guardians, and sheathed him. "Banishment."

He cried out, whether from pain or relief it was impossible to tell.

"Ivo, give me your fan."

He leapt to his feet and took his fan out of his sleeve and handed it to her. Deliberately, she struck Yassai across the face with it so hard it broke. He fell on his side and lay there, whimpering. She stalked back to her place and took her seat once more. "I didn't want to dirty my father's sword on him," she said, as if to herself.

Sigon leaned forward. "Well done," he said quietly.

"Veh," Vorsa said, just as quietly. "Very good, impressive, even if fan gets broke."

"Better you should have taken his head," Michu muttered.

The sound of closed fans being tapped on knees filled the room. Lutfu and Nao-Pei sat stonyfaced while almost everyone else registered their approval. Second Lord Wha-Li did not applaud as the others did, but he did allow himself to look pleased. "We must remove the former First Lord to a place of security."

"Allow me, I beg you," said the young man who had been too eager to champion Javerri. "Let me redeem myself."

"The assignment is yours, Naka."

Naka assembled a guard of twenty Yellows in addition to the ones already stationed by Yassai. Two of them had to carry him from the room as he was completely unable to walk on his own.

"Now," Wha-Li said. "That still leaves the matter of the regency. Someone will have to rule during the new First Lord's minority."

An entire plan of action, audacious yet logical, sprang into Javerri's mind, begun at the moment she had given Yassai's worthless life back to him. Would the lords, long confirmed and set in their ways, listen to one so newly come to their ranks? "If I may speak," she said a little breathlessly.

"Of course. I will be interested in hearing what Old Vin— I mean, what Lord Qai's, er, son has to say."

"Things have moved with great swiftness," she said. "In less time than it takes to tell it, we have deposed one First Lord, executed him without spilling his blood, and found another. But the new First Lord is just an infant. Now I propose that the Council of Lords act as regents and further that the former Governor of the Third Province be named as the child's guardian."

"What?" Ka-jin exclaimed. "When Lutfu was so eager to become First Lord himself he all but knocked me down to step forward?" He drew his brown robe closer around him. "I think not. The child won't last a week in his care."

"I disagree," Fifth Lord said. "It might work. We must set down clear and binding provisions, of course. First things first, though. As regents, we need a president."

"We are all connected by birth or by marriage," Ka-jin said. "Seniz-Nan is my niece but I do not desire the presidency of the regents. You, Third Lord? Your sister is Lutfu's wife. Surely you would have a strong voice in the Heir's upbringing."

"Thank you, Fourth Lord, but there is another among us with even closer ties of kinship. Second Lord is cousin to Lutfu and the Sublime Heir as well. If Second Lord would agree to take the position, he could give both Lutfu and my sister the benefit of his great wisdom. And for the terms of guardianship of the heir, I suggest the following. First, Lutfu will enjoy the power his position will bring. And his wife, also." She inclined her head ironically in Nao-Pei's direction and was rewarded by her half sister glaring daggers at her in return. A little dizzy, she talked on, wondering at the way details of the plan were falling into place for her even before she heard herself say them aloud. A sudden suspicion hit her. **Uncle?**

Nay, this comes not from me. I only help thine own thoughts find clear expression.

I thank thee for it. She took a deep breath, and then continued. "Second, if anything unfortunate happens to the young First Lord, Lutfu and his wife also must be summarily executed and Quang qa Masfa will take his place."

"That is the law," Fifth Lord Lennai said, openly amused.

"Childhood ailments excepted, of course," Pei-lin added. "He must have the best physicians attending him at all times."

"This I promise," Seniz-Nan said. She clutched Sen-Ya even closer to her.

"Third, Lutfu must not be allowed to take any important step without the approval of a majority of the lords. He will, of course, be in the position of casting the deciding vote in case of a tie. Last, and perhaps most important, at least for me, making him Sen-Ya's guardian will remove Lutfu—and my sister—from Third Province where they abused their authority, to a place where their actions can be properly, ah, supervised by us all. I have no doubts that the tale General Sigon related is just a hint of the sorry situation I can expect to find once I return to my home."

"Your suggestions have merit," Second Lord Wha-Li said. "And I can find little fault with your reasons."

"I call for the vote on president of regents," Fifth Lord said. "The proposal is that this office be held by Second Lord. Third Lord presented it, and Second Lord cannot object. I agree. Opposition, Fourth Lord?"

"None."

Second Lord bowed to them all. "I will endeavor to be worthy of your trust."

Something touched Javerri and she jumped. Chakei. He had crept close and laid his hand on her arm. He cradled the crimson egg protectively. **son to son**

Ei? What meanest thou?

my son, to little son, give i

Ah. Yes. I thank thee. She turned to Wha-Li. "My Dragon-warrior was most reluctant to relinquish the egg to Yassai, but he will give it to the infant."

"I think this is a sign we do the correct thing," Second Lord said. "Have we had enough discussion on terms of the guardianship? Ei? Vote!"

"Aye," Fourth Lord said, and Fifth Lord echoed, "Aye."

"There are many lovely details to be worked out," Pei-lin said contentedly. "Such as Lady Seniz-Nan's pension, and her future. I suggest that she should not marry again during the First Lord's minority."

"As if I would want to marry again ever!" Seniz-Nan said with a sniff. "Once was quite enough!"

"You are very young and may not always feel that way, but yes, we have many details to be worked out. We will have to confer many times before we have everything settled. But let us leave that until later. In the meantime, will you please be good enough, as the foremost authority on legal matters, to draw up a list of provisions you think necessary?" Wha-Li indicated the room. The bodies of the headsman and the luckless courtier who had tried to stop the Guardians lay in pools of blood. The Guardians themselves still stood smoldering where Wande-hari had stopped them, and the guards outside pretended not to listen through the ruined doors. "Now, let us leave this charnel house and find more agreeable surroundings for these meetings we must have before we depart for our own homes. Let the innocent man who died trying to save Third Lord be taken away and burned decently, but leave the headsman to rot where he fell. Let this room be closed just as it is and let stonemasons build a wall to seal it away forever. Let a warning be carved into the wall to remind all that who see it that on such-and-such a day in the First Province of Monserria, a corrupt era ended and a new cleaner one began."

ii

The first person Javerri received privately was General Sigon so she could learn all he had to tell about Third Province, the former Governor Lutfu, and Nao-Pei. She approved the spy that Sigon had caused to be a part of Sakano's household. Then she allowed others bearing gifts and congratulations to see her as well. To her astonishment, one of these was Madam Farhat.

"Ladylord!" Farhat exclaimed. She opened her arms wide as if to embrace Javerri and then, apparently thinking better of it, bowed instead. "How happy I am to see you safe and sound. And how happy I am that I am able to give you my greetings and my utter loyalty now, here, in person!"

As happy as thou wouldst have been to give this same utter loyalty to Lutfu if I had perished, Javerri thought. She smiled and accepted the dish of dried fruit the woman had brought. Then she listened intently as Farhat told her in greater detail than Sigon could about Nao-Pei's antics while Javerri had been gone. "It is always good to have friends," she said, pretending not to be affected one way or the other. "I regret what happened to Safia."

"Yes, it is a great loss." Farhat said. She sighed elaborately. "I do not know if I can ever replace her."

"I will pay you twice her full contract price and will guarantee a like amount from the other three lords because of her great service to Monserria. It would be indelicate to ask Lutfu to contribute. Will that ease your disappointment a little?"

"I—I never expected such generosity!"

Javerri shrugged. "May I suggest that you give her half of the money."

Farhat's face registered dismay despite her best efforts to hide it. "Perhaps one-third—"

"Two-thirds, then."

"Oh, half, by all means. But that will make her the richest former courtesan in any of the provinces."

"Yes. I thought she might use it to set up her own Hyacinth Shadow World house. I think she can do so anywhere in Monserria, and that she will enjoy an enormous patronage."

Farhat swallowed hard, and then bowed. "As you wish, Ladylord."

"Thank you," she said, dismissing the woman.

A little later, Javerri summoned her half sister. Nao-Pei's face looked like a thundercloud as she entered the room.

"So you win after all," Nao-Pei said spitefully. "And now I suppose you have your own little punishment waiting for me?"

"Do you deserve any other than what you have brought upon yourself?" Javerri said. "Lutfu has grown tired of you. Now you will learn modesty and respectability and cease acting like a whore. This is the only way to regain his interest, and that you must have or you lose everything, life and all. Then he would be free to form an alliance with Seniz-Nan. He can fill her bed well enough even if he may not marry her, the way Sakano filled yours. At least she got her whoring ways honestly. She was born in Fourth Province, after all."

Nao-Pei blanched and Javerri knew she had struck a nerve.

"Oh, yes, I have heard all about your antics, down to the least detail. You are lucky he has not choked the breath out of you already. Don't you even know that the 'platform' you enjoy so much is nothing more than a raping bench?"

"No! You lie! In any case, he relishes it, with me."

"Perhaps he did, but no more. Not with you. I tell you, he has grown tired of these pranks. Now you will learn to become a decent woman if it kills you. As Third Lord I formally order you, my kinswoman and a lady of the Third Province, not to have any traffic with Hyacinth Shadow World mothers except to supply your husband with the sort of women he requires. I further order you to bear him children. And I further order you never to return to the Third Province."

"But—"

"But Baron Sakano? I will deal with him when I return. Your schemes to seize power and rule with him are known to me as well. You are lucky that I do not order you executed, which I have the power to do. I still can. It is your decision now."

Nao-Pei sat very quietly, her face pale. She blinked several times. "May—may I have some wine?"

"Of course." She nodded and Kyoko, her new maid, brought a heated flask at once. Nao-Pei drank off half of it immediately, not bothering with a cup.

"If Lutfu should die—of natural causes, of course—may I have permission to marry Sakano? If his wife should die?"

"No."

Nao-Pei took another pull at the wine flask. "You have grown cruel, sister."

"And you bear some responsibility for that as well. I will grant you one favor, though."

"What is that?" Nao-Pei said, brightening.

"If, after one year of living as I direct, you are still unhappy, I give you permission to end your life if you are not pregnant at the time."

Nao-Pei's lips quivered, and for the first time, Javerri saw her half sister's pride crumble. "Please," she said in a small voice. "Though I have desired Lutfu, I do not love him."

"That does not matter. You are his wife."

"It is not the same with me as it is with you and Ivo. You are not Ivo's property, to dispose of as he chooses!"

"No," Javerri said coldly. "No, our situations are not the same. Not at all."

But how could you, as wrapped up with yourself as you are, possibly know how it stands with my husband and me? she thought.

"Leave me," she said. "I have more important things to do than to endure your presence any longer."

iii

Her interview with Shab Vorsa went much differently than she had planned.

"But I thought you would be eager to return to your home," she said, a little bewildered at his refusal.

"Veh, Dekla, I think so too, once. But you need good fighter now to replace your General Half-foot. My men, we got nice place to stay in fine castle. You need *plandals* for riding. Very bad, no *plandals* in all of country. And—" His eyes gleamed as, obviously, he prepared to produce his best argument. "And, Mama Lidian good for looking after little Dekla and also for growing fannaberry plants your doctor bring back with you."

"Lidian. I daresay Lidian will not be pleased."

"She not mind. She likes little Dekla. Also, likes looking after Dekla's babies some day."

Javerri's mouth closed in a bitter line. "She may have a long time to wait."

"Well, no matter just yet anyhow. Winter comes. Birds not much good on roads, even worse on icy roads. They like soft ground, though. Maybe they like rice fields. Your home much closer than Vorsa's, veh! I send Imroud back, though, bring Lidian in springtime."

"And how do you think Lidian will take this news?"

"Oh, she scream, cry, throw things. Then she pack." He smiled at her slyly. "Bring new *larac-vil* with her also. That make your fellow happy, to have son once more. I think you are only lord in whole damn country with two of them!"

She tried once again. "You have my thanks, as you know. And you will be well paid for your efforts—not that you need or want payment," she added hastily. "But you should not bear the burden of paying the men, particularly those who aren't of your family."

He shrugged. The Monserrian garments still looked strange on him with his dark skin and black curling hair, but he was beginning to wear them more easily. "Pay, no pay, all the same. We have good time, interesting, tell many good stories for years later, veh, even if have to make them up. Also, was good thing to do. Time for step down anyway, let Inbar be shab. You remember son Inbar? He old enough, sure, almost as good as Vorsa, also. I stay, finish job for Dekla."

And there was no moving him. Bowing to the inevitable, she accepted his pledge of loyalty, honored him by escorting him to the door, and then gave the signal that the next person be admitted to see her.

iv

That evening she sat waiting in a room lit only by a brazier and a few oil-nut berries. A simple meal of pickled vegetables and noodles with bean sauce lay ready on the table. There were no more flowers, but a vase held several branches covered with bright green leaves among which a few red berries glowed. Outside, the winter storm pelted the shutters, and guards shivered at their stations. Chakei, as usual, crouched just outside her door with a small brazier to keep him company, comfortable in his huge quilted coat.

She had allowed Kyoko to bathe her, massage all the tiredness out of her body, and dress her in women's garments, and then to apply a little makeup to her face. Her hair was tied back in the simple style she preferred, held by a green ribbon. She wore her favorite perfume, one reminiscent of the scent of sun-warmed apricots. As she waited, a tangle of thoughts stumbled over themselves, racing through her head.

Her sleeping alcove was just beyond, separated from the main room by a paper screen. This screen did not quite conceal the opening, being left discreetly ajar just enough to signal that the inner chamber awaited, and she knew Kyoko had already turned her bed down. No, don't even think of that. That alcove cannot exist, does not exist, must not exist. I should pull the screen tight across the opening. I should send word that I am ill, I cannot see him after all. Will he want me? she asked herself for the thousandth time. So much has hap-

pened between us. Does he still love me? Can he love me
now? Can I love him, want him? I have drunk all the
fannaberry water. Did it heal me? Perhaps I should ask Vorsa
to find me some of his holy herbs. Or perhaps I should drink
date wine until I cannot think. I wanted him so very much
that night, and he wanted me, I am sure of it. Will he compare me to Safia? Will he think I compare him to— No, no,
I must not think that, I must—

The door slid open and Ivo entered, closing it behind him.
"Ladylord," he said, bowing.

"I thought we might take a little food together," she said.
Her heart pounded hard enough that he must surely hear it.
She hoped she could eat a few bites. "Unless you are not hun-
gry—"

"Oh, no, I haven't eaten all day."

"Nor have I."

"Let me serve you." He began filling two peach-colored
bowls. "I never dreamed that we would be peacefully sharing
a meal this evening instead of our heads occupying spikes on
the castle walls."

"Nor I." She cast about for something to talk about.
"You should know, Vorsa is returning to Third Province with
us."

"I'm not surprised. He told me, on the road, that he was
pleased with Monserria. He said he liked a country where
things grow all year round."

"Well, we do need somebody to cultivate the fannaberry
plants Lek brought back with him. And he has spoken more
than once of stepping down as shab."

Ivo laid aside his untouched bowl and his eating sticks.
"Javerri, do we really want to talk about desert people and
fannaberries?"

"No."

"I remember another time we ate together, just the two of
us. You served me then."

"Yes. We ate from pale green porcelain and the light shone
through the bowls." And I chose this meal with particular

care, because it is the same as the one we shared then, she thought. I longed to touch you, to stroke the smoothness of your face, ease the line between your eyes. There are more lines in your face now than then. And I am not as perfect as I once was. All of Kyoko's skill with makeup cannot hide the scar on my cheek. "We were not yet married."

"The porcelain was not as green as your beautiful eyes."

"You kissed me."

"I had to, that once, if never again."

"Never is too long a time."

"Is it?"

"Yes." Despite her best efforts, her voice trembled and broke. Tears welled in her eyes. "But you will think little of me beside Safia."

"Safia! Why?" He sounded entirely astonished.

"She was so beautiful, and so, so accomplished—"

"And it was a loving thing for you to do to give her to me. But I never enjoyed her."

Javerri just stared at him, open-mouthed. "W-what?"

"It is true. If by custom you must deny yourself our bed, then from the moment you accepted my offer of marriage I would not take pleasure with anyone else until you were free to accept me."

She bowed her head, humbled by him. "I am very, very afraid."

"I know."

"What, what that man did—"

"You are brave, the bravest person I have ever known, man or woman. And inside, you are still sweet and tender though you have learned to hide it well. If you can bear it, let me hold you until you feel safe once more."

Hesitantly, she allowed him to draw her into his waiting arms. The welcome warmth of his body crept through her. Her own perfume filled her nostrils and she found herself moving closer until she could catch the clean spicy scent of his flesh. "I do love thee."

"And I love thee. Only thee."

She felt as if she floated on a sea of love, alone with th
person whose presence made her complete. He held her ger
tly and she knew his feelings echoed her own.

She raised her head and he kissed her lips. Then, as he ha
before, he kissed her eyelids and touched her mouth with th
tip of his tongue. Moving as in a well-remembered dream, sh
turned her head away and he brushed the back of her nec
with his lips. She shivered. Beyond hope or expectation, th
flame between her thighs ignited in the Springing Up of th
Jewel Terrace and her nipples tautened to sharp points of de
sire. "Oh, Ivo—"

The oil-nut berries burned low and went out, one by one
though the brazier continued to cast a flickering glow of ligh
and shadow on the walls of the main room and also on th
occupants of the alcove beyond. The little meal, symbol o
their fresh beginning, scarcely touched and now forgotten
grew cold. The Ladylord of the Third Province of Monser
ria and Lord Ivo, her fortunate husband, were enjoying at las
the fullness of the love they had for each other.

TOR
BOOKS The Best in Fantasy

ELVENBANE • Andre Norton and Mercedes Lackey
"A richly detailed, complex fantasy collaboration."—Marion Zimmer Bradley

SUMMER KING, WINTER FOOL • Lisa Goldstein
"Possesses all of Goldstein's virtues to the highest degree."—*Chicago Sun-Times*

JACK OF KINROWAN • Charles de Lint
Jack the Giant Killer and *Drink Down the Moon* reprinted in one volume.

THE MAGIC ENGINEER • L.E. Modesitt, Jr.
The tale of Dorrin the blacksmith in the enormously popular continuing saga of Recluce.

SISTER LIGHT, SISTER DARK • Jane Yolen
"The Hans Christian Andersen of America."—*Newsweek*

THE GIRL WHO HEARD DRAGONS • Anne McCaffrey
"A treat for McCaffrey fans."—*Locus*

GEIS OF THE GARGOYLE • Piers Anthony
Join Gary Gar, a guileless young gargoyle disguised as a human, on a perilous pilgrimage in pursuit of a philter to rescue the magical land of Xanth from an ancient evil.

TOR
BOOKS The Best in Fantasy